A Lady Would Know Better

PRAISE FOR *A LADY WOULD KNOW BETTER*

"A witty, sexy, and delightful romp, with an entertaining cast of characters that are impossible not to love!"

–Liana De la Rosa, *USA Today* bestselling author

"Emma Theriault's *A Lady Would Know Better* is a wonderfully swoony slow burn of a romance!"

–Alicia Thompson, *USA Today* bestselling author of *With Love, from Cold World*

"An utterly delightful and fresh take on the beloved amnesia trope. Brimming with sparkling wit and simmering tension, *A Lady Would Know Better* is sure to sweep you off your feet from the first page!"

–Amy Lea, international bestselling author of *The Catch*

"A grieving family broken apart from each other and the world, a woman who doesn't know her name, and a love that softens the edges of the sternest earl [...] I'm going to need a book for everyone who lives in Mulgrave Hall!"

–Sarah Hogle, author of *Old Flames and New Fortunes*

"A tender, heartfelt journey full of all the yearning and pining we crave from Historical Romance. Theriault combines fantastic tension with a superb cast of characters and puts you right in the middle of Mulgrave Hall for a snowy, forced-proximity romance that will have you turning pages till the very end."

–*USA Today* bestselling author Emma R. Alban

"Swoony, sexy, and full of heart! Fans of Lisa Kleypas will love Emma Theriault's rich and romantic historical romance."

–Alexandra Vasti, *USA Today* bestselling author of *Ne'er Duke Well*

A Lady Would Know Better

Emma THERIAULT

Copyright © 2025 by Emma Theriault. All rights reserved, including the right to
reproduce, distribute, or transmit in any form or by any means. For information
regarding subsidiary rights, please contact the Publisher.

Entangled Publishing, LLC
644 Shrewsbury Commons Ave., STE 181
Shrewsbury, PA 17361
rights@entangledpublishing.com

Amara is an imprint of Entangled Publishing, LLC.

Visit our website at www.entangledpublishing.com.

Edited by Erin Molta
Cover illustration and design by Elizabeth Turner Stokes
Stock art by artMari/Shutterstock
Interior design by Britt Marczak

ISBN 978-1-64937-744-9
Ebook ISBN 978-1-64937-748-7

Manufactured in the United States of America

First Edition January 2025

10 9 8 7 6 5 4 3 2 1

To my parents, who knew I was a writer before I did.
And to Byron, who reminded me when I forgot.

A Lady Would Know Better is an unforgettable romance about a woman who forgets who she is. However, the story includes elements that might not be suitable for all readers. Amnesia, deaths of family members (off page), and themes of grief are mentioned and discussed in the novel. Readers who may be sensitive to these elements, please take note.

Chapter One

JASPER

SURREY, DECEMBER 1877

"Jasper, are you ready?"

His eyes lifted from the tired correspondence without much reluctance. "I rarely am," he replied to his sister, who stood framed in the doorway to his father's study.

Jasper's study this past year, to be more accurate, now that he was the Earl of Belhaven.

Hell of a position for a second son to end up in.

"You promised," Helena said, her tone doing much to remind him of all his inadequacies. It wasn't supposed to be like this. His brother Anthony was the heir, Jasper the spare, and they had taken to their roles with vigor.

But that was before.

Their younger sister Isobel stepped around Helena and into view, frowning at him. The expression crinkled her features, so like their mother's that it made Jasper's heart ache. "What did I tell you?" she asked Helena. "It wasn't a promise he ever intended to keep."

Jasper leaned back in his father's imposing chair, his bones creaking with the effort of it. Surely a man of six and twenty should not feel so withered. He could recall lying on the deck of a sun-drenched yacht in the Mediterranean less than two years ago, wondering when he might have to face reality and cede to his parents' wishes and carve a place for himself in the world. He hadn't imagined that reality would be thrust upon him so violently.

He pinched the bridge of his nose. "What exactly did I promise?"

Helena sighed. "It's the seventh of December." Their mother's birthday. When she was alive, the Countess of Belhaven had been a famous hostess of the Ton, and each year, Society had descended on their snowy corner of Surrey in order to celebrate her. It had been a festive few days of sleigh rides and tree trimming and mulled wine. Jasper was quite sure that after last year's tragedy he'd never enjoy frivolity like that again.

Helena continued. "I can't bear the thought of letting the day pass unremarked upon. It was her favorite."

It took Jasper a moment to remember his hasty promise, uttered in the bitter reaches of the night some weeks ago, when he and his sisters had let their shared grief tether them together, rather than drive them to separate corners of their dark manor. They would visit their mother's grave on her birthday, after their youngest sister had gone to bed, so as not to upset her. At the time, Jasper had been making an effort, spurred by the pain he'd witnessed in his sisters' faces. They needed him to be strong, like Anthony had been. But Jasper had lived his life almost fitfully, as second sons were wont to do, until he'd met Annabelle, the daughter of the vicar of Wrayford. After so much time spent shunning virtue and chasing vice, at last he had stilled, and his world had irrevocably changed.

But that was before.

Jasper glanced out the window, where snow fell down like a heavy rain. Decidedly not the best time to visit the graves of their parents and brother. Perhaps he could convince them to postpone a day. But then he looked to the stack of letters he had been making his way through, all written by his impatient man of business, and thought a tromp through the frigid sludge would be preferable.

"Let me get my coat."

. . .

Jasper regretted his choice as soon as he stepped out the door and the icy chill cut right through him. His sisters, on the other hand, looked quite content in the frigid winds.

"How is it that the two of you seem to be managing so well?" he asked, wrapping his arms around his body in a futile effort to trap whatever heat remained in him.

Helena smiled weakly, her cheeks rosy and her halo of red hair a rare shock of brightness in the gray of winter. "Our cloaks were made with warmth in mind, Brother, not fashion."

Jasper looked down at his gray broadcloth frock coat and grimaced at how little it did to shield him from the cold. Having spent much of the last five years in the milder climes of the Continent, he had hoped he would never suffer through another unpredictable English winter. But then he'd lost almost everyone, and the thought of staying in Surrey permanently was no longer a nightmare to be avoided but rather an obligation he had to the family that remained. And in the year since the tragedy, Jasper hadn't gotten around to updating his wardrobe with more appropriate garments. His duties as the Earl of Belhaven had taken precedence, and he had the calloused palms to prove it.

"You'll freeze to death without Annabelle here to remind…" Isobel began before sputtering to a stop, her hasty, careless words dying in her throat. "I'm—I'm so sorry, Jasper…"

He said nothing, his own words buried beneath a knot in his chest, thoughts of Annabelle's pale, sickly form filling his mind, thoughts he had steadfastly avoided all year.

Because when scarlet fever swept through Wrayford, noble Annabelle had stayed at her father's side as he tended to the spirits of those who suffered, and all Jasper could do was uselessly pray she was spared.

Alas, his prayers had not been answered.

In the end, the illness took not only Annabelle, but the safe harbor his parents had always been for him, as well as the steady influence of his brother. It had been in those dark moments after Anthony had taken his last breath that Jasper had realized there were no new beginnings left for him. Nothing but an unrelenting reminder of what he'd lost, and what he could still lose, if he wasn't careful.

Their path to the chapel took them to the edges of their land, with Mulgrave Hall all but impossible to see behind them, veiled as it was by the falling snow. Before them, similarly shrouded, was the cemetery.

He knew Isobel meant him no harm, but for the past year, Jasper had done his best to stay strong for his siblings by closing off the parts of himself that felt too deeply. He was able to continue moving forward only because he'd never looked back. How would he be able to ignore the depths of his loss when standing at the graves of his parents and Anthony? The thought of it was almost too much to bear.

"What are our plans for the holiday?" Isobel asked, seeking a distraction from her earlier blunder. His throat tightened. He hadn't planned for anything more than survival.

"Freddie will be home soon," he offered. Their brother Frederick was away at Eton, while their other brother studied law at Oxford. "I still haven't received word from August, but I predict he will find his way to us eventually."

Isobel frowned. "Viola has been planning her outfit for Christmas dinner with the Banfields for weeks now."

Jasper grimaced, thinking back to the unopened letters that littered his desk, invitations from well-meaning friends who likely thought that since the Maycotts would be emerging from their year of mourning, they would soon be returning to Society. Nothing could have felt more impossible to him. "Surely having all of us back at Mulgrave Hall will be celebration enough."

"Will *all* of us be back, though, truly? Or will some remain locked away?" Helena asked, her eyebrows raised meaningfully.

"I would hardly say I'm locked away in father's study like some recluse," said Jasper defensively, knowing precisely what his sister meant. It was time for him to step into their eldest brother's shoes. But he would never be like Anthony, so constant. He knew that. It was why he'd sworn an oath to the darkness the night they'd lost their older brother. As the new Earl of Belhaven, he would care for his siblings. He would find them respectable matches and ensure their happy futures. But the line would pass to his younger brother when he died.

Because Jasper would never again give his heart to another. Whatever love he had left was for his siblings. He could not dilute it further. He would be a shadow of what Anthony could have been, or what his father *had* been, before the fates had cruelly taken them, but it would have to be enough.

A year had passed since he'd made his solemn vow, and while he could not claim the Maycotts were thriving under his care, they were at least surviving.

But is survival enough? Was it not his responsibility to do *more*?

He buried the thought, along with the rest of his unhappy memories, as Isobel gave him a cutting look.

"I think perhaps she meant it metaphorically."

He began to offer his sister a cutting look of his own when he stepped into Helena, knocking her slightly.

"Jasper, I think there's something in the road," she said, her eyes never leaving a distant point ahead.

He gazed in the same direction but saw nothing save for the swirling snow. "Your eagle eyes will never cease to amaze me, Helena. I can't see a thing."

"It looks like…" She paused, her already-pale skin blanching. Jasper looked in the same direction but still saw nothing.

"What, Helena?"

Her next words were bleak. "It looks like a body."

By then they had traveled enough for Jasper to make out a dark form in the middle of the road. It *did* look like a body. His skin went even colder, and the feeling of dread pooled in his gut.

Not another one.

And then he was running. His sisters shouted behind him, but he didn't register what they said over the hammering of his heart. He stopped short of the figure, gasping from the sudden exertion, and bent to his knees, gingerly turning the body over.

The first thing he noticed was dark crimson blood coating half the woman's face, and how it pooled in the snow where she had been lying.

He pulled her closer to him, desperate to ascertain if she was still breathing.

"Please," he whispered, his voice catching in his throat.

Then, to his immense relief, there was a tickle of breath on his cheek, like a whisper of spring against his frozen skin.

"My God," he heard Helena gasp behind him. "Is she all right?"

Isobel bent next to him and placed her ungloved fingers on the woman's exposed neck. "Her pulse is weak, but I can feel it."

Jasper took a second to study their surroundings, noting the erratic markings in the snow. "She must have been thrown from a horse. She's still warm, but that won't last."

Helena's expression was grave. "She should be dead."

"She isn't," he said, willing it to stay true. "She isn't."

He stood, lifting the woman with him as though she weighed nothing at all. "Isobel, run ahead and rouse whoever you can to send for a doctor." She nodded and ran from them without hesitation. He turned to Helena. "You must go and prepare a room. We want it warm. She's half frozen."

His sister paused. "I don't want to leave you." But he knew there was more to it than that. Helena had watched her husband die tragically in an accident not so very different from the one they had just stumbled upon. Surely the sight of the bloody woman was dredging up bad memories. But they didn't have time to sift through the heavy emotions.

"Go, Helena. I cannot risk moving much faster than this. You'll be more useful at home, preparing for our arrival."

She swallowed, her throat bobbing, and nodded, her decision made. She took off in the direction of Mulgrave Hall.

The woman in his arms was deathly still. They stood in a

sliver of moonlight peeking out from behind the clouds. He knew he had to get moving. She needed medical attention, but more than that, she needed to get warm. His embrace wasn't going to be enough to stop her from freezing to death, to say nothing of her obvious injuries. He waited as patiently as he could to feel her breath once more.

And then she opened her eyes, and the world around him stopped, confined as he was to those pools of gray, so luminous they appeared almost silver in the pale light. Snowflakes clung to her eyelashes. It took a moment for her gaze to focus on him, but when it did, her pupils dilated fully.

"Don't let them get me," she begged, fear weighing heavy in her soft voice.

The words were a shock. Jasper looked up in the direction she had come from but saw nothing. He looked back at her. "Who, my lady?"

She took a shuddering breath, wincing. "Please," she whispered, before slumping into unconsciousness once more.

Jasper didn't know what foe she spoke of, but as he held her in his arms, his path was clear. She was a woman in distress who had been injured on his land. He was duty bound as a gentleman to aid her. But it was more than that. When Annabelle had fallen ill, there wasn't anything Jasper could have done to protect her or spare her the pain of it. She'd suffered as he sat by, unable to help her. Her fate had rested unmercifully outside his control.

But the woman in his arms? The one who still breathed? Whose blood was hot on his skin?

She could still be saved, and he would do everything in his power to ensure she was.

Chapter Two

JASPER

The march back to Mulgrave Hall was arduous.

The woman was not an issue. Jasper had been an athletic man all his life. He barely registered her weight as he cradled her to his chest, more worried about the paleness of her skin and the steady trickle of blood from her wound.

Christ, she needs a doctor.

It was the snow he struggled against, knowing that each passing minute could be bringing her closer to death. He couldn't lose someone else under his charge. He banished even the thought of it from his mind. He must focus.

He forced his labored breaths into a rhythmic pattern, the puffs of white reminding him of the cold he no longer felt, due to his exertion, until finally the arches of Mulgrave Hall came into view. It was a stately Georgian mansion, classical in its design and understated in its elegance. His mother had never liked the sedate symmetry of the building, choosing to plant climbing ivy the day she'd arrived, newly wedded to the Earl of Belhaven. The veins of that ivy now spanned the entirety of Mulgrave Hall, spiderwebbed over the stone facade. In the summer, the leaves were lush and covered the estate fully, lending the graciously proportioned mansion an air of whimsy his mother strove to cultivate. In the winter, the ivy looked almost ominous, but never more than now, as Jasper approached with a bloodied woman in his arms.

They were met by Helena and Battersby, Mulgrave Hall's long-suffering butler.

"Come, Jasper. Every pot has been set to boil and I've had a fire built," said Helena, guiding him into the dwelling, where Nash, his valet, awaited. They walked to the grand staircase and Jasper paused, adjusting the woman in his arms. Helena walked backward ahead of him, efficient as ever. "I thought we'd use the Lavender Room, as it has the best light and a great deal of space."

Jasper nodded and turned left at the top of the stairs. "And the doctor?"

"Has been sent for, shouldn't be too long, if he remained in the village tonight. But the snow will slow them down."

"And Isobel?"

Helena gave him a tiresome look. "She went with the carriage."

"I should not be surprised," he replied, picturing his sister atop the boot with the footman Thomas. She was never one to miss the action by sitting safely in a carriage.

They reached the Lavender Room and Jasper walked right to the bed, laying the woman on it gently. He gazed down at her, his heart in his throat as he waited to see her chest rise and fall. And then she took a shuddering breath, sinking deeper into the mattress, and Jasper himself breathed again.

He pulled the covers over her small frame as maids lifted the sheets at the bottom of the bed and placed two warming pans with fresh embers alongside her. Helena removed the woman's boots, revealing her delicate, stockinged feet, and Jasper's eyes shot back up to the top of the bed.

Who is she? And why on earth is someone chasing her?

Helena came to stand beside him, handing him a warm, damp cloth. "I'm sure she'd appreciate someone cleaning her up a bit."

He removed his frock coat and rolled the sleeves of his shirt up over his forearms before taking the cloth and kneeling next to the woman, forgetting about propriety or etiquette or anything else, for that matter. He was careful, never scrubbing too firmly, but sure to get as much as he could without causing her any more pain. He couldn't help but note that her features were quite pleasing when not covered in blood. Despite the bluish tinge, the stranger's lips were full and welcoming. She had a fine dusting of freckles over her cheeks and nose, uncommon among the sun-shunning ladies of the Ton, and strong, almost incongruous brows that framed her delicate bone structure. Taken as a whole, she was memorable, unforgettable even. He only wished she were conscious.

"There, that looks a great deal better," said Helena, perhaps a bit too brightly. "Blood can make even a minor injury look terribly dramatic." Jasper looked back at his sister but he did not speak, knowing she was likely lost in memory.

Helena had faced the life-altering loss of her husband, the duke, before they'd lost their parents and brother to scarlet fever. Since that day, she'd borne the evidence of the carriage accident that had taken the duke's life in a long scar that cut from her temple to her jaw, as well as the pain she suffered—the pain she did her best to hide from the world.

"Marcus's injury looked like nothing at all." It was almost a whisper. It had been a little more than three years since her husband had died. She brought her fingers to her scar absentmindedly.

In a way, she and Jasper were alike in their losses, both altered by the trials that had befallen them so early in their lives. But where he knew Helena's warm heart would see her through her grief, his own heart had hardened into something cold and unrecognizable in order for him to survive.

Before Jasper could comfort her, a commotion at the door stole their focus.

Battersby appeared, looking perturbed. "My lord, the doctor has arrived—"

"Wonderful, send him in," replied Jasper.

"—and your sister requires your attention," he finished.

"Isobel?" It wasn't like her to admit to needing help, but it was entirely like Battersby to frame his disapproval of her as something that required Jasper's immediate action.

"No, my lord. I am referring to Lady Viola."

Jasper winced. His youngest sister was not yet thirteen, and Jasper feared he was failing her most of all. A child so young needed a parent, not an errant brother balancing far too much responsibility on unworthy shoulders. He stood just as the doctor was ushered into the room, bringing the outdoor chill with him.

"Welcome, Dr. Ramsay," said Helena, when words failed her brother.

The doctor was a tall man with extravagant whiskers and a kindly countenance. He had delivered each of the Maycott siblings and for the past two decades had tended to their various illnesses and accidents. After seeing the remaining Maycotts through last year's tragedy, he had become something of a de facto uncle in the absence of their parents. Jasper swallowed thickly, banishing the memory of the doctor holding Annabelle's impossibly small hand in his rather large one, as he'd checked her wrist for a pulse he hadn't found.

"What seems to be the problem?" Dr. Ramsay prompted, looking from Jasper to Helena when he, once again, proved incapable of speech.

"We came upon this young lady on the road to the cemetery," Helena spoke for Jasper as Dr. Ramsay approached the bed. "We surmised that she must have been thrown from her horse, not too long before we found her, though she's been unconscious the whole time."

Not the whole time, but Jasper didn't correct Helena. Only *he* had been privy to the young woman's plea, and it didn't feel right to share it with everyone else. Not yet, at least.

Dr. Ramsay rubbed his hands together for warmth and placed them at various points of the woman's head and neck. After some gentle prodding, he looked back to Helena. "Neither her skull nor neck bear any signs of fracture." He moved on to cradling the girl's face, opening her eyelids and studying her pupils in the light. He lifted the counterpane at the foot of the bed and tapped on the soles of her feet. He looked up to Jasper and Helena and grinned. "Her reflexes are intact," he told them as he stood. "She doesn't seem to have entered a lasting stupor."

"Then what ails her? When will she waken?"

"She is in shock, Belhaven." Jasper managed not to wince at the doctor's use of his father's title, somehow both too familiar and too formal in that moment. "Her condition is delicate. You must take pains to ensure she is not distressed or excitable for the foreseeable future." Jasper thought back to the fear in her eyes when she had begged him to protect her from *them*, whoever they were. Distressed barely covered how she had appeared then. "She must remain recumbent, and warmth should be applied to the legs. If she worsens, then strychnine can be administered, though I'd start with camphor—"

"Yes, yes, good, but when will she waken? We know nothing about her, or where she came from. Surely her family is worried about her."

Dr. Ramsay shook his head. "She cannot be rushed into wellness, Belhaven. An impairment of the head can be immensely damaging, so she may awaken confused." He rose to his full height and sighed. "Her injuries are largely invisible but they must be treated as if they were observable. She needs rest. Her symptoms must be managed and she must not be overly stimulated."

Ramsay was being professional but there was no stopping Jasper's descent into panic. He had been here before, had watched helplessly as first Annabelle, and then his parents and Anthony had died. He could not bear to stand by and lose someone else, even if that someone was a perfect stranger. "You say she will recover but then you speak as if she could succumb to her injuries. Which is it, Ramsay?"

Helena gave him a look that suggested he was being unreasonable, while the doctor's expression was pitying, reading all too easily into Jasper's true meaning. "There is always a risk of hemorrhage, Jasper." The use of his given name smarted. If anyone outside his family had a right to it, it was Dr. Ramsay. But to go from Belhaven to Jasper in the span of a conversation only served to remind him of what he had lost, and how adrift he had become. "The best thing you could do for her is to let her rest comfortably."

He pressed his lips into a firm line. "Then that is what we will do." She would be the most rested woman in all of bloody England. He'd make sure of it. But the moment she awoke and revealed who she was and where she came from, Jasper would see to it she was returned to her home—and the relative peace he had fought so hard for would be restored to Mulgrave Hall.

Battersby cleared his throat from the door. "My lord, your sister—"

"Right, I must attend to that—"

Dr. Ramsay clapped his shoulder. "I will clean the young lady's wound while you do, and perhaps instruct your sister in the proper application of camphor."

Jasper nodded, but found himself reluctant to leave the woman, even in hands as capable as the doctor's and Helena's. She seemed so small in the large bed, so defenseless. But it wasn't as though whoever pursued her could get to her in Mulgrave Hall.

She was safe for now.

The walk to Viola's chambers was short and didn't leave Jasper much time to come up with a plan for how best to explain the events of the evening. His sister must be near hysterics, especially if she had caught a glimpse of the woman.

Her door was very nearly closed, the room within dimly lit. Jasper took a deep breath and knocked softly.

"Come in," came a small, trembling voice.

He steeled himself against his fears of inadequacy and put on a brave face as he entered the room, expecting to find his sister consumed by fear. Instead, Viola sat bolt upright the moment she saw it was her brother who had come to her, her eyes alight and her body practically vibrating with excitement.

"Jasper, is it *true*? Did you really save a woman's life?"

He swallowed his shock at finding her so unaffected. "I don't know about *saving* her life but yes, Isobel, Helena, and I did come upon a woman who needed our assistance." He came to her bed and sat on the edge.

"Isobel said she was covered in blood, I heard her. And there's blood on your shirt!" She pointed, her eyes wide. "And she's *here*? In Mulgrave Hall? Is she dying?"

He had anticipated her curiosity but he hadn't expected her to be so frank and unafraid. Viola had only been eleven when their parents died, and Jasper had long assumed her to be the most affected by their loss. But here she was, full of questions and glee, as though a strange woman falling from her horse was the most interesting thing that had happened to her in months. "No, she is not dying, Viola. She has a head injury and must rest in order to recover."

"And she will do that here?"

He frowned, not wishing to encourage an attachment. "I daresay once we discover who she is, she will be on her way."

She pulled out a piece of parchment and a pen from beneath her pillow. Viola was always scribbling away, recording her thoughts and observations. Jasper sensed it was a symptom of the vast amount of turmoil that she had been through at so young an age, a way to make sense of what remained. She licked the tip of her pen and pressed it to the paper. "What is she like?"

He sighed. "I haven't the faintest idea, Viola. She's been unconscious this entire time."

"I suppose she's quite brave," she said dreamily, chewing on the pen.

Jasper poked her lightly in the ribs. "And you got a sense of that from what exactly?"

"Well, she was alone on horseback. Have you ever heard of

such a thing?"

"No," he said, thinking it was a rarity indeed. "And don't you go getting ideas."

"I'm not allowed on horseback as it is," she said, her eyes narrowed, but Jasper didn't take the bait. After all that had befallen their family, he thought he had a right to be a tad overcautious as a guardian. "Do you think perhaps she was running from something?"

Jasper froze, though he supposed he shouldn't be surprised by how close his acutely observant sister had come to the truth. "Why do you ask?"

"As brave as she may be, fleeing into the night couldn't have been her first choice. She must have been very frightened."

Jasper cleared his throat. "Or perhaps she ignored the warnings of a wise older brother and now she's paying the consequences," he teased, but Viola was barely listening to him, lost in her own train of thought.

"She's all alone and she could be in danger," she mused, not entirely unexcited by the woman's plight. She looked up at him, her eyes wide. "We'll help her, won't we?" she pleaded, and when Jasper did not immediately respond, she reached for his hand. "It's what Annabelle would have wanted."

Hearing her name was a shock, though it shouldn't have been. In the course of Annabelle's work with her father, she had always been drawn to widows and unwed mothers and other vulnerable women, insisting that Society failed to protect them at every turn, if not outright harmed them with unjust and prejudiced laws.

Before Annabelle, Jasper might have felt a shred of sympathy or made a nominal donation for some women's charity or another, never giving it a further thought. But Annabelle had opened his eyes to the injustice of it all. It had only been four years since the

Custody of Infants Act had passed in Parliament, allowing mothers access to their own children in the event of a divorce. Hell, it had only been twenty years since Parliament recognized that *violence* was grounds for a divorce. And while, in Annabelle's eyes, any progress made was to be celebrated, the passing of these laws had not been the dawn of a new utopian age. Rather, they were too little and came far too late for the many thousands of women who had suffered for so long without any other choice.

But this was different. He thought back to the woman's fine clothing. "She has a family, Viola. We simply need to find them."

"When can I see her?"

"Certainly not tonight. You should be asleep." He rose and pulled the pen and paper from her hands, placing them out of reach on her desk, knowing very well she'd retrieve them the moment he was gone.

"It's quite a lot of excitement, isn't it?" she asked innocently. "Almost makes you forget about—"

"Good night, Viola," Jasper interrupted. He swiftly kissed her forehead and left the room, never giving her a chance to speak, but acknowledging to himself that she was right. The last two hours had been the first in a long time he hadn't spent consumed by memory. And it wasn't as if he hadn't thought of Annabelle, or his parents or Anthony, but the pain was almost bearable. Maybe his sisters were right. Maybe he should open himself up again. Perhaps there was enough left in the world to distract him from his misery.

Then again, perhaps not.

Helena met him in the hall.

"Dr. Ramsay left," she said before he could ask.

"Has she woken?"

"Not yet, Jasper, but look." Helena held out a small gold ring in the palm of her hand. He picked it up and held it to the light, noting the initials carved into the facade: *JHD*. "This was in her pocket," Helena offered.

"*JHD*," he said. "Who do you think that is?"

"I don't believe many women wear signet rings of their own names."

He met Helena's eye. "You think she is betrothed? Married?"

Helena shook her head. "Betrothed or married women don't take their rings off, least of all before a journey on horseback."

He closed his fist around the ring and looked back at Helena. "What does any of this mean?"

"We have no way of knowing," she said. "Save for what she may tell us when she wakes up."

Isobel reappeared, her cheeks pink from the cold. "Dr. Ramsay is quite the conversationalist; I doubt I've spoken as much in the past month as I did while walking him to the carriage." She noted their grim expressions. "Have we determined the identity of our mystery guest?"

"Not even close," said Helena, before telling her about the ring.

"Why, how dramatic," exclaimed Isobel. "Perhaps she's a bandit."

"Perhaps, but her clothing suggests otherwise," said Helena. "She wears the finery of a lady, even if a lady would never ride horseback alone during a snowstorm."

"My kind of woman," remarked Isobel. "There must be an interesting story behind her late-night sojourn."

Jasper thought back to the woman's desperate plea and tried to piece together a theory. Was she fleeing an abusive fiancé? Heavens, an abusive *husband*? There wasn't much the Maycotts could do for her, if it was the latter.

Helena nudged him. "I can see the wheels in your mind turning, Jasper. We don't know that she's a damsel in need of rescuing."

"Who said I mean to rescue her?"

Isobel smirked. "More so than you've already done?" She gasped when Helena pinched her. "I simply mean it's rather romantic, isn't it?"

Jasper went cold. "There is nothing romantic about this, Isobel."

Something in his tone must have warned his impertinent sister against arguing further. By then, they had reached the Lavender Room only to find the woman stirring within.

Isobel began to speak but Jasper shushed her. "She's waking," he hissed as he and Helena crept toward the bed.

"Are we perhaps aiming to frighten the girl to an early grave?" whispered Isobel.

"We should let her come to awareness gently, Jasper," said Helena, straightening.

His sister was right, but Jasper was entranced by the fluttering of the woman's eyelids in the candlelight. He should leave, heavens knew she would be distressed if the first thing she saw upon waking was a strange man. But perhaps she would remember him as the one who had carried her from where she lay injured in the road.

He didn't have time to make a decision before her eyes opened in earnest. He froze, waiting for them to focus on him as they had in the road. Her brow creased as her eyes darted around the room. An arm escaped the counterpane and moved sideways until her hand slapped the nightstand.

"What is it?" Jasper asked without thinking. "What do you require?"

If she was frightened to hear a man speak in her immediate vicinity, she didn't show it. "My—my spectacles," she croaked, her voice entirely hoarse.

Helena stepped closer. "You've been in an accident."

"An accident?" The woman raised herself up on her elbows only to gasp out in pain.

Isobel stepped closer and eased her into a prone position. "Thrown from your horse, we suspect. You mustn't overexert yourself. Dr. Ramsay was very clear about that."

The woman was understandably confused. Helena sat on the side of the bed. "If you tell us your name, we will be able to inform your family of your whereabouts. They must be worried."

"My name?" she asked as though the question itself were perplexing.

"Yes, your name," replied Jasper, perhaps a little too forcefully. But he couldn't help her unless he knew who she was. Helena gave him a look nonetheless.

"I..." she began, and Jasper braced himself for the information that would set his course. He had said as much to Viola. If she was the daughter or wife of a peer, haste would have to be made in order to inform her family of her accident and injury. Then, they could come retrieve her and the Maycotts could return to their quiet mourning, surviving one day after the other. Enduring as best they could. All he needed was for her to speak her name.

She looked around the room, her brows crinkling, before speaking at last. "I do not know."

Chapter Three

"You *what*?"

The room was unbearably hot, her thoughts intolerably muddled, and the pain in her skull as sharp as a knife. And she had no earthly idea what was happening or where she was.

Or *who* she was.

"I do not know," she forced out again. She could barely make out any of the features of the room or hear anything over the dull roar in her head.

"You don't know your own name?" The voice that reached through the haze of pain was incredulous. Angry even. She couldn't see clearly enough to make out its owner. Where were her bloody spectacles?

"Jasper—" another voice warned, this one kinder.

"You mean to tell me you have no memory of your own self? Who has ever heard of such a thing?"

The kinder voice became firmer. "Jasper, Dr. Ramsay said she would awaken confused. He was also adamant that she not be distressed, and I must say, the tone you're taking is distressing."

There was an exasperated sigh from the man's direction.

A warm hand found hers. "You must be feeling terrible; we should let you rest. But first you should have some water."

The weight of her confusion hit her like a solid wall. Her heartbeat quickened and a sickly heat bloomed over her skin. "I should know who I am, shouldn't I?" she asked in the direction of the kind voice.

"Well, let's start with some facts, shall we?" said another voice, this one raspier and somewhat mischievous. "My name is Isobel Maycott. The nursemaid holding your hand is my angelic sister Helena, and the stern bastard—"

"Isobel!" cried Helena.

"Well, if she can't remember her own name it stands to reason she won't remember any of this," muttered Isobel. "As I was saying, the stern bastard is my brother Jasper."

She ventured a question, one that felt more manageable than queries about her own identity. "Where am I?"

"Mulgrave Hall, home of the Earl of Belhaven."

The name tickled in her mind, like the memory she sought was buried under miles of muck, but still present, if only she could reach it. She tried to sift for it, but the strain made her dizzy.

Isobel continued her patient explanation. "As we said before, you were in an accident, but you're safe now. We had our physician take a look at you and he doesn't suspect there will be any lasting damage—"

"He didn't say anything about memory problems," grumbled Jasper.

"In any event, you'll need to stay here until you recover—either physically or mentally."

She could hardly make anything out, and yet the room seemed to shrink around her. Something was wrong, something beyond her lack of memory or current predicament. It was as though her bones knew it even when her mind did not. A primal instinct told her she was not safe in the least, though she also knew this fear had nothing to do with the three people surrounding her bed.

Jasper stepped closer. "Anything yet? A name? A location?"

His question was a test, she surmised. One she would fail. "Nothing," she admitted. "It is as though there is a veil upon my mind I cannot penetrate." The room ceased its shrinking and began to spin instead. She let out an involuntary moan, causing Jasper to step even closer, tugged toward her as though against his will.

"Is everything all right?" he began, his tone sharp. "Are you well?" he added, the sharpness somewhat dulled this time. It seemed even in his frustration the man did not forget his manners.

He was close enough now for her to make out his features. Stern bastard was right—disapproval radiated off of him like a punishing heat, made evident by the firm line of his mouth and his dark, sharp gaze. She felt herself flush under the intensity of it, and only then, as concern creased his brow and his eyes softened, could she see a hint of what lay under his mask. She knew at once there was a good man beneath the austerity. It was the first thing she could see clearly since waking.

He bent close enough for her to smell him. Clean linen and sweat, like he had recently exerted himself. It was not displeasing, she noted, feeling a pull toward him. His steely facade continued to crumble, much like how the rest of the room faded from her knowledge, until the only thing that remained was the hot press of his hand on hers. His touch sparked, his skin rougher than she expected for the son of a nobleman. "My lady?"

The form of address stuck in her mind. *Not right*, came a persistent thought. And then the room rushed back in stark relief. She felt the heat of a bedwarmer upon her legs, the drip of sweat on the back of her neck, the pain that seemed woven into her very bones.

It was agony, and no earthly or heavenly power could have prevented her from emptying the contents of her stomach over the side of the bed, right onto his boots.

• • •

When she next awoke, she was alone.

Her hand stretched out again out of habit, but the familiar shape of her spectacles was still absent. It was odd to think of anything as familiar, when she lacked a foundation of memory. But perhaps some things were too deeply ingrained to ever be lost. She still knew how to speak, after all, she simply lacked a sense of self. It was disconcerting, but she could function, at least.

The pain was still there, but it had lessened some. She felt the urge to stand, if only to prove she still could, but a cursory wiggle of her legs suggested she was still too weak for that. She recalled blearily making use of a chamber pot sometime in the night, though God knew how she had managed it alone. Instinct, she suspected.

She thought back to what she had been told about her injury. *Found in a heap. Thrown from a horse. Alone.*

She wished she had the words or evidence to prove how very unlike her that was. Perhaps the conviction that she was not the kind of woman who did things like flee into the night on horseback was as deeply ingrained as her ability to speak. But the fact remained, she had no proof of the contrary, and while she had some idea of the kind of woman she *wasn't*, she still had no earthly notion of what kind of woman she *was*.

The hall beyond her room was quiet, but she knew she must be in a manor of considerable size if it was the residence of an earl. She hoped not to encounter said earl or his countess during her, hopefully, brief stay. She prayed he was a busy man, preferably kept in London, far away from the mess she had unwittingly made. The shame of seeing a man like the Earl of Belhaven in her current state would be enough to kill her.

Morning light poured in from the window, so she did her best to make out her surroundings, blurry as they were. She was in what appeared to be a well-appointed room with sumptuous pastel-colored furniture and lavender floral wallpaper.

No, she thought, squinting. *Not lavender.* The color erred too closely to violet to be a true representation. It was more like lilac, a shade morose and cold beneath a whimsical name. In any case, it was a fine room.

A fine room she didn't belong in.

The counterpane that covered her was made of a thick and richly stitched brocade, and she wore a soft frilled nightgown that must have belonged to someone else. She tried not to dwell on thoughts of any of the Maycotts seeing her in a state of undress. They had also seen her vomit on a man's boots, and that seemed the greater injustice at the moment.

A thick braid lay over her shoulder—someone had tended to her hair. She reached a tentative hand up to the bandage at her temple. The skin around it was swollen and warm, but not hot with infection as far as she could tell. She swallowed, allowing a small amount of relief to blossom in her chest. Her throat was parched. There was a carafe of water on the table to her right, and a full glass before it, demanding she drink it.

As she gulped down the tepid liquid, she noted it was a tranquil space she found herself in. But the peace of the room did nothing to assuage the fear that gripped her by the throat. She still didn't have the faintest recollection of who she was, nor how she came to be in the care of the Maycotts, but if she knew anything at all, it was that a woman in a predicament such as hers was in danger, even if her surroundings were quite placid.

"Oh, you're awake," called a kind and familiar voice from the door.

The figure approached and she made a guess. "I suspect you must be Lady Helena."

Lady Helena stepped closer to the bed and unfurled another quilt, laying it overtop her already covered body. "What gave me away?"

She nodded toward the blanket. "I believe your sister referred to you as my nursemaid."

There was a warm smile beaming in her direction. "In truth, I am Her Grace, the dowager Duchess of Pembroke. Well, one of them, at least, but we don't stand on formalities here, so Helena will do." Helena sat on the edge of the bed and extended a hand toward her. "Do you mind?"

She shook her head. "I don't believe I'm feverish but I'm also not the best judge of things right now."

Helena's hand was gentle on her skin as she probed for fever. "No, I think you're quite right about that. What a relief!" She withdrew her hand and settled it on the folds of her skirt. "Now what about your memory?"

She frowned, still feeling lost in the mire of her own unknowable mind. "Still nothing."

"Please do not feel pressured on my account. Not all of

the Maycott siblings insist on a superhuman recovery from our guests."

Heat colored her cheeks at the mere thought of Helena's brother and his penetrating gaze. She had to get a grip on herself. "Where is the stern bastard, then?"

Helena cleared her throat lightly. "After the *incident*, he decided to go out and search for your spectacles in daylight, surmising that as you were likely wearing them when you fell from your horse, they can't have gone far."

The heat on her cheeks deepened. "Did I truly vomit on his boots?" She knew she had, but with her mind so empty of other memories, that particular one stood out all the more in terms of clarity and agonizing precision.

Helena was as charitable as she was kind. "Unfortunately, yes."

"And I presume he's the kind of man who would take great offense at that sort of transgression?" She was a stranger in his home with a mind so addled she could not even tell him her own name. And she'd gotten sick on his boots. He must hate her. But his hatred paled next to her shame, which coiled around her like a great serpent, threatening to suffocate her.

"You needn't worry; my brother is not as stern as he would have you believe." She patted the bed with a start. "Now, are you hungry? I'll have a plate sent up to you."

The query was intolerably simple, but it smarted when she was forced to reckon with how well the Maycotts were treating her, a stranger. She couldn't help but ask the question that had been needling at her since waking. "Why are you being so kind to me? I'm a nuisance."

"You were injured on our land. It is our duty to see you well."

She wrung her hands together against the soft linens. "I

might not have my memories, but I know enough to know I'm an imposition."

"Please don't think of it like that. We couldn't possibly send you on your way in your current state." She scooted a bit closer. "If I'm being honest, you've given us a welcome distraction from what would normally be a particularly somber time of year."

The words were meant as a kindness, even if they did contain a hint of mystery. She didn't feel comfortable asking for elaboration, not after they'd asked so little of her.

"Well, please do not hesitate to send me on my way should I become a burden." Never mind that she had no earthly idea where she would go. "I cannot begin to imagine what the Earl of Belhaven would think of all this."

She didn't need her spectacles to see that Lady Helena was giving her a puzzled look. "Why, you don't have to imagine—"

A knock at the door surprised them both, and Lord Jasper entered the room. Helena shot to her feet as he strode unerringly toward the bed and deposited something in her lap.

She looked down to see he had retrieved her spectacles.

"How did you find them?" she asked while hurriedly placing them upon the bridge of her nose. The clarity of her vision came as a shock after straining miserably. There was Helena, her auburn hair tied up neatly, exposing the graceful line of her neck. She was beautiful, with porcelain skin marked by one long scar that spanned from her temple to her jaw, and bright blue eyes that held within them a gleam of sadness.

"They weren't that far from where we found you," came his stern voice. She was almost afraid to look at him. But she was a guest in his family's home. She could not ignore the son of an earl for much longer.

She turned and felt the full intensity of his gaze like a blaze of heat. He was terribly handsome, the kind of man who could hold a room in his thrall with naught but a glance. His golden brown hair was a touch long to be considered fashionable, as though such matters were beneath him, and she had to stop herself from reaching out to tuck a soft curl behind his ear. His cheeks were deeply red from the cold, and his warm brown eyes glowed like embers as they grazed her skin. She had never seen a man's jaw so finely carved, nor shoulders so artfully broad. She wanted to touch him. No, she wanted him to touch *her*.

She swallowed thickly and cast her eyes downward, hoping he could not sense her indecent thoughts. "I must thank you, my lord." Did he notice her voice catch? She peeked back up at him, finding his expression unreadable. "I fear my debt to you has only grown."

He looked surprised by her words. "There is no debt," he said gruffly, as though he spent every morning searching through snow for a woman's errant spectacles.

"Surely, I owe you at least one pair of boots, my lord."

The look he gave her then was icier than the Arctic, and yet it warmed her as well as any fire.

Her mind was distressingly empty, but she did know one thing: Lord Jasper and his beguiling eyes were trouble, indeed.

Chapter Four

JASPER

Jasper's eyes narrowed upon her, and when he spoke, his voice was rough. "I'm sure we will find a suitable form of repayment."

In the distance, Helena made a choking sound.

The woman nodded reasonably, as though he hadn't said something deeply improper. "I have no doubt," she replied.

He found it difficult to look away from her now that her vision was restored. For someone who had allegedly woken up terribly unmoored, there was a welcome surety to her now. It had only been twelve or so hours since he and his sisters had come upon her bloodied form in the road. *Don't let them get me* had been the very first thing she'd said to him, and now she had the cheek to parry words with him about his ruined boots.

She was something of an enigma. A woman so lost should not appear so assured.

It meant he would never trust her fully, even as he felt himself warm in her presence like the first thawing of spring. Was it truly possible for someone to become untethered from their own mind? Did that mean she'd forgotten the distress she'd been in as well? He would not forget the fear in her eyes. That had been real. But what about the rest?

His hands still ached from the cold. It had taken longer than he'd anticipated to dig through the snow in search of her spectacles. And then joy had coursed through him when he'd found them, a feeling of elation like he had won a sizeable bet at a gambling table. He had marched through the manor, intent on using the spectacles as a means of forcing the woman to remember herself. But when he'd rushed into the Lavender Room filled with purpose, the sight of her had stolen every thought from his mind, leaving only one: she was particularly beautiful.

It was a ridiculous notion to have filling his head, especially when there were far more important matters to focus on. But he couldn't help it. She was stunning even with a bandage covering the side of her head, even with dark bruises under her eyes, even in a too-large nightgown in the middle of a bed that seemed intolerably empty with only her in it. But it was deeper than that, too. Something about her tugged at the parts of him he'd thought long buried. Something about the way she spoke to him chipped away at the walls he had so carefully constructed.

Standing there, dumbstruck by her, he struggled to banish the thought from his mind. She was either a liar or a liability. Each possibility was reason enough to keep his distance from her. His sisters could keep him informed of her progress. He had work to do. He didn't have time for damsels in distress.

But then she had mentioned her debt to him, and all thoughts of leaving her to Helena had faded. His reply had been a desperate attempt to make clear there was nothing transactional about his finding her spectacles or providing her with a place to recover.

And when she had teased him, a long-forgotten flicker of roguishness had flared in him. He hadn't meant for his comment about her repayment to sound so sinful. Jasper needed to get a grip on himself, and quickly.

"I presume you have yet to recover your memory?" he asked, perhaps harsher than he'd intended.

She looked hurt by his sudden shift from playful to stern. With inhuman strength he managed to ignore the desire to put her at ease once more. "Not yet, my lord. But not even a day has passed since my injury."

"Quite right," said Helena, giving Jasper a look of irritation. "Take all the time you need."

Jasper didn't like the sound of that, but it wasn't as if they had a choice. Where could they send her? If word got out that the Earl of Belhaven had sent an addled woman away after she was injured on his property, it would be the height of scandal, and the sort of thing that would tarnish his siblings' prospects. Which was to say nothing of the woman's vulnerability in her current state. There were any number of criminals and charlatans lying in wait for women like her, hoping to press a nefarious advantage and bring harm upon her.

No, he wouldn't allow it. Perhaps she just needed some more prodding.

"My lady," he began, causing her to wince. He paused, waiting for an explanation.

"I need a name," she said at last, her frustration evident in her tone. "I need to start thinking of myself as someone."

"Well, what do you suggest we call you? Since I don't imagine you're very close to simply remembering who you are, despite how much trouble that may save us."

"Call me whatever you like, my lord," she replied through gritted teeth. "I have no preference."

Jasper was sure the honorific had never sounded quite so insulting, giving him leave to match her enmity. "What about 'Patience,' then, since you seem to have it in droves."

Her cheeks reddened. "I find I have *some* preference, my lord."

Jasper suppressed a smug smile. "I thought you might."

Helena cleared her throat as if to remind them both that she was there. "There was an item in your pocket that may help shed some light." She held out the ring. The woman accepted it eagerly, studying it as though it held all the answers.

"*JHD*," she said aloud, though not with a tone of sudden understanding. Despite his pessimism, Jasper did his best to not visibly deflate. "This was in my pocket?"

"Yes," Helena answered.

"It reveals very little about your identity," Jasper pointed out.

"That much is clear," she replied without tearing her eyes away from her careful consideration of the ring. "There is a maker's mark inside," she said, squinting to read the faded engraving. "B & K. I don't suppose you are familiar?"

"Isobel already combed through our parents' jewelry; none bear the same mark," replied Helena.

"Pity," she said, holding her hand out and slipping the ring over her little finger, the way men wore signet rings. It fell off as soon as she turned her wrist. Furrowing her brow, she closed her hand over the ring in disappointment.

"Try your ring finger," Jasper suggested. Her eyes widened as she slid the gold band over her finger. It fit, but barely. Her hands were very small.

"Whomever it belonged to, you must have deemed it

important enough to take with you."

She looked over to him, her spectacles slightly enlarging her gray eyes, making them appear almost unnaturally silver like when he had found her in the storm. "What if it belonged to me?"

"You think you're *JHD*?"

She looked slightly affronted. "It's not impossible, is it? At the very least it's a clue." She held her hand up to gaze upon the ring, and something in Jasper's chest snagged at the thought of her being married before he dismissed it as yet another ridiculous thought. She looked up at Helena and then back at him. "I could be a Jane," she said, a bit defensively.

Helena nodded. "An entirely suitable name—"

"I'd have thought you more of an Elizabeth," Jasper muttered.

Her brow creased as she considered his words. "Elizabeth Bennet?" she scoffed as she realized his meaning. "I hardly believe I possess even one tenth her cleverness."

"But you *are* familiar with Jane Austen?" He didn't mean for it to sound like an accusation, but *his* patience was wearing a tad thin.

Helena sighed in annoyance. "Jasper, you'd be hard pressed to find a woman in all of England who wasn't."

The woman—he supposed he should start thinking of her as Jane—began to speak as she picked at the stitching on her sleeve, her gaze vacant, lost in thought. "I suspect there are two categories of memory within my mind: the first pertaining to things like my ability to speak or recollect the works of Jane Austen, memories that are either too ingrained or inconsequential to be taken from me, and then the second pertains to the things that matter a great deal more, but are perhaps the most fluid, like my sense of self or memories of my family." She stopped the nervous fiddling and looked up at them both, clear-eyed through her pain and obvious exhaustion. "The injury couldn't alter the first category, but devastated the second, leaving me rather adrift, I suppose."

Jasper knew nothing of what she purported to be experiencing, and yet he recognized some of his own suffering in her words. There was an unwelcome tightness in his chest when he thought about how his own memories ruled him, and how, if given the opportunity, he might wish to rid himself of even the happy ones if it meant relief. He had too many memories while she had too few, and yet there were commonalities between them, things that could tie them together if he wasn't careful.

Helena stepped to the bed and sat on the edge, taking the woman's hand in hers. "Well, we do know one thing."

Her eyes brightened a bit. "What's that?"

"You were wrong about lacking Elizabeth Bennet's cleverness."

The woman smiled, but it did not quite reach her eyes. Jasper could see how she was fading, and understandably so, given her injury. "So what shall it be, then? *JHD*," he mused. "Jane Harriet Danvers? Or perhaps Jane Hazel Debenham?"

The woman shook her head and then winced, raising a hand to the borders of her injury. "No, just Jane, if you please. I wouldn't want to delve too far into fiction and build my life upon a falsehood." She paused, seeming to reflect upon the prospect until her skin blanched. Why was it he could read her so easily? Jasper had never considered himself a particularly astute man when it came to the feelings of others. Not for lack of skill but rather a lack of interest. It wasn't a flattering evaluation of the person he'd been before he'd met Annabelle, but it was an accurate one. She took a deep breath. "Jane somehow feels right, even if it is incorrect."

He summoned a smile for her, quite certain that he had never referred to a woman he barely knew with such intimacy. "Jane it is, then."

Helena stood. "We should let you rest, but can I bring you some food? A reviving broth perhaps?"

Jane had already sunk into the bed at the mere mention of rest. "Broth would be lovely," she said, her fatigue evident.

"And your dressings will have to be changed soon—" Helena started before Jasper pulled her away from the bedside.

The two of them paused in the doorway and looked back at Jane. "She's already asleep," he whispered.

Helena glared at him. "No doubt exhausted by your constant interrogation," she whispered quite harshly.

Jasper folded his arms over his chest. "I hardly think my desire to aid her can be construed as an interrogation," he whispered back.

"And I hardly think you have any idea how to treat a convalescing guest, but I assure you it isn't by demanding they recover on your schedule."

"I only wish to return her to where she belongs," he hissed. "With her *family*."

"And if she has none? Are we to turn her out into the streets with little more than the clothes on her back and our sincerest wishes for a swift recovery, only somewhere else so as not to burden us?"

"That is not what I meant..." He paused, noticing Isobel over Helena's shoulder, her attention rapt.

"Oh please don't cease your whispered quarrelling on my account. I rather like seeing you both so lively."

Jasper pinched the bridge of his nose, a sure sign of irritation he must have picked up from his father, since he couldn't recall doing it before the demands of his unwanted title fell upon his shoulders. "What is it, Isobel?"

His tone must have suggested he wasn't in the mood for whatever it was she came to tell him. "It's nothing," she assured him, her own falsely bright tone betraying her as she straightened.

"Isobel, please." It was better to get whatever it was out of the way so he could focus on literally anything other than the thoughts of Jane that clouded his mind. Was she a brazen charlatan? An immensely creative fortune hunter? A madwoman? Or more distressing yet, was she someone on the run from something he couldn't save her from? And if so, what then?

Christ, I need a distraction. He'd spent much of the last year working the land with his tenants, a backbreaking effort that had done much to silence his troubled mind. But it was winter now, the crops had long been harvested and the fields planted. There were no more fences to be mended, no more leaky roofs to be fixed. His tenants, as grateful as they had been for a helping hand, were likely tired of his zeal.

With Christmas around the corner, chaos—in the form of Freddie and August—would be descending upon them soon. Jasper shook his head, emptying all thoughts of escape from his mind. He was the Earl of Belhaven and the head of his family. Mulgrave Hall was the only place for him now.

Isobel looked like she wished to disintegrate on the spot rather than speak as a sharp bark of a rather unkind-sounding laugh echoed from below. Jasper's blood went cold. Behind him, Helena swore for the first time in living memory.

Isobel clearly saw no reason to obfuscate any longer. "Aunt Adelaide is here," she told them, rather uselessly.

"Who invited her?" Jasper asked, still gripped by the shock of it.

"I'd say I suspect Battersby penned one of his 'helpful' letters the moment you brought a broken, bleeding woman across the threshold," said Isobel bitterly, "but even she couldn't traverse the Channel so quickly." She paused, her eyes widening. "Perhaps we should consider that she may have crossed riding a broomstick."

Jasper laughed darkly, taking a moment to shut the door to Jane's room. He turned back to his sisters, their faces both mirrors of his own shock. "So she's a witch or it's just disastrous timing."

"We must do something," said Helena, her voice small.

Jasper sighed, resigned to the misery of a rare visit from their father's younger sister, a formidable woman the siblings had only spent scant days with over the course of their lives, as Lady Adelaide Maycott had made her home in Bordeaux. England was too pedestrian for a woman of her stature, she'd claimed.

"Short of abandoning our home and identities, I don't believe there is much we can do, Helena."

The sound of their aunt's voice grew closer, and with it, Jasper's impending sense of doom. His father had never tolerated any of their complaints about her, but Jasper knew their relationship had been strained since before any of them were born. Something about how she had treated their mother in the beginning of his parents' courtship. The most Jasper ever got out of his father was that Aunt Adelaide had been her father's daughter through and through. It was not a flattering comparison. She hadn't even returned for the funerals, citing an illness Jasper had uncharitably hoped might keep her away forever.

As she entered the hallway, Jasper was certain he saw Viola's door—which was never closed entirely, lest she "miss anything"— shut rather firmly. Battersby trailed behind her, his arms laden with her various trunks and cases, with a similarly burdened Nash behind him, no doubt roped rather forcefully into service. Adelaide's cheeks were rosy and her shoulders dusted with snow. Her red hair glowed like firelight against the drab traveling gown she wore, and her blue eyes pierced right through them, searching for flaws or weaknesses, as she was wont to do. She looked younger than he remembered, or was it that Jasper in his weariness had caught up to her in age? Despite it all, her presence was a bit like having a part of their father returned to them. It felt like a knife to Jasper's gut.

She paused before them, expectantly. Isobel and Helena braced themselves, but Jasper stepped around them, prepared to take the full blow of their aunt's scrutiny.

"Welcome, Aunt. What an unexpected joy."

"I'd say I'm rarely an expected one," she sniffed, though there was a gleam of mischief in her eye. "I thought you could do with a visit. Wouldn't want my nieces and nephews to face the holiday alone."

Jasper looked out the window to the swiftly falling snow. "I would have thought the storm would slow you down." Hoped, more like.

"*Psh*! Nothing a little grit can't overcome." He wondered if her coachman would agree. "Ready my room, would you, Battersby? My legs are aching and I'll need a maid to draw me a bath."

Battersby, who often acted as though the requirements of his position were beneath him, hopped to her service at once, disappearing down the hall for the Verdigris Room, her favorite. Nash reluctantly followed, giving the siblings an encouraging wink as he passed, leaving them at their aunt's mercy.

"Let me get a look at you."

It was nothing short of a demand and they heeded it quickly, forming a line for her to inspect. She walked it, beginning her assessment with Isobel.

"Too thin. Men don't like a frail woman, despite what they may think."

Isobel's defiant streak, likely inherited from Adelaide herself, pushed to the surface. "I find I don't much care for the opinions of men."

The corners of Adelaide's mouth tugged upward until she beat the grin into submission. "How old are you, Isobel?"

She stuck out her chin. "I turned nineteen last month."

Adelaide tsked. "Nineteen and without a single Season under your belt." She let the statement hang in the air ominously before moving on to Helena, her imperious gaze softening a bit. "You wear your grief upon you like a corset, my dear." She extended her gloved hand and rested it on Helena's shoulder. "Not that I blame you, but you must take care to loosen the laces before it smothers you."

Jasper watched as Helena flinched with each subsequent word, and felt his anger boil over. Their aunt was not overtly malicious, they could not point to a particular cruelty, but her tone was wielded like a weapon. He'd been forced to tolerate it when he was simply Mr. Jasper Maycott, second and most wayward son of the Earl of Belhaven. But Jasper was the earl now, and he would go to war to protect his sisters from even the barest of slights.

"Aunt Adelaide, you must be exhausted from your long journey. Perhaps a rest before supper is in order." He gave her a half bow out of respect and moved to take her arm in his. "Please allow me to escort—"

"Not so fast, boy." She stood as firmly as a mighty oak.

"There are a hundred things I could say to *you*, but I wish to see the girl first."

So Battersby had ensured she was informed. The desire to protect Jane from his aunt's clutches flared in his chest. "She is resting."

Adelaide shook her head. "I must see her—"

"She doesn't need to be seen, Aunt," he replied as sternly as he dared, not knowing how much his aunt knew about the state of Jane's mind, but wanting to protect her regardless. "She needs rest."

She gave him a look so cold it seemed to darken the hall. "What she needs is a chaperone." The word hung heavily between them, a reminder to Jasper of what was truly at stake. Adelaide continued, sensing his weakness. "Because as soon as word gets out that an unaccompanied, unwed woman has taken up residence in the home of the Earl of Belhaven without the benefit and protection of a chaperone, your options will be limited to either marrying her or ruining her."

If pressed, Jasper would have had to admit that she was right, and that he should have thought of the matter first. Helena was a widow and could have served as one if needed, but he knew from his days as a rake that the most unimpeachable chaperone in the eyes of those who counted was a spinster aunt with a spine of steel.

Much like the woman standing before him, who looked at him as though he were an intolerable fool. And perhaps she was right. The issue with Jane was precarious indeed, but nearly all of the risk fell on her shoulders. He pictured her again, bandaged and bruised in that ocean of a bed.

He scratched his neck, feeling very exposed. "We seek only to protect her."

It had been the wrong thing to say, judging by Adelaide's exasperated expression. "And tell me, nephew, who will be protecting *you*?"

The question fell with the heaviness of a cudgel, and even Jasper had to admit it was a fair one.

Chapter Five

JANE

When Jane awoke, it was to the thick scent of smoke choking her.

Her eyes flew open as her hand reached for her spectacles, shoving them on her face as she sat bolt upright, ready to pour her carafe of water on an escaped ember before it became something unmanageable.

Instead, she found a severe-looking woman she had never seen before smoking a cheroot in the armchair beside her bed. The woman wore a satin morning gown in deep plum with an ultra-high neckline, her hair styled in an efficient knot with ringlets artfully placed at her temples. She was older, but with a slightly less vibrant version of Helena's red hair and something of Lord Jasper in her eyes. A relation, no doubt, but Jane couldn't imagine the Countess of Belhaven smoking, at least not so openly.

The woman let a lungful of smoke out. "My, but you are excitable."

It did not sound like a compliment. "I don't believe I've ever seen a woman smoke a cheroot," she countered.

"I daresay you still haven't, as this is a *cigarette*." She said it with the crispest of French accents before taking in another puff. "They're all the rage in France, but like everything else, they will arrive in England ten years after we've deemed them unfashionable."

Jane's mind was groggy. She could have been asleep for an hour or a day. "How long was I—"

"Unconscious?" Another exhale, filling the room with a haze of smoke. "I arrived yesterday afternoon and you stubbornly slept through the evening and night, waking only to take your medicine, but I'd have hardly called you 'awake' then."

That explained how ravenous she felt. But she presumed her body had needed rest more than sustenance. "Would you mind opening the window?" Jane asked, her eyes watering as the woman's plume of smoke reached her.

"My dear, the conditions outside would rival the Arctic. I will do no such thing."

"Then perhaps you could take your *cigarette*"—she used the woman's exact pronunciation, impressing even herself— "elsewhere, as I do not believe that smoke is conducive to healing."

The woman gave her a long, assessing gaze before allowing a small smile while she stubbed the cigarette out in a glass dish. "I wasn't expecting much bite," she mused. "I'll admit it is refreshing. Too often Society robs young girls of their teeth long before they've had a chance to sharpen them."

Now that the excitement of waking to a potential inferno had faded, Jane was left to contend with the pain in her head and the hunger roaring to life in her belly. She slumped back onto the bed, not much caring what the woman thought of her, considering it was *she* who was intruding on an invalid.

"What is your name, girl?"

She bristled at that. "I assume you've heard tell of my misadventure, my lady," she offered before the woman nodded. "Well, then you know I am not exactly certain of much, but you can call me Jane."

The woman seemed to already know her name and was merely seeking to have Jane confirm it. "Of all the names in the world to reinvent yourself with, you chose *Jane*?"

"I am not seeking to reinvent myself. I would much prefer it if my memories were restored to me." Her stomach growled, and she found herself hoping the woman heard and would perhaps be moved to action on her behalf. Where was blessed Helena when she needed her? "Jane is simple, and I find I need a bit of simple in my life."

The woman barked out a laugh. "Too true."

Jane shifted uncomfortably, all too aware of her pressing need to visit the water closet. The woman noticed her mild distress but said nothing.

She raised a brow imperiously. "Aren't you a bit curious as to whom you are conversing with?"

"I assume Society bleeds the curiosity out of girls as well."

The woman's laugh was genuine this time, and loud. "I didn't expect to like you this much," she confessed. "I am Lady Adelaide Maycott."

A relation, then. "A pleasure to meet you, my lady. May I ask what brings you to my bedside?"

"I am here to observe. My arrival so soon after your incident was a happy accident, seeing as how you'll be needing a chaperone during your recovery."

"Surely you needn't go to the trouble," Jane started. "It's not as though I'm some fine lady with a reputation in need of protecting." Though, even as she said it, she knew she could be wrong. All she had to go on was a too-big ring and a hunch. And just because she didn't *feel* like a lady didn't necessarily mean she wasn't one.

"You are a woman of marriageable age and questionable origin at the mercy of Lord Belhaven. It is both for your sake and his that I will exercise my duty as chaperone."

Jane hadn't thought of it that way. "I suppose that's logical," she offered with a sigh.

Lady Adelaide did not seem to hear her. "You are aware, of course, of what normally happens to women like you?"

"Women like me?" she asked, bracing for the reply.

"The ones without a past, desperately chasing a different future for themselves." Her gaze was appraising and somewhat cold. "In the end, they get found out."

Jane hardly had the energy to be insulted. "It's my past I seek, my lady. Without it, I am lost."

Lady Adelaide's features seemed to soften at that. "No, my girl. Without it, you are in danger."

That she knew in her bones. What protection existed for a woman who did not know herself? Where could she turn for assistance? Who could she lean on for support? If she dwelled upon it for too long, Jane was certain the panic that simmered just beneath the surface would overtake her.

"It is a lucky circumstance you have found yourself in, to be injured on the grounds of Mulgrave Hall. My nephew numbers among the scant few aristocrats who would feel honor bound to assist you."

Was it honor, then, that spurred Lord Jasper? He seemed far

more driven to view her as an irritation to be rid of at the earliest opportunity. Not that she blamed him.

"I shall endeavor to count my blessings, my lady, but I do find myself in need of a bit of privacy at the moment."

Lady Adelaide stood. "I shooed your caretakers away so I could get a sense of your character without their influence."

Jane understood now where Lord Jasper's suspicious nature came from. "And how did you find it?" Pity that she had no idea where her boldness came from, but it seemed an inexorable part of her.

Lady Adelaide gave her a shrewd grin. "Far better than I'd anticipated."

"I am relieved." She said it with a mixture of sarcasm and honesty, strange bedfellows indeed.

Lady Adelaide continued. "You are a puzzle, my dear. And whether that is intentional or not, I do intend to solve you." She swept toward the door, pausing at the threshold. "Oh, I had a bath drawn for you, though I imagine the water is tepid by now." With that, she was gone, leaving Jane with the certainty that a tepid bath had never sounded so heavenly.

Jane rose carefully onto her unsteady feet, testing her full weight before committing to a few uneasy steps. She was weak, to be sure, but it didn't seem like a lasting ailment. She chanced a walk to the window, eager to feel even the pale winter sun on her sallow skin. It was latched tight, but her hard work was rewarded with the iciest of breezes, filling her lungs with crisp, reviving air.

"Jane! My goodness!" Helena rushed over to her, latching the window closed and setting her incredulous gaze upon her. "I cannot abide an open window in the heart of a Surrey winter."

"I found I needed fresh air, even if it was frigid."

Helena sniffed the air, nose wrinkling. "And what did you

think of dear Aunt Adelaide?"

"A most charming woman," offered Jane slyly.

Helena gave her a conspiratorial grin. "Come, now that the air is clear and we have surmised that you can walk, we can get this nightgown off of you and get you into a bath. My lady's maid will happily assist you, after which you will no doubt need to rest once more. I'll check in on you in a few hours." She smiled and departed, leaving Jane at the mercy of a stranger.

The maid simply guided her to the water closet and allowed her a few moments of privacy before aiding her into the waiting bath—tepid indeed, but a relief nonetheless—where the maid bathed her skin and washed her hair with practiced ease.

None of it felt familiar to Jane, not being scrubbed nor oiled nor waited upon. The maid took special care when washing around the dressings covering her wound. When finished, she lightly peeled back the damp bandage and let it fall to the floor. Jane looked down at the rust-stained fabric and felt her stomach lurch.

"It does not look too poorly, my lady," the maid assured her with a smile. "Shouldn't be a nasty scar."

She returned the smile. "Just Jane, please." It might not be her real name, but she found it fit her better than being referred to so formally. The maid nodded but Jane was certain she had made her uncomfortable. She did not speak again while she wrapped a clean bandage around her head, dried her off and helped her into a silk dressing robe.

Back in the bedroom, the maid sat her before the vanity and stepped away, allowing Jane a moment to contemplate her reflection for the first time since her accident.

The bandage, bruising, and slight swelling stole most of her immediate attention, but it didn't take long for Jane to surmise that her features, like the ring, were not going to lift her buried memories to the surface. Nothing about the way she looked shocked her, but her face was about as familiar as a stranger's. She peered closer, noting that her eyes were a peculiar shade of gray, her lips were an entirely acceptable shape framing a generous mouth, and her brows were perhaps a tad strong for the rest of her features. She traced her fingers along her cheek, wondering if it was a love of the sun that had her freckles staying with her well into the winter. She tucked a lock of dark, wet hair behind her ear. It was longer than she'd expected when unbound from the braid, reaching down to the small of her back.

Overall, not recognizing herself was not as distressing an experience as she'd anticipated. After all, she was a foreigner in her own mind, residing in the country manor of the Earl of Belhaven, a man she hadn't even met.

In many ways she was lost. Adrift. Alone.

Sitting straighter, she resolved to *do* something about it. What, she wasn't precisely sure. But she could walk now, and while her head ached, there was much that could be done in the face of a little pain. She couldn't rely on the kindness of the Maycotts forever. Surely, Jane was beginning to overstay her welcome.

The maid returned and tended to Jane's hair, pulling the strands into a serviceable braid. By then, she was so famished the gurgling in her stomach did not go unnoticed.

"I've sent for a plate, my lady," the maid assured her, steadfastly choosing to let Jane's request regarding her name go unheeded. "Should be here shortly. You should get some rest."

Jane thanked her and watched her leave in the reflection of the mirror, intending to ignore the suggestion as soon as she'd had something to eat.

It didn't take long for a tray of food to arrive, and even less time for Jane to devour it in its entirety. The dishes were hearty, if bland, but something as simple as porridge and oatcakes verged on the sublime now that Jane's appetite had returned. She washed it down with three cups of strong tea as she decided what to do next. Finding something tangible to jog her memory seemed a reasonable course of action, but she knew every inch of her chambers now. She needed something new.

A cursory search of the wardrobe showed it was stuffed full of gowns, varying from relaxed, flowing morning gowns to robust hunting costumes made of thick and hardy fabrics, to tiered evening gowns adorned with lace trimmings, all of them in pristine condition, if not unworn entirely.

Jane wondered who they once belonged to, and if it was appropriate for her to borrow one. She considered that as everything she had worn since her arrival had been lent to her, surely the Maycotts wouldn't mind this time. She selected the plainest-looking tea gown she could find in the sea of finery, hoping she would be able to manage putting it on without the benefit of a maid.

It was made of pale pink silk, with fitted sleeves, a modest neckline, and a medium-length train. She pulled it on over her head without much trouble, feeling scandalized by the idea that she would have to go without undergarments or a corset, though relieved when it settled around her and she saw that the excess planes of fabric acted like an outer robe, somewhat shielding the curves of her body from view.

By the time she was clothed, Jane was exhausted. She poured herself another fortifying cup of tea and shot it back like a dram of medicine. She didn't have time to be tired, or to languish and let the world pass her by. Until she knew who she was, Jane was vulnerable. She needed answers, and answers would not be found in this room.

Stepping into the hall felt like an accomplishment after days abed. Wandering down the corridor was a feat of strength, strength she hadn't been sure she possessed, and navigating the stairs was a welcome revelation. She moved slowly, careful not to exert herself too much, and eager to take in all of the magnificence of Mulgrave Hall. Her sense of awe was proving to be a mark against the possibility of her being a lady who would be used to such extravagance. Everywhere she looked, she found herself shocked by the beauty of the architecture or the intricate furniture or the masterfully rendered paintings lining the walls. The grand windows she passed revealed a snowy landscape of rolling hills and frosted trees, none of it familiar, but none of it so dissimilar from how she had imagined it from her bed. Did that mean she knew the area? Perhaps she had not traveled very far on horseback before her accident. Or perhaps she had been riding for days. It infuriated her to no end that she had no way of knowing.

She was relieved not to pass any of the Maycotts, though she didn't think what she was doing was wrong. Jane wasn't a prisoner, and while Helena would likely faint to see her upright and very much out of bed, she didn't think anyone would seek to stop her exploring. They wanted her memories restored as much as she did. Lord Jasper most of all.

Thoughts of his heated gaze sent a flush to Jane's cheeks, making her feel woozy in her already weakened state. She braced herself against a doorway, taking deep breaths through her nose until the feeling subsided. She had to get a grip on herself. If the mere thought of him gave her the vapors, she wouldn't survive seeing him in the flesh again. It was his intense manner that dizzied her, she told herself. Not one inch of Lord Jasper was nonchalant. She suspected that he didn't do things by half—he felt the full breadth of his emotions, be it his frustration with the gaps in her memory or his tireless zeal to see her healed and out of his home.

She wondered if positive emotions would elicit the same intensity in him, and what it would be like to be on the receiving end of his joy or his passion. Could his love for a woman ever match the force of the cold fury he had directed her way, brief but potent as it was? That woman would be lucky indeed, she suspected, feeling a flash of jealousy she refused to acknowledge. Because regardless of their mild enmity and Lady Adelaide's assumption that she wasn't aware of how lucky she was to have been injured on his land, Jane knew that Lord Jasper was a good man. Another might have taken advantage of her or left her to fend for herself, but something in his nature made either of those options an impossibility, and it was that part of him that intrigued her.

But that was where she had to leave it. Nothing good would come from her exploring how the man made her feel. It didn't matter. Once she recovered her memories, the Maycotts would themselves become a happy one. Surely, she had a life she needed to get back to.

She straightened her spine and left the safe embrace of the doorway.

Instinct led her to the manor's library. Her heart warmed at the thought of being surrounded by books and she tucked away the notion that they brought her joy, adding to her meager foundation from which she hoped to rediscover herself.

As she neared the library's doors, voices from within slowed her down. She didn't wish to intrude if any of the Maycott siblings were receiving guests. Heavens, what if the earl and the countess were present? Jane felt herself shrink at the possibility, desperate as she was to not meet a man of his stature in her current state.

Still, curiosity got the better of her. She stepped as close as she could to the entrance, pressing herself to the wall and straining to hear what was occurring inside.

"Aunt, Jane is harmless, I assure you." That was angelic Helena, defending her as usual.

"Be that as it may, no one can know she is a stranger suffering from an ailment of the mind, discovered alone on the grounds of Mulgrave Hall. Women have been confined to asylums for much less."

Jane's heartbeat quickened. How close was she to being shut away? Her mind rioted at the thought, and she knew then that she would rather flee into the bitter cold and the unknown than face that certain misery. She had already lost enough autonomy; she could not stand to lose any more.

"Too true, Aunt Adelaide. We live in a society that punishes women for mere eccentricity, labelling it 'hysteria' and deeming us ungovernable shrews in the process," said Isobel, her voice dripping with contempt.

"That was not an invitation for a political screed, Isobel."

"And yet I never seem to let an opportunity pass me by."

"We won't be advertising that information, Aunt." Lord Jasper's voice was as stern as she remembered, the kind of voice that belonged to a man whose every command was heeded. It made her want to defy him, if only to see how he would react.

"How fortunate you are that I arrived in time," said Lady Adelaide sagely.

"You certainly seem to believe it an act of providence," came Lord Jasper's exasperated reply.

She sniffed. "If rescuing wayward maidens is how you were spending your time prior to my arrival, then I'd say I couldn't have come soon enough."

Jane bristled at the thought of being considered a "wayward maiden" before the logical part of her mind reminded her that it was somewhat of an apt description.

"This is novel, even for him, Aunt Adelaide." That sounded like Lady Isobel's raspy voice.

"We haven't had a visitor in ages," sighed a dreamy, childlike voice Jane hadn't heard before.

"No callers whatsoever?" asked Lady Adelaide in an incredulous tone.

"We've been in mourning," said Lord Jasper in a tone that brooked no further conversation. Jane hadn't known they were in mourning. She hadn't seen enough of Lady Helena or Lady Isobel to note that they wore black or gray exclusively. Her skin heated. If Jane had considered herself an imposition before, it was nothing compared to how she felt now. *Who had passed,* she wondered. *Their mother?* Her heart clenched at the thought.

"To be sure, nephew. But it is your duty as the—"

"We will not discuss duty." It was said rather quietly but Jane couldn't imagine that Lady Adelaide would argue further.

"I simply desire to impress upon you the seriousness of the situation, Jasper."

"What is it about my behavior that suggests I'm not taking this seriously?" It was a good point, Jane thought, given his tone.

"It is not simply a matter of concealing the truth. You must also lie. Turn the mysterious woman into a dull story before a more interesting one emerges."

There was a weighty pause as the Maycotts considered her suggestion. Jane felt odd, standing on the threshold of a conversation about her future. But making herself known to them seemed the worse option. Better to listen and make her decision from there.

"We can say she is an old friend from Cheltenham, come for a visit," Helena offered.

Lady Adelaide made a noise to indicate her disgust. "What a waste that was. Sending the two of you away for no reason at all."

"It was my only chance to learn advanced chemistry," Lady Isobel argued.

"And did you return a chemist, Isobel? Or did you return a budding suffragist?" Their aunt said the word as though it were a disease.

"Which would you have preferred, Aunt?"

"Neither. Married is how I'd prefer you."

"Ah, but how could I be wed without a single Season under my belt? I'd say I'm well on my way to becoming a spinster." She did not sound displeased at the possibility.

"Nineteen may be too old to have never had a Season, but it is still *young*, Isobel."

"Back to the subject at hand, I'd say my idea is a sound one. No one would know that Jane isn't an old friend."

"Yes, that seems reasonable, Helena," Lord Jasper replied, causing Jane's heartbeat to flutter. They were deciding her fate, after all.

"It will be very difficult to control the situation should the truth come out," warned Lady Adelaide.

"Well, then I suppose it is a good thing that Mulgrave Hall will house only a few wayward Maycotts over the holiday," sighed Lord Jasper, sounding overwhelmed by the prospect already.

A noise behind Jane startled her nearly out of her skin. Mulgrave Hall's tiresome butler passed her without acknowledgment. He announced himself to those within by clearing his throat.

"Yes, Battersby?" asked Lord Jasper. Jane was still holding her breath, pressed against the wall rather uselessly now that her hiding place had been discovered.

"Your guests have sent word that the road has proven too perilous for their carriages, so they plan on completing their journey when the storm abates."

"Our guests?" Lord Jasper asked as though the word were foreign to him.

Then Lady Isobel swore most impressively, causing Lady Adelaide to gasp as though her niece had pulled a revolver from within her skirts. Jane couldn't see anything, hidden as she was.

"I completely forgot about the surprise," came Lady Isobel's distressed voice.

"Isobel?" A name had never sounded so threatening to Jane's ears.

"I planned it so long ago, it seemed like such a good idea then," Lady Isobel protested.

"Tell me you did not invite your friends to a holiday party at Mulgrave Hall."

"I didn't," she said defensively, as though the suggestion was an insult. The silence that followed was nigh unendurable. Jane could picture Lady Isobel squirming under the weight of it. She herself felt ready to crawl into the earth to avoid the rest of the conversation.

"Well?" asked Lord Jasper, ever stern.

Has he ever had a bit of fun?

"I didn't invite my friends, Jasper," she said contritely. "I invited yours."

Chapter Six

JASPER

Isobel's confession was a blow to the gut. He stood, walking around his father's desk to confront his sister. "You *what*?"

"You were so miserable!" She pointed her finger at him in accusation, as though he was the one who had done something wrong in this scenario. "And I knew you'd never do anything about it, so I took matters into my own hands."

"Who gave you the right?" he demanded, his anger bursting to life in his chest. It had been so long since he let himself feel the full force of it. So long since he had allowed himself to feel anything other than solemn sufferance. The anger, in contrast, felt almost cleansing.

Almost.

"Let's remain calm, shall we?" said Helena, ever the peacekeeper.

But Jasper could not find even a thread of serenity within

him. "How many?" he asked.

Isobel had the sense to look ashamed. "Six."

"You invited *six* of my friends to our home without discussing it with me first?" The idea of welcoming his old friends into his home as though he were a person whole and not simply a shell of a man was intolerable. Jasper was no longer equipped to handle the nuances of etiquette or the niceties of social interaction. It seemed a lifetime ago that he'd been anything other than empty. He didn't think he had it in him to be the Jasper Maycott they remembered.

Meanwhile, Isobel was moving past contrition to righteous indignation. "Can you at least admit that if they had arrived without warning, you wouldn't have had time to be cross with me?"

His anger met her indignation blow for blow. "How could we possibly know that?" He sat on the edge of the desk and yanked on his collar, feeling like he needed more air than the suddenly stifled library provided. "Your selfishness knows no bounds, Isobel."

"You think me selfish? You're the selfish one, Jasper. Keeping the best version of yourself locked away in your memories as though the only family you have left doesn't deserve you."

He stood without thinking, his anger a pulsing, uncontrollable thing. "There is no better version of me left!"

His words cracked through the library like a musket shot. Isobel's face fell, her features twisting with pity. Jasper turned away abruptly, unwilling to accept any of it. He closed his eyes and forced his breathing to slow, desperate to regain some control over himself.

"Have you had quite enough?" asked Aunt Adelaide between them, her rather light tone pouring an icy calm over Jasper.

"Quarreling doesn't change the fact that Mulgrave Hall is about to play host to a holiday party you've done precisely nothing to prepare for."

Jasper shot Isobel a look that made it clear where he thought the blame lay.

"Aunt Adelaide is right," said Helena calmly. "We have much to do and scarcely any time to do it. Battersby?" In his anger, Jasper had all but forgotten the butler's presence, yet another witness to his outburst. Would the indignities never cease? "Instruct the cook to prepare a menu for"—she paused, counting—"at least twelve. I'm sure Freddie and August will arrive at the most inconvenient time, so we should act as though they are already here. Heaven knows we will need to replenish our stores but there should be enough for tomorrow's meals. Isobel, go arrange with the housekeeper to have rooms aired out and prepared for guests. Viola and I will see to it that the rest of Mulgrave Hall is up to snuff."

"What would you have me do, Helena?" asked Jasper. He sat in his father's armchair, suddenly exhausted.

Helena's eyes were soft on him, making his skin itch. "You will procure for us a tree, Brother."

"A tree?"

"For trimming. Whether you like it or not, Jasper, we're hosting a version of Mother's famous fête."

Battersby chose that moment to clear his throat. Unfortunately, Jasper's patience had worn thin since discovering Isobel's meddlesome plot. He pinched the bridge of his nose. "Yes, Battersby?"

"What shall I do about Miss Jane?"

Jasper's heart thudded to a stop. He had forgotten about Jane and her beguiling eyes and mysterious past. Jane, a woman he didn't quite trust but who captivated him nevertheless, mixing with the friends he hadn't spoken to in a year. How was he going to endure any of it?

"The plan does not change," replied Aunt Adelaide crisply. "She is Helena's friend from school, come for a visit. It is the only option we have, save for turning her out into the street."

A thought came to Jasper, insistent and pressing. "It is important to me that we do not discuss Annabelle with Jane." A part of Jasper still belonged to Annabelle, a part he did not wish to share with anyone, least of all a virtual stranger. He still wasn't convinced that Jane wasn't a conniving fortune hunter seeking out his weaknesses to use against him. And given that a part of him was already drawn to her without much effort, he didn't think she needed any more ammunition in that regard.

His sisters exchanged worried glances. Helena spoke first. "Won't that be very difficult once your friends have arrived?"

He shook his head. "Not if they follow our lead with respect to the subject."

"So your plan is to prevent anyone from mentioning Annabelle by sheer force of will?" Isobel scoffed. "It's hardly how she should be remembered."

He refused to acknowledge Isobel's words. "I expect everyone to respect my wishes." When they didn't acquiesce right away, he continued. "We still don't know for certain that Jane isn't a liar."

Isobel glared at him. "Her gruesome head wound was fairly convincing."

"Jasper, you cannot mean that," Helena admonished. "I've spent time with Jane, and she is the furthest thing from a liar—"

"A fortune hunter would hardly own up to her plot," Jasper argued.

"That's assuming you're worth the effort," Isobel replied cuttingly.

Aunt Adelaide sniffed. "In any event, it would hardly be proper to discuss such matters at a country house party."

For once, etiquette was on Jasper's side, and by extension, so was Aunt Adelaide. It was all the army he needed at the moment.

Helena smiled brightly but unconvincingly. "We should probably inform Jane of our years-long friendship. Would you send for her, Battersby? I suspect she's had enough rest."

"No need," came a small, sheepish voice from behind the butler. And then Jane stepped into the room looking deeply ashamed, and Jasper's heart ceased its beating altogether. He leaped to his feet as she offered the room a wobbly curtsy. "Apologies, my lord and ladies. I was on my way here and stumbled upon your conversation. Not wishing to interrupt, I found myself..." She paused, her cheeks reddened with shame.

"Eavesdropping," Isobel finished for her with a grin while Helena shot an immensely concerned look his way. He *had* just finished calling Jane a potential fortune hunter and demanding his family not bring up his dead fiancée. What a disaster. He prayed she had missed the worst of it. Isobel continued. "As we spent a great deal of time discussing *you*, I find myself disinclined to blame you, Jane."

The world tilted on its axis when Jane stepped into the light of day. There was the monstrous bruise, stealing a great deal of the attention that should have been paid to the woman beneath it. He noticed her dressing had been changed—a good sign, he supposed—and her hair was damp. She'd had a bath. The mere idea of it robbed him of critical thought. Had Helena arranged for a maid to help her, or had she managed it on her own? Had the water been warm enough? Did she have access to everything she needed? *Christ, why am I so concerned?*

Distantly, he heard his aunt mutter something that sounded

like *déshabillée,* but he couldn't be certain.

Jane smiled a small smile and cast her eyes around the room. When they fell upon him, his heartbeat quickened like a lovesick schoolboy being given an ounce of attention. But she looked away quickly. Guilt slammed into him as he worked backward, trying to ascertain whether or not she had heard anything catastrophic. Would she understand who Annabelle was to him? Did she hear him call her a potential fortune hunter? He couldn't be certain, but he suspected she knew enough not to broach either topic with any of them. Which was what he had wanted, but then why did her shuttered gaze sting so much? He supposed it was just as well, if she sought to avoid him. Perhaps then he'd stand a chance at avoiding her as well.

"I am terribly sorry," she offered to no one in particular.

"Think nothing of it, Jane. I suppose that means you heard of our accidental party and how we plan to handle it?" asked Helena.

"Ah, yes. School friends, was it?" It was then that Jasper noticed what she was wearing. Ladies' clothing rarely elicited much reaction from him. He was far more likely to notice the lack of it, when the occasion warranted. But Jane was wearing a dress from Annabelle's trousseau, which Helena had been helping his former fiancée assemble, and for the first time since discovering her bloodied in the road, Jasper was forced to think of the two women at once.

They could not be more dissimilar. Jane was slight and dark-haired, and Annabelle had been tall with long golden curls, a veritable ray of sunshine. Where Annabelle had been polite and reserved, Jane was curiously sharp-tongued and quick-witted. But most obviously, Annabelle had been steady, a woman with her feet planted firmly in the earth, whereas Jane was terribly unmoored. But even as he thought it he knew it was an unfair juxtaposition, given that Jane's insecurity was not, strictly speaking, her fault.

Christ, but the devil had him comparing two women who by rights never should have been pitted against each other. But it was hard not to tie them together in some way when Jane stood there in Annabelle's clothes. Jasper began repeating their differences in his mind as though they were marks against Jane, a litany of her faults. He was far less willing to admit that there were commonalities between the two women, things he had seen in Annabelle that he sensed in Jane. He dismissed them as nebulous similarities. Not anything worthy of further study, surely.

His last shred of sense made him hold his tongue about the gown. Jane didn't know it had been made for his bride-to-be, or that seeing her in the clothing intended for Annabelle felt like a betrayal deep in Jasper's wretched heart. He felt quite certain that in this matter, Jane was an innocent. And besides, the thought of bringing up Annabelle again in so short a span of time was unbearable. So he would keep the pain to himself, as he had been doing for the past year, letting it sour and fester in the deepest parts of him.

"Miss Jane, that is such a lovely gown," said Viola, finding an opening in which to insert herself at last, having been failed in that regard by her older siblings.

"Why thank you," said Jane, fanning the skirt out a bit for effect. She seemed to catch herself, perhaps embarrassed by the overly familiar gesture. She straightened, her cheeks a tad red. "I do not believe we've had the pleasure of meeting, my lady."

"This is my sister, Lady Viola. She's been most curious about you, Jane." He spoke without intending to, his voice rough.

Something he couldn't explain made him eager to smooth over Jane's slightest discomfort. Perhaps it was that he knew how precarious her position was—he didn't wish to add to that feeling. Whatever the reason, he sounded like a desperate fool.

"I do believe you meant *Miss Jane*... What is it then?" asked Aunt Adelaide pointedly, doing her damnedest to remind him of blasted etiquette.

"Oh, we never assigned Jane a surname, Aunt," said Helena, attempting to close the matter.

"Well, that won't do. We can't have you referring to her by naught but her Christian name."

But even before he knew her as the name she chose, nothing about Jane had felt so very formal as that. Hell, he had carried her in his arms, her blood had stained his shirt, and he knew something about her even *she* didn't. Jane was not someone he felt distant from, even if it would have been better if he did.

Jane quirked her brow at him as if to agree with his very thoughts, an expression that hit him square in the chest like a bolt of lightning, but then she diverted her attention to his sister. "A pleasure to meet you, Lady Viola."

Viola beamed at the attention and Jasper felt a pang of guilt over how neglected the youngest Maycott had been since the tragedy.

"Jane, feel at liberty to explore the library while the rest of us see to our duties," said Helena, once again adopting a leadership role that had Jasper wishing *she* had been their father's heir.

"Please let me know if there is anything I can do to help," offered Jane. "Fortune hunting only takes up so much of my time, you see."

Jasper froze. He had assumed Jane had heard his less-than-flattering suspicions of her, but to have her address them outright? It was...unexpected. Jasper's blood warmed at her boldness. His first, most pressing thought was that he wanted to silence her impertinent mouth with a kiss. It didn't matter that they weren't alone. Their eyes met and he knew in his bones that Jane felt the same spark between them. He hungered for more of it, more of *her*.

"No need," said Isobel, sounding as though she were choking on suppressed laughter. "Especially since we've got the Earl of Belhaven himself offering his assistance."

The warmth bled from Jane's eyes as she stiffened, looking away from Jasper and to his sister. "Oh, is your father coming?"

The room fell deathly silent.

It was a question none of the Maycotts had expected. Not after a year of wading through the grief that had accompanied the most devastating of losses, careful not to mention their names lest the waters rise and the current take them. Jasper hadn't thought he would hear someone speak of his father as though he were living ever again.

It was a cruel impossibility that cut to the core of him, straight to the pain he did so much to bury for the sake of his siblings.

Jane sensed she had said something terribly wrong. "I'm sorry," she began, her distress evident. "I didn't mean to—"

But Jasper refused to hear what came next, choosing instead to silence her with the truth. "My father is dead."

It was the only weapon he had.

Chapter Seven

JANE

Jane's mind screamed for her to hold her tongue. It was more than a faux pas or a simple misunderstanding. She could tell she had struck at the deepest hurt of this family. And after all they had done for her.

She was a bloody fool.

Helena came to her rescue, as always. "We lost our parents and eldest brother a year ago," she explained, her voice terribly small in the sudden vastness of the library. "Scarlet fever."

Jane's heart shattered at the thought. Her eyes drifted from Helena to Isobel to Viola, each of them seeming far too young to have lost both of their parents. The grief of it could have smothered her, and yet the feeling was familiar, as if she, too, had experienced such a tragedy. She pushed it away for now, choosing to focus on the people she had harmed with her carelessness.

"I am so terribly sorry," she offered, knowing her meager

apology would do nothing to soothe their pain. "I cannot begin to imagine..." The words died on her tongue. The Maycotts didn't need her empty words.

"How could we blame you, Jane? In your current state?" said Helena, offering Jane far more grace and understanding than she deserved.

She searched her mind for some hint of a memory of the tragedy that had befallen this family. Surely the deaths of the Earl of Belhaven, his wife, and his heir would have been much talked about. But there was nothing, only a stark emptiness that served to taunt her, reminding her that pertinent memories such as this were still hidden from her as if by a veil, one she could not penetrate. But as she thought about it, a different realization sank like a stone in her gut.

"But that would mean..." she whispered to herself, unwilling to finish the sentence aloud as her eyes found Lord Jasper's across the room. She quickly looked away.

He was not Lord Jasper, *he* was the dratted Earl of Belhaven.

She had, in truth, intruded upon an earl's home, defiled his boots, and been nothing but a source of frustration to him. For Christ's sake, an *earl* had dug through the snow for her blasted spectacles, and Jane had thanked him by exchanging barbs with him.

Jane's skin heated, her chest tightened, and sweat dampened her palms. It was difficult for her to comprehend the extent of her mortification.

Jas—*Lord Belhaven* shifted in the corner of her vision, and it was only then that she allowed herself to *really* look at him. The glances they'd shared since her shameful entrance into the library had been fleeting, but now Jane was seeing him not as the eventual heir to an earldom, but rather the earl himself, and suddenly everything changed for her.

It became clear to her that while his pain was the best hidden, it was perhaps the deepest among them. But he was an earl. He had responsibilities beyond those of an heir. So he masked his sorrow with his impenetrable sternness, which she now understood made him less like a bastard and more like the rock that held what remained of his family together.

As she recalled his frustrated claim that there was no better version of him left, Jane had to wonder who it was that held *him* together.

It was a ridiculous query, she knew, but nothing could prevent it from filling her mind. In that moment, Lord Belhaven's eyes found hers, the locking of their gazes seeming inevitable, as though a force neither of them understood pulled them together. There were no cracks in his armor, and no slipping of his mask. Here was the Earl of Belhaven, solemn and steady. Why was it she could see right through him, then?

And who was Annabelle to him?

Seeming to read her thoughts, Lord Belhaven's brow furrowed and he broke their gaze, choosing that moment to turn on his heel and stride from the room, eliciting a *tsk* from Lady Adelaide. Whoever she was, a part of him still belonged to this Annabelle. A part he would never get back, perhaps.

Jane had no desire to pry into this family's pain any more than she already had. But her curiosity regarding Lord Belhaven flared to life. She should never have jested with him about his fortune-hunting comments. Christ, he was the bloody Earl of Belhaven. If anyone had a right to assume the worst of her, it was a man like him. And yet, she could tell that he felt that same pull to closeness that she did, and how shamefully easy it was for them to acquiesce to it. He tried to put distance between them, and she didn't blame him. She didn't trust whatever it was that drew them together, either, not when she could recall nothing of her own life to compare it to.

She thumbed the ring in her pocket. While she hadn't conceded Lord Belhaven's unspoken belief that its existence meant that she was married in the life she had forgotten, it had seemed the obvious origin of it. But when Jane had slipped the ring onto her finger, all she felt was the thudding certainty that whoever *JHD* was, they were not her husband. And so the ring remained in her pocket and not on her finger. A tantalizing clue, but nothing more.

"We should see to the preparations," began Helena awkwardly, studiously avoiding mention of her brother's abrupt departure.

Jane swallowed her third apology, knowing it wasn't needed. "I will do my best not to add to your burdens."

Isobel's melancholy lifted, and she gave her a wry grin. "If you need anything, truly *anything*, please don't hesitate to call for Battersby. He is most helpful."

The butler looked as though he would murder Isobel if he could, and Jane resolved to never ask anything of the man, lest she make another enemy in Mulgrave Hall.

The Maycott sisters smiled at her and departed, Viola giving her a small wave at the door.

Her least favorite Maycott remained in the library, however, looking at Jane as though she were a creature in a cage she sought to understand through careful study.

"Come," Lady Adelaide ordered, gesturing for Jane to take her arm. "You and I can conduct some experiments."

"*Experiments*?" Jane ventured as Lady Adelaide guided her toward the pianoforte set in a corner of the library.

"You told my niece that you believe there are memories too ingrained to be lost to you, such as the ability to walk or knowledge of the works of Jane Austen?"

Jane nodded, beginning to understand Lady Adelaide's intent.

"Then surely we can trick your mind into remembering more of your past by performing certain tasks that might also be deeply rooted within you."

"And you believe the pianoforte is where to begin?"

Lady Adelaide pulled out the bench. "I've yet to meet an accomplished lady who possesses no skill in this regard."

Jane hesitated. "And if I'm not a lady?"

"Then at last we will know something about you. Right now, we know very little." She stepped away from the bench and gestured for Jane to take a seat.

It was a beautiful instrument, made of rich, gleaming wood, scalloped gold trim, and extensively carved legs, with the word ERARD intricately embellished in gilded script above the keys. But it did not call to her like she would have expected if she were a great proficient. The cushioned bench, upholstered with pale green silk, was comfortable, and bore signs of having been used for years—small frays in the fabric, a permanent dent where someone had sat for many hours, some minor scuffs on the legs.

"Who plays?" Jane asked as she took her seat.

"Played," Lady Adelaide corrected. "The countess played beautifully."

Jane tried to imagine her, a woman possessing Isobel's coloring and Helena's grace, with perhaps a hint of Viola's curiosity. *She must have been a wonderful mother*, she thought, feeling a pang of emptiness for having no memories of her own.

"I'm told my nieces and nephews inherited my brother's

distinctly non-musical ears," Lady Adelaide said, sighing sadly. "You may begin."

Jane raised her wrists and held her hands above the ivory keys, waiting for some sense of rightness or understanding to come over her.

But nothing did.

"Are you perhaps waiting for the instrument to invite you to play?" asked Lady Adelaide impatiently.

Jane pressed a few keys, the notes sounding discordant to her ears. She pressed a few more, hoping for harmony to emerge, but it was clear she did not know how to play. She looked up to Lady Adelaide, who was wincing.

"It would seem I am not familiar with the pianoforte," she said, standing up and away from the bench, so as not to blaspheme further.

"We simply cannot leave it at that," said Lady Adelaide, taking her vacant seat and beginning to play. The difference was stark. Her fingers moved deftly over the keys, each tone weaving together to create a melody of great beauty, her expression locked in deep concentration. As Lady Adelaide played, Jane allowed herself to simply listen and enjoy it. She didn't think about her missing memories, her accident, the guilt or her shame or her fears. She thought of nothing save for how the music managed to transport her, giving her a feeling of lightness she hadn't known since before she'd awoken in Mulgrave Hall.

Lady Adelaide finished and released a sigh of relief, as though she'd had no choice but to play after Jane's disastrous attempt, lest the gods of music take offense.

"What was that?" Jane asked, in sudden awe of the woman.

"Schubert's 'Ungarische Melodie,'" she said with a sniff. "His compositions could make anyone sound gifted." She paused.

"Well, I suppose not *anyone*."

Jane ignored the jab. "You play beautifully, my lady."

She closed the fallboard. "I play technically well, but I lack a true passion for the instrument. Rebecca played as though she couldn't live without it, as though it fed her, body and soul." She let the sentence linger, lost in memory.

"It must have been a joy to hear her," said Jane.

"I hardly ever had the chance to," Lady Adelaide replied. "I rarely made the trip from Bordeaux."

"It's a long journey," offered Jane.

"Longer still when there is no warm welcome at the end of it." She shook her head. Jane knew better than to dig further. "That is enough delving into unhappy memories. Our first experiment was a failure, but worry not, I have a few more theories."

And so she and Lady Adelaide spent the next hour learning that Jane was similarly incapable of playing the harp, hopelessly bad at all forms of needlework, and unable to converse in French, which, according to her inquisitor, was beyond the pale for a proper young lady. Despite her lacking in that regard, Jane got along quite nicely with conversational Italian and German (she also had high hopes for Ancient Greek and Latin, but Lady Adelaide refused to investigate further as they were, in her words, the purview of men). Additionally, she was capable of performing an adequate waltz and lively polka (much to her dancing partner's chagrin), able to solve arithmetic problems with ease, and well versed in the art of penmanship, all things a proper lady would be trained to do.

But none of her successes or failures added up to an answer about who she was. It was as though she was half accomplished, half ordinary. She would have been grateful to know one way or another, but to have some skills that suggested she was a lady, yet be lacking others was infuriating.

Lady Adelaide did not seem any less frustrated by the results. "I would say your ability to dance competently would make you the daughter of a peer, but your utter lack of skill with a needle surely precludes you from that."

"Perhaps I am a natural dancer only because I excel at fencing—"

Lady Adelaide pretended not to hear her. "And yet, your penmanship suggests ample instruction, but who has ever heard of a lady who couldn't play an instrument?"

"I don't mean to disappoint you, my lady," she replied, her tone dripping with sarcasm as she sank into a plush armchair.

Lady Adelaide waved her hand lightly. "Do not trouble yourself, Jane. I did say I enjoyed puzzles."

But Jane was tired of being something that needed to be solved. She wanted to be a person whole.

Lady Adelaide looked pensive. "You know, we have not yet tried painting—"

"If you don't mind, my lady, I think I am done experimenting for the day." There was a crushing pain in Jane's head. She would have happily murdered someone for a cup of tea, but she drew the line at summoning Battersby.

"I will escort you to your room, then."

"I think I'll stay here for a while, if you don't mind." The books that lined the shelves were still calling to her, and though her head ached and exhaustion tugged at her, Jane intended to do *something* of her own volition that day. Something that might serve to deepen her understanding of herself, more so than needlepoint and dancing had.

Lady Adelaide raised her chin at her in assessment. "Very well. I shall have tea and sandwiches sent to you."

Jane stopped herself from exclaiming in delight, knowing Lady Adelaide would not deem an outburst like that to be proper. "Thank you, my lady." She paused, considering how the woman had spent the last hour. What had been frustrating for Jane was surely tedious, thankless work for Lady Adelaide, who had arrived at Mulgrave Hall to grieve with her nieces and nephew and had instead been saddled with a burden in the form of a rootless woman. "And I must thank you for aiding me in getting a bit closer to discovering who I am."

Lady Adelaide stood, her palms flattening any errant wrinkles in the bodice of her gown. "Think nothing of it, Jane. We will get to the bottom of it eventually."

"Still, I know I'm a burden to you and the rest of the Maycotts."

Lady Adelaide didn't disagree. "As burdensome as you may be, I believe you are giving the family something else to focus on during a trying time. We recently marked a year without my brother and his wife and son."

"Only a year?" When Helena had said it, a year had somehow seemed longer. Jane could recall nothing of her life, but like the ability to speak, she was beginning to think that grief was too ingrained in her to ever be truly forgotten. If she had learned anything that day, it was that she knew intimately the pain of losing someone she loved. *But who?*

"Indeed," replied Lady Adelaide, furrowing her brow as if piecing something together. "I called my arrival an act of providence, but perhaps mine wasn't the only bit of divine intervention."

Jane couldn't help but choke on a laugh. "I hardly think the earl would agree with you on that account."

Lady Adelaide's face fell, and Jane held her tongue, having

learned her lesson earlier. "Tragedy befell us all, but none so much as Jasper."

"What do you mean?" asked Jane before she could stop herself.

But the woman shook her head. "I cannot say more without betraying his confidence. It is his story to tell."

She could accept that. Even as she had asked the question, it had felt wrong. If she ever got the truth of it from someone, she wanted it to be Lord Belhaven himself. Not that she thought she was entitled to it, or that he was liable to tell her anything. In truth, the man didn't trust her. And why should he? She scarcely had leave to trust herself.

Interpreting her silence as acceptance, Lady Adelaide bowed her head slightly. "I'll leave you to your browsing, then."

She departed, leaving Jane in Mulgrave Hall's well-appointed library, totally alone. She approached the shelves nearest her and ran her fingers along the leather spines, reading titles and authors silently to herself and hoping for something to stick out, like Jane Austen had.

But nothing did.

Perhaps the library was too vast, the titles too obscure, shelves climbing to the ceiling in places. She had scanned the titles of books on one shelf in a room fit to bursting with them. She'd need a ladder in order to see them all fully.

A maid brought a tray of pastries and sandwiches and a pot of strong tea. Jane nibbled on a biscuit and pondered her current predicament.

Maybe it had been a mistake to think she'd find some hint of her former self so quickly. It had barely been two days since her accident, and while she was in a hurry to return to the life she had surely left behind, it would seem her mind did not agree with her.

After devouring most everything on the tray, Jane sighed and flounced into the chair behind the grand desk. Perhaps if she began writing, this time unconsciously, memories would be forced to rise to the surface. As she began to clear a space to work in, she picked up a book that had been carelessly left face down, possibly damaging the spine. Resolving to remind the Maycotts of how to properly care for a book, she closed it, placing it atop the rich mahogany desk for its owner to find it, unbesmirched.

And then she noticed the title.

It was *Pride and Prejudice*. Had Lord Belhaven left it there? She assumed it was his desk—it was rather masculine and covered in a mess of papers that appeared to pertain to earlish matters. Whoever was reading it was about a quarter of the way through the book. Jane scanned the page and felt a rush of that same sense of familiarity she had been seeking. She decided not to fight it. If the words of Jane Austen were all she could remember, then so be it.

She sank back into the chair and flipped to the beginning, letting out a comfortable yawn as she did so.

It is a truth universally acknowledged, that a single man in possession of a good fortune, must be in want of a wife...

She smiled at that delicious bit of irony while images of the brooding, uncompromising yet handsome Lord Belhaven unwittingly filled her mind, and she thought, if any among them resembled one of Miss Austen's creations, it was he.

Chapter Eight

JASPER

He found his valet in the kitchens.

"We've a mission," Jasper told Nash solemnly.

Nash, who had been flirting rather brazenly with the cook, stood at attention as he hastily swallowed an entire roll, his eyes watering. "What is it, my lord?"

Jasper sighed. "We must procure a tree."

Nash waited a beat before speaking. "A tree, my lord?"

"For trimming," he added morosely.

Nash nodded. "I'll fetch your coat, shall I?"

"Meet me at the stables, we'll be needing a horse." Nash set off, and Jasper took a moment to stuff a roll—still warm from the oven—into his mouth and another two into his pockets, managing a wink for the cook before leaving.

The bread did not go down easily, though it may have been Jasper's mood that prevented him from enjoying it. The day had been one for constant vacillation. He'd awoken feeling apprehensive. Jane had slept through Helena's attempts to engage her the night before, accepting only a spoonful of laudanum before succumbing to sleep once more. Helena had assured him that Dr. Ramsay had told her that bouts of prolonged sleep were to be expected as Jane healed, but he still had to be talked out of sending for the doctor once more. And then in the morning, Aunt Adelaide had fought her way into Jane's room, insisting that she alone be present when Jane woke up. It had left Jasper feeling rather unsettled. He had hoped to see how Jane was feeling himself, but then the day had gotten away from him.

Isobel's plot regarding the imminent arrival of his friends had only served to unnerve him further. And he'd scarcely had time to run through the potential consequences of her meddling before Jane had appeared in the library as if conjured from his mind, a vibrant apparition that had stolen all sense from him.

And then she'd parried words with him, revealing not only that she'd heard the terrible ways he'd insulted her character, but also that his words had not injured her as he'd thought they would, and a potent mixture of guilt and desire had fomented in his mind. It had been enough to overwhelm his senses, enough to make the rest of the library vanish until they were all that remained, two strangers pulled together as if by nature itself.

Her very eyes beguiled him. The way she looked at him was both intoxicating and infuriating. Somehow, she knew things he never said aloud, things he suspected he didn't know himself. If Jane knew nothing of her own origins, how was it she managed to read him like a book?

But when she'd mentioned his father, any feelings of desire had drained from him. It was clear then that Jane was not lying about her missing memories. How else could she be so unaware of the Maycott tragedy? He'd avoided polite company for a year simply because he could not bear the sad stares and empty expressions of pity. He didn't think a corner of England remained that didn't know what had happened to the Earl of Belhaven and his wife and son. News of their deaths had traveled as quickly as salacious gossip. People reveled in the agony of others as much as they did their shame. Jasper had a mile-high pile of unopened correspondence to prove it.

But Jane didn't revel in it. No, the pain she'd shown when Helena told her the truth mirrored his own. It was the kind of guileless display of emotion that precluded her from the sinister machinations he had suspected of her. Potential motives aside, Jane knew something of the kind of grief that had been drowning him, and in that moment in the library, all he'd wanted to do was speak that pain aloud to someone who would understand but not be harmed by it. He had been hiding it from his siblings out of a sense of obligation, but what if he and Jane could lessen their respective burdens, together?

But then he remembered that while Jane felt the heaviness of grief, she did not know the origin of it. She and Jasper could not commiserate, not when she knew nothing of her past and even less of her future.

Disappointed, he'd watched as she'd come to several realizations in quick succession, including the fact that he himself was the Earl of Belhaven, and all at once his body had felt too large for his skin.

He'd had to get away from her, even if his retreat had felt like a coward's move.

And now he stepped out of the manor and into the winter wind. The weather was not so bad as the night they'd found Jane twisted in the snow, but it could hardly be called an improvement.

A stable hand was harnessing one of the sturdier workhorses for them, having perhaps been tipped off by Battersby.

Nash arrived behind him, an axe in one hand, a coat in the other. Jasper shrugged it on and relished the immediate improvement.

"Is this new?" he asked, admiring the thickness of the wool.

Nash frowned slightly. "It belonged to your brother, my lord. I thought it would serve you better than your frock coat."

Jasper nodded, seeing the sense in his valet's choice, even if donning his brother's clothing made him feel like a child playing dress-up. He brushed past that feeling. "You know you don't have to call me that, Nash."

"A hard habit to break, my lo—sir." Nash had been his brother's valet before Jasper had inherited him, but they had known each other for years, Nash having been something of a friend to Jasper, back when the mantle of Earl had seemed very far away from him. They were near in age, and while Nash wore the years a bit worse than Jasper, anyone could see the man was handsome.

"Just Jasper will do, I think. At least when we're alone."

Nash nodded, taking the reins the stable hand offered him. "Of course."

The men began their trudge through the snow. Cold as it was, the horse seemed eager to stretch his legs. Jasper found he felt the same.

"I assume by now word has gotten out about our impending guests?"

Nash swung the axe upward and rested it on his shoulder. "The house is in a right frenzy. Never seen such a fuss, though I reckon it *was* all rather sudden."

The next question could not be asked delicately, not when

Jasper so desperately needed the answer. "What do the servants say of Jane?"

Nash looked at him out of the corner of his eye. "Not much is known of her. Some suspect she is one of your brother's past paramours, back to get one last piece of him."

It was a ridiculous theory, but perhaps not as ridiculous as the truth. "Do they know anything of her mind?"

"Her mind?" Nash looked genuinely confused.

Jasper paused, weighing his options. He believed he could trust Nash. The man had seen him at his worst, and when he had shut everyone else out of his world, Nash had been among the only people left who didn't share his blood. He needed to clear his head, and he suspected talking with Nash would help in that endeavor. "In truth, Jane is a mystery. She arrived here in such calamity, and the accident left her mind rather...blank."

"Blank?" Nash repeated.

"In that she has no memories. Not of herself or her life before we found her in the road. She could be anyone."

"And you mean to protect her." It wasn't a question, more of a confirmation of fact, as if Nash had already known it to be true. Jasper didn't like to think that he was that predictable.

"Well, what choice do I have as the Earl of Belhaven? Refusing to aid her could reflect poorly on me. On all of us. And yet, if word got out about her true condition, that would *also* reflect on me poorly. I'm in a bind either way."

Nash was suspiciously quiet as he fed the horse a ruddy apple.

"Something to add?" asked Jasper.

"Nothing," Nash said, hands raised defensively. "It's only that..." He stopped himself from finishing the sentence.

"You needn't fear angering me, Nash."

"I worry about her motives. You and your siblings have

suffered immensely and it's left you lot in a rather vulnerable position. I'd hate to think someone was using the tragedy as a way to get closer to you."

"You needn't fear that she's sunk her claws into me, Nash. Even if I fancied myself in love with her, I could hardly marry a woman who doesn't know her own name. She could be a laundress, for all we know." He wondered if it would be the worst thing in the world to marry a laundress. Jasper knew very well how love could erase the ridiculous rules drawn by Society. He had fallen in love with a vicar's daughter, after all.

But perhaps those rules were not so easily set aside for an *earl*.

When he'd been simply Mr. Jasper Maycott, second son of the Earl of Belhaven, he had not been so constrained as his brother. But now the title fell to him, and he had a responsibility to his siblings. He couldn't marry a laundress, even if he did love her.

He shook his head. None of his musings mattered. He had made a vow over Anthony's body to never love again, and while Jasper wasn't a religious man, he thought that macabre promise had to mean something.

They came to a copse of trees of roughly the right size for Mulgrave Hall's tall ceilings. They looked like they belonged in a painting of an idyllic winter scene, their branches dusted with snow like puffs of frosting. Helena could hardly find fault with a tree so perfect.

"These look suitable," he offered. Nash nodded as he tied up the horse and began to remove his coat, but Jasper extended his hand in his valet's direction. "Mind if I get it started?"

Nash handed him the axe. "Not at all."

The first swing of the axe was cathartic, reverberating up his arm like a bolt of lightning. The blade was sharp, slicing into the wood like butter. With his task at hand, his mind emptied like he'd hoped it would, but unfortunately it only took a few more frenzied swings before Nash was able to kick over the tree and sever it from the stump with a satisfying crack that echoed in the wood around them. By then, Jasper had worked up a sweat but he did not feel any less burdened by his thoughts. He pushed his hair from his eyes and wondered if he should take up pugilism once more. Surely a man could still find clarity by beating another man senseless.

Nash tied a rope to the base of the tree and attached both ends to the horse's harness. "Ready?" he asked.

They set off through the deepening snow, silent until Mulgrave Hall came into view, when Nash cleared his throat and began to speak, sounding as if he had mentally rehearsed what he intended to say the whole return.

"This Jane character has me concerned, if I'm being honest. Some women know how to spot a good man, whether he's an earl or a farmer, and sink their claws into them. And then they take and they take until there's not much left."

Jasper didn't think it was a flattering or fair description of most women, but Nash had seen a great deal more of the wickedness of the world than he had. "Your point?"

"Women like that know how to leave a good man when he's of no more use to her." They reached the stables and he took a deep breath. "You need to be careful, Jasper."

Jasper stopped himself from telling Nash he knew nothing of Jane's character. It didn't matter, when the meat of his message was true. Jasper *did* need to be careful. "I know."

"I don't want any of you to suffer more."

Jasper tried for levity, both for himself and for Nash. "I

hardly think the woman is capable of inflicting lasting suffering upon us. As soon as she is well again, she will be sent on her way."

Nash eyed him warily as he fed the horse an oatcake. "If you say so, my lord."

They exited the stables and entered Mulgrave Hall together. It was time for Jasper to ready himself for dinner, but after the earlier scene in the library, the thought of dining with Aunt Adelaide sent him into a cold sweat.

"Join me for a drink in the parlor, will you?" He tried not to feel guilty about his sisters having to manage their aunt without him. Helena would be up to the task, at least. Isobel would punish him later.

Nash nodded. "I'll have plates sent up for us," he added, thereby proving his worth as both valet and friend.

"And about Jane," he began. "No one can know of the ailment of her mind, Nash. Not a soul. It would end badly for us."

"I'll take it to the grave."

Jasper's heart settled a bit at his friend's promise. Because that was the thing about Nash. When he said something, he meant it. He might not trust Jane, but Jasper knew Nash would protect her simply because it was the right thing to do.

Nash had called him a good man, but Jasper knew the truth of it: there were hardly any better than his valet.

• • •

The manor's halls were quiet by the time he and Nash had finished their dinners, but Jasper was not ready to retire just yet.

No, the trials and tribulations of bloody Elizabeth Bennet were calling to him. Blast Miss Austen and her addictive prose, but at least now he could see what the fuss was about. As it turned out, the bits and pieces he had gleaned from his sisters over the years were not anywhere near the full picture. How could any of them have failed to mention how utterly obtuse both Elizabeth and Darcy were? If they went on to moon over each other from afar whilst trading barbs in person, he was going to chuck the book across the room.

As he strode into the library, peeling off his gloves and intending to settle into his leather chair in front of the fire and snatch a few more chapters before bed, something shocking stopped him in his tracks.

There Jane was, sprawled over the desk, dead asleep, her face using his copy of *Pride and Prejudice* as a pillow.

After the initial shock wore off slightly, he stepped closer to her to lightly nudge her on the shoulder with the blunt end of a letter opener. She stirred, but barely, proceeding to sink even deeper into the rigid embrace of the book.

"That's no way to treat the words of Jane Austen," he scoffed before searching the room for someone else, anyone else to handle this.

But he was alone. He nudged her again, meeting resistance once more.

"Jane," he whispered rather close to her ear, eliciting a groggy moan from the woman. "Jane, you've fallen asleep in the library."

Her response was unintelligible, though it did remind him of how she had behaved the night prior, when Helena had failed to rouse her fully in order to administer medicine. His sister had resorted to pinching Jane into wakefulness. Jasper could not fathom doing the same.

"Jane," he tried again, closer still. Close enough to smell the soap on her skin. Close enough to see the featherlight beating of her pulse against her neck in the dim firelight. Close enough to know he was too close.

Her next unintelligible response sealed his fate. Etiquette be damned, good sense be damned, he had to get her out of here before someone found them both. Alone.

Scooping her up was rather easy. She settled into his arms like she belonged there, though he banished the feeling of rightness from his mind.

He peeked his head out into the hall once more, confirming it was deserted. It was rather late. Heavens knew why no one had come to check on Jane. He supposed Isobel's plot had everyone turned upside down. He traversed the halls as quickly as he could. When he paused before the staircase, Jane had the temerity to nuzzle into his chest, as though being in his arms made her feel completely at ease.

Christ.

He took the stairs two at a time. He needed to deposit her into her room, needed to put some distance between them, needed to forget how her body felt pressed against his.

They arrived at the Lavender Room both too quickly and too slowly. Never before had Jasper felt so acutely torn between two emotions. It was agony and ecstasy both, having her in his arms. He placed her gently on the bed and made to leave before pausing and turning back to remove her spectacles. He hadn't gone digging through the snow for her to crush his hard-won quarry in her sleep. As he began to retreat, a small hand reached for his, trapping his wrist. He froze.

"I'm sorry I cannot play pianoforte," she muttered, her voice thick with sleep, her words nonsensical.

"Pardon?" he asked, not sure she was in a position to elaborate.

"Nor can I sew or speak French or..." she replied, sounding distressed but a great deal more conscious. "You must think me a great disappointment, my lord."

"Why would any of that disappoint me, Jane?"

She sighed and released his wrist. He didn't move an inch. "I know you're desperate to solve the mystery of Miss Jane without-a-surname. I hardly made much progress in that regard today. If anything, I am more confused than ever."

"I don't understand," he confessed.

"Lady Adelaide and I conducted a series of experiments. I cannot play an instrument or embroider or speak French, but I can write beautifully and do arithmetic and dance somewhat competently, but what does any of it mean? Perhaps I had a persistent mother who desired an advantageous match for me, or perhaps I taught myself out of spite."

Her distress would have been endearing if he didn't know himself to be at least partially the cause of it. But how could he put her at ease when he didn't have an answer for her? She was right, Jane without-a-surname was a mystery, one he was both desperate and apprehensive to solve. When Jane recovered her memories, she'd return to the life she had left behind, one that didn't include him. But the longer Jane spent in this unknowing limbo, the longer he got to spend with her.

He hated the thought almost as soon as it had formed. No part of Jane belonged to him, why should he desire to keep her here at Mulgrave Hall? As penance, he tried to placate her.

"Or perhaps you *are* a lady, Jane."

She waved her hand dismissively. "At least if I knew I was a penniless maid or a baron's daughter, I'd have a sense of where I belonged."

For reasons Jasper could not comprehend, a part of him

wished to tell her that she belonged here, with him. The realization made him take a step away from her, because how could they ever belong together? He knew nothing of her, and most importantly, she knew nothing of herself.

He cleared his throat. "I am certain we will get to the bottom of it." He willed it to be true. "Though, for the time being, I hope you don't mind too terribly that we'll have to lie about your origins."

"Of course not. I don't wish to put any of you in an awkward position."

He nodded uselessly in the dark. "It's late, I shouldn't even be here." But even as he said it, he knew he had found some of the clarity he sought in Jane's room, speaking with her plainly, even if the subject was one she found distressing. There was something about conversing with her that put him totally at ease. It was a calmness he hadn't felt since Annabelle, and that realization was as much a betrayal to his former fiancée as it was a comfort to him. He was drowning in his conflicted emotions. He had to leave. "Good night, Jane."

He made it to the door before she spoke.

"My lord?" Her voice was small but not coy.

Against his better judgment, he paused at the threshold. "Yes?"

"Thank you for..." She stopped, apparently not quite willing to admit that he had carried her through the corridors of Mulgrave Hall. "Just...thank you."

There was his pesky need to put her at ease. "It's nothing I haven't done for you before." As soon as he said it, he knew it was a mistake.

Jane picked up on his meaning at once. "You're the one who found me out in the storm?"

"I was out with Helena and Isobel. We came upon you in the road, yes."

"I had assumed…" He could hardly see in the dark, but he knew she stood as if electrified by his admission. "I had assumed a footman found me. It hadn't occurred to me to ask otherwise."

Jasper did his best not to stare as she walked across the room, stepping into the slivers of pale moonlight that shone in through the window, the light illuminating her for a few brief seconds, long enough to torment him.

He cleared his throat as she neared. "Yes, well. I apologize for not telling you sooner."

She shook her head, indicating it didn't matter. "Did I say anything to you?"

It struck him that deep down, she seemed to know that she had. And then the memory of her covered in blood, begging him to protect her, filled his mind. He blinked it away, dragging himself back to the present, and weighed his options. He could tell her the truth and add another layer of mystery to the story of Jane. Or he could preserve what little progress she had made. Would it even help to know she had been in some sort of danger? If Jane's memories were ever restored and she needed their aid, they would surely do everything they could. But for now it was safer for everyone that she be allowed to regain them at her own pace.

"No," he said, swallowing his guilt. "You were unconscious the whole time."

She nodded, tucking away the falsehood he had given her. Eventually, she offered him a small smile. "Thank you for telling me."

He couldn't speak lest he fall apart completely, undone by

Jane's trust in him, trust he did not deserve. She didn't seem to notice the turmoil he was in.

"I'm so very sorry about your parents and your brother."

The words wrapped around him, warm and comforting. Normally he would turn away from someone's pity, but he knew Jane was not offering something so hollow as that. Jasper's grief had been an intensely private thing, causing him to turn inward. Jane's words made no attempt to pull him out of it. They were words of understanding, coming from somewhere deep within her. "Thank you," was all he could say.

"For what it's worth, I consider myself very lucky to have been found by you and your sisters."

"Why's that?" His voice was a rasp. Did she notice? It seemed impossible for her to miss it, not when she seemed to catch everything else.

She looked up at him through dark lashes. "As I'm sure you're aware, it's a cruel world we live in. I could have been found by highwaymen or worse. Instead, I was found by the Maycotts." She paused, tilting her head as she tried to decipher him. "What I'm saying is you've done a good job holding your family together, my lord."

"Jasper," he corrected without thinking.

"What?" Even the hall candlelight couldn't disguise her blush, and nothing could have prevented him from noticing how it spread to her chest, sinking below her neckline. The sight of it set his own skin aflame.

To hell with it. "Call me Jasper."

"Jasper," she echoed, his name sounding like an incantation on her lips. "You know, a couple more rescues on your part and my debt to you will be impossible to repay."

There was a coyness in her voice this time, a slight teasing to suggest her words were meant in jest, but it did nothing to smother the uncomfortable awareness that flared to life in Jasper's chest, the one that told him there was no debt between them, and that he would have gladly ruined himself completely if it meant saving her.

He took the coward's route once more and fled.

Chapter Nine

Jane

Helena and Isobel intruded almost immediately on Jane's not entirely peaceful morning the next day.

"Oh good, you're awake," said a relieved Helena, moving a tray of biscuits out of the way so she could sit on the edge of the bed. "There is much to be discussed before our guests arrive, though, truth be told, the storm may yet delay them."

Jane had hardly slept after Jasper left the night before. He had fled in such a rush after she said his name, she worried she'd offended him, even though *he* had been the one to tell her to use it. The man was confounding. Every time she thought she got a bit closer to understanding where she stood with Jasper, the Earl of Belhaven emerged to remind her of the gulf that stretched between them. It would be easier to take if she never saw him, never felt pulled toward him, never had to imagine what the heat in his gaze meant.

Jane had decided to put the incident behind her. She had far more important things to focus on. Figuring out how Lord Belhaven felt about her registered very low on her list of priorities, or so she kept telling herself.

Even if a part of her couldn't help but wonder if hearing his name had felt the same to him as her saying it did. For her, it had been a confirmation of sorts, an erasure of a barrier between them. She had said it and it had felt right on her tongue, especially after learning he had been the one to carry her injured body all the way to Mulgrave Hall. There was an intimacy in the fact that he had seen her at her worst, bloodied and unconscious and utterly vulnerable. In her mind, she'd earned the right to call him by his Christian name, even if it was deeply improper.

"A maid changed my dressing," she said, indicating the fresh bandages. She had been assured she was healing nicely, though without her memories she could hardly put much stock in that assessment. Aside from the fresh dressing, she also wore another tea gown from the bursting closet, this one mint green and beaded in the bodice. Whoever it had been made for was a great deal taller than her, but it fit well enough and meant she didn't have to swan about in a nightgown like a Brontë heroine haunting the Yorkshire moors.

Isobel stepped farther into the room. "We need to get our stories straight."

"Regarding our very long and very real friendship?"

Isobel smirked but Helena frowned. "I should hope you do feel something like friendship between us, Jane."

"I do," she assured her, though she suspected the Maycotts would be happy to see her hearty and hale and very much on her way. It was obligation that placed them together, not the true bonds of fellowship. "I only mean—"

"That it will be difficult to invent a history between us when you have none of your own?" suggested Isobel.

Jane was sure women of Isobel's rank rarely spoke so frankly, but she found she liked that best about her. "Yes, that."

Helena clapped her hands together. "Well, we shall keep it simple then. You are Miss Jane…"

"Danvers?" she suggested, pulling a name from the ones Jasper had suggested only a few days before.

"Perfect. Miss Jane Danvers, daughter of a…"

"Vicar?" she offered, knowing that not many common-born girls had fathers who were wealthy enough to send them to boarding school.

"No," Helena said rather forcefully, exchanging worried glances with Isobel. "No, not a vicar."

Jane sensed she had treaded on a sensitive subject, and if her blunder in the library had taught her anything, it was to keep her mouth shut rather than dig further.

"What about an industrialist?" said Isobel. "Perhaps a man with a textile empire."

"I know very little about textiles," she confessed.

"*Psh*, my brother's friends are much like any other aristocrats, Jane. They are utterly uninterested in anything aside from the sounds of their own voices. Once you get past introductions, they will listen to almost none of what you have to say, and remember even less of it," said Isobel.

"Still, we must take precautions," warned Helena.

"Miss Jane Danvers of Buckinghamshire, a dear friend from Helena's time at Cheltenham, though we were lumped together in the dormitories. In fact, with Helena being named a snotty prefect on her very first day, you likely would have spent more time with me in the end."

Helena sighed. "I was not a prefect for my first three years, Isobel."

"Regardless, you were always Miss Beale's favorite and that took up much of your time."

"Likely as much time as you reserved for mischief and misbehavior."

Isobel shrugged. "What can I say, I was a dedicated pupil."

"Back to the matter at hand," said Helena, doing her best to steer her sister. "Miss Danvers, soon to be engaged to a Mister... Taylor," she offered. "That's for your protection, Jane. We must establish you as firmly off the market lest the men swarm you."

"Seems sensible," said Jane, not wishing to be swarmed by anyone.

"I suppose we must say *something* about your injuries, Jane," said Helena. "There is simply no disguising bruises such as yours, even though they have faded a great deal. And it's not as if you can do away with the dressing on your wound."

Jane nodded, having anticipated just that. "I suppose Jane Danvers can be rather clumsy, can't she? I think she was rather known for it at Cheltenham."

Isobel grinned. "Why, we had placed bets as to how quickly she would injure herself in Mulgrave Hall."

"Falling down the stairs on her very first day was sooner than even her most cynical friends had wagered," said Jane. "You know, it will be nice to have something of a disguise to hide behind."

"That's the spirit, Jane! If only my stern bastard of a brother could be so open-minded."

Battersby appeared at the door as Helena pinched her sister.

"My ladies, Miss Jane." He gave them a perfunctory bow. "You are needed in the dining room for final approvals, Your Grace."

"Thank you, Battersby." Helena stood, smoothing her skirts

and giving Isobel a stern look. "Can I trust you to behave in my absence?"

"Have I ever given you a reason not to trust me?"

Helena sighed in an indulgent manner. "More than one could count."

"We will simply establish a few key stories of the origins of our friendship that we can repeat ad nauseam until our guests are quite tired of hearing about our Cheltenham days and desire never to speak of them again."

"Nothing salacious," Helena warned. "We have reputations to uphold."

"Oh, Helena, I am certain a widow and a budding spinster have very little control over their reputations."

Helena's face fell, but only for a moment. Jane had the sense not to mention Isobel's use of the word *widow*, though she was beginning to think the Maycott family might be cursed.

Helena cleared her throat. "Do remember what stories you decide on, as I'll need to hear them as well," she said before departing in something of an unladylike rush.

"Damn," Isobel exclaimed once her sister was gone, eliciting a raised eyebrow from Jane, who, despite lacking memories herself, was quite certain she had never heard a lady swear as much as Isobel. She sighed and flounced onto the bed. "I always speak without thinking. It is my only flaw."

"I won't say a word about it," Jane assured her, not wanting a repeat of her earlier faux pas.

"Thank you for that. It's not as though it's a secret that Helena's husband died, but my sister has survived this long by never speaking of it. Perhaps she's forgotten that she can."

"The longer something goes unsaid, the easier it is to avoid altogether."

Isobel gave her an assessing look. "You've a keen insight into human behavior for someone without any memories to go off of."

"It would seem I've picked up a lot in my short time here." The Maycotts had provided much in that regard, from the minutiae of their everyday lives to the fullness of their tragedies. Jane suspected she would carry her time in Mulgrave Hall with her for the rest of her life.

Isobel exhaled sharply. "I don't doubt it. We've skeletons enough for three families, to be sure."

Jane felt she had some right to ask a question, if only to better understand her caretakers. "How long ago did her husband die?"

Isobel stroked her chin. "Three years ago, now." She let out a shaky breath. "She was married to the Duke of Pembroke for two years until he perished in a carriage accident."

"What a tragedy," whispered Jane, her heart breaking anew for Helena. "But she has no obligations as dowager duchess?" There must be a reason Helena was able to stay in Mulgrave Hall with her siblings in their time of need.

"The duke's heir is not yet of age, but their mother still lives. Neither has pressured Helena to take a more active role in the wake of our losses."

"That seems a small mercy," Jane offered.

Isobel nodded. "Time has not been kind to my sister. Her joys have been all too brief, while her sorrow stretches on. Sometimes, I think caring for us is the only thing that keeps her going." She paused, seeming to remember whom she was conversing with. "Forgive me, Jane. I shouldn't be speaking so candidly with you. I suppose we've uncovered my second flaw."

But Jane was beginning to feel a warmth between them that could be mistaken for friendship. She gave Isobel a small smile and nudged her arm. "It's nice to have someone to speak to, my lady. I'm not exactly drowning in meaningful conversation."

Isobel's eyes widened as though seeing Jane for the first time. "But yes, of course, you must be feeling your own kind of pain. Things have been so mad here lately. I hope you don't feel too neglected."

"Neglect is not a word I'd use," Jane assured her. "I already told Helena that I feel like a monstrous burden to your family."

"And where else would we send you, Jane? We live in a world that would label you a madwoman for your ailment, and I shudder to think where you might have ended up without the benefit of my brother's protection."

"Yours, too," Jane offered, not wishing Isobel to downplay the efforts of herself and her sisters.

"Do not mistake me, Jane. I would do everything I could to help you regardless of my own circumstances. But without my brother's title? His standing in Society? His *power*? We'd all be at risk, with or without you." She shivered, banishing the unwelcome thought. "Grief keeps me up at night, yes, but never as much as fear does."

"Fear?" The reply slipped out before Jane could stop it, but her confusion was genuine. From where she stood, Isobel and her sisters were well protected from the evils of the world, nestled away in Mulgrave Hall with every comfort they could ever desire at their fingertips. Tragedy had breached the walls of their loving home, but they were otherwise sheltered in ways Jane could only dream of.

Evidently Jane's assumption irritated Isobel, who quirked her brow rather derisively. "It is not lost on me that my security is reliant on the kindness of a man. Nor how quickly both can disappear. Imagine, heaven forbid, we had lost *all* of our brothers to scarlet fever in addition to our parents. The title would have gone to some horrid cousin of my father's, who would be under no moral or legal obligation to care for me or my sisters. We'd be on our own, our educations meaningless, our old friends little more than strangers to us, our futures bleak."

"You underestimate your resourcefulness."

"Perhaps," Isobel offered. "Helena couldn't move into Pembroke's dower house, not with the elder dowager duchess already taking residence there. But even if she could, would we be welcome to live there with her? And if not, where would that leave us? I've no actual skills beyond a sharp tongue, which already precludes me from most forms of employment available to women. I suppose I could charm my way into a position as a governess, but could I support my siblings on that pittance of a wage?" She met Jane's eye, some of her bluster fading. "There I go with another political screed, aimed at a woman already intimately aware of the precarious position we occupy in society."

"I needed reminding that my troubles are not unique," said Jane. "In a way, it helps to make one feel less alone."

"We women must stick together," Isobel replied with a grin. "All we have is one another. And please, do not fret about being a burden. If anything, you've been a blessing. I haven't seen my brother so lively since...well, since everything that happened."

Jane sensed that Isobel had been close to revealing Jasper's particular pain to her, and was glad she had not. It felt like Jasper's story to tell, but after last night, she wasn't sure he'd ever feel comfortable enough with her to do so. "I'm happy to be a distraction. I only wish—"

"You knew who you were." It wasn't a question. "I cannot imagine how you must be feeling, Jane. But Dr. Ramsay was adamant that you'd recover. He seems to think the mind is quite elastic in its healing abilities. I don't pretend to know a thing about the body, but I have to imagine that you'd appear quite worse off, if this were to be a lasting ailment."

"Yes, aside from the headaches and rare bouts of dizziness, I do feel well enough. I suppose I need to have more patience with myself."

"At least for the time being, I think it would be best for you to feel comfortable, not constrained by my brother's demands. I'll make sure he knows it as well." She stood, offering her hand to Jane. "He'll have to agree when I remind him our reputations rely on you pulling this off, so to speak."

Jane took her hand and stood, wavering a bit at the thought of the pressure being thrust upon her. "Oh, please do not trouble yourself on my account."

Isobel sighed. "The Earl of Belhaven will be so busy entertaining his guests he won't have time to prod you into wellness. Now, shall we go on a tour of Mulgrave Hall as we come up with our stories? I can't imagine you've seen very much of it."

Jane forced herself to accept Isobel's plan, even if her mind rioted at the thought of pausing her quest for answers. "That would be lovely."

They set a course through the immense manor, Isobel often pointing out bits of architecture or her father's favorite paintings. At first, mentions of the latter served only to wound her, but as time went on, and Jane proved an eager ear, speaking of her father seemed to revive Isobel, giving her a glow of happiness that Jane hadn't seen on her before.

"Ah, this one he picked up from a most unsavory curator in Vienna."

It was a lively village landscape. The artist had managed to capture the frenetic energy of a market, the sun-warmed skin of the peasants and the dusty roads they plodded on. His use of light and shadow was exquisitely wrought, and the way the blues of his sky interacted with the muted tans and browns of the buildings and stalls was breathtaking. He commanded so much detail with each brushstroke, the amount of care he devoted to each figure evident in how he managed to bring them to life even at such a distance. Jane couldn't get close enough to the painting. Something about it made her fingers itch.

"I swear he paid more than it was worth in order to get us out of there faster. But he did so love a Ferg."

"Why, the work of an Austrian master would surely have fetched a high price regardless?"

Isobel gave her a sly look. "Look at you, recognizing a painter's name."

Jane hadn't realized she'd done that. "Oh, it just...slipped out of me."

"While you were focused on something else, see?" Isobel gave a satisfied grin. "And yes, normally a work by Franz de Paula Ferg would fetch a high price, but see..." She pointed to the bottom right corner of the frame, where part of the canvas was missing. "This curator had no way to prove it was a genuine Ferg, and no storied provenance to add to its legitimacy. My father knew it was authentic the moment he saw it, but he never bought paintings for their monetary value. You see, he didn't hoard art like some aristocrats with masterpieces left to rot in country estates no one visits, never to be enjoyed again. He was in it for the feeling art gave him, and for the hunt that took him all across Europe and into the Orient."

"And he took you with him."

Isobel smiled a small smile. "Whenever he could."

She didn't need to say anything more; Jane already knew the former Earl of Belhaven had been a unique man and an uncommonly good father. What a tragedy that he had been taken from his children so prematurely. She wondered what Jasper would have been like had he not assumed his father's place, and if it ever felt to him like he was living a life he wasn't meant to. She recognized some of that pain in her own predicament. Who was she supposed to be? Was her fate one to be avoided, or had her future been ripped from her unwillingly?

After a while, their journey took them at last to the library, where they came upon three voices, only one of which Jane recognized, simply because she felt it all the way to her toes. Jasper had something of an effect on her, even when she couldn't see him. The other two were a mystery, until Isobel clapped her hands over her mouth.

"Goodness, my brothers have come home!" she whispered.

Jane looked askance. "There are *more* Maycotts I've yet to meet?"

"Two brothers, Freddie and August. They were away at school." Isobel leaned in close, whispering conspiratorially. "Do you mind terribly if we eavesdrop once more? I'd like to ascertain exactly how much trouble I'm in with Jasper without reminding him of my existence."

Jane had absolutely no desire to find herself in another awkward situation, but she didn't know how to say no to Lady Isobel Maycott, so she simply nodded and allowed Isobel to drag her closer to the door. As the voices grew louder the closer they got, it became clear they were talking about Jane.

"But is she comely, Brother?" The voice sounded a tad young, like a man who had not quite left the trappings of boyhood behind.

Isobel's eyes widened, but they were both frozen in place, unable to move away from the unfolding scene.

"She's a nuisance is what she is." There was no mistaking Jasper's stern tone. Jane thought she could have done an accurate impression of it, if pressed. Isobel reached for her hand involuntarily.

"A nuisance, eh?" The voice laughed. "You'll notice, Freddie, that our dear brother didn't answer the question, did he?"

"In fact, he did not," the other voice, Freddie, responded, sounding even younger than the first.

"Which would suggest to me that our addled guest"—Isobel's grip on Jane's hand tightened—"*is* in fact a comely lady."

"She's not a lady," Jasper argued, his words a punch to Jane's gut. She had suspected as much of herself, but last night in her chambers he had insisted she not dismiss the possibility outright. Why the sudden change of heart?

"Did you not just spend a quarter of an hour explaining to us that she very well might be?" Freddie asked, and Jane felt certain he was the younger of the two. He sounded a great deal less cocksure than August, the elder.

"What does it matter either way?" came Jasper's exasperated reply.

"I suppose it would matter little to me if you seemed less bothered," said August, sounding every inch the pompous aristocrat, so unlike his siblings. "Given your current state, I suspect you care a great deal more than you're letting on."

"Let me be perfectly clear, August: she means nothing to me. She is unworldly and tiresome to a fault." Jane's blood went cold. The words were exacting in their precision, leaving no room for differing interpretations. "I can't tell you how relieved I'll be when she's finally gone."

Isobel's hand squeezed hers even tighter, as if tethering her to her own shame. Jane couldn't bear it. The tone in Jasper's voice was more than disdain. It verged on loathing. She had thought she knew Jasper, or at least a part of him, one he might not reveal to many. But now she suspected she didn't know him at all. She was a fool.

Worse yet, a *burdensome* fool.

She wrenched her hand from Isobel's, the hot feeling of shame eclipsing whatever desire she had to preserve her host's feelings.

"Jane—" Isobel started.

"I think that's enough touring for me," she said, amazed at her own ability to speak without shattering. "I must be off."

To where, she didn't know. The only thing Jane knew was that she had to get away from the library. Away from *him*. Her only desire now was to prove she would not be a burden to anyone.

Mortification propelled her all the way back to her room, where she collapsed on the bed, though she knew she couldn't stay there, couldn't continue to rely on the Maycotts for anything. It was time to move on.

Jane's head ached as she packed her meager belongings into an old sack she suspected her hosts wouldn't miss. She didn't have much in the way of worldly possessions, but at least the dress she had arrived in had been expertly cleaned and pressed by a servant. She shed the silky tea gown that had never felt truly comfortable on her skin and donned the sturdy traveling gown, feeling immediately more capable.

Next, she wrapped the abandoned biscuits from her breakfast in a linen napkin and placed them in her bag, surmising that it wasn't theft if she had meant to eat them anyway, and that linen napkins were likely not in short supply in Mulgrave Hall. She didn't know how far it was to the village of Wrayford, but a glance outside told her the snowy road was packed down enough for walking, at least.

She shot back a frigid cup of tea for immediate sustenance and slung the bag over her shoulder, tapping her palm against her pocket, feeling for the ring that was nestled inside. Though the thought of selling the only piece of her forgotten life pained her, she would do what she must in order to survive. Because while Jane didn't know much about herself, she did know this: she had been alone before the Maycotts found her, and by God, she could be alone again.

She wrote a hasty note for Isobel and Helena, thanking them for their assistance and begging them not to worry after her, and left it on the nightstand. It was better this way. Jane didn't want a prolonged goodbye, and she suspected the same of her caretakers. Obligation had placed them together. They would be better off with her gone.

She took one last look at the lilac walls and sumptuous bed, feeling a bit like she was making a mistake. Perhaps she was being too hasty in her retreat. But then she remembered how Jasper's voice had seemed to curl with hatred, how it had become so unrecognizable to her in that moment, shattering any warmth she thought might have existed between them.

No, she thought, steeling herself for what was to come. *I cannot stay.*

If Jasper Maycott was too polite to send her away, she'd make it easier on him by choosing to leave.

Chapter Ten

JASPER

August let out a low whistle. "I take it back, Brother."

Of all his siblings, Jasper felt the most distant from August. Their personalities had been too alike and their vices too similar for anything more than a rivalry between them before their father died, and now that Jasper was the earl, it was their differences that divided them.

So he was in no mood for August and his uncanny ability to needle right to the very core of him. "Oh?"

His brother surveyed him lazily from the chaise, his hair artfully tousled in a way Jasper could never achieve, his clothing finely tailored and in keeping with the latest styles, his air nonchalant, relaxed even. Had August not suffered this past year? Had he been able to put the tragedy behind him in ways his siblings had not?

August smirked at his older brother. "I mistook loathing for passion. Easy to do with the tightly laced Earl of Belhaven. You know, you might think of loosening up a bit. Couldn't hurt."

Frustration rose in him as inevitably as the tides. "Tell me, August, would you rather take on the title yourself? Because—"

"I think the role of earl suits you fine, Jasper," August interrupted, his tone scathing.

"August only means that we wish to see you happy again," Freddie, a peacekeeper like Helena, interjected softly.

Jasper scoffed. "Happiness is the least of my concerns, Freddie." Happiness had been abandoned as he watched his fiancée, parents, and brother die, powerless to help them. Happiness was as foreign to him now as the thought of a new beginning. No, Jasper meant only to survive and see his siblings settled. Though, as that conviction solidified, an image of Jane filled his mind, both unwanted and unexpected. Jane and her impertinent tongue had something of a hold on him, one he meant to sever or embrace, depending on the moment.

His youngest brother offered a pitying frown, but mercifully a commotion at the door stole their attention. Isobel marched in, hands on her hips in a manner that had Jasper bracing for the blow.

"You really are an idiot sometimes," she announced, her gaze on him direct and blistering.

August offered her a hearty "Hear hear!" before Freddie smacked him.

He waited for elaboration, but she didn't offer any. "I suppose there is a reason behind the insult?"

She huffed. "Jane heard every unkind thing you said about her!"

Jasper's blood went cold. What he had said to his brother was an attempt to get him off Jane's scent, as he was desperate to make her seem uninteresting. Dull. Unworthy of a second glance. Because he knew his brother. August Maycott had left a trail of shattered hearts from Wrayford to Mayfair and all the way to Oxford, and while Jasper had been something of a libertine himself in his younger years, August was a great deal more callous about it. Cruel, even. He had heard the whispers of his brother's cold heart, had read of his escapades in the gossip rags. Perhaps, he thought, his earlier evaluation had been unfair. The tragedy weighed upon them in different ways. August was a rake, yes, but he was as broken as the rest of them. The difference was his skill at hiding it.

In that very moment, said rake was eyeing him suspiciously, reading Jasper's distress as easily as ever. He had to do something, but he was torn between his efforts with August or racing to Jane's side to ensure she knew he didn't mean it.

Isobel went so far as to stomp her foot angrily. "You need to apologize to her, Jasper."

Deciding August was the larger threat at the moment, Jasper feigned disinterest. "I refuse to apologize to an eavesdropper who didn't learn her lesson the first time."

August tilted his head at their sister. "Hello, Izzie, I've returned from Oxford, if you hadn't noticed." His tone was lightly perturbed. They hadn't seen him in months, after all.

She held up a finger to him. "We'll get to you in a moment," she said, never taking her eyes off Jasper. "But for now, let me assure you that you will get no peace from me until you make this right, Jasper."

He believed her, but he didn't know how to move forward without stirring August's interest. He couldn't rely on his brother being a gentleman, not anymore.

A decision was made for him in the form of a maid appearing

in the doorway, clutching a bit of paper.

"My lady, I went after Miss Jane like you asked, but…" She held the paper out toward Isobel, lost for words.

"She's gone, hasn't she?" he asked, already rising—to hell with trying to deceive his brother. The maid simply nodded, her face frozen. "Damn it." He strode from the library without a backward glance, cursing himself and Jane both for jumping to conclusions and failing to act rationally.

He looked out a window as he traversed the hall, noting the grey heaviness of the sky. There was a storm coming. "Damn!" he said to no one in particular. "Nash!" he shouted, hoping his valet was near. "I need my coat!"

"Where are you going, Jasper?" Isobel had caught up at last.

He didn't slow down. "Where do you think?"

"There's a—"

"Storm coming, yes, I am aware." He pushed his hair back out of his eyes. "Keep August occupied, will you?"

"You don't want me to come with you?"

He was of two minds on the matter. On the one hand, he could use all the help he could get. Jane couldn't have gone far but he wouldn't put it past the woman to wander in the wrong direction. The road to Wrayford wasn't as obvious as she might have assumed. But on the other hand, Jasper understood keenly that convincing Jane to return with him would require much penance, and that was not a scene he wanted anyone witnessing.

He looked at his sister out of the corner of his eye. "I think it best I go alone, don't you?"

She nodded. "Though I think Aunt Adelaide would have much to say about the matter."

"Well, she isn't here, is she?"

"Only by the grace of God himself," Isobel muttered.

They had reached Mulgrave Hall's imposing entrance. Nash stood at the threshold, coat in hand, having heard Jasper's shouted request.

"My lord—" his valet began.

"Not now, Nash," he replied, slipping into the heavy garment. He looked to his sister and Nash both. "If I'm not back in an hour, send footmen in either direction."

"If the storm's set in, it will be difficult—"

He clapped Nash on the shoulder. "I'll have found her by then, surely. How far can a woman go?"

Nash and Isobel looked at each other, their expressions grave. Outside, the wind howled and snow began to fall in earnest.

Jasper cursed. "Don't answer that."

• • •

Jasper's words came back to haunt him almost immediately.

Jane had made it a great deal farther than he'd thought she would. He found her almost two miles away from Mulgrave Hall, trudging through great drifts of snow. The Smithfields' farm stood as a lonely sentinel on the hill above her, without even a fire flickering in the window. It took a moment for Jasper to recall that Roger Smithfield and his eldest daughter had died last year, taken by the same scarlet fever that had ravaged Mulgrave Hall and the village of Wrayford. Had Mrs. Smithfield and her son moved away? It seemed unlikely, given their circumstances, but the home looked abandoned. Jasper had helped repair a damaged fence on the northern end of their land not two months prior. He made a mental note to check in on them at the earliest opportunity. But for now, his mind was occupied with quickly reaching a stubborn, likely frozen woman.

"Jane! Bloody hell, Jane, come back!" he shouted, but the

wind ate his words. Christ, but the air was biting, and she was clad in only a traveling cloak, and a thin one at that. He battled against the wind and rising snow, the storm he had been hoping to avoid now upon them.

Jasper dashed the last fifty yards or so and managed to take her by surprise, causing her to slip in the sleet. He caught her before she fell, pulling her hard against his chest to keep them both upright. She barely reached his chin when she looked up at him, her brow furrowed in surprise. Her eyes were that uncanny silver once more, veiled by dark lashes heavily laden with snowflakes, despite her spectacles. All Jasper could think of was how similar it was to when he'd found her in the snow before, covered in blood and begging for him to protect her.

I'm bloody trying.

"Christ, Jane, it's freezing—"

He watched as her eyes narrowed and she wrenched out of his grip rather ungracefully. "I hadn't noticed." But her red cheeks and strands of frozen hair betrayed her. She had a great deal of pride for someone on the verge of losing several toes to frostbite.

He took a steadying breath. "Jane, what you heard back in the library—"

"I know perfectly well what I heard, my lord." He hated the way the honorific rebuilt the wall between them. "It should please you to know I won't be imposing upon you any longer."

"It certainly doesn't please me, and you're the furthest thing from an imposition. What you heard wasn't the truth." His feet were soaked by the slush beneath his boots, sending an icy chill up his legs. "Christ, how did you make it this far?"

"Sheer grit, I suppose," she offered through chattering teeth. And yet, she took up her angry march once more. He'd have to try a different tack.

"My brother August is… Well, he's a scoundrel in every sense of the word. I didn't want him to make a challenge out of you."

"You supposed I needed protection from him?" She cocked her head, glaring. "Or was it August who needed protection from *me*? I am a brazen fortune hunter, after all."

That thought hadn't even occurred to Jasper, though he supposed it should have, if he'd had anything resembling a clear head these days. "You cannot think that, I would never—"

She paused mid-stride. "I cannot think of anything, my lord, without feeling taxed." Her frustration was evident, and he understood then that not all of it was reserved for him. "It is a devilish affliction, to be parted from my true self, and I understand why you would think me a charlatan. Hence why I am relieving you of your duty." She gestured to the road, as if the logic in her plan was obvious.

The woman was maddening. "You cannot be serious. Do you have any idea what could happen to you?" She ignored his entirely valid query, so he continued. "How did you imagine you'd make it through the storm you're marching straight into?"

She looked up at the dark sky through the swirling mists of falling snow and grimaced. "I thought perhaps I'd find an inn. I assume there are lodgings in Wrayford."

"And how were you planning on paying for your accommodations?"

She fidgeted, as if reluctant to respond. He raised a brow. She relented. "Surely a room is worth less than a gold ring," she replied miserably. Jasper hated to think she would have parted so easily with the only material object she had left from her past. *Is she so desperate to get away from me? No.* She was as beguiled by him as he was her. He saw it every time she looked at him. Heard it in the way she said his name. Jane didn't want to leave any more than he wanted her gone. She was simply angry, and he could handle anger.

"And what name would you have given them? Have you thought of how others might receive your tale of woe? Because I can assure you, most anyone you meet would seek to take advantage of you once they learned you lost your memories." He stepped closer, gesturing to her relatively well-made cloak. "It's plain to see you are not a pauper, Jane. Your speech is refined, your clothing finer than you'd find on a servant or shopkeeper. One could assume you come from money—"

Anger flared in her eyes. "That may be the kindest thing you've said about me since our meeting, my lord."

"Worse yet," he continued, ignoring her jab, "you might find yourself confined to a madhouse. All it would take is the word of one man to have you declared insane." Annabelle's work with so-called *fallen women* had taught him as much. Any behavior deemed abnormal was scrutinized. Annabelle had met women who were punished for the crime of challenging their husbands or fathers, or for being interested in politics, or not smiling enough—all of which filled him with a non-trivial amount of concern for Isobel's prospects, to say nothing of Jane's in this moment. "They'd paint you with the brush of hysteria, and you'd be stripped of your rights. Did you consider that?" She pressed her lips together, as if preventing herself from speaking. "Is Mulgrave Hall so abhorrent that you'd rather risk your freedom than recover there?"

She glared. "I am but a tiresome and unworldly girl, my lord." She stepped even closer to him, the distance between them barely a breath now. "To know me is to be burdened by me."

But he didn't back down. "I've already told you I didn't mean any of that."

She had to look up to meet his eye. "It's not only what you said to your brother. You retreat each time we…" She seemed unwilling to finish the sentence.

"Each time we…what?" he asked, his voice rough.

A flare of defiance kindled in her gaze. "Each time we get close, my lord."

She *had* noticed his cowardice. Had been hurt by it, perhaps. "That has nothing to do with you, Jane."

"No?" she scoffed as though disdain were the only possible reason for his hasty retreats. He hated how easy it was for her to assume the worst of him, and how much the desire to correct her eclipsed every other thought or feeling he had.

"I retreat not because I do not wish to get closer to you," he said, stepping even nearer still, willing her to be the one to pull back this time. But her feet remained rooted in place. "I do it because I know I should not."

Jane's breath hitched in her chest. They stood improperly close now, but neither of them withdrew. Rather, her eyes seemed to feast upon him, grazing over the contours of his jaw, his throat, his shoulders. For once, he didn't smother the heat that was building inside him. For once, he let himself feel it, let Jane feel it. He banished his doubt, his guilt, his regret. Damn the consequences. They were two people standing in the heart of a storm. What could possibly reach them there?

"Because I may yet prove a conniving fortune hunter?" she asked, breathless.

"Because you deserve my protection, not my—"

"Attention?" she offered, though they both knew the word to be a weak representation of what was unfolding between them, that blossoming of warmth when he had found her spectacles, that rush of heat when she'd parried words with him in the library, the sparking inferno when she'd first spoken his name...

"My attention, yes," he conceded.

He watched as she bit her lip, felt himself stiffen at the gesture. Jasper burned to feel those lips on his, to know what she tasted like, and hear what she sounded like when she surrendered to ecstasy in his arms. He blinked, trying to throttle the rising desire in him, but it had been a mistake to allow himself to feel even an inch of it. Now it had unleashed in him an entirely different kind of storm.

Her hands rose up to rest on his chest. They stood in the middle of a tempest and still he felt the heat in her touch. His arms wrapped around her waist without conscious effort, as if holding her were the most natural thing in the world.

When she spoke, her voice was small but clear. "And what if I desire your attention, my lord?"

Jasper's own unspent desire threatened to level him. "Jasper," he managed to choke out.

"What?" she asked as though in a daze.

"I told you to call me Jasper, none of this 'my lord' nonsense."

She looked up, her smile undoing him. "Jasper," she repeated, and he suspected then that he was doomed. "I find I do prefer it. But what would Lady Adelaide say?"

"I find I do not give a damn about her opinion, Jane." She smiled and then frowned slightly. "What is it?"

"It's nothing," she started, but he persisted with a nudge. She sighed. "Saying your name feels right in a way I can hardly quantify."

"But my saying Jane does not compare?" he guessed.

"I'm afraid there's only so much I can fool myself."

All at once, Jasper felt the brutal cold that surrounded them. He hadn't been thinking about Jane's past, caught up as he was in her more immediate future. He was a fool for letting his guard down, and even more a fool for giving in to the desire to touch her, hold her. He would spend the rest of his life haunted by how right she felt in his arms. He forced himself to step away from her warmth. "We cannot do this."

Her brow furrowed in confusion. "What's wrong?" She began to follow him, but he turned from her, not letting her get close—there was witchcraft in her touch. She paused, hurt by the distance he forced between them.

"This is a mistake, Jane," he said. She opened her mouth to argue but he didn't let her. "And not because of who you are, but because of who you could be."

"What does that mean?"

How could she not see that they stood on a precipice and that one terribly selfish move on his part would mean her ruin? "What if you're engaged? Married, even?"

She placed her hands on her hips. "What if I'm not?"

"We cannot dismiss the possibility," he said. "This..." He gestured between them. "This was a moment of madness. A fantasy. It would never work."

She looked to her feet. "Because you're an earl and I'm—"

"Jane, don't." His last shred of reason prevented him from telling her that her dubious background meant less to him now than it ever had. That truth wouldn't help matters.

"Is it because of Annabelle?" she asked. She didn't wield the name like a weapon; if anything she said it delicately. He wasn't sure which would have been worse. "You loved her, didn't you?" she pressed lightly. "What happened to her?"

But he couldn't bring himself to tell Jane about the girl he had loved, even if he suspected it would serve to heal him in a way he long thought out of reach. He couldn't find the words.

"I..." he began, choking on all the things he wished to say. "I cannot..."

Watching him struggle, Jane rushed toward him. "I'm sorry, Jasper." She stroked his shoulder. "I don't have any right to ask you about her."

But his first thought was that she did have the right. Jane was correct about how he chose to retreat from her each time the barriers between them were knocked down. Jasper was afraid of what this woman could do to him, if he let her.

Still, he pulled her into a tight embrace as he sorted through his thoughts. She sank into his arms and accepted the comfort he offered, the shelter from the cold.

He'd kept Annabelle's memory locked in his mind because he couldn't bear others' pity. For months he had been waiting for some great sense of quietude to settle upon him. Then, he thought, when his grief became bearable and the memory of Annabelle did not wound him so, he would be able to move on, whatever that might mean.

But how could he ever find peace without remembrance? And standing here before him was someone who had felt loss, but not *his* loss. He could not burden his siblings with the pain they shared, but Jane had felt a loss of her own, one deeper than the erasure of her memories. It was impossible to miss how she winced when the subject of family came up, or how the sheer force of her empathy could only mean she had suffered similarly. He could help her remember the things she lost in the accident, even if remembering them brought her pain.

But this was neither the time nor the place to unburden themselves.

"I cannot talk about her, Jane. Not yet," he murmured into her hair.

She nodded into his chest. "I understand."

"All I want right now is for you to get well, and you cannot do that out here in a snowstorm." He stepped back, holding her by the shoulders. "Come back with me, please."

She sighed. "I suppose I'm not very close to Wrayford, in any event."

Jasper swallowed his grin. "Another hour, at least."

"And I do already have a rather comfortable bed at Mulgrave Hall," she ventured. After a moment of consideration, she spoke again, her voice a bit smaller. "Will your brothers think I'm mad?"

Jasper let out a laugh. "I don't mean to offend you, Jane, but you're a woman who cannot remember her own name. They likely didn't think you particularly sane to begin with."

Jane let out a genuine laugh, loud enough to echo off the snow-covered trees that surrounded them. "A harsh assessment, but a fair one," she told him with a nudge from her shoulder.

Jasper tried to ignore how her laughter filled his own heart with joy. He could not risk being further charmed by this woman. "Let's head back, shall we?"

They began their march back toward Mulgrave Hall, both of them too cold and tired to say much of anything. Jasper was relieved that Jane had listened to him, in the end, but he worried there had been an irreversible shift between them, the consequences of which he could not yet fathom. At least he hadn't taken the coward's route this time, choosing to be honest with Jane. He didn't know what that meant for them going forward.

They hadn't been walking long before Jane stopped dead in her tracks, her head craned toward the snowy wood beside them. "Jasper, do you hear that?"

He hugged himself for warmth. "How can you hear anything

over the howling wind?"

"*Shh*," she hissed, moving to the side of the road where an old, rotted log rested. She bent toward it and gasped, reaching in.

"What is it?" he asked apprehensively.

Jane's arm emerged clutching something small and orange. "Oh, Jasper, look at the poor thing!" she exclaimed, holding the ball of fluff out to him.

He accepted it with great reluctance. "A kitten."

"We must save him!" she pleaded, stepping close so she could scratch him behind the ears. He was a weedy, shivering thing, with great big eyes and ears far too large for his head. "Look at him, he's freezing and starving, and it has fallen upon us to rescue him," she added matter-of-factly.

He raised a brow. "Has it now?"

"Indeed it has!" she practically shrieked, snatching the creature back and nuzzling him close to her chest in order to button her cloak around him.

Jasper sighed. "I suppose he could find employment as a mouser in the stables." Jane was suspiciously quiet. "Jane, that animal will not reside in Mulgrave Hall."

"Of course not," she cooed at the kitten, scratching under his chin as he peeked out from within her cloak.

Jasper found he lacked the energy to argue further. He set off once more, with Jane following close behind him—ready to defend the creature with her life, should she need to.

But they came suddenly upon a figure in the road, one whose approach had been veiled by the storm. Jane froze, but Jasper could see at once it was a boy, and one he recognized.

"Charlie?" he called through the wind. "Charlie Smithfield?"

"Yes, my lord," the boy called back warily, looking very much like he wished to run. He held a brace of rabbits over his shoulder that he tried in vain to keep from view.

"You needn't hide them, Charlie." The boy was ill dressed for the weather, and thinner than he had looked only a few months before. The Smithfield farm had seemed abandoned when he passed it earlier. His heart broke for the boy, only twelve, and his mother, forced into such dire straits. "Where is your mother?"

The boy swallowed, his throat bobbing. "Home, my lord."

"Is she well? I didn't see a fire in the window."

"She doesn't like to waste the wood or coal when I'm not there, my lord. Says the house holds the heat just fine for her."

"Nonsense," said Jasper, understanding a little of why Mrs. Smithfield would make that kind of sacrifice for her child. "Come with us back to Mulgrave Hall and we shall send you home with a wagon full of fuel and food."

"But my lord, the storm…"

The boy was right. A wagon would be useless in those conditions. "Do you have wood enough for the night?"

Charlie nodded. "Yes, my lord."

"Then build the biggest fire your hearth will hold for the night and come tomorrow when the storm abates. I will make sure everything is ready for you." The boy nodded, his expression one of exhausted relief.

"Thank you, my lord," he said with a grateful bow.

"Does your mother require a doctor?" The boy hesitated. "It will not cost you anything," Jasper added.

"The cold pains her, could a doctor help with that?"

"Certainly. I'll make sure of it," Jasper replied, making a mental note to have Dr. Ramsay drop by. "And Charlie? It's not poaching if you're on my land, and please don't ever hesitate in coming to me if you need anything at all. Understood?"

Charlie nodded again.

"Keep warm and well, Charlie," said Jane as the boy departed. Even in the dark of the storm, Jasper could see his cheeks flush.

When he was all but a speck in the distance, Jane turned to face Jasper.

"You really care for them, don't you? Your tenants, I mean."

They started back toward the manor as the question scraped against him, demanding an answer. "What kind of earl would I be if I didn't?" he offered somewhat flippantly.

Jane shrugged. "The ordinary kind, I'd imagine."

She wasn't going to let him off easily. "Ah, well, most noblemen didn't grow up under my father's shadow. He never minded getting his hands dirty and liked to see that everything around him ran smoothly and efficiently."

"It's more than that," she started, studying him thoughtfully.

"Is it?" he tensed, sensing where she was going.

"Yes. It would seem the protection of the Earl of Belhaven extends well beyond the walls of Mulgrave Hall."

How did she do it? How did she see right to the core of him? "I have a responsibility to them," he offered.

But she was right. It *was* more than that. The Maycotts had not been the only family to lose loved ones when scarlet fever had ripped through the village of Wrayford. The tragedy had bonded them. Whereas the Jasper of before might have been content to remain ignorant of the suffering of others, to do so would have been impossible now. Especially when he was in a position to help.

But why then did he chafe against the recognition of his hard-won decency? Perhaps it was because he suspected the closer Jane got to seeing the real him, the more difficult it would be for him to lose her.

"I know," she said. "And they are lucky to have you."

He did not argue against her assessment, but he did not agree with her. Instead, they were silent as they crested the last hill before Mulgrave Hall. Jasper felt a great sense of relief when the manor appeared just where it should be. He and Jane had shared a moment of weakness, of madness, one that promised an irrevocable change between them, but the rest of the world still stood.

They made a spontaneous mad dash the rest of the way, only to be greeted by his siblings, all of them evidently bundled in preparation for a search party. Everyone descended upon them in a rush, speaking over one another and wrapping them in blankets for warmth as they dragged them both inside.

Isobel gave Jasper an approving nod for a job well done as she and Helena shepherded Jane toward the nearest hearth. August and Freddie hung back with Nash, content to allow the scene to unfold around them. Jasper needed a stiff drink and to warm up, in that order.

"We were so worried, Jane," said Viola, her eyes wide with something akin to awe. "To set off into a storm—"

"Was rather foolish," Jasper finished for her, careful to nip any ideas that might emerge in Viola's developing, all-too-curious mind. "But it worked out." He didn't dare look Jane's way.

"Indeed it did, my lord," Jane replied rather demurely, causing the hair on Jasper's neck to stand on end. "In fact, it was lucky we were out there," she added, her voice thick with innocence.

"Oh?" Viola asked, hanging on Jane's every word.

Jasper realized immediately that he'd made a mistake. Jane pulled the small ball of fluff from within her cloak and held the creature up for all to see. Helena gasped in a rather motherly fashion and Viola squealed.

"We found him shivering in the cold, and your brother kindly offered to give him a home here in Mulgrave Hall," Jane said as though the matter were settled.

Jasper glared at her over Viola's head, knowing she had won and promising swift retribution.

"How splendid!" Viola cried, accepting the small bundle and cradling him to her chest. The kitten looked quite content indeed. "What's his name?"

Jane looked right at him when she answered, her eyes alight with mischief. "Mr. Darcy."

Jasper had been right about being doomed.

Chapter Eleven

JANE

Warming up was taking far longer than Jane was willing to admit.

She sat bundled before the hearth, inching ever closer, hoping the Earl of Belhaven didn't notice how her limbs shook and her teeth chattered beneath the protective shawl of blankets Isobel had wrapped around her.

Perhaps her hasty departure into the thick of a storm had been a mistake, but it wasn't as though she was going to tell Jasper he was right. Surely the man knew it already. It would do her pride no good to speak of it again.

"Cold, Jane?" he asked, reading her thoughts.

She made a show of shrugging out of the nest of blankets. "Why, it's positively tropical in here."

They sat in one of Mulgrave Hall's parlors (she assumed a manor of its size had many), toasting themselves before a roaring fire. Jasper was seeing to his earlish duties, reading from an intimidating stack of correspondence, his brow furrowed in mild irritation. Jane was relieved she wasn't the cause of it, for once. Helena had departed to see to her own duties, but not before hastily introducing Jane to August and Freddie, the former as cocksure then as he had sounded in the library, the latter even more timid than she had surmised, though it seemed that Maycott men did not come in a homely variety: they were both handsome, with dark hair and light eyes, but August was tanned and freckled, and Freddie a great deal paler. Once introductions were made, Helena had tasked her brothers with various duties, leaving only Isobel, who dozed on the settee, and Viola, who tossed a string of yarn for Mr. Darcy to chase, the kitten having taken quite quickly to his new, pampered life.

Jane thought his name was a nice touch. It had come to her in a fit of inspiration, and the look on Jasper's face when she'd announced it had almost made the entire frigid endeavor worth it. But that didn't mean she wasn't currently freezing. Could someone become permanently cold, she wondered, as Jasper stood up from the desk and walked toward the fire.

Ha, she thought. *At least he's as cold as I am.*

But he bent to the woodpile and tossed another log on the fire, looking back at her with something resembling concern on his face.

So the stern bastard wasn't doing it for himself. She made an effort to look less chilled but deemed it likely pointless before shifting even closer to the flames.

"I have an idea," announced Viola, standing and depositing Mr. Darcy in Jane's lap. "I'll be back."

"Brace yourselves," Isobel muttered absently from the settee, her eyes closed and head resting on a pillow.

Playing with the kitten did much to warm Jane, but she knew

the creature must be starving. As if conjured, a maid appeared with a saucer of milk from the kitchens, one that Jane had not requested.

She looked questioningly toward Jasper, who shrugged.

"I suspect he's hungry," he offered noncommittally before shuffling the papers on his desk.

Mr. Darcy lapped up the milk eagerly. "How thoughtful," she remarked lightly.

"Don't go thinking this means I've warmed to him." He pointed his finger in warning, not looking up from his work.

"I wouldn't dream of it," she assured him.

Satisfied, the kitten settled back into her lap and promptly fell asleep, and without his frenzied energy or Viola's constant stream of conversation, the room felt entirely too quiet. Jane wracked her mind for something appropriate and neutral to say to fill the growing silence, but the only thing she could think of was how good it had felt to be in Jasper's arms. She had been chilled to the bone when he reached her, but it had taken hardly any time at all for the heat in her belly to spread all the way to her toes as they'd argued, stepping closer together until they could step no more. The storm had raged on around them, but Jane had felt none of that cold.

She'd suspected that Jasper's passion would eclipse the fury she elicited in him, and she'd been right. There had been something in the way he had stood his ground, letting her close the distance. Jasper had let himself *feel* rather than flee, and meeting him in the middle hadn't been a choice she'd made so much as a compulsion that ruled her, forcing her to close the gap as though it were the most natural thing in the world. Her mind had emptied save for one theory that begged to be proven true: she belonged in his arms, as he belonged in hers, and she wouldn't deny either of them any longer.

Emboldened, Jane had taken what she desired greedily, bringing her hands to his chest, not knowing if she'd ever get the chance again. He had felt so hard against her softness, so steady, as if an earthquake could not shake him. And when his arms had wrapped around her waist and he'd pulled her tight against the firmness of him, her sanity had left her.

No, Jasper Maycott did not do things by half.

Sitting in the parlor, Jane wondered if the Earl of Belhaven knew how close she'd been to erasing what little distance had remained between them and pressing her lips to his. She had spent sinful moments imagining how it might feel to be in Jasper Maycott's arms, but the reality had been all the more tempting.

He'd been right, it was madness. But she couldn't bring herself to regret it, even though she knew he did.

And so, Belhaven needed to stop coming to her rescue before the debt between them became impossible to repay. Or perhaps she was the one who should stop needing to be rescued. After all, Jane had first awoken in Mulgrave Hall with one essential truth woven into her bones: she was not the type of woman prone to setting off into the unknown without a plan. Whatever had befallen her on the road to Wrayford had been an anomaly. An aberration from her normal course. That knowledge had been the first thing she could cling to.

And yet she now had ample evidence to the contrary. Perhaps she *was* that kind of woman.

Or perhaps the Earl of Belhaven brought out the absolute worst in her.

She felt the heat of his gaze before she knew he was looking at her, as though he knew the very nature of her thoughts. *Can he read me so easily? Does he think of me the way I do him?*

She met his eye boldly. How could she not, after the embrace they had shared?

The truth was, she wanted so much more than an embrace from Jasper. She wanted everything he had to offer—the wicked heat of his gaze, his soft lips trailing across her skin, his hands exploring parts of her she hadn't considered sharing before...

Jasper cleared his throat and studiously returned to the papers before him, breaking whatever spell had taken hold of her. Jane was shocked to discover she had been touching her neck, tracing the line she desired Jasper's lips to take. Suddenly, the room was intolerably hot. She needed a gulp of water or a plunge into an icy bath if the mere thought of Jasper had her behaving like a wanton.

He had made his own feelings abundantly clear, and she could not blame him for setting a boundary. It didn't matter what either of them wanted when so much of Jane's life remained a mystery. She would simply have to stop thinking about how it felt to be held by him, or imagining what could have happened if she hadn't brought up her minor, inconsequential discomfort.

"Well, I think we've learned a thing or two about jumping to conclusions," began Isobel, thereby dousing the heat that threatened to consume Jane.

"Couldn't agree more," replied Jane too brightly.

"You've never been more right, Izzie," replied Jasper at the same time.

She sat up and looked at them both suspiciously, seeming to piece entirely too much together from their brief exchange. "What exactly happened—"

But they were spared by the sudden reappearance of Viola, who clutched a heavy red book in her arms.

"Oh, Viola," said Isobel, pinching the bridge of her nose. "I don't think any of us are ready for another treatise on the decline of the aristocracy—"

"I haven't brought it out for that," Viola interrupted defensively. "I thought we might read through the *D*s, see if Miss Jane recognizes any of the names, seeing as we've yet to identify who *JHD* is."

Isobel narrowed her eyes at her younger sister. "How do you know about that?"

Viola shrugged. "You all speak over me as though I cannot hear you. It isn't my fault that I pay attention."

"Indeed," Jasper added. "Rather it is ours for underestimating you."

Viola preened and then noticed Jane's bewildered expression. "This is *Burke's Peerage*. It's an exhaustive list of all the aristocracy. Family trees, ducal lineages, things like that." She placed the heavy book on the side table and opened it with practiced ease, landing on a page with the name "Renwick" emblazoned in the top left corner. Sensing Jane's hesitation, Viola continued. "It's really quite interesting, you can trace families—"

"Viola, Jane does not care for the utility of *Burke's*, I assure you," Isobel interrupted. "Surely *no one* cares for it as much as you."

Viola gave Jane a sheepish look. "I like to know things."

Jane leaned in conspiratorially. "Speaking as someone who currently knows very little, I understand completely."

Viola brightened. "I care little about rank or titles. I simply like to know how it fits together. The Ton is a puzzle, you see. A lot can be learned from the pages in this book."

Jane imagined it would take weeks of dedicated study to get through the weighty tome. "Have you read it all, then?"

Viola nodded. "This is our most recent edition, probably

obtained by my grandmother, who cared very much about rank and titles." She closed the book and pointed to a gilded *1843* on the cover.

"You mean to tell me they publish this annually?" asked Jane.

Isobel gave her a sardonic stare. "A book listing the blue-blooded lineages of the Ton? I'm surprised they don't publish it seasonally. Better yet, immediately after an advantageous match is made. Why, the impatient mothers of American heiresses would be overjoyed if they didn't have to wait an entire year to see their daughter's names listed beside the titles their fortunes bought for them."

By then, Viola had found the beginning of the *D*s. "Shall I begin reading them aloud?"

Jane hesitated, and the ever-observant Jasper noticed her discomfort. "You needn't take part, Jane, if you don't think anything useful will come of it."

But Jane suspected that hearing her surname would knock her memories back into place, and she was keen to test the theory. She just didn't know if this was the best way to do so. "I only worry that you won't find my surname in there. It is for aristocrats, after all."

"Well, it's not as though you'll be punished either way," Isobel assured her. "Read away, Viola."

Jasper caught Jane's eye from across the room and gave her a small but reassuring smile. It was a welcome departure from his previous impatience to see her memories restored. The smile suggested to Jane that there was time to discover who she really was. Time she hadn't felt like she'd had before.

"Stop me if something sounds familiar," said Viola before clearing her throat and beginning. "*Dalhousie, Dalrymple,*

Darnley, Dartmouth." She paused and looked up at Jane, who shook her head. "*Dashwood, Davy, De Bathe...*"

On and on it went, with none of the names sparking a single memory. Mr. Darcy was up and about again, causing mischief and seeking more milk from the saucer. Viola soldiered on until the very end, never wavering in her dedication to solving the mystery of Jane-without-a-surname.

"*Dunmore, Dunraven, Dunsany, Durrant, Dyer*, and *Dynevor*." She looked at Jane once more, who gave her customary shake of the head, before closing the book rather firmly, waking Isobel from her stupor.

"Any progress?" she asked blearily.

"I'm afraid not," Jane confessed. Wanting to end on a more productive note, she looked to Viola. "Will you show me your family's entry?"

Viola lit up and opened the book at once. "You won't find our names in it, we'd need a later edition for that, and even still they'd likely only name the eldest son, but our father's name is listed as the heir..." She trailed off, having found the right page. "I suppose the most recent edition would name Jasper as the earl."

She turned and pushed the book toward Jane as the rest of the room failed to acknowledge the heaviness of what she had said. At the top of the left-hand column was the name she had been seeking.

BELHAVEN, EARL OF, (Augustus William Maycott,) Viscount Belhaven and Baron Wrayford, of Wrayford in the county of Surrey, m. in 1824 to Caroline Helena, daughter of John, 4th and late Earl of Lorraine, by whom he has issue Stephen Augustus, Viscount Belhaven, b. 17th March, 1826, and one daughter. Succeeded to the family honors upon the demise of his father on 11ᵗʰ June, 1820.

This ancient and illustrious house is descended from

ROBERT DE MORTAGNE, who, in the eleventh century, was Lord of Mortagne, in Normandy. The successor of this nobleman was his son,

RICHARD, who accompanied the Conqueror to England, and distinguished himself at the decisive Battle of Hastings, subsequently obtained a large portion of the spoil, in numerous English lordships.

Jane's vision blurred at the exhaustive lineage that followed, but the most pertinent information stood out starkly. "The earldom dates back to William the Conqueror?" she asked, unable to keep her voice neutral.

"Conferred upon our ancestor by King Henry II himself," Isobel replied, her own tone sarcastic. "Our grandparents never let anyone forget it, whereas our father made sure we understood it didn't mean much."

"No?" asked Jane. "I would have thought such a lineage would mean a great deal."

"To the wrong kind of people," said Jasper, not looking up from his papers.

"Our father was something of a radical," said Isobel with a grin. "The Ton didn't know what to do with him, but our mother ensured that they always had a place in the ballrooms of Mayfair. People loved her a great deal, you see."

Viola sniffed at the mention of her parents. Jane placed her hand on the girl's shoulder, not caring if the gesture was improper, especially when the girl leaned into her palm, seeking comfort. "Do you have any portraits of them? I'd dearly like to see them."

"Oh, but you haven't been to the gallery!" exclaimed Isobel.

"You simply must see it!" cried Viola, clapping her hands together in glee.

"Will you take me?" Jane asked, but before they could reply, Battersby appeared at the door, his face looking particularly pinched, like he had sucked on a lemon before entering the room.

"Lady Isobel, Lady Viola, Lady Adelaide has requested you attend tea in her chambers."

They both wilted, but they could not refuse a summons, especially not one from Lady Adelaide. Jane was immeasurably relieved to have been left out.

"You can take me another time," she reassured them.

"Nonsense," replied Isobel, her grin alight with mischief. "Jasper can take you." Jasper grunted behind them, but Isobel was undeterred. "Who knows how long we'll be stuck at tea? Taking Jane on a tour of the gallery is the least you can do after calling her an unworldly—"

"That is quite enough, Isobel," Jasper interrupted. "We were all there."

"I wasn't," argued Viola.

Isobel gave her a look that suggested she'd fill her in shortly, before continuing. "And besides, you so enjoyed seeing the Ferg and the other paintings in the rest of the manor." Battersby cleared his throat and Isobel and Viola moved to depart. "Did you know Gainsborough was induced to paint some four of our ancestors long after he'd transitioned to landscapes? Think of the cost!"

It was true that Jane desired to see the gallery, but she didn't wish to force Jasper into it.

But it seemed she wouldn't have to. He set down his papers and looked right at her. "I need to see to this list of supplies for Charlie Smithfield and his mother, but then we shall visit the Gainsboroughs."

"Don't forget the van Dycks!" called Isobel over her shoulder. "And the Dobson, and the Lely!"

"The tour will be robust, Isobel, I assure you," Jasper called absently after her, already penning his list.

As Jane waited for Jasper to finish, her eyes drifted back to the lineage of his family. It seemed to go on forever, spanning more than two columns and spilling over to the next page. It wasn't every aristocratic family that could trace the roots of their nobility back to the days of William the Conqueror. At last she came to the end of the entry, where something other than a man's name caught her eye.

Motto — We endure.

When she thought of everything the Maycotts had been through, she couldn't help but find the maxim apt, though she wondered which came first, the words or the lived reality. Had generations of ill-fated Maycotts suffered innumerable tragedies? Or had the adage been adopted as an aspiration, only to become more cruelly fitting as time went on?

She looked up at Jasper, his head bent over the desk, the perfect image of endurance. He was a man who knew how to keep going, how to forge ahead through adversity. But what good was endurance if one forgot how to live?

She looked back at the Earl of Belhaven entry and wondered what the entry looked like in its most recent iteration, with Jasper's name etched permanently as the earl.

Succeeded to the family honors upon the demise of his father.

So simple a phrase for something so tragic. Again, she found herself wishing she had met the old Jasper, the one without an earldom on his shoulders, the one who wasn't left to raise his siblings at so young an age. But by the same token, she felt lucky to know this version of him, too.

"Ready?" She jumped a little, startled by his sudden closeness. He laid his hand on her shoulder to steady her, managing to send a wave of calm through her. "Apologies, I didn't mean to frighten you."

"You didn't." Her hand rose to cover his without conscious effort. Neither of them wore gloves. He pulled away first, almost reluctantly, and when he dropped his hand to his side, he flexed it as though she had burned him.

"Shall we?" he asked, his voice rough.

Her cheeks heated. "The supplies will be procured, then? For Charlie Smithfield and his mother?"

He nodded. "They won't go without coal again; I've made sure of it."

"Among other comforts, I'd wager," she added.

He didn't disagree. Jane imagined a much-overburdened wagon would be making its way to the farm at the earliest possibility, which gave her a sense of relief for the boy and his mother. He had seemed so small there in the road, with his quarry hung over his narrow shoulders. She hoped he'd lit a roaring fire when he got home, knowing the Earl of Belhaven would be replenishing their stores of fuel the next day. Seeing Jasper's unconscious generosity on display had warmed her heart. It wasn't often a nobleman concerned himself with the plights of the less fortunate.

The silence between them stretched rather thin while Jane

pondered his virtues. She cleared her throat, desperately seeking a new subject for them to broach. In that very moment, Mr. Darcy scampered up the leg of Jasper's trousers, clinging precariously to the front of his vest. Jasper looked at the creature bemusedly as he wailed the world's squeakiest wail.

"He does not wish to be left out," Jane translated.

Rather than depositing the kitten on the nearest cushion like she thought he would, he simply perched Mr. Darcy upon his shoulder and began to walk.

"What if he falls?" Jane asked, scurrying to catch up.

"He'll learn quickly not to."

They walked in somewhat strained silence all the way to the gallery, which was mercifully not very far. Mr. Darcy adapted quickly to Jasper's cadence and looked quite cozy there on his shoulder.

Jasper paused at the threshold and beckoned her to enter before him, bowing slightly as she passed, stilted, so as not to disturb the kitten. It was rather formal for them after the events of the storm, but perhaps formal was the direction they should be heading in. They needed to build back the walls that had come down between them. She passed him with a straight spine and a polite nod. *So very proper.*

But Jane's breath caught in her chest the moment she stepped through the doors. The gallery was immense, its proportions difficult to take in all at once. Her eyes flew from painting to painting, not sure of where to settle first.

Where the rest of Mulgrave Hall was for the paintings acquired by the former earl—the storied works of Dutch Masters or masterpieces crafted by penniless apprentices—the gallery was its living, breathing history, a room dedicated to the Belhaven lineage, dating back centuries, as far as she could tell. It was a stark reminder of what Jane sorely lacked.

She pushed that feeling aside in order to devour the visual feast that was before her, terribly overwhelmed as she was.

The storm clouds outside did nothing to add to the light of the room, but Jane imagined that sunlight would have painted the walls and their blanketed canvases brilliantly. Some were the length and width of the walls themselves, depicting past earls in the heat of glorious, bloody battles or breathtaking portraits set against pastoral landscapes so real she could smell the summer wind in the air.

After depositing Mr. Darcy on a plush armchair and dutifully pointing out the Gainsboroughs, the Lely, the van Dycks, and the Dobson, Jasper seemed content to let her wander, and so she did, from painting to painting, ancestor to ancestor, some bearing the same title as Jasper, others marrying into the bloodline with even grander ones behind them. All of them connected, bound together by the blood in their veins.

It wasn't long before a queer feeling of loss came over her. Jane had believed there were things that tied she and Jasper together, things they felt more acutely than others, things that could not necessarily be put into words but could be sensed, perhaps. A shared understanding of grief, of feeling adrift.

It almost seemed a betrayal to discover how very rooted he was. How, if he ever felt unsure of his place in the world, he could simply walk to this gallery and be reminded of the centuries of solidity that held him up. Jane didn't have anything like that to lean on, and she felt that disparity to her core.

It was the most alone she had felt since arriving at Mulgrave Hall.

Eventually, she came to a dominant portrait of three men positioned menacingly above her. One had Jasper's chin, the other his nose, all three possessed his eyes, though none had his warmth. Ancestors, to be sure, but she didn't think any of them were his father, a man purported to have been kindhearted. None of these men could claim the attribute, if the artist had painted them honestly.

Jasper came up behind her and spoke over her shoulder. "Remember the Belhaven entry?" he asked, his breath warming her neck. She nodded, not sure if she'd be able to speak. "The youngest is Augustus, my grandfather. That's his father, Bartholomew." He pointed, his arm coming around her. "And the oldest is Bart's father, Laurence. All of them were, by most accounts, cruel, indifferent men."

"The painting all but screams that," she remarked as she studied their expressions, noting the peculiar, haughty angles of their chins, the way their shoulders were braced as if for attack, and how the artist managed to convey disdain in the lines of their mouths. It was a painting that most likely pleased its subjects and spoke the truth of them to those who chose to see it. A masterful work, really.

Jasper hadn't moved away, formality be damned. She felt his presence as though they were pressed together like they had been in the storm. Her body remembered everything about those stolen moments, and the aching need that had accompanied her since they'd parted.

"My father rejected the things that my grandfather valued most. My mother was the daughter of a well-to-do landowner, but my grandfather expected nothing less than a viscount's daughter for his son. It didn't matter that my mother defied his predictions and was embraced by the Ton. In his mind, the Maycott name had been tarnished, and it fractured his relationship with my father. Even my aunt Adelaide treated my mother poorly at first, and my father never forgave her for it." He let out a bitter laugh. "The irony is my grandfather's cold dismissal is likely what made my father so determined that we would have a place in Society." He let out a small huff, as though coming to a realization. "I do believe if my grandfather had lived to see my father's successes, he would have been proud of him."

Jane paused, unsure if she should speak the words on the tip of her tongue. In the end, she decided she had nothing to lose. She turned her head, not quite looking at him. "I suspect the same could be said of your father and your successes."

Jasper did not speak for a long while, though he likewise did not move from her side. Eventually, he sighed. "I'm not sure he'd agree with you, and besides, we were never fractured like they were. I was the spare, after all."

It seemed a prevarication to Jane, but she wasn't about to quarrel with him over it. He stepped away at last, and Jane turned to face him, noting that Mr. Darcy was playing rather violently with a curtain's tassel over Jasper's shoulder.

He held his arms out and gave her a grin that did not quite reach his eyes. "Well, Jane, was it all you wished for? I know Isobel did her best to sell it to you, but it is merely a farce designed by my ancestors to justify our place in the world."

She knew he spoke lightly, almost teasingly of the grandeur around them, but she found she could not jest in return. She took a deep breath, letting her lungs empty entirely before speaking. "In truth, I find myself somewhat disturbed by the inequity between us, my lord."

He frowned. "Because of your missing memories?"

She tilted her head at him. "You cannot deny that I am at a disadvantage."

"And why is that?"

She gestured to the vastness of Mulgrave Hall's gallery. "You know exactly who you are and where you came from. Your bloodline has doubtless imbued you with an ironclad sense of self." Jasper might like to pretend that he was different from the Ton, not so absorbed in pedigree and lineage as the rest of them, but he still benefited from it. "Your family fought at the bloody Battle of Hastings."

Jasper stepped a bit closer, his brow furrowed. "And who is to say you don't possess a similar blood in your veins, Jane? Who is to say that the woman who is veiled from you is not as sure of herself as you perceive me to be?" He leveled her with his hard gaze, his sternness back in full force. "And how can you hold it against me?"

A part of her wanted to assure him that she didn't, but Jane was tired of his dogged persistence in believing she was secretly a noblewoman, and how she had begun to suspect that he needed her to be, and that everything would change when they discovered otherwise. "I am a mere woman in a world built by men," she began. "The women in these portraits held little value beyond what they could offer their husbands."

He nodded. "A sad truth, but that is the way of the world."

"But what if a woman has nothing to offer the man she loves?" she asked, her voice a bit smaller than it had been before.

"What if the same could be said for the man? Surely you know the inequity can work both ways, Jane."

She hadn't expected that response. "Why, then true love would be separated, I suppose."

He paused, taken aback. "Do you believe in it?"

"True love? Of course," she replied incredulously. "How could you not, when your own parents were said to be a love match?"

He grimaced at her words. "Their love did not protect them. True love could not save them."

It was then that she understood his hesitance. Jasper may have been born into a prestigious bloodline, but it was loss that shaped him. And Jane was familiar with loss; it was what they shared, the feeling that tied them together. But as relieved as she was to find the connection again, she was all the sadder for them both.

"I'm not sure we can place the blame on love, Jasper," she replied softly.

"Where, then?" he asked, drawing his mouth to a firm line.

She searched her mind for an answer to a philosophical quandary that neither man nor religion had fully satisfied yet. "The indifferent stars? The cruel hand of fate?" she offered. "Humanity has spent millennia fighting both, Jasper. I daresay it is love that makes the fight worthwhile."

She hadn't meant to speak so passionately with the Earl of Belhaven about matters such as love, but Jasper had looked at her in such a way that she found herself desperate to make him believe that love was a gift, not a curse. She needed him to understand that the risk of losing it was not reason enough to avoid it altogether.

"Will you take me to the portrait of your parents?"

It was placed in the brightest part of the gallery where it hung alone opposite the largest window, bracketed by plush velvet curtains and with a settee laid out before it, so the observer could stay a while.

"The Earl of Belhaven and his loving wife," Jasper presented, not sarcastically, but perhaps bitterly.

Lady Belhaven was a beautiful woman with ink-black hair and kind eyes of deep indigo. Jasper might have inherited eyes the color and shape of his father's forebears, but he inherited the kindness of his mother's. The painter had also captured the gleam of mischief Lady Belhaven shared with Isobel. They looked remarkably similar, more like sisters, though Jane supposed the painting was likely decades old by now.

Lord Belhaven was a bear of a man with auburn hair and warm brown eyes. She saw so much of Helena in him, and Lady Adelaide. There was no mischief in him; instead the painter had captured his steadiness, and so she saw Jasper in him, too, despite the obvious differences.

Unlike similar portraits of noblemen and their wives, Lord and Lady Belhaven were not posed stiffly; instead they bent toward each other, his mother's head resting on her husband's shoulder in obvious affection, his hand wrapped around her waist protectively.

"It is plain to see they loved each other deeply." She looked back at Jasper, whose gaze was locked upon her rather intently, avoiding the portrait altogether. "You may not believe in true love, Jasper, but you are the product of it."

"You speak of love as though intimately aware of it," he said, stepping closer. Was that jealousy in his tone? "Have you loved someone, Jane?"

"I—I could not say," she stammered, surprised by the question. "Without my memories, I—"

"But what do you *feel*?" he interrupted. "Is love as familiar to you as grief?"

Her heart thudded in her chest, to hear him speak so openly of the truth she had been trying to avoid. "How do you know grief is familiar to me?"

"Having experienced so much of it myself, how could I not recognize it in you, Jane?"

"I do not know who I lost," she whispered, eyes on the floor. "I only know the ache of their absence. It is like a physical pain. Something I cannot forget, even when the origin of it is hidden from me." She looked back up to find Jasper studying her, scarcely even breathing, as though he needed her answer more than he needed the air that filled his lungs. "But I did not love them, not like that," she concluded with a sigh.

By then, he had come to her, tentatively reaching for her hand. She took his, and as he rubbed her palm softly, the touch was as intoxicating as a glass of champagne rushing to her head.

"I did not mean to upset you," he said, inclining his head to meet her gaze.

"I'm not upset," she replied. Being aware of her loss was not the same as feeling it, at least not in that moment, when she had so much more to think about—like the man standing before her, holding her hand as though it were the most delicate thing in the world. "I would accept even my unhappy memories if it meant gaining some clarity. I suppose that means I should not flinch away from the subject. But—"

"But?" he echoed, one hand encircling her wrist now, the other cupping her chin, tilting her head up slowly.

"It does not seem to be the time," she whispered, losing herself rather steadily in the warmth of his gaze. "Does it?"

"No, I do not wish to talk about grief any longer," he agreed with a tempting smile.

"Is there a subject you'd prefer?" she asked, her voice a mere rasp as he ran his thumb along her jawline.

"I can think of a few," he said, pulling her to him until their bodies notched together, both hands on either side of her face now, cradling her. She felt his touch over every inch of her body, felt herself blush beneath his hands. "The most pressing being that I cannot seem to loosen your hold on me, Jane, however much I may wish to." She understood his meaning. She felt the same pull in her, and the same reluctance to be free of or to give in to it entirely.

"I'm not sure if I should apologize—"

"I don't want an apology from you, Jane. I want..." His thumb was on her bottom lip, tugging gently downward as he weighed his options carefully. All she wanted was for him to be reckless, but she couldn't push him or beg him to give her what she desired. Nor would she be the one to save them both by retreating. The earth could have opened up around them and Jane would have stood her ground, daring him to take what he wanted, what they both needed.

In the end, the decision was made for them.

"My lord?" came the butler's voice from very far away.

Jasper did not move, did not tear his eyes away from Jane's. "Yes, Battersby?" he replied, his mouth mere inches from hers.

"Your guests have arrived."

Between their legs, Mr. Darcy howled his displeasure, reminding them both that they had never truly been alone.

Chapter Twelve

JASPER

Jasper stepped away from Jane hastily, suddenly very aware of how it would have looked if one of their guests had been the one to walk into the gallery and seen them doing...whatever it was they had been doing.

For his part, Jasper had been smothering the desperate desire to lay claim to Jane's mouth under the watchful and unwelcome eyes of his parents. He had been ready to take her right there against a wall, damn the consequences.

"This cannot happen again," he told her, though he was mostly speaking to himself. Mr. Darcy howled again from the floor. "We cannot do this."

She looked disappointed but not surprised by his vow. "Because of who I may be?" she asked sarcastically, reaching to pick up the small kitten and cradling him against her chest.

"Precisely that," he replied seriously. "And especially

now that Mulgrave Hall is playing host to a party, filled with reprehensible noblemen."

"I must say, they sound charming," she said while tickling Mr. Darcy between his oversized ears.

"You cannot trust a single one of them, Jane." He couldn't blame his friends for what was in their nature. There was a time when Jasper might have behaved as callously. It was what had made him pull away from his friends when he'd lost those dearest to him. He couldn't bear to play at normality with them, which they would undoubtedly expect much sooner than he was ready.

"Truly?" she asked, her voice catching a bit.

He grimaced. "I've made them sound rather monstrous, haven't I?" Jane nodded. "I'm simply trying to prepare you for the reality of noblemen."

"Are they all?" she asked. "Noblemen, I mean."

"Of varying degrees," he replied. "If I had to guess, I'd say Isobel invited Clarence Meadows, who is an actor but also the illegitimate son of a duke, which is enough for most members of the Ton to accept him, even though he will never inherit the title. And then there's Mr. Edgar Ashwell, the second son of an earl, like I was, and Mr. George Selby, who is the son of a baron, and finally Sir Lucian Hill; as a knight and a physician, he is both the least and most noble among us. You needn't worry about him, to be fair. The rest I'd keep my distance from."

"Isobel said she invited six of your friends," said Jane, scratching Mr. Darcy under his chin. "You've listed four."

"Oh, then I suppose she's invited Edgar's sister, Lady Louisa, and George's sister, Miss Beatrice Selby."

Jane raised a brow. "Allies?"

"You stand the best chance with them, yes. Much more honorable than their brothers, in any event. They knew me before," he said, attempting to explain the gulf between who he was then and who he was now in as few words as possible. "It's more mischief than actually harmful behavior. I simply suspect you aren't ready."

"Perhaps you underestimate me, as you do Viola," she replied, not looking away from the kitten in her hands.

He thought it possible, but felt the urge to hide Jane away from the lot of them nevertheless. "Jane, I only wish to—"

"Shouldn't you go greet your guests?"

He could tell she was disappointed with him. "Will you be all right?"

"I can manage a simple walk to my chambers. I'm quite tired, really. Perhaps I'll take a nap. I suspect you'll be busy, so I will endeavor to keep my distance from you, my lord."

Is that what he wanted? Judging by the bolt of displeasure, it was the opposite of what he desired. But then, with Jane, he often found himself doing precisely what he shouldn't. Perhaps it was better this way. The house party could serve as a barrier between them. Christ knew they needed one, especially since he'd considered ravishing her in the middle of the gallery, under the imperious gazes of his many ancestors.

"You know you can ask for anything you require, anything at all."

"Just not from Battersby?" she teased, allowing a small bit of warmth between them.

It might as well have been a crackling fire for how it warmed Jasper. "May I suggest seeking a more agreeable servant first and only calling upon him as a last resort?"

Suddenly, Helena appeared in the same doorway that Battersby had departed from. "Jasper! You are being a terrible host," she hissed, wincing as she pressed her hand to her lower back. She still carried the pain of the accident that had taken her husband from her. But every time he tried to push her to seek a new treatment or consult with a new physician, Helena changed the subject. Still, he made a mental note to ask Lucian about what could be done.

"Is it really a mark against me if I never wished to be a host in the first place?"

"Why don't you ask Aunt Adelaide?" She looked over his shoulder and noticed he wasn't alone. "Jane, there you are. Are you ready to be Miss Danvers?"

Jane curtsied, wobbling a bit in the delivery, thanks to the furry bundle she clutched close to her chest. "Miss Jane Danvers of Buckinghamshire, pleased to make your acquaintance."

Helena exchanged a slightly harried glance with Jasper. "We'll do our best to keep you away from the hounds," she assured her, extending her hand for Jane to take. "Jasper, your friends are milling about like louts in the drawing room, aside from Lady Louisa and Miss Beatrice, who are no doubt being scandalized by Isobel as we speak. Oh, and Lucian."

"He didn't come?"

"No, I sent him to the Smithfields'," she said patiently, as though explaining to a child. "Do you think anything happens in this manor without my knowledge?"

Jasper was surprised but relieved, knowing Mrs. Smithfield was in good hands with Lucian. "Thank you, Helena."

She quirked a brow at him. "Believe it or not, it was Battersby's idea. Now go! There's only so long I trust any of your friends unsupervised."

He nodded. "Let it be known that I still plan on murdering Isobel for this."

"Your friends are under the mistaken assumption that you

want them to be here. Let's not make it so obvious that you don't."

Jasper nodded, and with one parting wave from Jane, they were gone.

Which left him alone under the portrait of his parents, the one he had done his best to avoid since they'd died. It loomed over him, demanding he be brave when he hadn't felt that way in ages. But that wasn't quite true. Jane had made him feel...if not *brave*, then perhaps daring. He had done things these past few days the old Jasper, the one laboring under the weight of his many tragedies, wouldn't have dreamed of.

He could look at a damn portrait.

He gave it a cursory, testing glance, not knowing how it would feel to see their faces again.

Pain enveloped him. Immediate. Crushing. Gasping.

But it was not the type of pain he had anticipated. It was not the all-encompassing agony he had felt in the early days without them, the pain he had worked diligently to avoid by building rituals and adhering strictly to rules he had made for himself. He had needed to survive and be strong for his siblings, and that pain had not allowed for it.

No, this was the pain of missing them, and while it robbed him of breath, it was endurable.

His mother's warmth and his father's steadfast nature reached out from the painting, like fine tendrils of memory wrapping themselves around him. It was the pressing of a bruise—it smarted, but there was strange relief there, beneath the hurt of it.

I miss you. He wasn't sure if he said it aloud or simply felt it with every fiber of his being.

A deep breath shuddered through his chest, and he stood taller, feeling a slight bit more capable now that he had faced them and survived. And Jane had seen them, too. He had shared a part of himself he hadn't thought he could, and she had seen them as they were when they were living. It was the best he could have hoped for.

Jasper turned on his heel and made to leave, feeling like something had been accomplished.

It wasn't until he left the gallery entirely that he realized he hadn't shown Jane the portrait of his brother. But perhaps that was for the best. There was only so much memory Jasper could endure in a single day.

• • •

Jasper spent the walk to the drawing room sifting through his myriad of feelings. It was not an activity he enjoyed, but he was beginning to suspect the sheer weight of them might drown him.

Namely, he focused on his feelings about Jane.

The woman was a hurricane who had stormed into his world and blown everything apart, including the carefully crafted defenses Jasper had been relying on in order to keep moving forward.

And she had awoken more than simple lust in him. Jane had the unique and maddening ability to dig deeper than Jasper was willing to delve, like, say, into whether or not he believed in the concept of true love. He could not recall having so frank and philosophical a conversation with anyone before. Even with Annabelle, the topic of love had not extended much further than that which they'd shared for each other. But Annabelle had known a different Jasper, a man who had been unmarred by tragedy.

Would she even recognize him now? Would it matter if she did, or didn't? Jasper had believed grief would always be a knife, but in the year he'd spent without her, he thought maybe it had changed its shape. Less a knife, and more like a stone sinking through him, weighing down his steps.

But these few days with Jane had somehow lessened the burden, causing him to feel light in a way he hadn't expected he'd feel again. Was it that she'd entered his life like the sudden brilliance of a comet cutting through the sky, but would vanish just as quickly? Could he be less guarded with her because she was a stranger? One who would recover and return to whatever life she left behind her, and so it was safe for him to tell her things he'd never tell someone who intended to stay? Someone permanent? Someone quite the opposite of Jane without-a-surname, who was as fleeting as she was beguiling?

So, if his grief was no longer a knife, what was it that stabbed through him now, and why did it carry with it the sour taste of guilt? He realized he didn't have time to parse that particular emotion, as he rounded the corner that would take him to the drawing room, where several of his friends awaited him after more than a year of silence on his part. Like Annabelle, they knew the old Jasper, but unlike Annabelle, they would have to contend with the new one. He would have to don a mask for them and hope it was enough.

He could hear them already, their laughter echoing through Mulgrave Hall's empty corridors. Jasper paused to steel himself at the doorway, then he entered.

Chaos erupted all around him, as three men shouted their raucous greetings. Five, if you counted his brothers, who joined in the chorus, as though they hadn't seen him at breakfast.

"There he is!" cried Selby as he crossed the room to grasp Jasper's arm, his full cheeks ruddy from the cold.

"The Earl of Belhaven himself!" added Clarence, his wry expression dimming none of his good looks. "Deigning to mingle with us lesser beings."

"Don't be so hard on yourself, Clarence. It's not as if you can help being a bastard," replied Edgar before Clarence whipped his hat directly in his face.

"How were the roads?" Jasper managed to choke out almost normally.

"Bloody awful, but Mother Nature herself could not deter us, Belhaven," said Clarence, automatically adopting the title in place of his name. His *father's* title. Christ, it was Anthony's more than it would ever be Jasper's. Clarence didn't mean anything by it. Jasper *was* the blasted Earl of Belhaven, and nothing would change it. Still, he found he couldn't bear it.

Selby seemed to pick up on his discomfort. "Our coachmen are recovering in your kitchens as we speak, Jasper," he said, switching to the name they had always known him by.

"We may have promised them copious amounts of ale and good company for their troubles," said Edgar. "So I do hope Battersby has retired. It's good to see you, Jasper."

"And you, Edgar." He stepped back, taking them in. "It's good to see all of you. Even Selby."

They all laughed, but Clarence quirked a brow wickedly. "That's *Lord* Selby, now."

Jasper looked to Selby. "No," he started, dumbfounded. "How?"

His friend looked at the ground. "We lost my father six months ago. Apoplexy."

Jasper clutched his shoulder, knowing news of Lord Selby's untimely passing likely lay in the pile of unopened letters he had been avoiding. He wished he could have been there for Selby. God knew he had some experience with loss. "I'm sorry, George."

His friend shrugged. "I knew you were overwhelmed with

your own affairs. And besides, we all know my father was a reprobate."

"But still." He knew his self-imposed exile meant he had missed their joys, but he hadn't thought he would miss their sorrows, too, or how it would feel to know he could have helped them. Perhaps becoming a recluse didn't only damage him. Perhaps it damaged everyone he held dear.

But it wasn't about how he felt. He swallowed whatever else he meant to say. "How does it feel to be Lord Selby?"

"A great deal like being his heir did, since I'd assumed his duties long ago. At least now I don't have to run everything by him first. It was a bloody daunting task finding a sober hour in the man's schedule."

Clarence clapped them both on the back. "You'll be heartened to know, Jasper, that my dear father still lives. Though I suppose his death will bring little material difference to my life. Might be nicer to say I'm the bastard son of the *dead* Duke of Rosemont. A drink?" he asked, taking on what should have been Jasper's duty.

"Yes, drinks for all," replied George. "And enough talk of our blasted fathers, dead or otherwise."

Clarence got to generously pouring scotch from the crystal decanter, passing libations out to his devoted friends.

"Yes, what's this about your sister's guest?" asked George in between sips.

"Heard about that, did you?" Jasper asked, eyeing August, whose eyes shot upward innocently.

"Come now, Jasper. It's not often we meet fresh blood outside of the Season."

"She's all but betrothed, George," he replied, with no small amount of menace in his tone. "Do try to behave honorably."

"Speaking of honor, where is Lucian?" asked August.

Clarence collapsed onto a nearby chaise, his scotch already drained. "Visiting the sickbeds of Wrayford's less fortunate. What else? You know, it goes against my better judgment to allow so upstanding a man into my confidence."

"He makes up for it in his lack of nobility, don't you think?" asked George.

"He does indeed, the scoundrel," replied Clarence. Jasper had not been in so lively a conversation in a year. It was as overwhelming as it was oddly welcome. Comforting, even, to be swept along without much effort.

"Are the rumors of his imminent betrothal true, do you think?" George asked Edgar, who tended to know these things because of his exceedingly well-connected sister.

"To Miss Abigail Bunworth?" asked Clarence.

"Indeed," Edgar replied. "She is quite accomplished, as it were. She runs a school for foundlings in Cheapside."

"Someone must, I suppose," said Clarence as he helped himself to another scotch. "How fares Lady Louisa?" he asked brightly.

Edgar glared again. "Why do you ask?"

"My aim is innocent!" he insisted, arms raised, scotch sloshing in his snifter. "I seek only to ascertain how many titled buffoons I must vanquish in order to win her."

Edgar did not laugh with the rest of them. "I would sooner see her wed to George, Clarence."

George brought his hand to his chest, deeply affronted. "How did I get dragged into this?"

"No offense, George," Edgar added, not looking away from Clarence.

"Much taken," George replied incredulously.

Edgar ignored him. "If you so much as glance at her,

Clarence, I will beat you within an inch of your life."

"You say that, Ashwell," replied Clarence, kicking his boots up onto the table. "But deep down you must desire me as a brother-in-law."

"I detest even the idea of it."

"You'll come around."

"My father would never consent to my sister marrying an *actor*, and I know you far too well to even entertain the notion. You forget we have seen you at your worst."

After considering it, Clarence shrugged as though Edgar had a point.

Edgar sighed deeply. "Christ, must we talk only of betrothals and women? I get enough of that from my mother."

"I'd much rather discuss *less* marriageable women," said August from where he was sprawled lazily on the chaise next to Clarence. Freddie sat next to him rather more upright, a faint blush dusting his cheeks.

"Have you made that opera singer your mistress yet, then? I saw her at Simon Griffith's club not three nights hence, looking rather lonely."

"Miss Clara Bradshaw?" August asked with a quick exhale, emptying his lungs. "She's far too expensive for me, Clarence. And besides, why would I want to be tied down by a woman?"

"I hear Simon will be the Duke of Radcliffe soon enough, now that his wretched father has taken a turn for the worse," said Edgar.

"Serves the devil right, but I doubt Simon will much enjoy his new title," replied August with a wicked grin.

The conversation faded as Jasper tried not to be bothered by the idea that, in his absence, his brother had assimilated rather fully into his group of friends. It was a rather childish emotion, jealousy. It only bothered him that August had seemingly had little time for his family, but perhaps all the time in the world for carousing with Jasper's friends and entertaining opera singers.

In a way, it made Jasper feel replaced, but he swallowed his discomfort. It would serve him no purpose.

"Have you met her then yet, Jasper?" asked George. "She's a sight to behold."

"Who?" he asked, George's description conjuring up images of Jane's silvery eyes in the moonlight.

"Clara Bradshaw," George replied as though it was obvious. Jasper supposed it was.

August cleared his throat. "I hardly think an opera singer of less-than-stellar repute would entice my brother out of the bowels of Mulgrave Hall."

"Come now, Jasper used to have a soft spot for winsome sopranos," said Clarence. "There was a time when we couldn't get him out of Covent Garden without a bit of muslin on his arm."

"Yes, well, that was before..." Edgar paused and the room fell suddenly silent. There was little Jasper could imagine doing to remedy the situation, save for evaporating into thin air. "That was before," Edgar said, a note of finality in his delivery.

They were spared further agony by the sudden appearance of Lucian and the ladies.

"See, what did I tell you," Lucian began as the room jumped quickly to their feet. "Of course, the gentlemen are prepared to receive the company of four lovely ladies."

It took not even a second for Jasper to note that Jane was not among them. There was Helena, giving him a searching look, and there was Isobel, looking as mischievous and unbothered as ever. To their left was Edgar's sister, Lady Louisa, a woman famous for her lush figure and sparkling wit, and George's sister,

Miss Beatrice, a pale slip of a woman with a sour countenance and a grievance tucked away for every occasion.

While the rest of the room greeted the women, Lucian found his way to Jasper's side.

"Mrs. Smithfield's joints are arthritic," he said, dispensing with pleasantries altogether. "Taking up her husband's share of the farm work has not been easy on her. I advised that she apply heat and stay off her feet as much as possible so as to avoid a flare-up. She didn't seem to think rest was possible."

"I'll see to it that she does," said Jasper, already formulating a plan to ensure she and Charlie got all the help they needed. "You went on horseback?"

He nodded. "And Helena sent me with a basket of food and warm clothing. Their spirits were lifted, at least."

Jasper clapped him on the shoulder. "Thank you, Lucian."

"Gentlemen, apologies for the delay, though I can assure you we are worth the wait," quipped Isobel with a slight, rather masculine bow and tip of her nonexistent cap. "Now which of you would like to pour me a scotch? I fear we don't have much time."

Miss Beatrice blanched as Clarence jumped to action, procuring snifters for Isobel and Lucian in record time. Jasper had learned long ago not to attempt to limit his sister, as she would do what she liked, regardless of his intervention.

"Where are your lovely chaperones?" asked George, looking over their shoulders fearfully, having been on the receiving end of Aunt Adelaide's wrath on more than one occasion.

"Blessedly engaged in a game of whist," said Lady Louisa. "It would seem my aunt and Lady Adelaide have nurtured something of a grudge between them that dates back many decades."

"Who is their fourth?" asked Clarence, sidling closer to Lady Louisa.

Isobel grinned. "Battersby, naturally."

Edgar cleared his throat. "Where is your school friend, Helena?"

It was then that Jasper emerged from his stupor. Keeping up with his friends had tasked his mind so fully that he hadn't thought of Jane since determining she hadn't arrived with his sisters. Which meant she was somewhere else entirely, and that was an ominous thought indeed.

Helena offered a placid smile. "Oh, Jane is retiring. She should join us soon."

"Is she ill?" asked Miss Beatrice, her lip curling in a sneer.

Helena and Isobel exchanged a quick glance. "There was an accident," interjected Isobel. "But she is much recovered, if a little fatigued." Miss Beatrice did not look convinced. Isobel continued. "I assure you, she is in quite good health."

But Jasper didn't believe her.

After their abrupt parting in the gallery, Jasper had walked straight to the drawing room, which didn't leave Jane much time to get to her room and change for dinner, let alone fall asleep. Had she finally tired of his constant vacillation and left Mulgrave Hall for good? Having only recently regained feeling in his toes after following her out into the storm earlier that day, Jasper was not prepared to do so again. He clenched his fist at his side, knowing he couldn't ask his sisters without raising suspicion.

"I daresay I spend much of the winter burdened by one illness or another," offered George diplomatically.

But illness was a topic Jasper did not wish to tread upon. Sensing his discomfort, Helena took over. "Miss Beatrice," she said brightly. "Do tell us about your latest charitable endeavor."

Miss Beatrice sniffed mildly, but anyone could see she was pleased the conversation had steered her way. "Myself, along with the other members of the Belgravia Benevolence Committee, seek to raise funds to restore the grounds of St. James's Park. We will be hosting a series of musicales and bazaars to that end. I'm sure you've all received your invitations."

"Are the grounds not in rather good shape to begin with?" asked Clarence with a bemused smile.

Miss Beatrice glared at him. "And what do you think prevents a sudden decline into disrepair, Mr. Meadows?"

The rest of the conversation was lost on Jasper, who was facing a sudden decline of his own. Was Jane truly unwell? Had he not noticed due to his own damn selfishness? He thought back to the heated moment they had shared in the gallery—she hadn't seemed ill. If anything, she had seemed wholly alive, glowing despite the pale, wintry light, her cheeks and nose still pink from the cold—or was it desire?—and Jasper himself alive with the all-consuming need to warm her, touch her, hold her. And she had certainly *felt* vibrant—her skin so perfectly soft and delicate, her body deliciously curved and supple. Standing there, cradling her between his hands, everything Jasper wanted had felt within reach. He needed only to grasp it. Why hadn't he?

And what if it was too late?

But he and Jane were an impossibility. A man could not be too late to seize something that would never be his. How many more times would he come to the same realization?

It didn't matter. Jane was still missing from the drawing room, and until he knew she was all right, he would be unsettled.

Slowly but surely, Isobel found her way to his side, drawn perhaps by the look of unbridled concern he was unable to disguise.

"She was sleeping when we went to retrieve her," she said in a voice so low that no one but Jasper would have been able to hear her. "And it didn't seem wise to wake her. Viola has been instructed to watch for her and send for one of us if needed."

"I must go—"

"You mustn't," Isobel replied as firmly and quietly as she could. "Please remember, Brother, that Mulgrave Hall is no safe place for secrets at this time." She looked around them to be sure none were listening. "Not when everyone present has brought a ladies' maid or valet who would love nothing more than to ingratiate themselves with the household servants, namely Battersby, by providing a bit of choice gossip, like, say, the Earl of Belhaven visiting an unmarried woman's chambers."

Jasper clenched his jaw so tight his teeth ached. "What if she needs me..." Isobel's eyes widened. "Us," he corrected hastily. "What if she needs *us*?"

Isobel's mouth was a flat, disapproving line. "She is a grown woman, Jasper. You need to trust that she can handle herself." After a beat, she continued. "Speaking of which, I must say you're handling yourself rather well."

Everyone else in the drawing room was engaged in conversation, laughing and sipping their drinks happily, utterly unaware of Jasper's rising panic. In a way, it was the rousing success he had thought impossible before his friends had arrived. He should be relieved, but all he felt was worry.

Jasper gave her the smallest glare out of the corner of his eye. "I feel as though I am barely treading water."

Helena stood and the room fell silent. "Shall we retire and ready ourselves for dinner?"

Everyone rose as Isobel whispered out of the corner of her mouth. "But you don't *look* it, and that's what's important."

It wasn't the reassurance she thought it was.

Chapter Thirteen

JANE

Perhaps I'll take a nap.

The suggestion had been a lie, as Jane had been attempting to shrug off the pain of Jasper's latest rejection. Christ, how often was she going to allow the man to make her feel so bloody foolish? And so, the nap was a shield, a play at ambivalence. She certainly wasn't planning on sleeping while Mulgrave Hall filled with strangers. She had a role to assume and a room full of noblemen to fool.

And yet, when she reached her chambers, the events of the day and the pounding in her head caught up with her, and she found herself slipping beneath the counterpane, intending only to snatch a few restful moments. Mr. Darcy voiced his disapproval until she got settled and he claimed his spot curled up on her hip. And then they were lost to the world, utterly unaware of the goings-on of the rest of Mulgrave Hall, both sleeping quite heavily for what was supposed to be a brief afternoon nap.

When she awoke, it was to the faint echo of a dream leaving her, one that felt oddly familiar for a woman for whom familiarity was a foreign concept. Jane stared out the window into the gathering darkness as she clung to the fading fragments of the dream—a man's laugh, the smell of pipe smoke thick in the air, the taste of champagne on her tongue—hoarding them like bits of treasure, trying to understand if they were memories brought to the surface of her mind while she slept, or a fiction invented by her mind.

They certainly *felt* like memories. She had heard that laugh before, been comforted by it, laughed along with it. And the smoke tickled her nose even though it wasn't real, making her think of a pipe peeking through a substantial moustache. Jane knew that man. Had loved him, too.

And lost him.

Alas, she knew it was a memory because of how it hurt her. Surely an invention of her mind would not pain her so. The grief she had carried through her injury was bound up in her memories of him, she knew that now. Which meant he was someone important to her. Someone dear to her.

Had Jane dreamt of her father?

But the rest of the memories faded like mist in the morning sun, too tenuous to remain rooted in her mind. Sadness arrived in their wake, because it felt like a whole new kind of pain, to have had this small taste of who she was before, only to lose it again. She wiped her useless tears away, wondering if she'd ever feel like a person whole. A part of Jane wanted to crawl under the blankets and drift back into the dream, as it was as close as she'd come to knowing who she was.

But she knew it wouldn't be so easy. Instead, she went to

the desk in the corner of the room and wrote down everything she could remember from the dream. If she had to rebuild her old life from the smallest scraps of memory, so be it. Let it be the painstaking work of inches. Jane was simply glad to have *something* to hold on to.

By then, her tears had stopped. By putting pen to paper, Jane had given herself a purpose beyond simply existing. Isobel had meant well when she suggested Jane stop pressuring herself to recall everything, and it had helped to have a few unencumbered moments in which she felt a bit like a normal woman, but it was not the solution. Letting her guard down had felt invigorating, even when it had also felt foolish. Making choices for herself had felt freeing. But it was an illusion.

Until she knew who she was, there would be no freedom for her.

Until she knew who she was, she had to keep her guard up, lest she let Jasper in again.

I will endeavor to keep my distance from you, my lord.

Another lie. Another play at nonchalance, even though the idea of steering clear of him struck her as an impossibility. She was living in his home, taking her meals with him, wearing his sister's clothing, reading his books. But she would have to try. She could not remain entranced by a man who would never be hers, even if thoughts of him made her knees weak.

A soft knock on her door startled her as much as a sharp rap would have.

"Come in," she called, her voice still thick with sleep.

Viola stepped into her room. "You're awake!"

Jane looked once more out her window. "Have I slept through dinner?" Jane wanted nothing more than to avoid it altogether, sore and tired as she was. But she owed the Maycotts her presence at the very least.

"No, I received strict instructions to ensure you woke in time to dine. It is nearing eight o'clock."

"Have I kept you from your own dinner?" she asked, knowing Viola was too young to attend a dinner party with the Earl of Belhaven's friends.

Viola shook her head. "I will eat after." She took a few tentative steps toward the bed, and suddenly Jane understood her intent.

"Please take Mr. Darcy. I'm sure he's grown quite tired of my company."

He protested ever so briefly as the girl picked him up, but settled immediately in the crook of her arm. "I've made him a bed out of my sewing basket," Viola explained.

Jane pushed her chair back to face her. "Are you an accomplished embroiderer, then?"

"No, and Jasper seems to have forgotten that I ought to be." She and Mr. Darcy sat on the edge of Jane's bed. "When we are forced to tea with Aunt Adelaide, I take one of my older projects and do my best to seem like I'm working very diligently on my stitching when really I am doing nothing."

"That's quite clever," Jane replied with a grin. "What is it you prefer to do?"

"With all of the time in which I am not embroidering, you mean?" Viola looked at her appraisingly, trying to decide if Jane could be a trusted confidant. She leaned in a bit closer, even though they were alone. "No one knows this, but I so dearly wish to become a novelist."

"A novelist!"

Viola blushed. "It's silly—"

"Of course it isn't, Lady Viola. So you spend your time writing?"

"Writing, yes, though I hardly think myself ready for such a task," she added.

Jane was puzzled. "No?"

"No, I am only thirteen and, if the works of Mary Elizabeth Braddon are to be believed, I am rather sheltered. So for now, I am an observer. I write what I see, what people speak about, what they do, how they might feel, and especially how they act with one another. I wish to understand people before I invent sensational stories for them."

"That seems logical," Jane replied. "I hope you've taken ample notes, as I've likely provided you with priceless material for your first novel. Though, may I suggest making me an *actual* fortune hunter in your version? Much more compelling stuff than the reality. That is, if you believe me when I say I am not."

Viola smiled kindly at her. "You may be a mystery, Miss Jane, but I've known you weren't a fortune hunter from the start."

Jane was a bit surprised to hear it. "No?"

"No, a fortune hunter would not be so bewildered as you." Her eyes widened at her own boldness. "I mean no offense—"

Jane patted her hand. "You have not offended me, Lady Viola."

"It's only that I have read all sorts of lurid tales about highwaymen and rogues and mollishers and doxies—"

"I'm not certain your brother would approve of you using the word—"

"And I simply cannot fathom counting you among their ranks. It isn't as if you're attempting to woo my brother with your womanly charms, as a swindler would. And you're hardly grasping or mercenary with your methods."

"Which are?"

Viola pondered. "Well, I'm not sure you have any, Miss Jane."

"If I do, I am certainly unaware of them," she replied with a sigh.

They sat in contented silence for a few moments, Viola softly petting a very put-upon Mr. Darcy, Jane surreptitiously stretching her aching muscles.

Eventually, Viola spoke, her voice small. "May I ask you a question?"

Jane sat up a little straighter. "Please do."

"Have you ever lost anyone?" So small a question, and yet it fell so heavily between them.

Jane wasn't sure how best to serve Viola. The girl had suffered more tragedies than most people would face in a lifetime, and she was barely out of childhood. Jane had felt loss, too, but as devastating as it was, she thought it paled in comparison to Viola's, as she'd lost her parents and brother in one fell swoop. "I can't say for certain, but I suspect that I have."

Viola nodded and gazed wistfully out the window. "I wish I could forget."

Jane got up from her seat at the desk and sat beside Viola on the bed. "But I didn't just forget the pain. I forgot everything." She would not cry in front of Viola, not when the girl was in desperate need of a bit of hope. "I think you'd be sorry to lose your happy memories, too."

Viola nodded. "Perhaps what I actually want is to forget how we were before. Jasper especially. He's very different now. He used to be so...light."

Jane couldn't imagine that version of Jasper, the very antithesis of the stern bastard she knew. But that didn't mean Viola was wrong. "I don't know much, Lady Viola, but I do know that humans are capable of change, even when it feels impossible. So who you are now may not be who you are in a year, or ten years. You keep growing and changing and adapting all your life. Your brother, too."

"You think?"

She nodded. "Similarly, the way you feel now isn't how you will feel forever. Time can dull the ache in your heart. It will never disappear completely, but then, why would you want it to? Without that pain, you wouldn't remember the joy."

Viola gave her a sly look. "Are you sure you don't remember? It seems as though you might."

"I remember the pain," Jane said sadly. "It's the joy I forget."

Another soft knock at the door surprised them both, reminding Jane she had somewhere to be.

"I hope that's not Battersby," whispered Jane.

"His knock is much more insistent," Viola whispered back.

"Come in," Jane called, reasonably sure she wasn't ushering the supercilious butler into her room.

But it was only a maid, the same one who had helped her bathe. "Hello, Miss," she said with a quick curtsy. "Her Grace sent me to assist you."

"She left you a gown behind the screen," said Viola, pointing. "Lottie will help."

Lottie gestured for Jane to follow her. Once ensconced, she stripped Jane down to her chemise and stockings and took a step back, allowing Jane to consider the gown. It was a beautiful creation, composed of dark green silk skirts and tidy bell-shaped sleeves tied off with bows. "The gown is Helena's, you said?" she called over the screen.

"Yes," replied Viola. "Chosen to suit your coloring."

By then, Lottie had gotten Jane into the corset and laced her gently. Next was the crinolette, which she cinched around the natural bend of her waist. She looked in the mirror, noting the bustle was modest, which pleased her. Next, Lottie added a petticoat, and in hardly any time at all, she had Jane in the gown itself, moving on rather quickly to tend to her hair, which she fashioned into a knot that sat at the crown of her head, leaving a few curling tendrils to frame her face. She finished the look with a gold comb fastened before the knot, inlaid with pearls of various sizes, which looked a great deal like a tiara.

"This isn't...too much?" Jane asked, worried she would be reaching far above her station.

"It's terribly fashionable, Miss." Jane must not have seemed convinced. "Her Grace was very specific." Jane nodded. Who was she to argue with Helena? "And there's this," she said, holding out a delicate silver chain. "Her Grace said it's for the ring, if you'd like."

Jane reached for the signet ring that was never very far from her and looped the chain through it. Lottie then attached the clasp behind her neck and let it settle on her. The chain was very long, allowing for the ring to remain hidden in her bodice, but closer than ever before, and safer than when it was tucked into her pocket.

"It's perfect," she breathed, her thumb rubbing the engraving.

When Lottie was done and the transformation complete, Jane couldn't help but be transfixed by her own appearance in the mirror. Aside from being slightly tight in the arms (she resolved not to lift them for God or country that evening), the dress fit her perfectly, and for once, Jane felt almost normal.

"You look lovely, Miss," said Lottie. The maid gave her a final small curtsy and departed, leaving Jane a moment more to revel in her borrowed gown. Helena and Viola had been right to choose that particular shade of green—emerald suited her dark hair and golden skin well. Even the bruises and bandage could not detract from the overall effect. She would be lying to a room full of noblemen tonight. At least she looked the part. It was enough to shore up her meager supply of confidence. Enough to get her out from behind the screen, at least.

Viola gasped when she came into view, crushing Mr. Darcy against her chest in excitement. "Oh, Miss Jane! How splendid you look! But you must hurry!"

Jane rushed to the door and paused, looking back at Viola and Mr. Darcy. "Thank you for your assistance. I hope I'll be able to repay your kindness."

"I expect a full report on tonight's dinner," she replied with a grin. "For research, of course."

Jane delivered her most flawless curtsy yet. "Of course."

• • •

The closer Jane got to the drawing room, the harder her heartbeat hammered against her ribs.

Miss Jane Danvers of Buckinghamshire.

My father is in textiles.

I am very nearly betrothed to Mr. Taylor, who is...also in textiles.

She repeated the lies over and over in her mind until they began to feel like truths, reminding herself that the effort would likely be in vain, as Jasper's noble friends would not care a whit about her. Still, she liked to be prepared.

As she turned a corner, Helena came into view.

"There you are, Jane!" She hurried to her side. "I only just realized that you may not know the proper etiquette. I'm so relieved I found you." She escorted her to a nearby alcove. "Now, since you are an unmarried woman, you cannot speak to a gentleman without a proper introduction. I will try to make yours in a timely manner, but there are a great many guests within, so please do be careful. The last thing we need is for Miss Beatrice to witness you breaching etiquette. The woman is a viper. Worse yet, a tediously dull viper." Helena shivered at the thought. "As for dinner, I suspect you know at least basic table manners, but when in doubt, do *not* look to Isobel for guidance. I've seated you across from me and I will keep an eye out and try to help you in any way I can, *discreetly.*" She reached for Jane's hand and gave it a reassuring squeeze. "We simply need to survive tonight. The first dinner of a country party is always the most rigid. Are you ready?"

Jane swallowed thickly. "I suppose so."

Helena hooked their arms together and held Jane's hand, guiding her toward the drawing room. "And may I say, you look almost too lovely in that gown."

"Thank you for lending it to me."

"Nonsense, it's yours now."

"I couldn't—"

"Oh, *psh*, it's not like I'll be wearing emerald green any time soon." Helena's half mourning dress was a pale lavender, almost gray to the naked eye. At least she wasn't in full mourning, forced to wear the stiff and itchy black crepe gowns that seemed less an honor to the dead and more a punishment for the living.

They reached the doors and Helena paused, wincing. She reached a hand behind her to the small of her back and seemed to press on an injury, her breath shaky as she did so.

"Are you all right?" Jane whispered. "Do you need to sit down?"

Helena took a deep breath and plastered a smile on. "Nothing more than a stubborn ache, Jane. Shall we?"

Servants opened the doors before them, and they were met

by a wave of noise. Jane's heart was in her throat. It was a mere gathering of people, but to Jane it was pure chaos. Helena pulled her into the room as the men stood up to greet them.

But in a sea of new faces, Jane could only focus on one.

She had never seen Jasper so polished—his hair was combed from his face, his skin was clean-shaven, his black dress coat and trousers were more close-fitting than any she had seen him in. He looked every bit the stern bastard she had met upon waking, though she understood now that it was a mask. But nothing could disguise the fact that the Earl of Belhaven was an absurdly beautiful man. He stood by the fireplace with two of his friends who appeared to be locked in some deep conversation, but Jasper could not tear his eyes away from her. She watched as his friends tried in vain to reengage him before following his gaze toward her, knowing smiles on their faces. Seeming to remember himself, he looked away and loosened his collar, and Jane's blood heated at the thought of having had some effect on him.

"Jane?" came Helena's voice, much closer.

She turned away from Jasper and faced his sister, who stood next to a man with warm brown skin and closely cropped dark hair. "I'm terribly sorry," she began, somewhat distracted.

Helena interrupted as gracefully as she could manage. "Sir Hill, may I introduce Miss Jane Danvers, a dear friend from Cheltenham."

"Just Lucian, please." He gave her an indulging bow and smiled. "A pleasure, Miss Danvers. May I ask after your injury?"

Jane's hand unconsciously came to the bandage on her head. "Oh, this?" she asked with a nervous laugh. It was one thing to come up with the falsehood on a whim; lying about it to a physician was a different matter entirely. "I simply slipped and fell on the staircase."

Lucian frowned. "Were you seen by a doctor? A head injury can be deceptively serious."

"Yes, and promptly. He advised rest."

"Our family doctor is quite modern in his methods, Lucian. I assure you Jane was in good hands."

Lucian's arm positively twitched with the desire to examine her himself. "Please do not hesitate to come to me should you feel unwell, Miss Danvers. I would be happy to treat you."

"Lucian is a physician, Jane, to the Prince of Wales."

Jane was startled by that. "In truth?" she asked before thinking better of it.

"Last I checked," he said with a smile. "But I am little more than a cog in the machine, not one of the Prince's physicians-in-ordinary, merely an assistant to Dr. William Gull."

"But then you must have had a hand in the Prince's recovery from typhoid fever?"

Helena's eyes were saucers at Jane having remembered something, but Lucian did not notice. "Indeed I was, Miss Danvers. But the credit must go to Dr. Gull, who 'possessed an energy that never tired and a watchfulness that never flagged,' if you'll forgive me for quoting the *Times*."

"How fortunate for the Prince to have had you both," Jane replied.

He nodded his head congenially. "I thank you for the compliment, but I must let you carry on with your introductions."

Helena smiled serenely as she guided Jane away. As soon as they were out of earshot, she inclined her head. "Was that—"

"I remembered something."

"And not something so ingrained as breathing or reading, Jane, nor so recent so as to be fresh in one's mind. The Prince's illness happened years ago."

It felt like a victory over her own mind, to have had a memory slip through the cracks when she was least suspecting it. Joy surged through her and all she wanted was to tell Jasper of this latest development. But he was across the room, a distance which may as well have been an ocean for how much it separated them.

"Oh, prepare yourself," Helena hissed. "Clarence Meadows approaches and none are immune to his charms."

Jane was skeptical. "None?"

"Even Aunt Adelaide swoons in his presence."

Jane doubted that, but then they stopped before a man who seemed to have been built by the collective desires of all women. He was trim but broad shouldered, with a generous mouth that tilted in a crooked smile, eyes as green as fresh spring, veiled by indecently long lashes for a man, and a head full of cherubic golden curls. The look he gave them left no room for debate: Clarence was entirely aware of his gifts.

"Mr. Meadows, may I introduce Miss Jane Danvers, a dear friend—"

"From Cheltenham, yes." He took her hand and brought it to his lips. It was not altogether unpleasant. "Where has the duchess been hiding you, Miss Danvers?"

Flustered, Jane grappled for her senses. "In—in Buckinghamshire, sir."

"Miss Danvers's affections are engaged, Clarence," said Helena in a tone that brooked no argument.

"Pity," he remarked lightly, as though the matter were of no consequence. He still hadn't relinquished her hand. Jane noticed then that Clarence wore a great number of rings, one for almost each finger. But it was the signet ring on his pinky that caught her eye, a gold ring with engraved initials, *CGM*. His, she supposed.

He noted her curiosity. "Are you a lover of glittering baubles,

Miss Danvers?"

"Clarence is famous for his discerning eye when it comes to jewelry, Jane," Helena said.

"Indeed?" she asked, an idea forming in her mind.

Clarence offered her something of an arrogant smirk. "You'd be hard pressed to find someone more knowledgeable than I, it's true."

Without further ado, Jane pulled the chain from within her bodice and brandished her ring before them. "Do you recognize this maker's mark?"

Clarence, perhaps surprised by her brash delivery of the question, cleared his throat and took hold of the ring, holding it up to his eye to study it closely. "Ah, yes, B & K, Bailey and Kitchen. You needn't be an expert to know of them."

"No?" Jane prompted, impatient to learn even a sliver of information about the only artifact she had left from her old life.

"Why, they're one of the best-known American jewelers. Based in Philadelphia. They famously designed the mortuary medal for President Lincoln's casket, if I recall correctly."

"American," Jane echoed, wondering what it meant that the ring had crossed an ocean.

"Indeed, they are quite renowned. Is this a family heirloom?"

Jane looked down at the ring, desperate to feel connected to her past. "Something like that, I suppose," she said, tucking it back under her neckline as best she could, while remaining modest.

"You know," Clarence said, leaning in as though they were the closest of confidants, still holding her hand. "If you ever have any additional queries about other priceless gems or bijoux, I do often find myself in Buckinghamshire on affairs of business—"

"What business would a bastard son of a duke have in

Buckinghamshire?" asked a man of middling height with ink-black hair and a moustache.

"Plenty, George," he replied, his jaw clenched.

"Lord Selby," Helena cut in, "may I introduce Miss Jane Danvers."

He took Jane's free hand, forcing Clarence to let go of the other one or be party to looking quite ridiculous. "Charmed, Miss Danvers," he said, his tone warm and welcoming.

It was less intimidating than Jane had feared. Jasper's friends seemed to regard her as a welcome distraction, but she wasn't fool enough to think that their attention meant anything. She was simply a new, shiny toy, being the first unmarried woman the men had met outside of the Season. She was happy to find she quite liked Lady Louisa, and to confirm that Helena was right about Miss Beatrice. She was feeling almost confident in her ability not to make a hash out of the evening. A bit premature, perhaps, considering the meal had not yet been served. But things seemed to be falling into place.

Except that Jasper was avoiding her like the plague.

He hadn't said one word to her, or even acknowledged her existence. To the casual observer, they appeared to be little more than acquaintances, barely more than strangers. Perhaps he thought others would be able to sense the way they were pulled together if he got too close.

It shouldn't hurt her. She had told him she would do her best to keep her distance from him. Perhaps he was making her task easier by staying away.

But she did sense his eyes upon her, even without looking his way. Jasper might be avoiding her, but all evening his gaze had tracked her around the room. Was he worried she would say the wrong thing and reveal herself to be a fraud?

Out of the many introductions, only one man remained, and he was standing right next to the Earl of Belhaven. Helena pulled her toward them by the crook of her arm, but Jane would have rather avoided them altogether. She didn't want to face the stern bastard again, not after she had peeled back his layers and seen him for what he really was, only for him to don his mask once more.

They stopped before the men, Helena silent, waiting for her brother to speak. He was the host, after all. Yet he seemed almost reluctant to introduce them. His friend was neither handsome nor homely, his looks residing somewhere in the middling range.

After an intolerable delay, Jasper spoke. "Mr. Ashwell, please allow me to present Miss Jane Danvers of Buckinghamshire, a friend of Helena's."

She had expected flattery, whether hollow or sincere, like she had received from the rest of Jasper's friends. But Mr. Ashwell looked at her with unvarnished curiosity, like she was someone worth knowing. His genuine smile transformed him into a captivating man, and she decided to listen to her instincts and extend her hand to him.

"A pleasure to meet you, Mr. Ashwell."

Ashwell seemed delighted by her boldness and shook her hand most eagerly. "The pleasure is all mine, Miss Danvers."

Jane couldn't help but notice Jasper's expression held a hint of displeasure. She knew ladies were not, strictly speaking, supposed to shake hands with gentlemen, but it wasn't as if Lady Adelaide were there to witness the spirited gesture. Though, thinking on it, Jane suspected she might have approved in this particular instance. The woman made it plain that she did not care for shrinking violets. And besides, it was a handshake, not an invitation to her chambers.

Mr. Ashwell let go of her almost reluctantly. "Do you come often to Mulgrave Hall, Miss Danvers?"

"This is my first time, sir."

"And are you enjoying your stay? I can't help but notice your injury."

She couldn't stop her fingers from rising to trace the borders of the bandage. "An unfortunate accident, but I can think of no better place to recuperate."

"Quite right, and as unfortunate as the accident was, I cannot help but think we may be the fortunate ones, if your injury is the reason you extended your visit."

It was a circuitous compliment, but after Jasper's cold reception, Jane found herself needing one. "I do hope I don't disappoint."

"I daresay that's not possible," he replied with a warm smile.

The stern bastard cleared his throat. "Miss Danvers will be returning to her home at the earliest opportunity."

The room stilled. Even those not a party to their conversation had heard the finality in Jasper's tone. Mr. Ashwell looked between the two of them, attempting perhaps to deduce the nature of their relationship. Acquaintances did not merit such antipathy. Enemies did, perhaps, but then what would an enemy of the Earl of Belhaven be doing in his home?

"Oh, didn't we tell you, Brother?" Isobel called out, her tone firm.

"Tell me what?" Jasper ground out.

"Miss Danvers has been freed of her obligations and can stay as long as she likes!" Her jovial timbre did not match the atmosphere of the room, but Isobel was not daunted. "Isn't that splendid!" She did not pose it as a question, but rather intended to force her brother into acquiescing.

Waiting for his reply was agony. Torment. Torture, really. The whole room was on tenterhooks. Hadn't they come to an understanding when Jasper had offered her the time she needed to recover her memories? And yet he was acting as though her very presence displeased him. She thought back to the gallery, when they had come so close to succumbing to desire—she hadn't displeased him then.

"Indeed," he replied through a clenched jaw. "How very fortunate."

It was then that her heart sank fully, for Jane realized he must not have felt the same way she had. Not in the gallery, not in the storm, not in her chambers. Those stolen moments that had come to mean so much to her had been mere distraction for the Earl of Belhaven. Whatever force pulled them together had relinquished its grip on Jasper.

All she could hope for now was to be similarly freed.

Battersby appeared at the door, dissolving the tension of the room. "Dinner is served."

Everyone stood and began pairing off, performing that strange dance of etiquette that Helena had warned her about. Rank dictated that Jasper should depart first, as earl. But he was frozen beside her, seeming to want to speak but forcing himself to stay quiet. She could not read him, now that he had retreated behind the stern mask once more.

"Shall we?" asked Mr. Ashwell, offering her his arm.

"Please," Jane replied, taking it gladly.

Before they turned from Jasper, he opened his mouth to say something. Jane inclined her head searchingly, willing him to say whatever it was he wished to. But he only cleared his throat and stepped around them to walk away.

In a way, she felt relieved. It was better that she understood her place with him. She would do them both a favor and avoid him for the rest of her stay. Mulgrave Hall was a manor of considerable size. They shouldn't find themselves in close proximity too often, especially if Jane found a way out of the rest of the planned activities. He'd forget she was even there, and as soon as her memories returned, she'd be gone.

All she had to do now was survive dinner.

Chapter Fourteen

JASPER

Jasper didn't know how he was going to survive dinner.

Not with Jane standing there looking like she belonged in the stuffy grandeur of Mulgrave Hall.

Like she belonged with *him*.

In vain, he had attempted to banish that thought and regain his composure, but it was a lost cause the moment Jane had stepped into the drawing room and the world around him faded to nothing next to her sharp brilliance. One glance was all it took for Jasper to feel that peculiar tug—the one he was beginning to realize would have pulled him anywhere, so long as it was in her wake.

There she was, wearing a dress that suited every tempting inch of her, donning a smile that he recognized as a mask to cover her bone-deep apprehension. All he wanted was to go to her, to put her at ease, to take her arm in his and present her to the room as she ought to be presented, as his equal.

As *his*.

Christ, the thought was intoxicating, even though he knew Jane belonged to no one save herself. Jasper had watched as she met his friends and the apprehension faded and Jane's confidence at last shone through. He should have known she'd handle herself admirably, and that his worry had been for naught. Even disadvantaged as she was, Jane was a force to be reckoned with. He knew that.

He simply didn't want anyone else to know it.

Christ. I need to get a grip on myself. Jasper should feel no ownership over her and had no desire to mark her as his, like some lesser man might do. So he avoided her, like a coward, because avoiding her was easier than acknowledging what she meant to him.

The problem was Edgar.

"Jasper, she is exquisite," his friend had whispered in his ear as Jane conversed with Lucian, her smile ready and her eyes alight. Jasper could hardly blame him for noticing, but it was unlike Edgar to be so immediately entranced. He was famous for his ability to judge character, so it was both distressing and reassuring that he was drawn to Jane based on so little.

"She's attached," he had replied through gritted teeth.

"To you?" Edgar always had been vexingly perceptive.

"Of course not," Jasper had said, his irritation obvious. "She is all but engaged to a man back in Buckinghamshire." The words, though false, felt like poison on his lips. He cleared his throat. "I merely wish to make her status known."

Edgar had nodded, his brow raised. "Duly noted."

It only got worse once Helena and Jane had made it through the rest of the gentlemen in the room, save for Edgar. Somehow the fates had contrived against him and Jasper had been forced to introduce them himself. And then Jane had offered his friend her bloody hand and whatever good sense remained in Jasper had left him entirely. He had been an unforgivable ass. He knew that now, but in the moment, he could not have helped himself.

Charitably, he could put it down to wanting to protect her. But it was more than that. Jane had walked right through the walls he had built to keep others away, and she had done it without him noticing. How easy it had been to let her in, and how welcome her presence had become. But she deserved so much better than a broken man such as he, a man of sternness and barbs and impenetrable grief. Jane deserved a man whole.

He'd watched as her face fell and knew he was the cause of it, silently swearing he would atone for it in due course, starting by treating her as she ought to be treated, not like a prize to be won. When Edgar had offered her his arm, Jasper had forced himself to stay silent. When Jane's eyes had begged him to say the words that might as well have been emblazoned on his chest, he had done the impossible by walking away, his hand burning with the unspent desire to take Jane's.

Isobel was right. Jane was a smart woman. She would not be wooed by any of his friends, because in the end, none of their attentions or intentions mattered when Jane had no foundation to stand upon without her memory.

Let Edgar charm her. Let Clarence make an utter fool out of himself. None of them knew the real Jane. They might see her as a prospect now, but her lack of memory would preclude her from any serious form of courtship, and they couldn't very well reveal the truth to any of the guests.

The best thing Jasper could do for her was give her room to find herself again.

He walked the short distance to the dining room alone, knowing there'd be another gentleman to escort Lady Louisa, as he had been meant to. He needed a moment to clear his head and forget the look on Jane's face when he'd been unforgivably rude.

The dining table sagged under the weight of all the dishes and candles. Mulgrave Hall had not seen a feast such as this since Jasper's mother was the lady of the house, and he was surprised by how pleased he was to see it restored to its former glory. Helena had more than outdone herself, especially on such short notice.

As he waited for the rest of his family and guests to settle around the table, he did his best to avoid looking at Jane. Isobel squeezed his shoulder reassuringly as she passed, seeming to sense the turmoil he was going through. He hoped she was particularly perceptive, and that the strain wasn't obvious to everyone.

But no, his guests seemed content. Jovial even.

Before anyone else could contemplate it, August stood, raising his glass. "A small toast to good health and good company," he began. "May both endure."

"Hear, hear," called George, his glass raised. The rest of the table echoed him. August caught Jasper's eye and gave him a small nod. It was all the sentiment Jasper could handle, and he was surprised August had taken it upon himself to deliver it. Perhaps his brother was more observant than Jasper gave him credit for.

Thankfully, the rest of his friends sensed that was enough toasts for one evening. The servants placed steaming bowls of carrot soup before them, and the guests began to serve themselves from the many dishes of salads.

"This is quite a full table, Jasper," Lucian called, his voice carrying over the heads of many.

"The proper number of guests should be more than the Graces, less than the Muses, as they say," Miss Beatrice replied through pursed, disapproving lips in between minuscule bites of anchovy and endive salad. "Any more than nine is not particularly well bred."

"Ah, but surely the men at this table count as half a Muse at best, Miss Beatrice," said Clarence with a wink. "Which makes our number of guests an entirely appropriate eight and a half."

"Miss Danvers, how are you liking a Surrey winter?" asked Lady Louisa warmly.

It seemed to take Jane a moment to recall her alias. "I find I am liking it a great deal. It has been a nice respite."

"Though, I imagine it's not altogether different from a Buckinghamshire winter," drawled George, and Jasper could have smacked him.

"No," Jane began, placing her soup spoon back in her bowl. "But you must agree that any deviation from one's regular life can feel a great deal like a holiday, even if the climes are so similar."

"I find a house party at the estate next to mine to be a genuine escape from reality," Edgar added in support of Jane, who gave him an appreciative smile in return.

"Is your estate very far from here, Mr. Ashwell?" she asked. Did she look pale to anyone else?

"It is very close indeed, near the village of West Clandon, if you are familiar. But I tend to reside at my townhome in London far more often."

On that note, the table dissolved into many different conversations. Jasper forced himself to loosen his grip on his knife as he watched Edgar make Jane laugh. He was making a mess of the rump of beef he was meant to be carving. Had Jane ever laughed so freely with him? Doubtful, as he had been a stern bastard for much of their time together. If Jane were to bless him with a laugh so sincere, he'd probably devote his life to pursuing it.

Eventually, he realized he had to stop studying her, seeking even an ounce of her discomfort. What could he do about it, anyway? Half of the guests surely believed he hated her, and the rest were likely able to see through his miserable attempt at disguising his true feelings. Better to trust her to handle herself.

As he sat through courses and disaster did not strike, the pressure he felt to perform lifted somewhat. Now he was able to observe, to breathe. George and Lady Louisa engaged him in mindless but pleasing talk of the minor scandals he had missed in his months away. It almost seemed normal, to have the room filled with his friends and family, to feel something other than the crushing weight of grief upon his shoulders.

What pleased him most of all was to see Helena and Isobel smile. There hadn't been much occasion for their joy the past year, but to see them so engaged and lively bestowed upon Jasper a sense of peace that had long eluded him. Perhaps he wasn't failing them. Perhaps this was what his parents would have wanted, though Jasper would loathe having to admit it to Isobel. She had pushed him out of his seclusion, and he was beginning to suspect she had been right to do it. Was he ready to tear down his walls entirely? To acknowledge what they'd lost? No, that seemed a distant occasion indeed. But the fact that he was able to sit here at a table filled with people, more specifically, the people who knew him *before*, seemed a decent start, one that had felt impossible even a week ago.

After all, Jasper's only goal upon ascending to the earldom had been to see his siblings well situated, but he couldn't do that if he was shut up in Surrey, allowing the world to pass them by. Isobel should have a proper Season, though the thought of it both horrified and delighted him. Perhaps he could induce Aunt Adelaide to stay and aid him in presenting his vexatious sister to the world. God knew he'd need all the assistance he could get in that regard, even if his better senses rioted against the idea of prolonging her stay. She was the only family they had left, and so he must draw upon his well of patience and ensure his siblings felt closer to her, even if her relationship with their father had been less than loving.

And Helena would have to see to her duties as the younger Dowager Duchess of Pembroke, duties she'd been avoiding for too long now, as Marcus's brother was still a year or so away from taking them on himself. Surely the elder Dowager Duchess's patience toward Helena was wearing thin. Jasper would do what he could to help her, but seeing as he himself was floundering as a reluctant earl, he couldn't imagine he'd be much use to the dukedom Marcus had left behind. Still, Helena shouldn't have to face it alone.

And lastly, he needed to get his brothers in line. He glanced over at Freddie, marveling once again at how much he had grown in the last few months. He had left in September a mere boy and returned a man, or something close to it. What were they feeding him at Eton? Freddie didn't seem as wayward as August, but as Jasper recalled, he *was* susceptible to his brother's dubious guidance. Jasper had grown up under the unflagging, dutiful influence of Anthony and he had still fallen off the path from time to time. If August was all Freddie had to look up to, it didn't bode well. The boy was sixteen. He needed structure, and August needed a firm hand, even at twenty-one.

That settled it. He would have to reenter Society, for his

siblings' sakes, and to take his place in the House of Lords, as duty now required of him.

It had nothing to do with Jane without-a-surname and Jasper's increasing concern for her. Though, he was beginning to wonder what they would do if her memories never returned. The human mind was a complex instrument. Perhaps her recovery would take months. Months in which she would need stability. Comfort. The best doctors money could buy. The Maycotts were in a position to help her, should she need it. It wasn't the most displeasing prospect, to think of her as a more permanent fixture.

But all feelings of warmth and progress faded when Jane rose suddenly from her chair, looking as pale as she had when they'd come upon her in the road. Their guests fell silent as she took two or three unsteady steps before wavering and collapsing onto the ground. All at once, the table descended into chaos, but Jasper heard nothing, his focus only on Jane as he moved with an impossible haste to her side.

As her seat mate, Lucian was already tending to Jane, feeling for her pulse as Edgar stared down at her in shock.

"What happened?" Jasper managed to gasp out, falling to his knees beside her.

"I—I do not know," Edgar replied, fear weighing his words. "One moment we were discussing bloody Gainsborough, the next she was excusing herself. Said she needed some air."

Lucian gripped Jasper's forearm, forcing him to return to the present, to let panic loosen its hold upon him. "She's fainted, Jasper. Likely something to do with her head injury." He picked her up in one swift motion. "Show me to her room, she must rest."

As they left the dining room, Jasper heard Helena speaking, likely calming their guests with her signature steadiness. It didn't work on Jasper, however. Not when Jane seemed to be deteriorating rather than improving. When she woke, he was going to give her an earful about setting off into a storm to prove a point. *If* she woke.

No, he would not fall victim to despair. Not yet. Not when she had been a light for him. A beacon through the dark. If anything, Jane had given him a reason to hope again. He would not dishonor her by retreating to his previous ways.

They made it to her chambers in record time. Lucian laid her down on the bed gently and began rolling up his shirtsleeves. He pressed his fingers along various points on Jane's head.

"Get me my kit, will you?" he asked, not looking away from his patient as Jasper retrieved the case of medical supplies Lucian never went without. "There are contusions all over her skull, Jasper. Her hair hides most of them. I can hardly believe she's been upright since her injury."

"Will she be all right?" His voice cracked as Lucian unstoppered a vial. He was ready to send for a whole team of physicians, if necessary. Damn the storm. He could not lose someone else.

Lucian sighed. "She shouldn't be so stimulated." He pulled back the bandage on her temple, revealing a somewhat healed wound. "The cut has not reopened," Lucian offered, dabbing at it with a gauze smelling strongly of antiseptic before he got to the process of dressing it with a new bandage, taking care to shape it with the surgical scissors from his kit.

After a time, he covered Jane with the counterpane and stood, which Jasper understood to mean the crisis was averted for now. "I'm surprised her physician approved of her attendance this week. Head injuries are quite difficult to manage."

The truth lay heavy on Jasper's tongue. If anyone should

know it, it was Lucian. What if Jane worsened? He would have to know the extent of her injuries in order to truly help her. But what if the truth put Jane in danger? No, he thought. Out of everyone, Lucian was the most noble. The most trustworthy. He could help Jane. Dr. Ramsay wouldn't get to them in time, and there was hardly a better doctor than one of the Prince of Wales's own personal physicians.

"It's worse than you think, Lucian." He pushed his hair back from his face and took a deep breath. "We discovered Jane in the road not three days ago, unconscious, likely having been thrown from her horse."

"My God," he exclaimed. "She's lucky to be alive."

"Indeed, though her injury is more severe than meets the eye." He paused. Took another deep breath. "Jane is a stranger to us, and she has yet to recover her memory."

Lucian let out a low whistle. "Amnesia, is it? I've not come across that in my career. How extensive is the loss?"

"Well, to begin with, Jane isn't even her real name."

Lucian waited, perhaps for Jasper to admit he was joking. "You mean to tell me she remembers nothing?"

"She can recall inconsequential things, like books and artists. But her own past is a mystery to her."

Lucian looked back over at Jane. "Remarkable," he whispered. "And Dr. Ramsay believes she will recover?"

Jasper's eyes narrowed. "Do you not?"

"I didn't say that," he began. "But head injuries are pernicious things. I should think the ability to recover lies with each individual patient. We don't know anything about Jane's health prior to this. Perhaps this is one of many concussions she has suffered. If that was the case, then I'd imagine this could be the culmination of many different injuries, and perhaps a full recovery wouldn't be possible. But if this is her first, then I should expect her mind and body to be up to the task, but only if she is given the proper time and space to heal."

Jasper's heart sank. "She went out into the storm today." It felt like he was admitting to some great sin, even though it had been Jane's choice.

"Why in God's name was she out in the storm?"

"She overheard me trying to get August off her scent. You recall how he is." Lucian nodded knowingly. "I may have said some unflattering things about her that aren't, strictly speaking, true."

Lucian studied him. "She overheard you insult her?"

"It wasn't as if I meant any of it."

Lucian scoffed. "It's not as if that matters."

"Fair point," he admitted. "In any event, I went after her. She had been out there for some time. Could that have anything to do with her fainting at dinner?"

"I hardly think one would need to have studied medicine to know that walking headlong into a snowstorm isn't conducive to good health in the physically fit, let alone an invalid." Jasper winced. "But it does help to paint a more promising picture for her outlook going forward."

Hope flared in his chest. "What do you mean?"

"I think we can chalk up her current condition to the events of the day. I do not think it means she will continue to decline." He reached for her hand, his fingers encircling her wrist as he pulled his pocket watch from his vest pocket. "Her pulse is no longer racing. I should expect she needs a good night's rest and a hearty breakfast before she feels more like herself."

Jasper let out the breath he had been holding in, letting relief soften his posture. "Thank you, Lucian. I trust that I do not need to express the danger Jane would be in if the truth about her were revealed."

He paused. "You don't think any of your guests would pose a threat? They are your friends."

It wasn't Jasper's friends that concerned him. He still hadn't forgotten Jane's plaintive plea for protection when he held her in his arms. That hadn't been Jane without-a-surname. That had been the real Jane, the one even she did not remember, and she had been in some sort of danger. Until Jasper knew what it was, keeping the truth about her a secret was the best way for him to protect her.

It didn't matter if Lucian didn't understand his motive. "I need to know you'll keep it to yourself."

Lucian's eyes narrowed. "Like it or not, Jane is my patient and that means she is entitled to my discretion."

"I didn't mean to slight you—"

"You haven't," he interrupted, putting his dinner jacket back on.

"I only wish to see her well."

Lucian nodded, and they both looked to Jane, who appeared to be sleeping peacefully.

After a time, Lucian nudged him. "What about you?"

Jasper sighed. "What about me?"

"You seem...agitated."

Jasper let out a mirthless laugh. "It's been a trying few days."

Lucian looked at him pensively. "Bad memories rising to the surface, I'd imagine."

He was treading upon dangerous territory. Jasper didn't take the bait. "I don't know what you mean," he replied with a sniff.

"I hope you..." he began. "I hope you feel like you can talk to me, if ever you need to."

Could I? The mere idea of it had been an impossibility for so long, but many of Jasper's long-held beliefs had been shattered during the past few days. Perhaps he was wrong to think he could not unburden himself with his closest friends, the very ones he had spent the last year shutting out.

Sensing a lack of resistance, Lucian continued. "Losing Annabelle and Anthony and your parents in quick succession was a tragedy, the magnitude of which many of us will never face, but that does not mean you are alone, Jasper."

Jasper's throat was clogged with all of the things he wished to say to Lucian. He had survived this long by never speaking of the loss that had shattered his world, never letting himself feel the full breadth of pain that had invaded his body, woven into his bones and stitched into his tissue. *Could it even be excised?* Did the Jasper from before, the one untouched by death, remain underneath?

Lucian continued, steadfastly ignoring Jasper's discomfort. "Pretending they didn't exist won't work forever."

"I know that," Jasper interjected.

"Do you?" he asked. "Helena tells me otherwise."

"Helena's one to talk," he muttered. But he had to wonder if they were right. By not allowing himself to feel, had he been preventing himself from healing? Had he been prolonging his suffering, or worse yet, the suffering of his siblings? It had felt necessary, the silence surrounding what had happened, what they had lost. But was it serving a purpose any longer?

That exploration would have to wait.

"Speaking of my sister, has she spoken to you of the pain that plagues her? Three years have passed since her accident and she is yet to make a full recovery. How much longer will she have to wait?"

Lucian raised his brow. "Helena is also entitled to my discretion, Jasper."

Jasper sighed, having known what his friend's reply would be before he spoke. "I had to try."

"I'll do everything I can for her. You have my word."

"Thank you, Lucian. For everything." He hoped his meaning was clear.

Lucian nodded. "Jane shouldn't be left alone tonight. Perhaps Helena, or a maid—"

"I will stay with her." He had already decided, but saying it aloud was another matter entirely.

Lucian hesitated. "Do you think that's a good idea?"

"I can't leave her, Lucian. I can't..." He didn't know how to put into words the trauma that was watching Annabelle die while he sat there powerless to stop it, or how similar it felt to see Jane suffer with no end in sight.

But Lucian was a doctor. He had borne witness to his fair share of suffering and helplessness. He had felt the cruel sting of fate, the indifference of God's will. He placed a hand on Jasper's shoulder.

"I'm not going to stop you, but I am going to remind you that you must be careful, Jasper. Jane is an unmarried woman. She has no power here, while you have it in spades."

"I would never do anything to harm her."

"That much is clear. But you can hurt someone without intending to."

Jasper knew that much. After letting his words settle uncomfortably around them, Lucian tipped his head.

"Don't hesitate to send for me if she worsens. And make sure she drinks a good deal of water when she wakes."

"Thank you, Lucian. Will you make some excuse to explain

my absence? Something of plausible importance but utterly dull to prevent further investigation?"

"I will." His friend turned to leave but paused at the door. "Be careful."

Lucian was correct, but it didn't change the fact that Jasper wasn't leaving her side until he knew she was all right.

But it wasn't only Jane he needed to protect.

If he wasn't heedful, Jasper was at risk of erasing the progress he had fought so hard for. To lose someone again, whether by calamity or circumstance, would wound him in a way he suspected he would never recover from. He couldn't go back to the darkness of a year before. The Maycotts wouldn't survive it.

A soft knock on the door interrupted his thoughts. After a moment, Isobel stood beside him.

"All is well with our guests?" he asked absently.

"Helena managed them quite efficiently. Only Beatrice made any fuss while everyone else soldiered on through dinner and parlor games before retreating to their rooms."

"Lucian offered a sufficient explanation?"

"He said you'd received a most urgent missive from your solicitor that you needed to see to immediately." She let out an uncharitable laugh at the thought. "Lucky for you none of our esteemed guests have witnessed you quite literally flee in the face of any correspondence from dear Mister Sheridan." She dragged another armchair over to Jasper's. "So your scandalous secret is safe for the time being. Shall we take turns, then?" she asked, gesturing to Jane's sleeping form.

His heart swelled, but guilt stole in behind any warm feelings. "You don't have to stay, Isobel."

Isobel gave him a doubtful look. "Tell me, Brother, who will hide you under the bed when Aunt Adelaide arrives unannounced at the crack of dawn?"

A dry laugh escaped him. "And you think you're up to the task?"

She gave him a knowing grin. "Let's just say I have experience in the matter."

Jasper could guess what she meant by that. "Have I failed you so thoroughly as a guardian?" It was asked lightly, but they both knew there was a deeper meaning to the question.

"I hardly think I needed one," she began, her tone light. But then her face fell slightly and her tone turned more serious. "I was a girl of eighteen when we lost them. Many girls that age get married, some mother children. Do I feel delayed, in some respects? Yes, but that wasn't your fault, Jasper. Time seemed to freeze for us all a year ago. But I suspect it's thawing now." She didn't prod him or expect him to assure her that things would be different. For Isobel, it was enough that he had shifted, even if it was by mere inches. Complain as he had, Jasper had accepted the arrival of his friends in the end. "So no, you have not failed me, Jasper. I suspect you've more to fear in failing yourself."

He couldn't respond to that, not when the truth of it sat heavy on his chest. He cleared his throat. "You don't mind sleeping in a chair?"

She wiggled deeper into it and put her feet up on the ottoman. "You're not the only one who's concerned about our Miss Danvers, you know. I've come to like her a great deal, mostly because she doesn't hesitate to put you in your place."

"That she doesn't," he replied, thinking Isobel didn't know the half of it.

They spoke a little more of trivial things before succumbing to sleep, both falling into it rather easily, considering they sat upright.

After a restless night spent jerking awake every half hour or so, Jasper awoke in the predawn light, the room hardly brighter than it had been in the deepness of night. He wasn't confused; even the stolen stretches of sleep hadn't robbed Jasper of his awareness of Jane. He looked to her bed now, where she stirred slightly. Isobel snored lightly, sprawled as she was in her chair, Mr. Darcy curled in her lap.

Jasper stood, intending to check more closely on Jane. He took a step toward the bed. The floor creaked. Jane's brow furrowed, but it was Isobel who woke.

"Jasper, what are you doing?" she hissed, her words turning into a yawn.

"I wanted to make sure—"

"You need to leave before anyone catches you in here. Aunt Adelaide is very fond of her morning inspections."

"You're probably right." Still, he hesitated.

"I'll make sure she's all right. And that she eats. You can come check on her at a less scandalous hour."

He nodded and left the room, intending to put as much distance between himself and Jane as he could before he ran into anyone.

But then he heard her speak, and his feet stopped moving before he could think better of it.

"What time is it?" she croaked out. Jasper stepped back toward the door, not revealing himself but eager to hear a bit more from Jane before he departed.

"Indecently early. How do you feel?" Jasper hoped Isobel gave her water.

Jane audibly drank what sounded like the entire glass. "There is a dull thud in my head..." She paused, realization dawning. "I fainted, didn't I?"

"I'm afraid you did," replied Isobel with false gravity. "But the doctor tended to you, and he thinks all will be well after a rest and a hearty meal."

"Oh, what a menace I am," she cried lightly. "And I ruined your brother's first dinner with his friends in ages."

"I don't think he cares about that, Jane," Isobel replied warmly.

"You don't?" she asked skeptically. "I'm sure I made a spectacle of myself, which is precisely the opposite of what I intended to do, and yet it seems to be all that I am capable of these days."

Jasper couldn't help but smile. Isobel spoke as though suppressing a laugh. "I assure you, we are only relieved to see you well."

"You were here all night?" Jane asked in between sips of water.

"We had to ensure you recovered."

"We?" Jane missed nothing.

Isobel paused. Jasper wasn't sure if she would reveal the truth. She seemed to think the less Jane knew of his attentiveness, the better. He wasn't sure her concern was misplaced. Maybe it would be better if Jane didn't know how affected he was by her.

"Jasper and I stayed the night," she said lightly.

But Jane could not have been more surprised. "The stern bastard was my caretaker?" Had he been so convincing when he pulled himself away from her? The distance he strove to put between them seemed the greatest farce to him, but Jane appeared to believe it, and thus, the worst of him.

"You're surprised?" Isobel asked, playful skepticism lacing her words.

Jasper's heart stilled. A part of him felt guilty, hearing Jane's unguarded thoughts without her knowledge. But a larger part of him desired to know where he stood with her, not that it would change anything. Besides, she had eavesdropped on him more than once. He'd consider them even.

"I just didn't think he cared."

Her words gave him pause. Because he did care. More than she knew.

Far, far more than he should.

Chapter Fifteen

Jane

Isobel's words had shocked Jane to her core. She looked down, somewhat relieved to see she still wore her gown from the night before, though the buttons at the back had been undone. It hadn't made for the most comfortable sleep, but at least she hadn't unknowingly revealed her undergarments to the Earl of Belhaven.

But Christ, Jasper had spent the night in her room, watching to ensure she still breathed.

It was as impossible a revelation as she could imagine. Jasper, the man who seemed to vacillate between desiring and disliking her, had slept the night in a chair in her stuffy room while she'd snored next to him.

But hadn't she known that the sternness was a mask he wore in order to protect the people he loved? Jane supposed she simply hadn't anticipated that she would ever be the recipient of that protection. She had assumed she was a distraction. An impermanent diversion from the weight of his duties and responsibilities as earl. Jane hadn't dared imagine that the Earl of Belhaven's attention might mean that he truly *cared* for her.

"It seems Jasper has within him the capacity to surprise us all," Isobel added, reading her mind. It was then that Jane noticed how rumpled her appearance was. A flicker of guilt passed through her, to have been the cause of anyone else's discomfort. Isobel took the empty glass from her hand. "You should go back to sleep. As I said, it is indecently early. I will be here when you wake."

"You don't have to—" Jane protested, not wishing to burden Isobel any more than she already had.

"I know I don't," she replied, tucking Jane back under the counterpane. "But I will."

And so she drifted back to sleep, safe in the knowledge that there was someone watching over her.

• • •

She awoke hours later, groggy but much improved. "What time is it?"

"Well after midday." Isobel wasted no time pulling back the curtains and stripping the counterpane from her tired body. "Let's get you out of that dress, shall we?"

Before Jane could argue, Isobel had hauled her rather unceremoniously out of bed, holding tight to Jane's arm as she swayed in disbelief.

"You know, the muscles in your arms are quite developed, Jane. I might have thought you a pugilist if I didn't know any better."

Jane attempted to breathe through her shock. "For all we

know, I am."

Isobel laughed and pulled her outer gown over her head and tossed it to the floor.

"You're efficient," Jane offered weakly.

"Plenty of experience," Isobel replied, already loosening Jane's corset. "May I?" she asked, and in no time at all, and certainly only because Jane felt rather incapacitated, Isobel had her out of the wrinkled chemise she had slept in and into a clean one, adding over top of it a plain dressing gown.

"That's better," she remarked as she helped Jane settle back into her bed.

Jane still didn't quite understand how she had managed it. "I did not expect the daughter of an earl to be so..."

Isobel began retrieving pins from Jane's hair. "Unabashed?" she offered. "Shameless, perhaps? Lord knows I've heard that before," she added with a wink, pulling a comb from her pocket and tending to Jane's hair. "I am no wilting violet, Jane. And besides, it's nothing I haven't seen on numerous occasions." Jane was reasonably certain that at least one of the occasions she was referring to was the manner of their meeting, when Jane had been rather at the mercy of the Maycotts, but she had tried to put that helplessness behind her. "Boarding school is an effective way of ridding oneself of any latent modesty, a particularly useless quality, if you ask me."

Jane winced as the comb got caught in a snag. "Helena still seems rather modest," she pointed out.

"Yes, well, there was never any hope for Angelic Helena," Isobel replied, not unkindly, twisting Jane's hair into an efficient, though perhaps unfashionable, knot. "How are you feeling after sleeping like the dead?"

It was a simple question, but thoughts of Jasper immediately filled her mind. The chair next to Isobel's was empty, but he might as well be sitting there still, for all the mortification she felt. Heat rose to her cheeks and spread to her chest. The man affected her even in his absence. She was torn between fury and gratitude. How dare he care so much for her well-being but only in secret. How dare he add another layer to her confusion.

Isobel gave her a quizzical look. "Should I send for the doctor?"

Jane slammed back into the present. "No, that won't be necessary. But I do think I should have passed on dinner last night. I was feeling dizzy almost as soon as Helena and I reached the parlor."

"And now?"

She paused, taking stock. "A slight improvement, perhaps."

"Well, that's a relief, then." Isobel stood and gestured to the water closet. "I'm sure you wish to see to your needs. I'll send for some food, shall I?"

Jane nodded, but her mind was still with the Earl of Belhaven. She could recall how he'd studied her from across the table, before she'd fainted like some overwrought heroine from a penny dreadful. She had read his behavior as needlessly watchful, as though he was waiting for her to commit a grave error. But had he simply been concerned for her? Was he capable of such gallantry?

He was indeed. She knew the depths he kept hidden. Why was she so surprised?

Perhaps it was because each time she took a step toward understanding him, Jasper was quick to turn away from her, relying on the rigidity of protocol and a mask of duty to sever their connection.

But a night spent at her bedside said so much more than

words ever could. Jane shifted restlessly under the weight of her sudden understanding. Jasper *did* care for her. What she had interpreted as animosity was perhaps better explained as a feeling of confliction in the Earl of Belhaven. She could not fault him for his hesitation. Even stripped of her memories as she was, Jane sensed he had more to lose than she did. More to fear, too, perhaps.

But that didn't mean that she would accept his reticence. He could not occupy both positions—that of trusted confidant or mere acquaintance—whilst also treating her fairly.

She stood rather unsteadily and stepped over the dress Isobel had failed to retrieve from the floor. It had served her well the night before, making her feel at least a little like she belonged among Jasper's friends. Lady Louisa had complimented her rather sincerely, and Miss Beatrice had not managed to find a way to snub her about it. Most importantly, it had seemed to stop Jasper in his tracks.

After she was done seeing to her needs, she went to the basin on the desk and splashed the frigid water on her face, taking care to avoid her bandage, which she remembered would have to be changed soon. Only, when she looked in the mirror, she saw it wasn't one of the maid Lottie's bandages. This one had been cut rather cleverly, leaving more of her skin exposed. She still didn't have the courage to look beneath it, but she hoped whomever had dressed her wound the night before would do so again. The smaller dressing helped her to feel less like an invalid. Even the worst bruising and swelling had reduced somewhat. Most was hidden behind her hairline, and when she pressed on the skin it smarted fiercely, but otherwise she looked almost normal. Very nearly healthy. So why hadn't her memories returned?

Isobel had returned and left a dress out for her, a dove-gray tea gown with white lace edgings and embroidered cuffs. The gown laced at the front rather sensibly, meaning Jane required no assistance. She donned it behind the screen while stuffing herself with the sandwiches that had arrived while she washed. Thoughts of her missing memories persisted. The small threads she had uncovered of her father weren't enough to paint a full picture, but they were *something*. And then the memory of the Prince of Wales's brush with typhoid had emerged, as if from a veil of fog, sneaking up on her when she'd least suspected it. She supposed that was progress. Infuriatingly slow progress, but progress nonetheless. It was certainly more than she had awoken with days ago. All she required now was an immense amount of patience, even if she suspected she'd never possessed that quality, and while that wasn't a memory, it *was* the truth.

A knock on the door interrupted her thoughts and her meal both.

"Yes?" called Isobel from where she was remaking Jane's bed.

A man spoke. "It's Lucian." He paused, cleared his throat. "Er, it's Dr. Hill."

And then it dawned on Jane. The doctor who tended to her the night before *would* be Sir Hill, not the anonymous, kindly old man she had been picturing in her mind.

Isobel looked to her for confirmation. Jane nodded, because what else was she going to do?

"Do come in, Sir Hill," said Isobel.

He walked in, just as handsome as she remembered, and gave them a quick bow. "Miss Danvers, I wanted to check on you after last night's events, if you are amenable."

She sat back in the armchair, wiping crumbs from her lap, noting he was even more handsome in the light of day. "Of course, Dr. Hill."

He stepped toward her, hands extended. "May I?" She nodded and he began feeling along her scalp and in her neck, twisting her head slightly, seeking any errant pain. He let go, using his fingers to tilt her head upward gently until he was peering into her eyes. "How are you feeling?"

Jane was beginning to hate the question, because she did not know how to answer it, not accurately at least. There was the polite, false response of *fine* or *more of the same*. But it wasn't true, was it? She might not be in immediate danger, but she was far from fine.

"Adequate," she said before thinking.

A small smile teased at the corners of Lucian's lips. "Simply adequate?"

"What I meant to say is—"

"I understand, Miss Danvers. The question is a complicated one. I should have been more specific." He removed his hand from where he held her chin in place and stepped back. "Have your memories returned?"

"No," she replied before she understood what he was asking. "Who told you?"

His hand came to the back of his neck. "Lord Belhaven. And only in the interest of helping you, I assure you." Oddly enough, she was assured. Jasper must have been quite concerned for her well-being to have revealed the truth of her ailment to someone new. It seemed to Jane that Dr. Hill and Isobel were describing a man she desired very much to know, if only Jasper would let her in. But grief had built a fortress around the Earl of Belhaven's heart, one Jane wasn't sure she could conquer, or even if she should. Between his siblings and his friends, he had enough people to care about. What exactly could she offer him?

For her part, Jane wanted Jasper to trust her with all of him, to understand, as she did, that they were kindred spirits. That they could help each other through the darkness, if only he would allow it.

Dr. Hill continued. "I don't have much experience with amnesia, but in my professional opinion, you will recover, Miss Danvers. It is simply a matter of time."

She was heartened to hear it. "Thank you, Dr. Hill. How lucky I was to be injured on the property of a man with such accomplished friends."

He quirked a brow at her. "I suspect you weren't the only lucky one, Miss Danvers."

All at once, another knock interrupted them, and Helena and Lady Adelaide entered the room, the latter looking a bit worse for wear with dark circles under her eyes.

"My goodness, Aunt, are you ill?" asked Isobel, her voice filled with mock concern. Helena shot her a look that demanded she behave, which Isobel promptly ignored. "Thank heavens there is a doctor present."

Lady Adelaide glared at her. "Achieving my long-awaited retribution kept me up much later than I am used to," she said, tucking an errant strand of hair—a true rarity for Lady Adelaide—behind her ear.

"By 'retribution' do you mean fleecing Lady Louisa's maiden aunt for all she's got in a game of whist? Best of eleven, was it?"

"That was vengeance decades in the making, Isobel, and I will speak no more of it." Aunt Adelaide shifted her flinty gaze from her niece to Jane, her eyes softening slightly upon her. "I hear I missed quite a spectacle at dinner."

"Jane can hardly be blamed for her injury, Aunt," began Helena. "I rather think the blame lies with us for pushing her before she is ready."

But Lady Adelaide was ignoring her, having just noticed a man among them. "Who are you?" she asked with a tone that suggested she had discovered something unpleasant under her shoe.

Lucian, who had been doing his damnedest to sneak away, paused and straightened. "Dr. Hill, my lady."

Helena leaned closer. "He's one of Jasper's friends, Aunt Adelaide."

Lady Adelaide eyed him appraisingly. "Yes, the Prince's physician, no?" she asked Helena as though Lucian himself were not present.

"Not quite," he began, seeming to sense that a correction would be pointless.

"Modest, too," she added, impressed. "A quality not equally shared amongst my nephew's friends. Tell me, Dr. Hill, is there a betrothal in your immediate future?"

"Aunt Adelaide!" Helena cried, entirely mortified. Isobel pressed her lips together in obvious delight at her aunt's antics.

Lady Adelaide waved her arm impatiently. "I've found I must be direct when it comes to you girls, what with all the years wasted."

Lucian looked to be caught somewhere between horror and amusement. "Not formally, no. But there is someone."

Lady Adelaide sighed. "I suppose I shouldn't be surprised that a man of…" She looked at him expectantly.

Sensing that he was trapped, Lucian gave a small sigh. "I am twenty-eight, my lady."

"That a man of twenty-eight, and once so accomplished at that, would be attached." She looked at him a bit longer than was necessary before speaking again. "You may go, Dr. Hill."

He nearly ran from the room. "Now then," she said, turning her attention back to Jane. "You are recovered?"

"From last night's spectacle?" Jane asked wryly. "Yes, Lady Adelaide. Overall? Not yet."

"As I thought," she replied. "No reason to keep you shut up in this room in the meantime, is there?"

A part of Jane wanted to bury her head under the bedsheets for the rest of the day, but it seemed the cowardly move to beg off with claims of a headache. As she weighed her options, she noticed Viola lurking in the doorway, perhaps seeking a way into the room, but fearing invoking her aunt's ire at her impropriety.

Jane decided to end her agony. "Lady Viola, do come in," she called, a spark of an idea forming in her mind as to how the girl might come to rescue her.

Viola, sensing opportunity, rushed in past her aunt and sisters. "Miss Jane, did you really faint at the dinner table?"

Jane couldn't help but cringe. "I'm afraid so."

"Why, you're like the heroine of a novel," she exclaimed.

"Do you only read novels with particularly dramatic and flighty characters, Viola?" Lady Adelaide asked with a sniff. Jane tried very hard not to read it as a slight against her, not after all the progress she had made with the woman.

"As a rule," Viola replied with a satisfied grin.

"I wonder if you might try novels with unflappable heroines," Lady Adelaide mused. "Good, sensible women possessing sound judgment—"

Viola scrunched up her nose. "I don't believe that would be very interesting, Aunt Adelaide."

"Nor I," added Isobel with a wink. "Give me a Marianne Dashwood or Catherine Earnshaw any day."

"In any event, I am much recovered," Jane said, willing it to be true. Needing it to be. "And I think it's high time you show me that piece of embroidery you've been working on." She raised her eyebrows significantly. "The one that's been troubling you."

To her credit, Viola caught on exceptionally quick. "Come with me," she replied conspiratorially. "I've left it in my chambers."

"Now what is this all about?" Lady Adelaide asked, her tone deeply suspicious.

Viola turned toward her aunt with a flourish. "It isn't proper to discuss a gift before it is ready to be presented, is it, Aunt Adelaide?" she asked innocently.

Lady Adelaide preened briefly before turning to Jane and pinning a distrustful gaze upon her. "And how might you be helping, Jane? I seem to recall needles bending in fright at your hapless touch during our previous experimentation."

Jane was at a loss for words before clever Viola swooped in. "It is in the act of teaching that we may find the clarity we seek, Aunt."

Lady Adelaide, incapable of detecting fault in her niece's sage observation, seemed flustered. "I suppose that is a suitable reason for missing tea, but only this once," she snapped, settling the matter.

As Viola and Jane left the room, even Isobel offered them a dubious look, likely well aware of her own sister's distaste for needlework.

But Jane did not regret her subterfuge. There was little she wanted to do less than face Jasper's friends after the drama of the night before. The relative peace of Viola's chambers would be a welcome refuge. Surely none would miss her.

As they left sight of the room, Viola reached for Jane's hand and broke out into an excited run. Jane allowed the girl to tug her along, unwilling to dampen her spirits after the solemn conversation they had shared before dinner the night prior.

They arrived in her room and Viola collapsed on her bed in a heap. Mr. Darcy—curled up in a tight ball near the pillows—hardly reacted to the disturbance.

"I hope you don't mind—"

She raised herself up on her elbows. "You crafting the perfect escape? Not in the slightest!" she exclaimed. "The most brilliant part of it is the fact that she can never ask me for her gift, not without being *intolerably rude*," she added in a frighteningly accurate imitation of her aunt's voice. "Now, let me get my things; we want them close in case Aunt Adelaide comes investigating." She pulled a haphazard pile of cloth and bundles of thread from beneath her bed. "What is it you'd like to *actually* do?"

"Anything you'd like," Jane offered. "Perhaps you could read some of your writings to me. I'm not sure how helpful I'll be, but I'd love to hear what you've been working on."

Viola's smile could have lit the darkest room. "If you truly mean it…"

"I do." Jane wanted nothing more than to be someone Viola felt safe with, as she felt safe with the Maycott siblings. "But only if you promise we can hide out here for the rest of the day. I'm not yet ready to face everyone." Jasper, specifically, but she kept that to herself.

"We'll dine here!" Viola exclaimed with a clap of her hands. "No one seems able to deny me my more reasonable requests."

"Wonderful."

And so they passed the afternoon and well into the evening together. Lady Adelaide had a lavish tea spread sent up to them, and Jane felt the smallest twinge of guilt, knowing she had only done so under false pretenses, before sampling the array of scrumptious biscuits.

They spent the rest of their time reading in contented silence or reciting the most dramatic of Shakespeare's soliloquies aloud. Mr. Darcy moved between them, seeking pets and mischief in equal measure. After Viola caught Jane up on a year's worth of Society gossip she had dutifully collected from letters written by cousins and friends, dinner arrived. True to her word, they dined at Viola's table, which was set with fine but mismatched china and a floral tablecloth. Jane suspected they would be served finer fare in the dining room later, but her meal with Viola was exactly what she wanted.

After dinner, Viola gathered her courage and read some of her writing to Jane, though she could not meet her eye as she did so. Jane, genuinely impressed by her prose and witticisms, offered praise freely and small suggestions only when needed. Eventually, they returned to reading silently next to each other in the bay of Viola's window, propped up by pillows and wrapped in blankets.

Viola, absorbed in her book, reached for Jane's hand, perhaps without conscious thought. She allowed her to take it, and before long, the girl was fast asleep, and Jane was left alone with her thoughts for the first time since waking.

She hoped it escaped everyone's notice that she'd spent the day hiding in a child's bedroom. It had felt selfish at first, but when she looked down at Viola's small hand in hers, and listened to her soft snores, Jane had to wonder if the girl had needed this as much as she had.

But it was time to go. She carefully removed her hand from Viola's, prepared to sneak away so as not to wake her, but a creak from behind startled her. It sounded like someone stood in the doorway, but there was no one there that she could see.

Jane made her way across the room and peeked out, but the hall was empty.

Her heart raced, but not from fear. Instead, it beat with anticipation. Like she had expected someone in particular to be looking in on them.

But that anticipation quickly shifted to disappointment when she realized she was, in fact, alone, and perhaps always would be.

Chapter Sixteen

JASPER

Never had a day passed so unbearably slowly for Jasper.

After spending the night by her side to ensure she continued breathing, he found he wanted nothing more than to know that Jane was all right. And yet, she hid from them, choosing instead to spend the day with Viola, he was told.

He himself had spent it with his friends, which should have distracted him from the aching absence of Jane, but even their antics could not shake his melancholy. He only hoped none of them had noticed, or if they had, they chalked it up to whatever bad news his solicitor's letter might have delivered the night prior.

Mercifully, Helena seemed more than capable of steering the day in a less grave direction. She was a natural-born hostess, he realized, as she guided them from a lively round of charades to luncheon to cards. He did his best to remain present and engaged, but all he could really think about was Jane. At least he had the sense to know he could not check on her, torturous as it was to go on without knowing how she fared. The night before had been a gamble. He couldn't rely on being lucky once more.

Eventually, the high-stakes poker game came down to Clarence and Edgar, which proved diverting enough, and Jasper was at last able to loosen his shoulders and watch as they sought to destroy each other most vigorously. Everyone else crowded around the table, even Miss Beatrice, though she seemed entirely perturbed by Isobel's passion for the game.

"I bet it all," said Clarence, pushing his remaining chips to the center of the table.

"He bluffs, Ashwell!" cried Selby. It was difficult to tell with Clarence, whose skill as an actor paled only in comparison to his ability to charm a room. Edgar studied him nonetheless, searching for a crack in his unruffled facade.

To Jasper's eye, Edgar himself was impenetrable—neither confident in nor panicked by his hand. But was it enough?

"I call," he announced, pushing the rest of his own chips forward. A hush fell over the room.

"Let us see, then, gents," said August.

Edgar turned over his cards, revealing four eights and a six of hearts, four of a kind. He sat back and allowed a satisfied smirk to play at his lips.

"Lady Louisa, I must apologize," Clarence began. Had he told her he would win in her honor? Jasper hadn't been paying close attention. "It must be difficult, being the sister of such a miserably bad poker player."

He turned his cards and revealed a bloody royal flush, and the room immediately broke out into both raucous cheers and accusations of cheating.

The rest of the afternoon carried on in much the same

manner, and then it was time for dinner. Truth be told, Jasper felt some measure of relief when Jane did not appear at the table, not because she had any reason to be ashamed or to avoid their guests, but because he was not sure how he would react to seeing her after spending an entire indecent night by her side.

Evidently, she needed her space, and he would ensure she received it.

Jasper was relieved when dinner ended and everyone seemed keen to return to their rooms rather than carry on playing parlor games. He waited for them all to depart, until only Isobel remained, eyeing him wearily from across the dining room.

He poured a glass of scotch and gulped it back in one go, seeking a reprieve from swirling thoughts of Jane. He looked to his sister and poured a new glass, raising it to her in offering.

She joined him by their father's bottles and took the glass, sipping slowly.

"Father would not approve of your lack of respect for his beloved beverage," she teased, continuing to savor her drink. "You did well today," she added. "One could hardly sense your inner turmoil."

He drank another glass, relishing the burn of the scotch on his tongue. "Good night, Isobel."

"Do not do anything foolish, Brother," she warned as she left, offering him no time to craft a response. It didn't matter. All Jasper intended to do was find his bed and silence his racing thoughts with merciful slumber.

The halls were dark, save for the light that leaked out from Viola's room. Not for the first time, Jasper moved to extinguish whatever candle his sister had left burning while scribbling away and subsequently falling asleep with ink-stained fingers. It was something of a ritual for them. But as he approached and caught a glimpse into her room through the crack in the door, his heart stopped.

Viola was not in her bed, nor was she alone.

There was Jane, lit by the soft glow of candlelight with a book in one hand, Viola's hand in her other. His sister was asleep, unguarded, and more at peace than he could recall seeing her.

He watched as she lowered her book and noticed that Viola slept soundly, Jane's face creasing with emotion. He felt that same warmth blossom in his chest to know that Viola was so cared for, and by someone like Jane, who had no reason to be so kind in secret. There weren't any schemes at play here, only a woman who knew the sharp pain of loss, attempting to soften it for someone else.

In that moment, Jasper knew with stunning clarity that he was both too far gone and not at all what Jane needed.

The weight of his twin realizations almost bowled him over. He stepped backward, the floor creaking beneath him. His eyes flashed back to Jane, who looked up in his direction. She couldn't see him, he was sure of it, but still he fled, not wishing to be discovered or to intrude upon her quietude. She had stayed away for a reason. He must respect that.

His chambers were cold, the fire in the hearth nearly burned out. He knelt before it, stirring the dormant embers back to life as he added a log on the grate and tried in vain to push thoughts of Jane from his mind.

Lucian had really struck a nerve with him earlier when he'd warned Jasper to be careful.

Jasper felt the need for caution in his bones, but he was beginning to worry it was too late for him to change course. He knew he was far too close to Jane for any sort of objectivity at this point. His path had been altered the moment he and his sisters had found her in the road.

No. They had not become entangled then, when Jane was simply someone in need of assistance. Their connection had not been an instant one. Hell, Jasper had thought she could be a criminal until yesterday morning. There had been plenty of chances for him to distance himself, opportunities to establish boundaries. But when it came to Jane, it was so much easier to simply give in and let the current take him.

If pressed, he wouldn't have been able to name what it was that existed between them. Some unholy marriage of traded barbs and desire and tension and a warmth he hadn't thought he'd feel again. He didn't think either of them had expected it, nor did he regret something that had happened so naturally.

But it scared him. Deep down, Jasper knew there were similarities between what he felt for Jane and how he had fallen for Annabelle. A headlong tumble into the unknown, a lack of control or conscious effort, a feeling of it being *real* long before it made sense.

He knew what he must do. Jane was at Mulgrave Hall to recover, and a gentleman would not do anything to impede her in that regard.

So he would resist the pull of her, for Jane's own good.

Whether it would be good for *him* was another matter entirely.

• • •

After a fitful night's sleep, all Jasper wanted was a cup of coffee and some solitude. So he rose early and made his way to the dining room seeking both, but not obtaining either. It seemed just about everyone was present, their plates full and cups steaming. George and Edgar were buried in fresh copies of *The*

Times, Miss Beatrice was deep into penning a letter, and Lucian was spreading marmalade on a thick slice of toast.

"My lord?" came a soft voice from behind him as he poured the final dregs from a pot of coffee into his still-empty cup.

He turned to find Lady Louisa looking as fresh as a daisy, despite the early hour. "How may I help?" he asked, wondering when Society had done away with the custom of guests sleeping late. Jasper had never been one to indulge in a lie-in, but he wasn't sure he liked the idea of tolerating Clarence Meadows before noon.

Perhaps their presence so early in the day was the mark of a successful party, he thought optimistically. Still, he could have done with a fresh pot at the very least.

"I only wondered if Miss Danvers is quite well? I know we all missed her yesterday."

Beatrice sniffed as if to indicate that she was not to be included among those who missed Jane, but otherwise he got the sense that Lady Louisa spoke for the room, and he had to admit it warmed his heart a little to know that Jane had made such an immediate impression upon his friends.

But saying as much would be a scandal.

"You'll have to ask Sir Hill, Lady Louisa. I'm afraid I have not been kept abreast of her condition."

He noticed Lucian's knowing smirk over Louisa's shoulder and cleared his throat in an effort to remind his friend of the importance of discretion.

Louisa turned to Lucian. "Well?" she asked. "How does she fare?"

Lucian swallowed some toast and took a sip of tea. "She was much improved when I checked on her this morning. I suspect we'll be able to entice her to join us soon enough."

Jasper wasn't so sure. In fact, he worried that without prompting, Jane might do her damnedest to avoid their guests, burdened by the incorrect belief that she had disappointed him in some way, or embarrassed herself. But he couldn't retrieve her himself, nor could he direct someone else to do so, not without arousing suspicion.

He'd have to get creative, and as Viola skipped into the room, flanked by Freddie and August, he knew exactly how he would do it.

"Viola, what do you think about trimming the tree today?"

His sister froze mid-stride and gasped. "Do you mean it?"

"It's not going to decorate itself, is it? And you've a room full of people ready to help."

She looked around at her unwitting assistants, her smile wide until it fell. "But what about Miss Danvers?"

Jasper feigned nonchalance. "Why, you should invite her as well." Not for his benefit, no, but for Jane to feel like a welcomed guest. He knew Viola would be most persuasive, given that she was running from the room before he finished the sentence.

August gave him a sly look. "I didn't think you were the trimming type, Brother."

"People can change, August."

He shrugged. "Usually not for the better, in my experience."

Jasper had to believe his brother was wrong.

Chapter Seventeen

JANE

Despite Viola's enthusiasm, Jane was not sure what to expect when she entered Mulgrave Hall's great room.

She had only agreed because decorating a tree did not sound like too taxing of an activity. In fact, she might be able to watch as Viola managed most of it on her own, especially after the girl revealed that it was a tree Jasper had chosen and cut down himself. She pictured a modest tree, something befitting the somber atmosphere Jasper had been cultivating before chaos had descended on his home against his will.

But...once again, he managed to surprise her.

Jasper had selected a mighty evergreen that towered above them, and every railing, doorway, and mantel was wrapped with boughs of fresh greenery, transforming the room into something out of a Christmas card. And his friends and family milled about, which she supposed should not have surprised her. There were, after all, only so many things to do in a country manor in December. Trimming the tree was an enjoyable way to waste a day, even if she would have rather avoided the lot of them.

The rest of the guests were more or less happy to see her recovered. Miss Beatrice, having convinced herself that Jane suffered from hysteria, recommended a rigorous course of smelling salts and brisk air, and to avoid the rest of the party altogether, lest her delicate condition progress to a nervous disorder. Clarence made a show of clearing space for her on the settee, should she find herself in need of a soft place to land next time she fainted. She made a silent vow to spend the afternoon standing just to spite him.

"Miss Danvers, I am delighted you were able to join us. Would you like to help me with the fruit garland?" asked Lady Louisa, a spread of dried cranberries and orange slices before her.

"The fruit garland has always been my favorite decoration," she replied, a curious sensation coming over her as she spoke without thinking.

Isobel caught her eye and tilted her head. *A memory?* the gesture asked. Jane nodded, clinging to its fine tendrils with a desperate grip. The smell of cinnamon and melting wax, the roughness of a pinecone in her palm, a fire roaring before her. Was it home she was remembering?

But just as quickly as it came, the memory was gone, leaving her colder in its absence. She looked down at the table to see Lady Louisa had pushed a pile of dried orange slices and a spool of yarn toward her. It was time to get to work.

Viola was her shadow as she strung the fruit and knotted the yarn, the girl prattling on about every subject under the sun, from botany to politics to local gossip. She had a seemingly endless well to draw upon, even after they had spent the afternoon and evening before in each other's company, but Jane suspected much of that had to do with the girl finding a more receptive audience than she was used to. Jane was happy to listen to her argue the merits of allowing girls to take up fencing (in Viola's mind it was only logical, especially in the apparently inevitable event of a duel) as she finished the garlands and hung them on the tree, feeling accomplished.

By then, Isobel had stolen her sister away to sort through the many boxes of ornaments that kept appearing, carried out from the bowels of Mulgrave Hall by a very perturbed Battersby, leaving Jane time to observe the room.

Clarence was pestering Lady Louisa as they continued with the cherry garland under the watchful and reproachful eye of her brother Edgar. Lucian and George were engaged in what appeared to be a ferocious battle of a baccarat game with Jasper's brothers Frederick and August, the latter looking increasingly frazzled as time went on, leading Jane to believe there was no small sum of money on the line. Miss Beatrice was stringing popcorn garlands alone, having refused assistance from all who offered, while Helena and her sisters were dusting beautiful glass decorations in preparation for the trimming.

It was a peaceful, if chaotic scene, but something was missing. Someone, rather.

Like her, Jasper seemed to be observing from across the room, holding himself at a distance from the people he loved. It was so bloody typical of him. And so, Jane decided to coax him into participating. She began to make her way toward him, careful not to cross his line of vision before it was too late for him to escape.

"I must commend you on your selection of the tree, my lord."

She didn't mean for the honorific to put distance between them, but in a room full of strangers, it didn't feel right to use his name.

He looked at her out of the corner of his eye, as if reluctant to see all of her at once. "You are feeling better, then?"

"'Better' seems a relative term, but yes, I am much improved." She tilted her head, silently attempting to catch his eye. "I am told I have you to thank for my quick recovery." A muscle in his jaw tensed. He still wouldn't look at her, still retreated behind a wall of propriety when she knew they were well past such things. "You and Dr. Hill," she added. "Thank you for coming to my rescue again, and my apologies for being in need of it. I hope to one day prove I am not always a damsel in distress."

Finally, he looked at her, his gaze sharp as a knife against her skin. She couldn't stop herself from gasping when she felt the full force of it. His eyes fell to her mouth. He opened his, and the words that followed were low and insistent. "Jane, I will never—"

But they were interrupted by the sudden appearance of Edgar. Jasper took a step back from her, swallowing something that sounded like a grunt. He stood straighter. Donned his mask once more.

Edgar didn't seem to notice the tension brewing between them. "Jasper, Miss Danvers," he said in greeting, offering them both a small bow.

Jane couldn't help but notice how Jasper's fist tightened against the table. Edgar turned his attention toward her. "Miss Danvers, would you mind helping me with the tree candles? I've been tasked with lighting them."

"I'd be glad," she replied, not sparing a look at Jasper. She had come to thank him for taking care of her the night before, and thank him she had. Her part of it was done, and it was clear he intended to pretend there was no closeness between them, despite the care he had shown her in private. Pride would keep her from begging him for more than he was willing to give. She took Edgar's arm and left him standing there, silent as the grave.

"Thank you for rescuing me, Mr. Ashwell," she whispered, not entirely sure what he had rescued her from.

"Edgar, please," he said. "And think nothing of it, it is *you* who is rescuing me from a task I am woefully unqualified for, Miss Danvers."

"Jane," she replied with a smile as they approached the tree. "If I may, how long have you known Lord Belhaven?"

"Oh, Jasper and I have been friends since infancy," he replied with a grin, handing her a thin taper. The tree was heavily laden with candles; their task would take them some time. He lit a match to light the tapers. "Our mothers were dear friends long before we were born," he replied before blowing out the match. "It was a happy circumstance indeed that saw them married to earls with estates so near each other."

"It would be so lovely to live near a friend," Jane remarked.

"And you, Jane? Do you have many friends close to your home in Buckinghamshire?"

This was what she had been hoping to avoid. Jane had no desire to invent a life for herself when her own was miserably out of reach. And the thought of lying to a man so kind as Edgar brought her no joy whatsoever. How could a friendship be built upon such shaky foundations? At least the Maycotts knew the truth of her affliction.

Still, she didn't have much of a choice. She would use it as an exercise of her mind. She would tell lies in the hopes that they would cause the truth to emerge.

"'Many' is a strong word, but yes, I am lucky enough to have some friends close," she replied, lighting her first candle, one that rested between a beautiful glass angel and a fragrant bundle of cinnamon sticks.

"Well, I hope that if we have not succeeded in scaring you off, you will consider your circle of friends widened. I know Louisa would like that very much." Jane couldn't help but feel a flare of guilt in her chest, knowing in her gut that Edgar truly meant what he said, even as she knew it could never happen. "Miss Beatrice I cannot speak for," he added with a grimace. "Though I am sure she would consider it an insult to be included," he added with a whisper.

Jane barked out a laugh. "I would never be so bold as to assume anything of Miss Beatrice, my lord, friendship least of all."

They crossed each other then, their paths around the tree having intersected. Jane hadn't expected him so close, and she tripped over her own feet in an effort not to bump into him. All at once, she was falling, cursing herself and her clumsiness in equal measure.

But Edgar caught her, righting her rather quickly and without much fuss.

"Thank you," she said breathlessly. "I'm still a bit unsteady on my feet."

"Think nothing of it," he said, his hand still gripping her waist. It took longer than it should for him to notice they still touched. When he did, he dropped his hand to his side and took a step back, offering her a small, formal bow as if to reestablish proper boundaries.

Jane looked around, fearing Lady Adelaide's razor-sharp gaze, but no one had noticed them.

No one save for Jasper, whose expression was unreadable. Blank, even.

Heat rose to Jane's cheeks, but she banished the sticky feeling of shame that accompanied it. She had done nothing wrong. Edgar had done nothing wrong. But why did it feel like a betrayal? And to *who*?

Ignoring that emotion, she carried on with lighting the candles, those within reach, as Edgar continued above her. He made conversation and slowly the feeling of shame receded. Eventually, Viola and Helena came over to them, remarking on their job well done, and the room descended again into its happy chaos.

Jane, caught up in the moment, smiled as she scanned the room for Jasper, seeking him out to share in the joy that bubbled all around them. But she could only watch as he left, his departure going unnoticed by everyone else. With so quiet and somber a presence in a room of boisterous activity, it was easy to understand why his friends did not miss him as of yet.

But Jane did.

Standing there among his family and friends, she felt his absence like a hollow deep within her. She would have taken his critical gaze over his leaving entirely. He should be with the people he loved, and if she had to force him, so be it. She saw it as her solemn duty, dragging him back into the world he'd left behind. Let him hate her for it. She owed him as much.

Sensing her opportunity, Jane excused herself. Given her condition the night before, no one pressed her to stay. She assured them she only needed a quick rest and she would be ready for dinner.

No one noticed when she turned left toward the library instead of toward her room.

Chapter Eighteen

JANE

Reaching her destination didn't take long, and Jane was pleased to note her instincts as to the Earl of Belhaven's whereabouts were correct.

She entered the library without saying a word and closed the door behind her. She didn't want an audience, or to incur the ire of Lady Adelaide. Jasper was at his desk, frozen, looking at her like he couldn't quite believe she was real. Had he not thought she would follow him? The path between them was worn down and well-trodden. Their coming together felt inevitable, didn't it? Or was that just how Jane felt?

Neither of them spoke for several moments. All of Jane's bluster faded when she entered the library and saw him hunched there, looking so utterly defeated.

"What is it, Jasper?" she asked, stepping toward the desk. He recoiled, and her stomach fell. Trust the stern bastard to treat her like a leper rather than actually tell her what he felt. "Is my presence so disagreeable to you?" she asked, sarcasm weighing her words. But his face was twisted with so much emotion, her bite fell back once more. "You need only say the word and I will leave," she added softly.

He stood so quickly his chair fell. "Do you honestly think your presence is *disagreeable* to me, Jane?"

His passion surprised her. "You have hardly spoken a word to me since your friends arrived," she started defensively. "Why, you all but revealed to your guests that I am an unwanted intruder!" He wasn't going to get away with it this time. Jane stood her ground, forcing herself to speak every word that was on her mind. "And then I am told that you spent the night by my side, only to have you rebuff me when I try to thank you for your efforts, efforts which so obviously strained your already limited patience for me. So why would I think otherwise, my lord, when you treat me thusly?"

He stepped around the desk. Another woman might have feared his approach, but Jane craved his anger, finding it all the more satisfying than his indifference. He stood mere inches from her, that all-too-familiar disapproval set in his brow.

When he spoke, it was barely above a whisper. "I avoid you, dear Jane, because I cannot be near you." She tried to reply, but his hand reached for her jaw, his thumb gently covering her mouth. He tilted her head upward, forcing their eyes to meet. "I cannot be near you without thinking of taking you in my arms and making you mine." Heat crackled between them. What had seemed like disapproval before, she read now as hunger. "Slowly," he added.

Jane blinked and swallowed thickly, causing Jasper to let go of her jaw and turn away from her. "Oh," was all she could manage to say.

"Oh?" he replied over his shoulder.

She stepped around him, forcing him to look at her again. "Is—is that why you avoid me?"

He turned his head away. "Everything about you sets me on a dangerous path." But then he looked at her, really *looked* at her in a way that was so heated it felt indecent. "But I cannot escape you, Jane, not when you occupy my every thought."

"That is your desire then?" she asked, breathless with need. "To escape me?"

His eyes fell to her lips. They were close now, so close to getting what they both wanted. Jane ached with desire; she knew he felt it, too. She placed her hands on his chest, an invitation. He looked down at them. Considered them. Pressed his lips into a firm line. He was on the edge; all she needed was for him to jump. Jane was already there, already drowning in him.

But the stern bastard won out in the end, pushing her hands away and putting distance between them. "I am doing my damnedest to stay away from you, Jane, because I cannot distract you from your purpose."

She had been following his retreat, but his words made her stop. "My purpose?"

"You are here to recover," he replied as though it were obvious. "How could I allow myself to selfishly muddle your desires?"

"Who are you to tell me what I desire?" Now it was Jane's turn to be angry. "Can a person not be ruled by more than one? A gentleman would defer to the lady in matters such as this, no?"

He studied her as if seeking permission, as if he couldn't quite believe what she was saying. "I do not wish to take advantage of you."

The man was infuriatingly cautious. "I may lack my memories, Jasper, but I know my own mind."

He stared at her, his brow softening as he considered her. He stepped closer. Her heart raced, but not from fear. "All I want is for you to heal, Jane. I do not wish to complicate your life any more than it already has been, so I feel like an ass for how I am constantly drawn to you, and how I can't seem to leave you alone—"

"I don't *want* to be left alone," she argued.

Another step closer. "And then I lash out at you as if any of this is your fault—"

"Yes, well, that *does* make you something of an ass."

Even closer still. "And then watching you with Edgar has been sheer torture—"

"Edgar?" Jane asked incredulously. "You are jealous of him?"

He looked sheepish. "I know I have no claim on you, Jane, and a decent man would step aside and let you pursue whatever it is your heart desires, but—"

"I desire *you*, Jasper." The words echoed around them, carrying so much more weight than she'd intended. Jane's heart was in her throat, but she did not regret her candor. If anything, it was like the breaking of a dam. "Not him. Not anyone else. I want you almost as much as I want my memories. Christ, I may want you more. It feels as if the wanting will kill me and I know you don't—"

He silenced her with a brand of a kiss, hot against her lips, and the world stilled. No, not stilled, it shifted, seismically and irrevocably. There would be no going back from this, no retreat into propriety. The kiss was a confirmation. An inevitability.

She felt shock course through him, as if Jasper himself

hadn't expected to be so bold. He began to pull away, but Jane was faster. She wrapped her arms around his neck and brought him deeper into her. He met her eagerly, lifting her off her feet, pulling her tight against the firmness of his body. His next kiss was not a shock. No, Jasper Maycott, a man who did not do things by half, took his time, teasing his lips against hers, the sensation so torturous, so heavenly, Jane thought she might faint again.

He pulled himself back, resting his forehead on hers. "Is this all right?" he asked breathlessly, his eyes soft and warm on her, no trace of the stern mask remaining. "I'm not hurting you?"

She shook her head and writhed against him in answer, her body begging him for more. Because Jane was a match, and Jasper's touch was a flame, and all she wanted was to burn. She wasn't thinking about her past or her future; she was unburdened by worry and fear. All she felt was *him*, and how the two of them fit together like they had been created for each other.

He kissed her again, and it was the culmination of the lingering looks they had shared, the barbs they had traded, the limits that they had pushed each other to, and something entirely new, something that could only exist because they had broken down every last wall that stood between them.

Her mouth opened against his, a sigh escaping her lips. Jasper swore so low it rumbled through his chest as his palm cupped her neck, leaving Jane to wonder if she had ever been here before. Had she felt this unbridled desire for someone else? It didn't seem possible. Surely, she would remember this feeling, this uncontrollable urge to give herself over to another. To surrender entirely.

He licked against her lips and she opened for him again, this time eliciting a low moan from him, one that unraveled a molten heat inside her. Even without her memories, Jane knew she had never been kissed like *this*. She reached blindly for his necktie, fumbling to gain access to more of him. He let go of her only to assist her, ripping it off and throwing it to the ground. She kissed his neck and breathed him in, tasting the salt on his warm skin. He let out a soft growl as his lips traced from her temple to the boundaries of her injury in a gentle, delicious exploration.

He turned her face and claimed her mouth once more, as if desperate to taste her. They were melting together, their bodies less different than they were the same in that moment. Her hands were in his hair as she arched against him, needing to feel more of him against her.

Swearing again, Jasper lifted her off her feet and walked until he had pushed her up against a wall. She wrapped her ankles around his hips, notching the two of them together in a way that was both deeply wanton and deeply right. He smiled against her mouth and turned his attention to her chest, trailing kisses along the edge of her neckline, his tongue licking under the fabric of her dress.

"Please," she begged, desire and need nearly overcoming her. Somehow, in a world of uncertainties, Jane knew exactly what she wanted. Him. Him. Only him. Jasper had said he had no claim on her, but that was a lie. The stern bastard had claimed her heart. Now she wanted to be the one to claim *him*.

He pulled at the laces at the front of her dress, loosening them enough for the chain she wore to escape from her bodice. The ring swung free and thudded against her sternum, glinting between them in the firelight.

He paused, raising his head to her, looking at her like no one had ever looked at her before. But he did not kiss her again; instead, he seemed almost puzzled.

"Please," she whispered again, needing relief from the

languid, torturous heat. "Jasper, I need you."

But if saying his name had tethered them together before, it severed that connection now, like the sudden slamming of a door. He looked down at the ring and back at her, his expression shuttered. Guarded, even.

He set her back down on her feet unceremoniously. A chill wrapped around her where his arms had been.

"I'm sorry," he began, but the silence only deepened after he spoke. He looked like a man tortured both by *what* they had done and the fact that they had stopped.

She found she had no patience for it, or him. "What is it you're sorry for?" she asked, an edge to her voice. "Because I wanted that. I wanted *you*. And I have been nothing but honest with you from the start, as limited as my honesty can be given the circumstances, whereas I'm not sure you've ever been fully truthful with me."

"I haven't been," he agreed, shattering what remained of Jane's resolve.

She stepped away from him, her anger leaving her, shame and hurt rushing in in its wake. She straightened her skirts for want of something to do with her hands, heat rising to her cheeks. "Oh," was all she could manage.

Jasper grasped her hand, halting her retreat. "It's not what you think, Jane—"

"Isn't it?" she asked, her voice small. "You have made it abundantly clear there is nothing between us. It is my fault for not listening."

"What exists between us is real. I'm the one who should be blamed for not—" He closed his mouth, swallowing whatever he had intended to say.

Jane was done with letting moments pass, or words go unsaid.

"For not what?"

He looked down at her hand, small in his, and back at her. "You're the first person I've kissed since…"

There was the pain, the grief she knew so well. "Since?" she asked softly, but not kindly.

His gaze left her for the first time since their lips touched. He looked toward the window, casting half of his face in shadow. "Since my fiancée—since Annabelle died."

Jane realized then that she had suspected as much. Jasper had clearly loved Annabelle, and only death had torn them apart. She thought back to the gallery, when he had cursed love for not saving his parents. She understood now that he had also been blaming love for not saving Annabelle, and by extension he had been blaming himself. *His* love had not saved her, not saved them, and he had been punishing himself ever since.

"I'm sorry, Jasper." And she was. He had lost so much. So had Jane, but somehow, standing in the library with a man so tormented by his past, she felt almost grateful for her lack of memories. Her pain was an echo she chased, his was a specter haunting his steps.

"The worst of it is that what I feel for you is real, Jane. God knows I tried to deny it and I will not do so anymore. But…"

"But?"

He still couldn't look at her. "When she died, I made a vow to never love another."

In all her imaginings of what would keep the two of them apart, she hadn't envisioned something as histrionic as a deathbed vow. And yet, so much of her life of late had felt like it had been ripped from the pages of a particularly sensational periodical. She shouldn't have been so surprised by the Earl of Belhaven's solemn promise, one that had shackled him to a rather grim future.

"Did—did she ask it of you?" She had to imagine that was the case if he felt obligated to uphold his end of the bargain. But how could someone exact such an oath from one they claimed to love?

He shook his head. "Of course not—"

"Then who was that promise for, Jasper?"

"You don't understand," he started, his normally neat hair falling across his brow in disarray, obscuring his eyes from her. She had never seen him so grieved. "This is how I've kept going. How I've survived."

She pulled her hand from his and wrapped her arms around herself, weighing her next words carefully. "Surviving isn't living, Jasper."

He began to reach for her unconsciously, but stopped, letting his arm fall to his side, his hand forming a fist. "I know."

But he did not say another word, did not give Jane even an ounce of hope for what might be. How could she have been such a fool? Hadn't he told her nothing could exist between them? That it was a mistake? She had told herself over and over again that the mantle of sternness he wore was a mask, but she knew now that it was also a shield meant to keep people like her out. She felt no victory at having broken through.

Not if it meant she had something else to lose.

The library was quiet, but Jane's mind was a riot of thoughts. Jasper only stared at her, his pain as evident as his desire had been. He did not hate her, no. Worse, she suspected that he cared for her in a way no one else ever had, or perhaps ever would. But it didn't matter. They were both of them tortured by things they could not change, haunted by lives they did not recognize.

This time, Jane was the one to leave.

Chapter Nineteen

Jasper

Jasper didn't move after Jane left him in the library.

The awareness that he had wronged her was so apparent his skin prickled with it, but he couldn't go after her. Not after what he had said.

Not after what they had done.

And yet, he couldn't bring himself to regret it. Not even a little. The moment their lips had met, he was hers and she was his, and in another life, they might have had a future together.

But reality was far more complicated.

Never before had he been ruled by such conflicting emotions. There was the ecstasy of having finally acknowledged the truth of what lay between them, of finally giving in to his desire and discovering Jane wanted him as much as he wanted her.

And then there was the wretchedness of his guilt.

Jasper had spent a year avoiding thoughts of Annabelle,

certain that if he gave in and truly felt her loss, he would never recover. He had done it in order to keep going. His siblings had needed him to endure.

And yet he had thought of her more times since Jane had arrived than the rest of the year combined, and it hadn't caused him unendurable pain. It was like looking at the portrait of his parents—the pain was there, would likely never leave him, but the remembrance also brought forth happier memories, or at least echoes of them. Someday he might be able to recall them at will and relive the goodness of knowing Annabelle, and the better person she had made him. He could almost glimpse it now. Almost.

He had sworn never to love again, building a wall around his heart. Enduring, as the Maycott family had always done. But had it served him? Had it made anything easier? Or had the wall kept others out? Others who needed his warmth more than they needed his strength?

Who was that promise for, Jasper?

Jane's words echoed endlessly in his mind. He had no answer. He had thought the promise was for the family he lost and for the siblings left behind. It was a promise made out of desperation, and he had clung to it in his darkest moments, sure it was the only way forward.

That was why he had pushed Jane away when all he wanted was to give in to the relentless pull of her.

He sank into the armchair by the fire and buried his head in his hands. His mind was clouded by guilt and desire, yes, but above everything else, Jasper was consumed by fear. Fear that he could come to love another the way he had loved Annabelle, and lose them, too. Surely that was the most compelling reason to reestablish the distance between him and Jane.

When Helena at last found him, Jasper wasn't sure how much time had passed. Minutes? Hours? Had he wasted a whole night in restless contemplation?

She came to his chair and he noticed she was bundled for the cold.

"You're missing an outing to the pond and what promises to be Clarence's long-awaited comeuppance for tripping Isobel three years ago. I've never seen her look *more* wicked than when Viola innocently suggested everyone go skating. What's more, I think Clarence has forgotten his transgression and is blissfully unaware of what's coming for him." She paused and looked down at him slouched in his chair, her brow creasing. "What's the matter?"

Lucian and Isobel both had offered themselves to Jasper as people he could talk with, but in the end, it was Helena he chose. Helena, who had lost her husband, would know the impossibility of what he felt.

"Do you believe in true love?" he asked bluntly, knowing there would be no easing into the subject. He had to act quickly, before he lost his nerve.

Helena let out a long breath and sat in the armchair next to him, removing her gloves as though aware she would be staying a while. "I do, Jasper."

It wasn't the answer he was expecting. "Truly? Even after losing Marcus? You still believe there is one person for whom your devotion will eclipse all others?"

"One person? No." She gave him a smile he tried not to read as pitying. "Love is not a finite thing, and loving again would not lessen what I felt for him."

The part of Jasper that wanted to believe her roared to life in his chest, but the rest of him worked to smother it. "It doesn't feel as though you would be dishonoring his memory?"

Helena's brows shot up. "Is that what you think?" she asked, her voice barely above a whisper. "Jasper, why are you holding yourself to a standard she would never have expected of you?" Images of Annabelle flooded his mind. Kind, loving Annabelle. Was Helena right? She leaned closer to him. "If your places had been exchanged, would you have wanted Annabelle to be alone for the rest of her life? Would you have expected her to close her heart off, living only for the memory of you?"

The very idea of it disgusted him. "Never," was his vehement reply.

"Then you dishonor her by acting as though that is what she would have wanted from you."

The sudden clarity Helena's words provided could have knocked him over. Annabelle had been as patient as she was kind, as generous as she was loving. Their time together had been unfairly short, but it had been long enough for Jasper to shed his immaturity, his selfishness, his greed and his vanity. He had grown as a person because of Annabelle's steady influence. In loving her he had transformed, and in losing her he had shattered. It hurt to think she would not recognize the man he had become, cold and guarded and shut away from the world.

"You're right," he remarked, still stunned by it. "And I am a bloody fool who has spent all this time refusing to speak of her, to even *think* of her, terrified that I was betraying her by...well, continuing to live, I suppose. As though I should have died with her." A tear escaped the corner of his eye. Jasper waited to feel shame, but none came. Another tear fell, splashing onto the back of his hand, unfurling a great knot in his chest. Why shouldn't he allow himself to feel this deeply after so long a time spent shunning emotion? "You see, that was what I wanted, Helena.

When she lay there dying, I prayed for it, because how could I live without her?" He looked over and watched as Helena wiped her own tears away, but he could not cease his dawning realization. "But then we lost Mother and Father and Anthony, and suddenly I had a duty to provide for the rest of us, and the only way I could fathom it was to seal off my grief and move forward."

"Enduring as we Maycotts are meant to," Helena added bitterly, echoing his earlier thoughts.

"I saw you as a grim burden I had no choice but to accept when I should have seen you as my salvation. Christ, who knows where I would be without you?"

A few heartbeats passed before she spoke. "You were our salvation, too, Jasper."

She seemed to mean it, but Jasper couldn't accept it. "A fine job I've done of that."

"Give yourself an inch of credit. It's only been a year since we lost them. We all needed one another to see our way through the storm. And the change I've seen in you since Jane arrived..." She let the sentence linger, inviting him to acknowledge the effect Jane had on him, should he wish to.

"She has been a welcome distraction," he said, knowing she had been a great deal more, but that saying it aloud would only serve to pain him.

"Only a distraction?" Helena asked, her voice heavy with skepticism.

He couldn't go down that road. "Nothing can come of it, Helena. Not when she might have a whole life to return to."

"One that doesn't include you?" Helena surmised.

"Precisely."

She tapped her fingers on the arm of her chair, tilting her head. "Perhaps she could have both, her past and her present.

Maybe they are not incompatible things."

This time, he could not stop the burst of warmth in his chest that accompanied Helena's words. Because that was what he wanted. A way forward with Jane, broken as he was by grief.

"It matters not. I've pushed her away too many times, Helena. I'm not even sure I want what it is I think I want, or if it's fair to her to keep getting close only to realize I'm not ready."

"Perhaps you should talk to her."

It was a dreadfully simple concept, speaking to the woman at the center of his every thought. And yet the Jasper of a half hour hence would have feared it. *That* Jasper had pushed her away, warm and wanting, in favor of self-imposed isolation.

Christ, Isobel is right. I really am an idiot sometimes.

Jane undoubtedly deserved better than a man who had needed another's permission to even fathom a different future for himself, but more than anything, she deserved an apology. He could give her that, at the very least.

He sighed. "I swore I'd never love again."

Helena shook her head. "An empty promise."

"And yet I meant it. Held myself to it, too."

"It's not that I don't believe you, Jasper, but rather that I don't think you have much choice in the matter. None of us do." She leaned forward, resting her elbows on her knees. "You cannot help how you feel, and if your heart is telling you Jane is the answer, who are you to deny it?"

He couldn't accept that. Not yet. Perhaps not ever.

"Without her memories—"

"I'm not saying you have to marry her, Jasper." She sat back in the chair. "I'm simply saying you needn't fear your own feelings. You dishonor no one by listening to your heart."

"Thank you, Helena." He looked over to her and out the

window. "You should join the others."

She grinned as she put her gloves back on. "I wouldn't want to miss Isobel's revenge." She stood and patted his shoulder as she walked past him.

"What about you?" he called out. Helena had been without her husband longer than he had been without Annabelle. He wanted to see his sister love again, should she wish it. "Do you think you will? Love another, that is."

She turned back to him, her smile small as she shook her head. "Perhaps someday."

. . .

The door to the Lavender Room was shut, so Jasper knocked softly, not wanting to startle Jane.

"Lady Viola?" she called. Jasper was not surprised by who she was expecting.

"No, it's me," he replied. "It's Jasper."

It was so quiet behind the door that he was sure she was ignoring him. He supposed he deserved it, and cursed himself once more for his blasted sternness. But then the door opened, and there she was, hair mussed, dress rumpled, eyes red-rimmed behind her spectacles. She was so beautiful, so vibrant, he almost ached to look at her.

"Jane," he breathed, desperately wishing he knew her real name so he could ensnare her with it the way she had him.

She folded her arms across her chest. "What do you want, Jasper?"

"May I come in?"

She said nothing as she moved aside to let him in. It was a start. He stepped into the warm room, pausing in the center and turning around to face her.

He took a deep breath. "I am so sorry."

"What is it you're apologizing for?"

Jasper wasn't sure where to begin. His sins were many, but he would start with the most egregious. "For my inability to confide in you long after you had proven yourself trustworthy." He swallowed the desire to leave it at that. "I should have told you about Annabelle from the start."

"Why didn't you?" He could see that she was hurt by it. "You speak of our shared grief but kept your deepest pain from me."

"I believed I was doing what I must. It's a poor excuse, but it was all I had to hold on to. I thought if I acknowledged the loss of her, everything I had fought bitterly for would crumble and I would fail."

"And? Did it? Did *you*?"

He shook his head. "All I have learned is that I should have spoken of her sooner, though I suppose now is as good a time as any, if you'll hear it." Jane nodded and moved to sit in the armchair by her bed. Jasper was far too anxious to sit still. He had spent most of their time together concealing a part of himself, but all he wanted now was to be known by her, and to know her, as much of her as he could before it was too late. "Annabelle and I were engaged only a short time before she died last year of scarlet fever, just before my parents and brother. Her father was the vicar of Wrayford and she liked to go with him when he traveled through the parish, tending to his flock, as it were. She had a particular fondness for women and children in need. She was always finding work for widows and unwed mothers, tending to their children when she could, making sure they understood the power of an education. She was the light of her father's life, and he hers. Even after we knew of the illness, she wouldn't leave him to perform his duties alone."

"A strong woman," Jane offered.

"Indeed. I was with her when she died, and losing her almost killed me. But then I lost so much more, and suddenly I had people depending on me, and I could not fail. I bottled up that sorrow and refused to acknowledge it, and it worked, for a time. Or rather, I thought it did. I distracted myself by aiding my tenants, felling trees, building barns, anything to keep my mind from what we lost. But then you arrived." It had only been days but Jasper felt in his bones that he had known Jane a great deal longer, like she had always been there in the orbit of his life. Perhaps they were two planets on converging paths, destined to align, however briefly. "At first, I saw you as another distraction, or better yet, someone I could save. An atonement, perhaps, for those I couldn't. But you are so much more to me than that, Jane." His voice cracked with feeling, but he needed her to understand him. "You forced me to recall the things I buried. But it did not hurt the way I thought it would. And I realized that acting the way I did about Annabelle almost made it seem like knowing her was a curse, but I was blessed to know her, as I am blessed to know you." Both women mattered to him in ways he could not yet put into words, but he was relieved to find that whatever he felt for Jane was different from how he felt when he thought about Annabelle now. They were not linked, as he had feared they would be. "Each time you speak of your debt to me I am almost overcome with the need to tell you the truth, Jane."

"And what is that?" she asked.

"That I am the one who is indebted to you, and I always will be."

It wasn't the sort of impassioned declaration one might expect from a man as besotted as he, but it meant as much to Jasper as more sentimental words would have. He suspected Jane would perceive the deeper meaning as well.

"Jasper," she whispered, her voice laden with emotion. But he was not done.

He stepped closer to where she sat and kneeled before her. "Please forgive me, dear Jane. I know my transgressions against you are many, but the fault has never lain with you."

She took his hand in hers. "There is nothing to forgive." He did not expect her pardon, but it was a balm for his wearied heart. Her thumb rubbed across the back of his hand. "I would dearly love to know more about her, about all of them, if ever you wish to tell me."

There was no heat in her touch, only a deep sense of caring. Jasper was surprised by how much he needed that from her. But then, that was how she had forced him to shed that protective layer, inch by inch, with her kindness and her stubbornness both, even when he had shut her out. Without it, his very soul was bared to her, but he did not fear her seeing him clearer. Jane had seen through his mask from the start. It was Jasper who hadn't seen himself fully until now.

"I only wish I could help you the way you've helped me."

She brought her hand to his cheek. There was that ache again, that feeling that his future was within reach, and yet also never further from his grasp. "You've done more for me than any stranger might deserve."

"Especially one who ruined a perfectly good pair of boots," he added playfully.

Her smile went wicked. "A first impression you'll never forget, I'd wager."

The ache deepened. "There isn't a thing about you I'll ever forget, Jane."

Her eyes fell to his mouth. Jasper hadn't dared to hope that they could return to what they'd left unfinished in the library. His only goal had been to apologize to her. But as he watched her bite her bottom lip, desire gripped him once more.

She pushed her fingers through his hair as though she could not help herself. There were no words to describe how it felt to have her touch him so intimately. Rapture, perhaps. Paradise. Utter bliss. "So soft," she remarked. "I've wanted to do this since you brought me my spectacles. The way you looked at me could have set my skin aflame."

"We spoke of debt then, too, do you remember?" His words were heavy with the desire he feared he could not contain much longer.

"It was hard not to feel like I owed you something," she whispered.

"You do not owe me anything, Jane. You know that, right?"

She nodded. "And yet," she began, trailing her fingers along his jaw, "I wish to give you everything."

He stiffened at the admission, knowing he was inches away from taking her in his arms and finishing what they'd started.

But a howling at the door interrupted them. Mr. Darcy was demanding entrance.

"He likes how the sun comes through my window," Jane said in the cat's defense.

Unwilling to disappoint either of them, Jasper stood and went to the door to let the tiny beast in just as Isobel rounded the corner, her cheeks deeply pink and her eyes wide.

"You're lucky it's only me," she chided lightly. "If Aunt Adelaide caught you alone in Jane's room—"

"Well, it's a good thing it's you, isn't it?" he replied smartly, snatching Mr. Darcy up from the ground and holding him against his chest. "How did your campaign of revenge fare? Is Clarence still breathing?"

She looked between him and Jane both before smirking in a rather knowing manner. "He'll live, but how long can a man survive without his pride?"

"Too long," he replied. "We are talking about Clarence."

Helena and August appeared behind Isobel, all of them as pink-cheeked as their sister.

"Oh good, you're here," said Helena, graciously not mentioning the impropriety of it. "Viola and Freddie are thawing out by the hearth in the great room, but I wanted to find you and tell you we ran into Lady Cordelia at the pond."

"Oh?" Her father, the Earl of Banfield, had been one of their father's closest friends. He and his wife had been most persistent in their efforts to lure Jasper and his siblings out of their seclusion over the past year.

"Her parents are hosting a ball and hoped we'd attend," said Isobel. "Lady Cordelia was *certain* we were sent an invitation. You wouldn't happen to know anything about that, would you, Jasper?"

Jasper had long given up on managing the tottering pile of correspondence on his desk, and Battersby knew better than to bring an *invitation* to his attention. "I'm sure I don't," he replied stiffly.

"In any event, it is tonight and since she encountered us with a number of guests of our own, I didn't see an easy way to refuse her."

"You cannot seriously be thinking of attending a ball," he scoffed. It was enough that their manor was filled with Jasper's closest friends. To venture out into the wider world seemed an impossibility, to say nothing of what it might mean for Jane.

"It's a masquerade, Jasper. You wouldn't even have to show

your face." Helena raised a brow at him. "Seems a decent choice to ease our way back into Society, no? Besides, everyone has already retreated to their rooms to ready themselves. You'll have a hard time dissuading them, Beatrice especially. She seems to think Lady Banfield will be an easy target for a sizeable donation to her charitable efforts of bettering the already immaculate grounds of St. James's Park."

August let out a low whistle. "Just think of what she could do with all that money."

Isobel *tsk*ed before taking Mr. Darcy from Jasper's arms and depositing him in her lap. "Waste it and her time both."

"A noble endeavor, then," August added.

"This is madness," Jasper muttered to no one in particular.

Isobel rounded on him. "Think, Jasper. A night spent at a ball is one less night you'll have to entertain your friends on your own."

"It's an easy win, Brother," August added.

"I wouldn't mind attending," said Jane. Jasper was sure no one else noticed how she wavered ever so slightly as she spoke.

"It would be a clever way to discern if Jane has any ties to the area," said August.

"Yes, of course!" Isobel exclaimed. "Why, we could solve the mystery of Jane-without-a-surname at last!"

Jane cleared her throat. "Or at least rule out some possibilities." She looked over to him, pleading with her eyes that he acquiesce. The whole room was waiting for his answer, but none of them knew of the danger Jane was in, not even Jane herself.

But he didn't necessarily want to reveal the truth to them all. Seeking a deflection, he cleared his throat. "I worry about—"

"You? *Worry*? What a surprise," Isobel huffed. "Precisely

what do you have to be concerned about, Jasper? It's a country ball, not an event in bloody Mayfair, packed to the hilt with hawkish Society mamas. You could hardly ask for a better or kinder reintroduction to the concept of a ball."

His sister made a compelling argument, one he would have trouble pushing against. "It's a very sensitive time of year—"

"All the more reason to seek out frivolity when and where we can," she shot back, her anger rising.

"What if—"

"Christ, Jasper, what if *what*?" She threw her arms in the air in exasperation. "Stay home if you must, but we are going, and that includes Jane. And if you try to stop us, I will simply enlist the help of Aunt Adelaide—"

"It isn't bloody *safe* for Jane, Isobel!"

The room quieted at once, and Jane stepped between them, looking pale. "Why not?"

There'd be no getting out of it now. "You said something when we found you in the road, something you don't remember, something that leads me to believe we should avoid things like balls until we know more."

Her brow creased. "What did I say?"

He pressed his lips together in a frown. "Should we perhaps speak about this in private?"

She shook her head. "Your family knows as much about me as I do; it would hardly seem fair to keep this from them."

Behind her, Isobel nodded in agreement. Jasper was far too aware that it would be impossible to change Jane's mind on the matter, but it seemed wrong to utter her own dire plea back to her in so inauspicious a setting.

"Jasper," she said, leveling him with the way her voice cracked over his name. "Please."

He couldn't keep it from her. Perhaps he never should have. He took a deep breath. "When I came upon you, you told me you were being pursued. I saw no one, but your fear was…visceral." He paused, waiting for her reaction. But Jane was silent. He watched her chest rise and fall, the only evidence of her shaky breaths. She was doing her damnedest to hold herself together. "You were unconscious again before I could ask more of you."

She nodded and looked down at the floor. Panic gripped him as he wondered if he was forcing her to relive her worst memory, one that had been buried for a reason. All at once he knew he never had a right to demand her past from her. Whether she remembered it or not, it belonged to Jane. If forcing her recollection was going to harm her, he wanted none of it. Let her be a blank slate. Let her forget that which would torment her.

But he would always remember that fear in her eyes. Anger filled him at the thought of Jane being in danger, but without knowing what had happened to her, he had nowhere to direct it.

If she asked it of him, he would tear the countryside apart to find those who sought to hurt her. Hell, he would go to the ends of the earth if it meant keeping her safe. He owed that to her, and so much more. Because back in the great room, when she had spoken in jest of him always coming to her rescue, Jasper had been struck by the truth.

Jane had been the one to rescue him, long before he knew he needed it.

Chapter Twenty

Jane

The Lavender Room seemed to shrink with each pounding beat of Jane's heart. She felt as if she were falling and nothing could stop her. There were too many people witnessing her descent, too many kind eyes looking at her with pity and fear.

Seeking solid ground, she looked back at Jasper. "What *exactly* did I say?"

His eyes were sharp on her, not with anger, but with concern. She wasn't disguising her rising panic well enough. "Your horse was nowhere to be found, but you were warm, your blood was still warm. It couldn't have been more than a few minutes since your accident. I sent Helena and Isobel ahead of me for help. When I picked you up, I waited to ensure you were still breathing, and when your eyes opened your pupils narrowed on me. You said *'Don't let them get me,'* before losing consciousness again."

It was as robust a description as she could have hoped for, so

Jane was not surprised when the room faded as a memory filled her mind, and with it, a sense of urgency that set her teeth on edge.

Hoofbeats cracking through snow. Heaving, gasping breaths. Ice filling her lungs. Tears frozen on her cheeks. And fear, true fear, gripping her as tightly as she gripped the reins.

She was being hunted, and there was no safe place left for her in the world.

"Jane?" Helena's voice broke her reverie. "Are you all right?"

"I—I remember fleeing through the woods. I was on a horse. I didn't know where to go," she spoke in fragments, trying to collect the pieces before they faded. "I was being chased," she concluded darkly.

Helena took her hand. "By whom?" she asked softly.

Jane's brow creased and she strained for more, but her mind was empty. "I do not know, but I was afraid." It was an odd sensation, to remember the fear but not feel it. "More than afraid," she added, parsing out her buried emotions. "I was desperate. I was without hope."

When she had first woken up in the Lavender Room, she had felt that something was wrong beyond the pounding in her head. Those feelings, that fear and hopelessness had been strong enough to follow her from her old life, through her injury, and stay with her when she'd emerged on the other side.

But she had dismissed them. She'd felt safe enough with the Maycotts to ignore the primal urge to flee. She had thought them phantom emotions, but now she knew they had been real.

"You didn't see anyone?" she asked Jasper, who was looking at her like he expected her to collapse or run at any moment. "You didn't hear anything?"

He shook his head. "I didn't stay in the road long enough to investigate. You were bleeding quite a bit."

"And you didn't think to tell the rest of us?" Isobel demanded.

"What good would it have done? Jane was already a mystery to us; I didn't wish to make a sensation out of her, or tell her something that may have delayed her healing." Jane nodded, still not able to look anyone in the eye. According to Jasper, someone had been chasing her. Hunting her. Maybe they were still. Jasper picked up on her unease. "For all we know, it was a group of robbers after what they thought would be an easy mark, only Jane was clever enough to escape them."

"Or Jane-without-a-surname has a salacious background the likes of which even Viola couldn't have dreamed of," said Isobel, her voice heavy with admiration.

"Or it's nothing," chimed Helena, aiming for a positive note but coming across as slightly hysteric. "Perhaps it was the result of her rather traumatic head injury. She did proceed to faint and lose her memories. It does seem as though an invented sense of impending doom might be a part of that."

Jane found she couldn't quite commit to any of the options. She didn't have enough information to dismiss anonymous bandits or a false memory or worse yet, people from her past who wished to do her harm. It was enormously frustrating to only have a small piece of the puzzle. All she knew for certain was that she had been alone, and that ultimately, she was still alone. Because what did it mean that no one had come looking for her? Had she truly traveled some great distance, making it impossible for the people she left behind to find her?

Or had that been the intent all along? To escape them fully?

It was the not-knowing that would kill her in the end. She couldn't live with so much uncertainty. Jane had to find a way to uncover the truth. Perhaps a ball wasn't the worst way to discover someone who might know her. If she could somehow get some answers about that night, perhaps she could move forward.

Jasper had been studying her as she collected her thoughts. She knew him well enough by now to know that he was holding himself back from comforting her in front of his family. She found she craved it nonetheless. Craved him. He had been so honest with her at last, and all she wanted was to give him that same honesty.

But she couldn't. Not until she knew what had happened to her that night.

Their eyes met and she thought he must have been able to read her mind for how quickly he crossed the room, closing the gap between them in three long strides. The others had the decency to step away and converse amongst themselves, offering them a modicum of privacy.

"Jane, my intention has always been to protect you, and I would have told you about what you said to me soon enough, sooner still if we had not been descended upon by a horde of unwanted guests."

She rested her hand on his forearm, an intimate, if a bit muted, gesture. She felt the heat of him beneath her fingertips nevertheless, felt as it spread through her, working to calm her frayed nerves. "I am not angry with you." She wasn't. She believed him when he said he would have told her.

Relief washed over him, smoothing his furrowed brow. "Then you must also agree that Mulgrave Hall is the safest place for you until you recover your memories."

"I don't disagree," she started, hedging a bit.

"So we won't be attending the ball, then," he added, reaching the logical conclusion of his argument.

He was going to be very angry with her. But it couldn't be

helped. "We *must* go to the ball, Jasper."

"I beg your pardon?"

"I hardly think whoever I may have been running from will be in attendance." It was, at the very least, a bit of a lie. Jane had every intention of ferreting out anyone who might know her and discovering the truth about that night. Whether or not she had any hope of success was a different matter. "And besides, we will be masked, no?" He refused to acknowledge the point. She would have to try a different tack. "I cannot go the rest of my life relying on your kindness and protection." His expression suggested that arrangement would be perfectly acceptable to him, but what mattered most was that it would not be acceptable to her. "I cannot live in fear, Jasper. I cannot live like *this*."

His lips were pressed in a stern, disapproving line. "You cannot think that being reckless is living, either, Jane."

"Neither is simply surviving," she said, aiming directly at the part of him that recalled their previous argument in the library, when he had hidden behind a promise no one had ever asked him to make.

He glared at her, his expression unyielding. She would have read it as sternness before, as annoyance, even. But after he had told her about Annabelle and the pain he carried with him every day, Jane found she understood him better. Jasper was not stern, he was a man who could not stand to lose anyone else, one who had protected himself and his family by shutting everything out. Had he been right to do it? Perhaps not, but Jane could not fault him for it. Not after what the Maycotts had been through.

But he had changed so much in their brief time together. She had, too, she suspected, both of them transforming into greater versions of themselves. It was lunacy, then, to expect more from this man who had given her so much of himself, but Jane couldn't help it.

He seemed to be waiting for her to speak, but Jane was floundering. She wished she had a way to convince Jasper that they needed to attend that ball without having to explain her true reasoning: that she would never fully trust him or herself until she knew who she was.

As if he had read her mind again, Jasper spoke low. "If you're doing this because you think I require it, you are mistaken."

His reversal on the matter of her past brought her comfort, but worse than what she had suspected of Jasper was what Jane suspected of herself. What if her background was as salacious as Viola's novels? What if the Maycotts were not safe with her entangled in their lives? She could not put them in danger, not after all they had done for her. Not when one more tragedy could break them fully.

"*I* require it, Jasper." The others fell silent in the wake of her emphatic declaration. She stepped closer to him, lowering her voice. "I cannot stand here in ignorance as my old life hangs over me like a blade, and I cannot move forward if a part of me is locked in the past." Jasper had been vulnerable with her, had trusted her with the deep, dark parts of him she had craved to know. She needed to be known by him in the same way.

She expected him to argue, to demand she see reason. But Jasper only sighed. "So be it."

"We're going to the ball?" asked Isobel from across the room, evidently having heard every word of their hushed conversation.

Jane didn't look away from Jasper when she replied. "Yes," she said, studying the man she was beginning to fear she loved, as he wrestled with indulging her supposed recklessness and his desire to protect her. It mattered to her that he understood her reasoning enough to swallow his own reservations. "Yes, we're going to the ball."

Isobel let out a triumphant squeal, sending Mr. Darcy racing from her arms and under the bed. "You know what that means."

"I cannot begin to imagine," replied Jasper with a groan.

"Jane's going to need one hell of a gown," said Isobel as she looked around the room, smiling wickedly. "And I have just the ticket."

• • •

After the gentlemen had been unceremoniously dismissed from the room and tea and biscuits had been ordered and devoured, Isobel wasted no time in wrangling Jane into a frothy concoction of berry-red velvet and black lace.

"I feel as though I am in a costume," Jane complained, examining the bits of herself that she could in the mirror. Despite its myriad folds and frills, she felt nearly naked, with the low neckline revealing all too much of her chest and the sleeves falling artfully off her shoulders. It was a magnificent creation, but meant for someone else. Someone who knew without a shadow of a doubt who she was and where she belonged in the world.

Someone distinctly unlike Jane.

"Think of it as armor," Isobel replied from behind her as she laced the gown. "Lord and Lady Banfield's estate is your battlefield."

"And my weapons?" Jane asked sarcastically as she tried to pull the dress over her almost indecently exposed bosom.

"Your charm and wit," Isobel replied with a wink.

"And us, of course," Helena added, eyeing Isobel sternly and looking very much like her brother.

"Of course," Isobel hastily agreed. "We will not leave your

side, Jane."

"If this is to be your first foray into Society since..." Jane paused, unsure of how to refer to their collective tragedy and opting instead to simply move past her blunder. "I should hardly think you'll enjoy being my chaperones."

"Nonsense," said Helena. "Like it or not, we are your friends, Jane. And we shall not leave you to the wolves."

"Besides," added Isobel, hairpins falling from her mouth as she twisted Jane's hair into something complicated and impossible to replicate. "I think you'll find we're as rusty as you are when it comes to socialization." She stopped and observed her handiwork. "Why, I'm positively feral compared to Lady Louisa. But will I let that stop me?"

Helena sighed. "Regretfully, no."

"Precisely," said Isobel. "Now gaze upon my masterpiece."

She stepped away from the mirror, allowing Jane to see herself for the first time, fully transformed. Her breath caught in her chest. The dress *was* armor. Better yet, it was a shield. No one would think she didn't belong in Lord Banfield's ballroom clothed as she was.

"This dress... It's like witchcraft." She studied her reflection, searching for even a hint of familiarity the fine attire might offer her. But she was a stranger to herself. Standing very still, she might have been fooled into thinking she was looking at a portrait of someone she did not know. Someone she had never met. She looked at Isobel in the mirror. "I don't think I deserve a gown so..."

"Perfect?" Isobel guessed. "Alas that it is only perfect for you, dear Jane," she said, gesturing toward the hem, which fell to Jane's ankles and would have barely covered Isobel's calves. "I had the dress made for my first Season. Had to go to a specific dressmaker on Bond Street. You see, the lacework is very intricate; not many seamstresses have that skill. Somehow, she got my measurements wrong, only I didn't notice until we had arrived back at Mulgrave Hall. By then the dress didn't seem to matter."

Jane shook her head. "I do not think I should—"

"Wear the gown, Jane." She put her hand on Jane's shoulder, giving it a squeeze. "I must have been saving it for you. It fits you like a glove."

"Speaking of gloves," said Helena, procuring a pair of black silk gloves from a pouch that had accompanied the dress.

The sisters helped Jane put them on, buttoning them up past her elbows.

"There," said a satisfied Helena. "All done."

Jane's hand went to the bandage at her temple. "What about this? I do not wish to field a hundred questions about my injury."

"Ah, but you haven't seen the best part," Isobel exclaimed, waving a black satin and lace mask before her. "You'll be in a mask so no one will even know you're injured."

"I assume that's not the only thing they won't know about me," Jane added.

"Yes, I suspect you'll have to take on an air of mystery, Miss Jane Danvers. If you're asked a question you don't have an answer for, may I recommend excusing yourself for some air. We delicate females are in constant need of it, and no one would dare pester a lady professing to that particular weakness."

"How exactly will this fit over my spectacles? I'm not sure if you recall but I am rather blind without them."

"Our mother wore spectacles as well. She had this mask made to accommodate them, see?" Isobel turned it over, revealing a great deal of padding on the underside of the mask, enough to cushion around her spectacles and hold them in place. "May I?"

Jane nodded and brought the mask to her face so Isobel could tie it around her head.

"Comfortable?" she asked.

Jane looked toward the mirror. The mask didn't cover her bandage entirely. She brought her fingers to the borders of it, wishing she could do away with it entirely.

"Only the most shameless gossips will press you on it, Jane," said Isobel with confidence. "Everyone else will politely pretend they do not see it."

Helena smirked. "A favorite pastime of the aristocracy."

"I do believe you're ready now," said Isobel.

"Wait!" came a screech from the hall. Viola burst into the room waving a ribbon in the air. "Miss Jane *must* wear this around her neck. All the ladies in London do." She held out the ribbon, revealing the star-shaped pendant inlaid with black jewels that hung from the center.

"It's beautiful, Lady Viola," said Jane.

"It's a costume brooch, not worth much," Viola told her sheepishly. "Stars are terribly fashionable," she added somewhat defensively.

"Do you know that from personal experience, Viola?" Isobel asked sarcastically.

Viola offered her a glare. "Cousin Effie sends me fashion plates."

"Well, who are we to deny the sartorial wisdom of Cousin Effie?" asked Helena as she took the choker from Viola and looked for approval to Jane, who nodded. Once secured, anyone could see the necklace completed the look.

Jane thumbed the brooch, marveling at the sparkle of it. "Thank you, Lady Viola."

"It's not much," the girl said.

"And yet it means so much to me," said Jane, hoping Viola understood.

"Will Jane be the only fashionable lady at the ball or do you have more ribbons and jewels for the rest of us?" Isobel asked.

"I have more," Viola replied, pulling scads of the same black ribbon from her pockets and delighting Mr. Darcy, who batted at the tendrils most ferociously.

"You and your ribbons must help me pick out my own gown," said Isobel. "You are tasked with making me look at least half as good as Jane does in my castoffs."

Viola pouted. "I haven't talked with Miss Jane since the tree trimming and I have much to report. I believe my lady's maid has developed a tendre for a footman, and I believe the footman has a tender regard of his own for my governess, it's very indelicate—"

Helena began to steer Viola out of the room. "Let's give Jane a moment to collect her thoughts, Viola. She'll be available to discuss matters of the heart with you tomorrow morning."

"Will you?" Viola asked, almost as sternly as her brother would have.

"Indeed," Jane replied. "Who else am I to share my research with?"

Helena and Isobel gave them both quizzical looks but Jane merely offered them a secretive smile.

Viola nodded sagely. "Over breakfast, then."

And then the trio left the Lavender Room, taking Mr. Darcy and any sense of frivolity with them, and suddenly, Jane was entirely alone.

She had hardly had any time to truly contemplate what Jasper had told her about Annabelle, to say nothing of what he went on to reveal about what she had said to him after her accident.

She thought she should feel more adrift than she did, given the circumstances. But having a plan, small as it was, served to ground her.

With a plan, anything is possible. She paused and pressed her hand to her stomach, a queer feeling coming over her. Was that an adage from the old Jane, uncovered as though she were an archaeologist of her own memories, sifting through layers of time? There was a certain unconscious familiarity to it, like walking a well-known path in the pitch dark. It did not bring her comfort. Was she doomed to remember only the smallest slivers of her old life, as inconsequential as they were brief?

A shiver ran through her. She didn't have time to dwell upon melancholy thoughts. But she could not drag herself from the mirror. It was not vanity that kept her there, but rather the promise of a future she wasn't sure belonged to her. She was mesmerized by it, by this version of herself that did not exist, but perhaps could. A woman in a beautiful gown, as sure of her place in the world as she was in herself.

Could it last? Could that future be hers? Jasper had been inching ever closer to letting her in, but was that love?

It didn't matter. If she did not know herself, it would never feel real. How could she build a new life upon a foundation that might crumble to dust beneath her feet? How could she expect another to trust her with their heart when she did not know her own?

She buried her fears and her desires both, choosing to cling only to the pursuit of the truth, and left her room. It seemed an eternity had passed since that morning with Jasper in the library. The halls of the manor were cold and dim, but Jane had her convictions to keep her warm. Regardless of what occurred that evening, she would have something resembling an answer. If she were the least bit noble, surely someone would recognize her. And if no one did, then perhaps that was answer enough.

She reached the staircase and saw all of the Maycotts, save for Viola and Freddie, waiting for her. Everyone was dressed for the ball, and Jane realized she had taken even longer than she meant to.

"We were about to send a search party," called Isobel, wearing an indigo gown and matching pelisse, her ivory gloves peeking through the heavy wool and a silver satin mask framing her eyes beautifully. It was the most polished Jane had ever seen Isobel, and it suited her.

Helena *tsk*ed as Jane began her descent. "You can never be too late for a ball, Izzie, but you can be entirely too early." Her gown was emerald, not unlike the one she had lent Jane before. On Helena, the color was a revelation. Her mask was dark like Jane's but without lace or other trappings. It was almost plain in its construction and would, Jane suspected, serve to make her stand out all the more.

It struck her then that the sisters were no longer in mourning colors. It had been a year since they lost their parents and brother, she reminded herself. But it was a welcome surprise nevertheless, and made her think that perhaps the Maycotts had turned a page.

Jasper and August looked sharp in their dark tailcoats and white bowties. Dressed so similarly, Jane was able to see that the brothers looked alike, despite their differences. August's mask was ivory trimmed with gold, Jasper's plain black like Helena's. August gave her a slight bow, and she thought she was beginning to see through his metaphorical mask, too, though he strove even harder than his brother to hide his true self.

"Where is everyone else?" she asked no one in particular.

"They've already left in their carriages. Beatrice could not be convinced to wait for you, and we sent the rest of them after her before she caused an incident. We'd rather like to remain in the Earl of Banfield's good graces," said Isobel.

"And Lady Adelaide?" Jane asked.

"Left with the other chaperones. I'd say she's not particularly dedicated to her duties, wouldn't you, Helena?" asked Isobel with a wicked grin.

"Likely thinks we're lost causes," Helena added brightly.

"Shall we, then?" August took a sister on each arm and guided them out the door.

"We'll see you there, Jane," called Isobel. "Don't dally!"

Jasper met her at the bottom of the stairs, his hand outstretched for her to take. He was achingly handsome with his dark golden hair combed back and clean-shaven face. She found his mask, like hers, made him something of a stranger. Perhaps tonight they could enjoy the ball as two people unburdened by their respective pasts.

She felt the heat of his hand through her glove as he guided her from the stairs. He smelled divine—cedar and bergamot mixed with the smoky scent of scotch.

"You are breathtaking," he said, his voice low despite them being alone. His breath tickled her neck, sending a shiver of icy heat through her. He retrieved her cloak, the one she had arrived at Mulgrave Hall in, from where it hung behind her, and settled it upon her shoulders. She went to button it but he shooed her away and took matters into his own hands. When he spoke, his attention was focused entirely on his task. "Let it be known that I still think this plan is foolish."

There were a hundred things Jane could have said to placate him, excuses she could have fabricated to smooth things over, but she was hypnotized by the steady motion of his hands, and the way his knuckles brushed along her collarbone a little too slowly. Desire flooded her. She needed him, craved his touch, was desperate for it. If the truth about her past was about to break the spell between them, she wanted to take what was hers before it shattered.

Instead of speaking, Jane stood on her tiptoes and pulled him to her by his tie, kissing him before she thought better of it. If he was shocked by her boldness, he recovered quickly, one hand capturing her jaw, the other curling around the base of her neck, angling her head back so he could kiss her more deeply. His tongue moved against her lips, teasing them open as a sigh escaped her and she felt the hardness of him against her hip.

Jane didn't think anything had ever felt so good. She was a woman without a past who spent most of her waking hours tormented by questions she could not answer, but when she was kissing Jasper, her mind emptied of every worry and concern, until all that was left was him and her and them together.

With Jasper she felt like a person whole, not a mystery in need of solving.

He moved his attention to her neck and she curled her fingers through his hair, cursing her gloves for keeping her from the softness of it. Her breath was heavy. Her breasts ached for his touch. She was wanton, need made flesh, and she felt no shame.

"Christ, Jane," he whispered against her neck, his voice rough. "At this rate, we'll never make it to Lord Banfield's estate." She felt him smile against her skin.

She pulled back so she could study his face. His eyes were hooded with desire; the hard line of his jaw had softened; there was almost no sternness left in him. She wanted to see him completely unguarded. Free. She wanted to be the one to make him feel that way. Jane almost told him to take her to his chambers, to hell with the ball. The words were on her tongue, begging to be said. She wanted to tear down the only wall left standing between them, to give herself to him and take him in return, forever sealing their fates.

But she forced herself to remember the real purpose of attending the ball. And how nothing could exist between the two of them until she knew the truth.

"I'm sorry," she whispered, not entirely sure what she was apologizing for.

He released her gently and brought a hand to her cheek. "You need never apologize to me," he said. "Unless it is regarding the destruction of a certain pair of boots," he added with a smirk.

Jane feigned innocence. "You'll have to be more specific, my lord. You see, I have amnesia."

He laughed at that, the kind that could not be forced. It was sweet as music to her, to hear him so unburdened. "A convenient excuse," he said, guiding her to the door.

The outside air was cold and crisp and did much to loosen desire's hold on Jane. She had a plan, a way forward. Regardless of what happened at the ball, she hoped she would emerge with answers. But for now, she was on the arm of the Earl of Belhaven, and she would let herself enjoy it while it lasted.

Jasper looked down at her and let his sternness fall back into place. "Let's get this over with, shall we?"

It didn't bother her. She knew the man beneath. "Let's," she agreed, trying very hard not to let fear of the unknown weigh down her steps. He wrapped his arm around her, sheltering her from the cold with his embrace. She felt protected, but how long would it last?

They walked toward the waiting carriage, but a persistent tapping noise broke through the howling of the wind. Jane looked back to see Freddie and Viola at a second-floor window, the latter holding a wiggling Mr. Darcy up to the glass and waving goodbye. It bolstered her meager supply of courage and tugged on Jane's heartstrings both.

She would dearly miss the feeling of belonging at Mulgrave Hall if ever she was forced to leave it.

Chapter Twenty-One

JASPER

Jasper had no words for the effect Jane had upon him.

Mere words were paltry compared to the feeling that had burst in his chest when she'd come into view at the top of the stairs, wearing a gown that seemed to have been made for her, the very air between them warming with each step she descended. It was the flick of a switch. She was incandescent, and he a man disarmed, basking in her light. There were no walls between them, no more masks for him to don. Jasper wanted only to protect her. Shelter her. Love her.

Christ, am I thinking of love? He tried to dismiss it, but once considered, the thought that he might *love* her would not leave him, and the closer they got to each other, the more feverish he became with the desire to tell her, tell everyone, and live the truth of it every day for the rest of his life.

He needed to get a grip on himself. Even if it was true, he

would not shackle her to it. Not when she had expressed so plainly her desire to know herself before she knew anything else. What kind of man would he be if he tried?

Instead he bottled the knowledge up, refusing to let himself feel it lest he get lost in it. Lost in the idea of loving a woman so singularly able to see him for who he truly was, a woman without memories but with convictions enough to make up for it. He could hardly be blamed for finding her compelling.

But Jane had more important things to focus on, and sitting across from her in the carriage, he could tell she was afraid. She didn't say it, but the closer they got to the Banfield estate, the smaller she became, as if by shrinking she might disappear completely. It was very unlike the Jane he had come to know, the one who had parried words with arrogant noblemen and discerning chaperones alike. Hell, she had taken him on as a challenge and won. But leaving the safe embrace of Mulgrave Hall was different.

He knew enough about her to guess that she feared what they might discover about her past at the ball. He wanted to tell her it didn't matter, but he understood that it did to her. Jane needed her autonomy more than his arguments or concern, and so he kept his protests regarding their attendance to himself.

Besides, she was likely right: whoever had been pursuing her through the woods would hardly be expected at the Earl of Banfield's ball.

And so, he forced himself to don a mask of light indifference, as though her past were inconsequential to him. In fact, it could not matter less to him, not after seeing how it might serve to hurt her. He would happily never learn the truth, if it meant protecting her. But if that was what she needed in order to move forward, with or without him, then he would ensure she got it. Despite her nerves and his misgivings, she would be safe. He would make sure of it.

"How is it we have a whole carriage to ourselves?" Jane asked far too brightly, seeking a distraction.

"I suspect we have Isobel to thank," he replied, intentionally not matching her energy.

She looked over at him, a defensive expression on her face. "Are you going to tell me again that my plan is a foolish one?" she asked. He wondered if she wanted him to be the villain once more. If Jane wished to use him as an excuse to avoid the ball altogether, he thought perhaps it was his duty to offer her a way out.

He quirked a brow. "Are you going to be moved by my arguments if I do?"

She pretended to consider it before shaking her head. "No, my mind is quite set."

Jasper had tried. He leaned back, extending his legs toward her. "Then I see no reason to waste what precious time we have alone together."

"What wouldn't be a waste of time, my lord?" she asked in mock innocence, leaning toward him. Even apprehensive as she was about what was to come, it would seem that Jane could not resist an opportunity to tease. How he wanted to kiss that impertinent mouth, taste the sweetness of her that had been haunting him since their stolen moments, have her come apart in his arms over and over again until all she remembered was the pleasure he gave her.

Jasper was rapidly losing his composure. The chill outside their carriage did nothing to quell the heat within it. He wanted to pull her into his lap and kiss the fear from her bones. He wanted to tell her nothing could harm her. He wanted to make her feel safe, truly safe, for the first time since he'd found her bleeding in the road.

But he didn't have that power, and in the end, they arrived at Lord Banfield's estate far too soon. For the first time since agreeing to go, Jasper wondered if he was making a mistake. He had been thinking only of Jane, and he had forgotten that this would be *his* first social event in more than a year. Knowing the aristocracy as he did, he was sure they'd cause a stir. The Earl of Belhaven, out of his seclusion and with a mysterious woman on his arm. It had all the makings of a scandal. Surprisingly, he did not care.

Jane reached for his hand unconsciously as she gazed out the carriage window and the estate came into view.

He rubbed his thumb along her palm. "If you wish to turn back…" he murmured, letting the choice be hers.

"No," she said, mustering her confidence. She looked back at him, her smile weak.

An idea came to him. "Shall we establish a code word?"

She tilted her head. "A code word?"

"Something to say if we need to make a quick escape." If someone were to insult her or make her feel unsafe, no amount of decorum would prevent him from defending her to his fullest ability. He hoped it wouldn't come to that. But they were crossing enemy lines, in a way. Back at Mulgrave Hall, Jane was a secret Jasper could protect. At the Banfield estate, she would be exposed, and all the more so for being on his arm. He wondered if he was being selfish, wanting her there rather than in the safer, more anonymous embrace of his sisters.

She pulled him from his worried thoughts with a suggestion. "Pemberley?"

For a moment, he couldn't recall what they had been talking

about. "Pemberley?"

She squeezed his hand. "For our code word, or is that too esoteric?"

Pemberley. Darcy. She was referring to bloody Jane Austen once more. This woman was, as he had long since accepted, going to be the death of him. He smiled. "No, I think it's just esoteric enough for something only we should understand."

"And I think we should use it more broadly."

The carriage was slowing down. "How do you mean?"

She removed her hand from his and let it fall into her lap. "We should use it in the event that a quick escape is necessary, to be sure. But we should also use it if I recognize something from my past, or remember something important. What if we're in the middle of a tiresome conversation with a viscount and I suddenly remember who I am?"

Jasper wasn't convinced it would be that easy, but there was no harm agreeing with her. "One quick 'Pemberley' and we shall make our excuses to the poor viscount."

A footman opened the carriage door. Light flooded in as Jasper disembarked first in order to help Jane out.

"A code word and a secret mission?" she whispered in his ear as he helped her down to the ground. "Why, what's a little light espionage between friends?" she added with a wink.

He tried not to let the word *friends* crush him. He would be her friend, if that was what she needed. But by God, Jasper wanted so much more with Jane.

"Ready?" he asked, hoping she didn't notice his voice crack.

She looked up at the imposing Banfield estate. He almost expected her to cower from it. But this was Jane without-a-surname. She had faced much worse than a nobleman's estate. Her spine straightened. She adopted a mask of her own, one of quietly assured confidence. He suspected only he would be able to see through it.

"Ready," she confirmed, taking his proffered arm.

They ascended the steps, and Jasper's heart began to race. The last time he had walked through these doors was with his parents. Today he was alone. Sensing his discomfort, Jane squeezed his arm, reminding him that he was wrong. With Jane at his side, he was the furthest thing from alone.

"Will we have to be announced?" Jane whispered as they joined a long line of people. So far, no one paid them any mind. That relative peace would not last, he was sure.

"Not typically," he replied. "I imagine it will be Lord and Lady Banfield greeting guests. Their daughters will likely be milling about within."

They paused at the threshold of the ballroom, waiting for the line before them to clear. Jane gasped quietly at the grandeur that lay mere steps away.

"It's magnificent," she breathed, taking in the golden glow of numerous crystal chandeliers reflected off the gilded walls. Lady Banfield, known for her love of tropical plants, had the ballroom lined with lush, towering palms surrounded by bouquets of jewel-toned flowers. It was decadent, to be sure, but Jasper thought it wasn't fair that Jane had never seen Mulgrave Hall live up to its full potential. Why, he wasn't even sure if she had *seen* their ballroom, and if she had she certainly hadn't seen it the way his mother had intended a guest to enjoy it.

"Just wait until—" he began, but Jane was distracted.

"I wish Lady Viola was here to see this," she said under her breath.

"Viola has seen plenty of decorated ballrooms."

"Not for the decor," she whispered. "But the people. Look

at them, Jasper! Dressed in all their finery, their inhibitions as disguised as their faces, the champagne flowing freely." She paused in breathless wonder. "It is a ripe night for research into human behavior."

"Research?" he asked, lightly perplexed.

"Oh, never you mind," she said, patting his arm. "It's between Lady Viola and I."

Jasper could hardly quantify how much it meant to him that his sister had brought Jane into her confidence, and that Jane seemed to have taken to her with equal warmth. They were kindred spirits, each with a hunger to know things, each seeking knowledge as a means of controlling the uncontrollable. It had been too easy for him to forget that out of all of his remaining siblings, Jasper was the one who had had his parents the longest. Loss was not a competition, but Viola was a child who had lost her mother and father. If it had been hardest on any one of them, he suspected Viola suffered the most, and was perhaps the most overlooked. He thought Viola could learn from Jane, a woman for whom loss was foundational. Perhaps they all could.

But it was not Jane's job to fix the Maycotts. Only they could do that.

All at once, they were at the front of the line. Lord and Lady Banfield awaited them wearing looks of joyful anticipation behind their masks. Jasper resisted the urge to transform into the terse man he had been for a year. His parents had loved the earl and countess, had treated them like family. Their smiles were genuine, their welcome effusive.

Still, he wished to make the introduction quick. "Lord and Lady Banfield, may I introduce Miss Jane Danvers of Buckinghamshire, a dear friend of Helena's from—"

"Cheltenham, yes," Lady Banfield finished for him, her keen

eyes evaluating Jane. She was a handsome woman a slight bit younger than his mother would have been. "Miss Danvers has already caused quite a stir," she added with a knowing smile.

Jane reddened and curtsied before the countess and her husband. "My lord, my lady, I thank you for the honor of your invitation."

"It was our pleasure. We were in need of some new blood around here," Lord Banfield said. He was quite a bit older than Jasper's father had been, and Lady Banfield was his second wife. He often spoke of how he had intended never to marry again, but fate and the future countess had had different plans. Jasper thought him lucky indeed to have had a second chance at love. Banfield's eyes were sharp upon him. "And to have Belhaven and his siblings in attendance is a special treat indeed."

"Indeed," Jasper replied evenly, not wishing to delve further into the subject.

Mercifully, the line wished to keep moving, and Jasper and Jane were swept to the grand marble staircase and into the ballroom.

"That wasn't so bad," Jane mused as they descended.

"They were our easiest test," replied Jasper, unable to keep the cynicism from his voice. But neither he nor Jane could let their guards down.

The room itself was abuzz with more activity than a country ball held out of the Season would usually warrant. It seemed that all of London was in attendance, and even with everyone masked, Jasper felt hundreds of eyes upon them.

"Just breathe," he whispered to Jane, who had stiffened like a corpse when they reached the bottom of the stairs as the orchestra's music swelled around them and they entered the wider room. "You must play at confidence. The key is to fool everyone, but most especially yourself."

Her posture softened. "I'm accustomed to that, at least."

It wasn't long before Isobel and August found them.

"I wasn't expecting half of bloody Mayfair to be in attendance," she said under her breath. She handed something to Jane. "Your dance card," she offered, looking to Jasper at once. "Before you start, it would be terribly ill-mannered for Jane to refuse every man who might ask her. Some might say it would make her stand out all the more." Her eyes narrowed on her brother, anticipating his disapproval. When he said nothing, she continued. "Fetch us some champagnes, will you?"

Jasper looked to Jane, who nodded. He supposed Isobel was as good a protector as he could have hoped for. If anyone attempted to insult Jane, they would find themselves on the receiving end of Isobel's cutting wit. More than a few of Jasper's friends had yet to recover from such an encounter.

"I will assist you," offered August.

"Fine," he replied. "Isobel—"

"Behave, I know," she intoned. "It's as if you expect me to hike up my skirts and dance a jig on a table whilst smoking a cigar. Think better of me, will you?"

"First you must give me a reason to," he replied before departing with August, heading to the north side of the ballroom.

· · ·

"Slow down," begged August. "Some of us are still recovering from the pond."

Jasper grinned, picturing his brother on skates. "Not as steady on your feet as you used to be?"

August only glared. When they made it to the refreshments without anyone stopping them, Jasper was relieved but confused.

Had he made pariahs of the Maycotts in their seclusion? He looked about the room, noting that they did not want for curious gazes. Perhaps no one quite knew how to navigate the vast ocean of grief he and his siblings had learned to tread through.

August downed an entire flute of champagne and wiped his mouth on his glove. "How is she?"

Jasper paused, not meeting his brother's eye. "We've been here all of ten minutes."

"And no disaster yet. Must be a good sign," said August. "I half expected an aged viscount to materialize the moment you entered the ballroom, eager to take possession of his wayward daughter."

"I hardly think Jane's background is as salacious as that."

"A mercurial baron?" he suggested. When Jasper merely frowned, he stepped closer. "Do you not think her noble any longer?"

Jasper looked around the table, but none were close enough to hear them. "Seems difficult to imagine that we wouldn't have heard of a baron's missing daughter, no?"

"Ah, but you forget that a woman's reputation matters more than her safety, Brother. If Jane's family wishes to protect her virtue, they might not advertise that she is missing."

"And so, what, they're simply hoping she turns up on her own? She could be in danger or languishing in an infirmary for all they know."

August shrugged. "I imagine they'd have a couple of discreet detectives on the case, but would otherwise be pretending Jane was visiting an aunt in Bath or a distant cousin in the Highlands. You said she had a ring, didn't you? Perhaps they are attempting to salvage a precariously balanced engagement."

Jasper's vision darkened at the thought. He looked back

toward where they had left Jane and Isobel, his gaze finding her directly. The Banfield ballroom was not lacking in beautiful women, but none could hold a candle to his Jane.

His.

There she stood, nodding along to whatever Lady Lydia Coventry was emphatically explaining to her, looking not out of place but rather like she belonged there.

It was then that he realized that Jane belonged everywhere. She belonged in the middle of a roaring tempest. In a sun-warmed corner of the library. At the head of a table, commanding attention. Alone in the wilderness, forging her own path. With him in Mulgrave Hall, should she wish it. She belonged wherever she went, because she was *Jane*. Grief had not shrunk her heart; loss had not shaped her into something unrecognizable. Jasper was certain that the woman she had been—before her memories were taken from her—was the same woman he knew now. Her spirit was indelible, and it mattered little to him that he did not know her real name or who her father might have been.

He admired Jane for her convictions, and so the relief he felt when he became achingly aware of his own should not surprise him. Jasper was a man who had spent a year shrouding himself in ignorance, afraid to know the depths of his own pain. His sorrow. He had numbed himself to the possibilities that lay ahead of him, but Jane had forced him to know himself. There was a strength in that awareness, a defense that even uncertainty could not shatter. Jasper did not know what would happen next; all he knew was this: he belonged to her.

They were not two planets on converging paths, as he had thought before.

No, Jane was the sun, and Jasper was caught in her orbit, and if he could, he would gladly stay there forever.

Chapter Twenty-Two

JASPER

August followed Jasper's gaze all the way to where Jane stood across the ballroom, her smile shining as bright as a beacon.

"You love her, don't you?" August asked without preamble.

The question should have terrified him. Fear had been his constant companion of late. But loving Jane didn't frighten him; only the thought of losing her did.

"We should get back to them," was all he said. August seemed to hear the answer in his evasion.

"I suppose we should." His brother's gaze was knowing. Shrewd, even. "But I worry for you, Brother. The fates have not been kind to our family as of late."

Jasper grasped two flutes of champagne and let out a small, mirthless laugh. "Now August, you strike me as a man who believes in making his own destiny."

August's expression darkened. "Much about me has changed."

If his tone had not managed to dissuade Jasper from further prying, his abrupt departure would have. August was halfway across the ballroom before Jasper caught up to him. There were a great many things he wanted to ask his brother, but he decided that the Earl of Banfield's ballroom was not the place to do so. When they approached the ladies, it was clear Lady Lydia was in the middle of speaking.

"—which is why we must campaign for more support, push for more aggressive private member's bills..." She abruptly stopped when she realized the women were no longer alone.

"My lady, do not cease pontificating on our account," said August with something of a smirk on his face as he handed a flute to Isobel.

Lady Lydia, a pretty, if severe woman they had grown up with, grimaced and turned toward him. "August Maycott," she said acidly. "I'm surprised to see you so very far from Covent Garden. Have you run through *all* of London's eligible ladies? Do not despair," she added with mock concern. "I'm certain there's a lady or two present whose reputation has yet to be tarnished by association with the likes of you."

Isobel choked on her champagne, while Jane froze, mesmerized by the exchange, her flute held awkwardly midair. Jasper rather thought his brother deserved it.

August chewed his bottom lip, the expression dripping with contempt. "My tastes run a tad bit more cosmopolitan these days, *Lydia*."

"I'm sure they do," she replied scathingly before turning back to Isobel. "I must be off. Think about what I said?"

"Of course," Isobel replied, delighting in the repartee between Lydia and August.

Lydia turned to Jane. "It was lovely to meet you, Miss

Danvers. I do hope your overall impression of the gentlemen of Surrey is not sullied by the likes of Mr. August Maycott."

The air positively crackled. Whatever there was between Lydia and August was more than mere dislike, which led Jasper to believe that she was yet another victim of his brother's coldheartedness.

"I shall wait before I make any official judgment," Jane offered diplomatically. Lydia smiled at them, glared at August, and was off.

"Something you wish to confess?" Jasper asked.

"Nothing you need concern yourself with," August replied through gritted teeth.

"If you're striking up dalliances this close to home—"

"I need a drink," August replied, his glass nowhere near empty, before turning on his heel and leaving as Edgar arrived.

"I just saw Lady Lydia Coventry storming off. I assume that's related?" he asked, pointing over his shoulder to August's retreating form.

Isobel laughed. "Perceptive of you."

Jasper looked between Isobel and Edgar, feeling like he was missing a piece of vital information. "Is there something I need to know about? A reputation in need of saving, perhaps?"

"Nothing as dramatic as that," began Isobel. "I suspect August has met his match, even if he doesn't know it quite yet."

Deciding he had more important things to worry about at the present, Jasper dropped the subject.

"Where is Lady Louisa?" Isobel asked Edgar. "Hiding from her suitors already? Does she have a particularly good spot? I'd love to join her."

Edgar gave her a sad smile. "Lady Adelaide has made me her messenger, I'm afraid. She requests your presence at her table.

There are some gentlemen she wishes you to meet."

"She's matchmaking this early in the night?" Isobel blanched. She turned to Jasper. "Permission to flee before I am subjected to such horrors?"

Jasper swallowed a laugh. "You don't need my permission, Izzie. But do consider if the consequences will be worth it. At least if you go to her now, you give the appearance of compliance."

"Perhaps you're right," she offered grimly before departing, looking as though she were walking to her own execution.

"I don't envy the gentlemen your aunt will offer her up to," said Edgar, watching her go. He turned back to Jasper and Jane. "Miss Danvers, will you favor me with the next dance?"

Jane looked startled, as though she hadn't considered it a possibility. She seemed at a loss for words, until Jasper nudged her.

"Pemberley?" he whispered.

She smiled and shook her head, turning back to Edgar. "With pleasure, my lord. Though I must warn you, it has been some time since I last danced."

"I pity the gentlemen of Buckinghamshire," he said with a smile. "I'm an excellent partner, I assure you." The orchestra started up again, a quadrille this time, and Edgar offered his hand. They left, Jane shooting a tentative smile over her shoulder, and Jasper melted away, leaning against a wall where he could watch to make sure she was all right.

He would have gladly spent the whole night dedicated to that task, but Lord and Lady Banfield's other guests had different plans. The distance they had maintained from him earlier in the night vanished now that he stood alone at the edge of the ballroom. At first, only the boldest mothers approached him, daughters in tow, seeking an introduction. He was only as polite as he needed to be, and when he did not proceed to ask any of them to dance, they largely left in a huff. He preferred them to their nosy husbands, who were not so easily rebuffed by his stern mask, asking after his tenants, his investments, his bloody horses, all inane subjects they wielded as weapons to pierce his defenses. It wasn't long before they began asking after Jane, circling around the mere idea of her like predators.

Miss Jane Danvers, Helena's friend from Cheltenham.

Jasper trotted out the same lie they had been telling everyone, but Jane's common status did not seem to deter the men. Only her status as a soon-to-be-married woman was enough to remove her as a prospect.

She's all but betrothed.

If there was anything a so-called gentleman understood, it was the matter of another man's property. Jasper bit his tongue to prevent himself from rebuking them fiercely. He wasn't going to change anyone's mind on the matter of a woman's autonomy. Not in a ballroom, at least. Instead, he did his best to communicate without words that he wished to be left alone. He was being terribly rude, but he thought the Maycotts should continue to be afforded a modicum of grace in that regard, at least for a little while longer.

Mercifully, no one mentioned his parents or Anthony. Everyone in attendance seemed to have been warned against such somber conversation. He suspected Lady Banfield had gotten the word out to a few of the likeliest offenders, who then spread it like wildfire. He still saw it in their lingering glances, their masks doing nothing to hide their pity. He thought he recognized several of them, people from his old life, people who didn't know the version of him that had loved Annabelle, let alone this version of him that loved Jane. The Jasper they knew was a stranger to him now. Perhaps they sensed that, and that was why, after some valiant but ultimately unsuccessful attempts, they kept their distance from him.

Meanwhile, his friends each took their turns dancing with Jane and Lady Louisa and Helena. Lucian was an adept partner, George less so, but they were all of them enjoying themselves. It did not distress Jasper to be left out. He had a task to perform, a duty to Jane that he must see through. He scanned the crowd for people who might recognize her, but so far he only watched as others became intrigued by her, taking note of those who were drawn to her, as he had been. How could he blame them? There was an unconsciousness to Jane's actions. She moved without hesitation, laughed freely, burned brightly. Jasper thought it was likely evidence that she had not been raised to make a debut in Society. Aristocratic ladies, through no fault of their own, had been molded from birth to be a gentleman's perfect bride. Pure, chaste, refined, and modest. It didn't leave much room for anything resembling Jane's gaiety, and he thought that if her instinct was to be so very different, it must mean something. As the night progressed and no one recognized her, he thought that was evidence of something, too.

Eventually, Helena found her way to his side, flushed from dancing with Clarence, who, as an actor, was known for his theatrics.

"Feeling dizzy?" he asked, recalling that Clarence had practically tipped her upside down in a swooping dip that nearly took out the aged Viscount Lumley. "Are you in pain, Helena?"

She ignored the question. "Your failure to ask any young ladies to dance has been noticed and remarked upon." She nudged him slightly with her shoulder. "You're lucky Lady Banfield adores you so, or she would have done something about it by now. It is her good word alone that keeps you from utter social ruin."

Jasper didn't look away from where Jane was dancing a lively polka with the Duke of Hereford. "I'm not here to dance."

"Surely not," she scoffed. "It's almost as if this were a *ball*."

He glared at her. "I'm here for Jane."

Helena held his gaze and then looked out to where Jane and the duke were putting on a rather spirited display. "It doesn't bother you to see Miss Danvers so occupied? I don't think I've seen her sit out a single dance."

He rolled his shoulders. "Why would that bother me?"

"Please, Brother. Do not be obtuse, at least not among family."

He paused, watching Jane lose herself in the dance. She looked so unburdened. Joyful. It was a delight to see her that way. "I suppose if anything, it brings me comfort."

"Comfort?"

He looked to his sister. "It's proof that Jane can be happy, even without her memories."

Helena was silent for a moment. "Proof she could be happy with you?"

"With or without me," he replied, and he meant it. "I have no claim on her future. I am merely relieved to see her so..."

"Unburdened?"

"Unburdened, yes." Jasper bristled at his sister's perceptive silence and sought a new topic to distract her from the truth. "Has Aunt Adelaide chained Isobel to the nearest gentleman in hopes of a betrothal?"

Helena grinned. "Last I checked, Isobel had managed to find her way into the card room, unbeknownst to our dear chaperone. Clarence told me she is currently fleecing Lord Trevayne in a game of écarté. August is brooding somewhere, but I've got Edgar keeping him out of trouble at least."

Jasper nodded, satisfied that the Maycotts had avoided disaster as of yet. "And you? Your dance card isn't full?"

She glanced down at the empty spaces and sighed. "Widowhood has its privileges, I suppose."

Before Jasper could say anything, Jane, Lady Louisa, Clarence, and Lucian descended upon them in a rush.

"I've worn right through my slippers," said Lady Louisa, rather breathlessly. "Join me in the retiring room, Helena?"

Helena gave Jasper a rather meaningful look as the ladies left. All at once, Clarence and Lucian began a lively discussion about Clarence's rivalry with fellow actor Henry Irving.

"I heard the Lyceum is reopening under his management," said Lucian.

"Yes, well, perhaps I should not have been so hasty in my shunning of the man." Thinking better of it, he continued. "He's a second-rate actor at best, but a cunning businessman, I'll give him that. Did you know he weaseled his way into Bram Stoker's confidence? The snake. Befriending a critic! The utter shamelessness of it!"

"Pemberley," Jane whispered in Jasper's ear when no one was looking.

"What is it?" he asked, barely controlling himself. Had she remembered something? Spotted someone?

She gave him a slow smile, her hand squeezing his discreetly as she pulled him back from his panic. "I simply need a moment's respite." She took a champagne from a passing tray. "Shall we take a turn about the room?"

He offered her his arm, noting the eyes that narrowed upon them when she took it. *Let them look.* The stares would be worth it if this venture ended up being what she needed to do in order to finally understand her place in the world. Jasper wanted to give her the belonging she sought. The peace she deserved. He wanted her to feel safe, to know she could have a new life, if she wanted. A home of her own, at Mulgrave Hall or otherwise. He'd build one for her with his bare hands should she desire it, as close to or as far from him as she wished.

But beneath his noble desires to see Jane safe and well situated lay Jasper's most vulnerable truth: *he* wanted to be her home, and he suspected she wanted the same.

But he could not force her into that realization. Jane had to come to it on her own. Had to want it as badly as he did. Time was on their side. He would wait for her forever, if necessary.

They walked in silence, both of them all too aware of the eyes that followed them around the room. Seeking a distraction, Jasper leaned in toward Jane's ear.

"How goes your secret mission?" he whispered.

Her face fell. "I rather forgot what I was here for. I've been so caught up in dancing and such that it hasn't occurred to me to look for people I might remember. Though I suppose anyone would make themselves known to me if they recognized me." She paused, perhaps realizing the fruitlessness of her mission. "Or that is what I hope for, at least. Obviously, I am still a mystery. Perhaps I always will be."

It cleaved Jasper's heart in two to see her so crestfallen. "Jane, it doesn't mean—"

"But it does, doesn't it? The great mystery of my life will go unsolved. I will never know where I came from, where I belong. I suppose I've known it all along, but denied the truth to myself." Her brow furrowed. "You suspected me from the start. In a way, you've been the most truthful, the most realistic. You should be commended for indulging me tonight."

Jasper shook his head, unwilling to allow Jane to abandon her pursuit of the truth entirely. "You've made improvements since waking, Jane. You must have patience. There is no hurry."

"I know that. You and your family have been uncommonly kind to a woman who cannot ever hope to repay it."

They passed a long row of palms, stares, and the whispers still following in their wake. If it had been summer, Jasper could have taken her out to the gardens for privacy, scandal be damned. They unconsciously paused before a window, watching as moonlight sparkled on the layer of snow that blanketed the balcony.

"My mother used to say that kindness is not a currency, nor is it scarce. You have not overburdened us, Jane. I rather hope it is in our nature to help others. Or, failing that, you have served as a welcome reminder of what we should strive for."

She smiled at that. "I do so wish I…" But she swallowed what she desired to say, choosing silence instead.

"What?" he asked, desperate to know.

She waved her hand. "It's silly, given everything your family has been through, but I wish I had gotten a chance to meet your parents and your brother." She watched him, waiting for a reaction. When he said nothing, she continued. "In a way, knowing them would have meant knowing you better."

Jasper hadn't believed he'd have something in his life that he wished to share with his mother and father and Anthony again. In fact, after he'd lost them, all effort had been made to not feel anything, lest he be reminded of their absence. But now he wished for them to know Jane, and for Jane to know them. There was an ache when he thought of how his mother would have loved her heart, and his father her sharp wit. Anthony would have relished her unique ability to put Jasper in his place. They would have also loved her for the same reason they had loved Annabelle—she pushed Jasper to become a man worthy of her.

He swallowed thickly. "I would have been a different person if they had survived."

If illness had not touched Wrayford, he would have married Annabelle, and he would've never known Jane. His mind could not reconcile it because it was impossible to desire something that had torn his life apart so ruthlessly, so viciously. The Jasper of before would never have chosen it, even knowing what he did now, knowing Jane as he did now. Of course, he'd choose to have his family still, to have Annabelle still, if the fates had offered it. But he could not regret the broken path that had brought him and Jane together. The alternative—a life spent alone, a husk of his former self, eager to push everyone he loved away before he lost them—was too grim to consider.

She saw the conflict in him, read it as clearly as one did words on a page.

"Much like kindness, I rather think love is not scarce, Jasper." Was that an admission? Or was Jane being philosophical once more, like she had been in the portrait gallery when she had done her damnedest to convince him that true love was real?

He knew that now. Much could change over the course of a few days.

"No, it is not," he said, less a concession and more a hopeful prompt.

But she began to walk again, and he followed, as he always would.

Jane leaned her head toward his. "I have a new mission for us," she whispered.

Jasper's heart thumped in his chest. "Oh?" Did she feel his

pulse racing beneath her hand? How he tensed at her words?

She didn't look his way, instead keeping her gaze outward. "I wish to dance."

"I'm not sure a person could dance more than you have," he offered.

"No, Jasper. I wish to dance with you."

He almost stopped walking. It was one thing to promenade through the room, arm in arm, inviting gossip and whispers. Jasper could manage that. But dancing? The very idea of it would court scandal. He couldn't imagine Aunt Adelaide approving, and they'd have more than mere whispers to be concerned about. He almost refused her, but then a depressing thought came to him: *What if this is my only chance to dance with Jane?* He could not say why, but this night felt like it was perched on a precipice. It was a night that made him feel as though everything could change, and perhaps not for the better. If he had a chance to tell Jane and the whole world—without words—that he loved her, and he squandered it for fear of what other people thought? His parents would be ashamed of him.

"Miss Danvers," he started, but the name felt wrong on his tongue. "Jane," he corrected, his head tilted, his voice low. "My dear Jane," he whispered, letting his breath tickle her cheek. "Would you honor me with a dance?"

"Why yes, my lord," she said, adopting a falsely formal tone that sent heat through the core of him. The woman could bend him to her will with naught but a few words and that beguiling smile. "The honor is all mine," she added, bowing her head prettily. "Shall we?"

They took their positions, the floor far too busy with couples for anyone to pay them much mind at first. It wasn't the dancers that worried Jasper, but rather his discerning aunt and others of her kind. He had spent the night declining unspoken requests that he dance with any number of eligible ladies, and due to his grief, the latitude he had been given in that regard likely vanished as soon as he took his position across from Jane. Even her false identity wouldn't shield her from scrutiny, because what was an earl doing dancing with a commoner? It wasn't as if the Maycotts were claiming Jane was an heiress, which could explain the pairing. From the outside looking in, it seemed the Earl of Belhaven was utterly smitten with a mysterious and penniless woman, which made them the talk of the ball. Before he'd lost his parents and Anthony, Mr. Jasper Maycott likely could have married a commoner without causing much of a stir. But he was the earl now, and like it or not, his association with Jane was scandalous.

The orchestra began a familiar waltz, the introductory notes soft and soothing as Jasper and Jane bowed before each other, and ascended into something forceful and bright when they came together.

Jane smiled up at him. "'*Geschichten aus dem Wienerwald*,'" she said, surprising herself. "'Tales from the Vienna Woods,'" she added, almost unconsciously.

Jasper smiled. "It would seem Strauss is as foundational to you as our friend Jane Austen."

She shook her head as they began to turn about the room. "I couldn't identify Schubert before, much to Lady Adelaide's dismay, yet here I am recalling Strauss in the original German."

Jasper tilted his head closer to hers. "Perhaps your mind has improved since."

"Perhaps," she echoed softly, her hand growing tighter on his shoulder.

He spun her outward and she returned gracefully.

"You don't seem to have much trouble with the steps, either." There was a charming confidence to her movements. Jasper had thought he would be leading her, but Jane was more than capable.

"That comes as less of a surprise, given that I spent nearly an hour proving myself an adept dancer with your aunt." Her expression was caught somewhere between a grimace and a smile at the memory. "It was a point of pride of mine that while I was hopelessly bad with a needle or at playing the pianoforte, I could hold my own in a waltz."

"Which of you led?"

Jane looked up, her grin sardonic. "Who do you think?"

When the solo violin began and the tempo changed, they had to focus on the steps lest they lose their footing. He hoped dancing was the distraction Jane needed. His mind was a flurry of thoughts, but he forced himself to appreciate having Jane in his arms. He had held her before, but this felt different. Perhaps it was that they were on display, and that even with their faces masked, he felt exposed. Perhaps it was the way he felt the warmth of her through their gloves, emanating like the glow of an ember. It was the undeniable luminosity of Jane—his sun.

It was all of that and more. It was the first time he'd held Jane without denying himself the truth of what he felt for her. She would know the extent of his feelings one day, he swore. But he would not crowd her mind with it yet. It was enough to simply hold her, studying the lock of hair that curled at the nape of her neck, wishing he could press his lips to the warmth of her skin as they turned together, carving their own arc across the ballroom.

Jane tucked her head as close to his as she could without collapsing into him. Something was wrong.

"What is it?"

"I fear I'll never know who I am, Jasper."

The ballroom seemed to fade around him, until all Jasper was aware of was Jane—her hand in his, the curve of her waist, the depths of her fears, the desperation he felt to make her feel safe. *Be* safe.

"I do not care who you were or what you may have done before, Jane. I care about who you are now—the person who brought light and life back into Mulgrave Hall. The person who reminded me what it is to live in this world." He cradled her cheek for the briefest moment, unable to keep from touching her even in the middle of the ballroom. She followed the ghost of a touch, tilting her head as if to find it again. "I know exactly who you are, Jane. I have known it since we first spoke, but I know that isn't enough for you. If you wish to enlist a detective in order to find the people from your past, I will help you. If you'd like me to publish a letter in *The Times* seeking information, I'll start composing one tonight. Christ, I'll plaster your face on every signpost in London, if it will bring you peace. But your past does not matter to me, Jane."

She did stop dancing then. They were still as statues in the middle of the room, the waltzing couples continuing around them. Time froze, trickled by them like the slow melt of early spring. Jane was breathing heavily; the gaze behind her mask was direct.

"Do you mean that?"

He took her hands. "You must know that I do."

"Why? Why would you do all of that?"

The words were there. They had come easily. Without thought or effort.

Because I love you.

But his wretched guilt reminded him that he should not shackle her to a future that wasn't meant to be, or tell her the truth of his heart before she was ready to hear it.

He took the coward's route for what he hoped would be the last time. "Because it is the right thing to do."

Did her shoulder slump? Had she been wishing for more? They unconsciously came together and began dancing once more.

"Thank you," she said, her voice small. "It helps to know I can count on your friendship."

There was hurt layered in her voice, and Jasper realized he could not wait for the perfect time to tell her how he felt. He couldn't be sure that what he was doing was right; he could only be true to himself and honest with her. Whatever happened would happen, but at least the unspoken words would not choke him. At least he would know he had said and done all he could.

He loved her. Not for her past, not for her future, but for who she was now.

Stay, he thought, or did he shout it? *Stay and make a new life at Mulgrave Hall with me. Stay and be my wife.*

"Jane," he whispered; the ache of her name was sweet to him. "My Jane..."

She looked up at him with tears welling in her eyes and all at once, doubt left him. There was his future. The woman he loved. He knew it in his bones. They were meant for each other. He simply had to say the words. They were on the tip of his tongue, the confirmation that had blossomed in his heart. He knew she felt it, too. Nothing had ever felt so certain to him.

"Don't cry," he began as he twirled her away from him. The arm that held her was a steady anchor, ready to pull her back in so he could whisper that truth to her.

I love you, my dear Jane.

But before he could speak, a figure froze in his periphery, too still to be ignored.

Reluctantly, Jasper tore his eyes away from Jane to see a man staring at them both, looking like he had seen a ghost.

"Hetty?" he choked as the dance brought Jane back to Jasper.

Time had passed slowly before, but now it came upon them in a rush, disorienting them, tearing them from the path they had been carving mere moments before. The noise of the ballroom was all at once unbearable as the man took a step closer.

"Hetty, is it really you?"

And Jasper realized everything changed when Jane went rigid in his arms, her heartbeat hammering against his chest. Their eyes met, and there was something unfamiliar there, something that told Jasper a new, unsettling truth.

He might still be hers, but she wasn't his any longer.

Chapter Twenty-Three

HETTY

The name was a tether.

It rooted Jane to the earth more than anything else since she'd awoken without her memories. Rooted *Hetty* to the earth. For that was who she was.

Hetty. She could hear her father's voice. *Hetty, my darling, my treasure.*

She looked to the man who knew her, expecting his face to have the same effect upon her that her name had. But she felt nothing. He might as well have been a stranger. She noted he was uncommonly tall, perhaps only a couple of years older than her, with dark brown hair and pale skin and a bit of a weak chin. But other than what she could see before her, he was a mystery.

"Hetty? My God, we thought you were dead!" he cried, looking at her like she was a ghost. She had certainly felt like a phantom with the Maycotts, haunting a life that wasn't meant to be hers. But this man knew her. Knew who she used to be. *He* could bring her back to life.

Her name had locked into place the moment he uttered it. An essential, undeniable truth. Why didn't she know him as well as she knew her name?

Jasper had not yet relinquished his hold on her. Strauss's composition built around them; the dancers continued. It was like no one else knew of the seismic shift that had occurred, to say nothing of the one that had preceded it.

Jasper had been ready to tell her he loved her. She knew it in her bones, just as she knew that hearing the words would seal her fate. But it hadn't brought her joy nor peace. If anything, Jane felt as though she had tricked them both into believing a future together was possible. All night, a new conviction had been building in her, one that whispered that she was unknowable, unlovable. How could she be the Earl of Belhaven's wife? How could they lie to everyone they met, claiming she was Miss Jane Danvers, then the Lady Belhaven, and expect their fantasy not to shatter? How long before someone discovered the truth? How long before they hurt Jasper's family with it?

So Jane had decided the dance would be their last. It was a way of saying goodbye. She didn't know what came next, but she would spare Jasper the pain of associating with her. Her past was a powder keg. She could not be so selfish as to pretend otherwise. But as they'd danced, Jane had let herself imagine a different future for them, one in which her past was not an obstacle. It was all the indulgence she would allow, a lifetime confined to one waltz. It would have to be enough.

It would never be enough.

Jasper didn't lead, but rather allowed her to contribute to the movement. It was better than she could have hoped, to be held by him, his arms steady, his spine straight, his smile only for her. Half the women in the room had fallen in love with the Earl of Belhaven, but only she really knew Jasper Maycott. There was little victory in having uncovered him so thoroughly. Ultimately, she would be leaving him and he would suffer for it.

Though thinking of him with another was like a knife straight to her heart, Jane had silently prayed that Jasper would move on from her betrayal. That he would not don his mask again. He deserved a wife to be proud of, not one who would require an intricate web of secrets. And while the Maycotts would have been enough for her, Jane would never have been enough for them. There was no future for her there, only pain.

Jane, my Jane...

The way his voice had scraped over her, so close to being everything she wanted, yet so far from the truth. She was not Jane. Would never be his Jane.

But then she heard her name. Her real name. It slipped over her like a well-worn cloak and filled the empty parts of her like a flood of warmth.

She was not Jane, but she *was* Hetty.

And what had seemed impossible only seconds before became possible. If she knew her name, the rest would follow. If she knew her name, she could perhaps let Jasper love her.

But her mind was quickly overwhelmed by competing thoughts, and the ballroom was suddenly stifling and shrinking.

The man was looking at her expectantly, waiting for the obvious response.

"I'm sorry, I was in an accident..." she trailed off, not sure how to explain her injury in the middle of the ballroom while her legs buckled beneath her and shock numbed her senses.

"Jane, not here," said Jasper in her ear.

The man looked between them, perplexed. "*Jane*?"

Jasper lowered her hand but did not let go of it. The constant pressure of his palm gave her strength as the world seemed to swirl around her.

"Let's find somewhere to speak more privately, shall we?" asked Jasper.

The man nodded, slightly bewildered, and followed them to a curtained alcove. It was the best they could hope for, given the circumstances. Hetty shrank away from the sharp eyes that followed them. If she had managed to avoid being a complete scandal before, she would not be so lucky now.

The alcove was shockingly silent; the noise of the ball was muffled there, but the pounding of Hetty's heart filled the quiet.

The man turned to face her. "I don't understand—"

"Who are you?" she asked, not able to stop herself from interrupting him.

He pressed his lips together. "Who am I? Hetty, this is ridiculous—"

"I fell from my horse," she blurted out. "I fell and injured my head and lost my memories. I awoke not knowing who I was or where I came from. Jasper—the Earl of Belhaven and his family have been caring for me as I recovered."

The man did not speak for several seconds, studying the contours of Hetty's face, looking for a jest or a lie. Eventually, he seemed to accept what she had explained to him. "You're quite serious, aren't you? You truly do not recognize me?"

She shook her head. "I am terribly sorry, but I didn't even know my own name until you said it."

He brought his hands to the ties of his mask, removing it. "I am your cousin, the baron, Lord Claremont." He offered her a small bow. "You are Henrietta Davenport. We've been at

Sutton House since your father died some three months ago." He grimaced, seeming to remember that this was new information to Hetty.

For her part, the news of her father's death abraded Hetty anew, even though she had suspected it. "How did he die?" she managed to choke out.

Claremont loosened his collar. "Apoplexy. I'm told it was quick."

As if that mattered. "And my mother?" she ventured, knowing the answer before he said it, but needing to ask it all the same.

He gave her a queer, if pitying look. "Your mother died nearly fifteen years ago, I'm afraid," he replied, his voice softer than before. "Scarlet fever when you were just a child."

She felt Jasper stiffen behind her, but he still offered her his silent support, keeping her upright when all she wanted was to collapse. "So I am alone," she concluded.

Claremont shook his head. "Not alone, Hetty. You have my mother and me, and we have been so distressed at your disappearance. You cannot begin to imagine the extent of our worry."

Something prickled in her mind, a question that needed answering. "Why was I out on horseback alone?"

He straightened, looking out toward the ballroom before replying. "That I cannot answer. I suspect only you can."

Hetty deflated, having hoped to learn the truth from her cousin. So far she was only left with more questions. Another one rose to the surface. "If you're a baron, what does that make me?"

"Well, nothing. Your mother married a commoner. My father, your mother's brother, inherited the title when our grandfather passed, but he only lasted a few years before passing himself. So my mother and I are all you have, in terms of family."

He said it almost apologetically, but beneath the shock of it, Hetty could hardly believe she had any family left at all. After thinking of herself as unmoored from her past, the idea of an aunt and a cousin was almost too good to be true.

"You really don't remember a thing, do you?" he asked again, studying her face with earnest curiosity.

"No," she replied with a sad smile. "I thought seeing someone from my past would break the dam in my mind that has kept my memories from me, but I am frustratingly unable to recall much else."

Claremont frowned. "I wish I could help you, Hetty."

"Oh, but you have!" she exclaimed, not wishing for him to feel any guilt about her current predicament. "I rather thought myself alone in the world, without a past or a future. You have given me both, even if I will have to work at it. I cannot thank you enough."

Claremont's cheeks reddened. "Hetty, you must return with me tonight. Mother will never believe me unless you do, and she has been suffering so much in your absence."

Hetty didn't need her memories in order to imagine that her aunt was in pain. Her only solace was that she could alleviate it. But it meant leaving Mulgrave Hall, and the Maycotts, behind.

Worst of all, it meant leaving Jasper. But hadn't she been planning to leave him forever only moments before? At least now she could fathom coming back to him.

The Earl of Belhaven tugged on her wrist. "Jane—Hetty," he corrected, speaking her real name for the first time. He said it almost hesitantly, as if he didn't quite believe it to be true. "Hetty, do you trust this man?"

Claremont scoffed. "Why wouldn't she trust me? I'm her family."

"All due respect, Claremont, but it was *my* family that took care of Hetty after her accident. Would you begrudge me for ensuring her continued safety?"

Claremont straightened, evidently affronted. "Why, of course not. And my family will undoubtedly wish to repay your kindness in due course—"

"No repayment will be necessary." The response was firm. In a matter of moments, Jasper had donned the mask of the stern bastard once more.

"How magnanimous of you," Claremont replied, his tone verging on sarcastic. "Hetty, I do not wish to upset you, but if I return to Sutton House with only my good word as assurance to my mother that you are safe, she will never forgive me. Hell, I wouldn't be surprised if she never recovered from the shock of it."

Jasper huffed, but he did not make a similar plea. Hetty knew his concerns. She could read him like a book. Jasper wanted her to be cautious, but Hetty was willing to rush headlong into a storm if it meant getting some answers. There was very little she wouldn't do in order to learn the truth. How could he expect her to turn her back on her past, now that it was in her grasp?

The answers she sought would not be found in Mulgrave Hall, but rather in Sutton House, the home she did not remember. Claremont would take her there. Walking the corridors she grew up in, sleeping in the bed that had always been hers, reading her father's letters... Surely, she would remember everything then.

And when she did, she could come back to Jasper, free of the suspicion that her unknown past could ever harm his family. It was better than she had hoped for. Hetty hadn't dared imagine a future in which she had Jasper and her memories both. It had seemed incompatible. She had always thought having one meant giving up the other, or living a life with neither.

But now her past had met her present, and it seemed she wouldn't have to choose.

Excitement built within her. "I'll return with you, Cousin."

Claremont grinned, but Jasper stepped between them.

"Could you give us a moment?" he asked, his tone allowing no room for argument.

Hetty nodded at her cousin, who seemed very reluctant to leave. It was sweet, she thought, how easily he had slipped back into his role as her protector. With her father gone, Claremont had likely stepped up in that regard.

"I will be just outside the curtain," he said with a shallow bow.

It didn't take long for Jasper to turn to her, his expression incredulous. "How can you trust this—this *stranger*?"

"He is my cousin, Jasper. He is practically all the family I have left in the world."

"But you do not know him, not like you know your name." So he had sensed the shift in her the first time Claremont spoke her name aloud.

"No, but how could he know me so well and be a stranger? I am safe with him; I am certain of this."

"How?" he asked, his tone verging on desperate. "How can you be certain? Do not forget that you were running from someone when I found you."

She risked reaching for his hand, needing to feel connected to him. "He knows me, Jasper. That is plain to see. How can I distrust someone who knows me better than I know myself? And besides, he could be asking me the same question about you."

He stepped back as though she had struck him. "I would *never* harm you—"

She squeezed his hand. "I know that better than I know anything. But from his perspective, you don't know me at all." She tried not to say it cruelly, but at the same time she knew it was the truth. The story of Jasper and Jane had spanned less than a week thus far. She wished for the story of Jasper and Hetty to last much longer, but she couldn't do that unless she knew herself. Claremont was the key.

Jasper frowned. "I feel as though I know you better than I've ever known anyone else."

She felt that, too; the connection between them was stronger than words. She needed him to understand it wouldn't fade if she went with her cousin. He might not grasp her motives now, but he would when she came back to him, her position one of strength. Wouldn't professing her love for him mean more to Jasper then? Instead of being uttered from a place of desperation in an unfamiliar ballroom?

"Jasper, I must do this. I cannot ask my family to suffer even a moment longer." She paused, searching him for the arguments she knew would follow. "Nor can I spend even one more night not knowing who I am and continue to put your family at risk by associating with me." He opened his mouth but she held a finger to his lips. "I need you to trust me."

He sighed against her finger, capturing her hand and bringing her palm to his lips. He pressed a kiss to the center of it, one she felt over every inch of her body.

"It's not *you* I don't trust, Hetty." This time, he said her name like he was certain of it. "Henrietta," he said, pulling her into an embrace. Hetty allowed herself to sink into him, to feel the hard lines of him against her, to feel safe in his arms one more time.

"If this is what you need, who am I to argue?"

"I'll be back before you know it," she whispered against his chest.

He pulled back and brought his hands to her cheeks, cupping her face like she was something precious. "You will always have a place at Mulgrave Hall. And that is not a conditional offer. Day or night, in the middle of a storm or not, if you need me, I will come for you and I will bring you home."

Home. Mulgrave Hall had begun to feel like it. Would Sutton House be as welcoming? Or would the absence of her father haunt the halls as well as any ghost? The only way to find out was by going to it and comparing it to the warmth she was leaving behind.

"You'll tell your sisters? Viola especially will think of it as a betrayal—"

"She will understand. No one will fault you for seeking out your family."

She looked up at him, almost overcome by the need to kiss him until her lips had memorized the contours of his face, and her hands his body. She wanted him to make an imprint on her very soul, so the memory of him became as ineradicable as knowing how to breathe, to blink, to smile. That was the thing about not remembering her past—Hetty feared it would happen again, and she couldn't bear the thought of forgetting Jasper Maycott.

"Jasper—" she began, her voice cracking.

But he seemed to understand her without words. "Go, Hetty," he said, lightly pushing her away. "Go so you may come back to me, in whatever way you can."

It took an immense amount of effort to tear herself from his side. A part of her screamed to stay, to find another way. But she pushed past the fear and doubt. Neither would serve her well. She was doing this so she could come back to him. That knowledge was the only reason she was able to leave.

When she stepped back into the ballroom, the roar of noise almost overcame her.

"Ready?" asked Claremont, jumping to his feet from where he had been leaning.

"Yes," Hetty replied, turning back to see Jasper over her shoulder as they began to walk away. Jasper held her gaze, his eyes burning like embers with something she knew but could not name. She felt it, too. He left the alcove, walking slowly, not following, but not wishing to lose her before he had to.

The rest of the ballroom could have been on fire, but Hetty did not look away. Claremont was speaking, but she did not hear him. Jasper paused in the middle of the room; Lucian stood beside him, his own gaze directed at Jane. Lucian's expression crinkled with concern, Jasper's still resolute.

They reached the top of the stairs too quickly. Hetty wasn't ready to leave the man she loved behind. He had been her tether, the thing that held her close when all that remained of her could have floated away.

"Come, Hetty." Claremont's voice was impatient as he guided her through the door, which closed behind them.

The tether snapped, and she felt all at once lonelier for having left him. But Hetty had to focus on her mission. It was her only way back to Jasper.

More than that, it was her only way back to herself.

Chapter Twenty-Four

HETTY

The outside air was frigid. Neither of them had thought to collect Hetty's cloak, and Claremont was in such a hurry that she was sure he wouldn't go back for it. Eager to get her back to her suffering aunt, she thought. The fact that he was a good son helped to warm Hetty as they made their way down the daunting line of carriages. Claremont's own seemed to be at the very end of it. By the time Hetty had been helped into it, warm thoughts of familial love or not, she was shivering violently and her excitement had faded, replaced by a slight feeling of unease.

Information, she reminded herself. She needed information. It was the end and aim of her very existence, to know things in order to feel a sense of control. And for the first time since waking, her questions would have answers.

After what sounded like a spirited discussion with the footman, Claremont got into the carriage and handed her a folded wool blanket, which she promptly wrapped around herself until only her head was visible. The footman placed a warmer between them on the carriage floor, looking at her curiously but saying nothing. Before long, they were moving, the delicious heat of the warmer curling around Hetty's frigid toes.

Hetty looked to Claremont, who studied her as if waiting for disaster. She supposed that was fair, given her behavior.

"Why were you at the ball tonight?" she blurted out, unable to even pretend to have a normal conversation with the cousin who likely had thought her dead.

He cleared his throat. "I was looking for you, of course. We have been hunting for you since you went missing."

"What did the search entail?" she asked, wanting to know what she had put them through.

He looked out the window, pulling at his collar. "This isn't exactly a proper conversation to have with a lady—"

"I recently vomited on an earl's boots, and was subsequently stripped down to my underclothes most efficiently by his sister. I can assure you, I am not at risk of being scandalized."

Claremont made a small choking sound. "Well, our search has been quite robust. Or at least as robust as one can be while still being discreet. By the time we knew you were gone there was little hope of following your trail. But we did our best, trying first the places we thought you might go, but there was no sign of you. Eventually we enlisted the help of a detective, who suggested we might try to find you in a mortuary." He shuddered. "That unfortunate task was left up to me. Clearly, I did not find you there."

Did he seem almost vexed by that? His tone was confusing. "Did you believe me dead?"

"No," he replied quickly. "But we were desperate for answers.

Not knowing if you were dead or alive was perhaps the most difficult part."

"Did you have reason to suspect I'd run away?" She thought back to the memory she had of her hopelessness and fear, and Jasper's claim that she had said she was being pursued. She wanted to ask Claremont outright if he knew anything about that, but her gut told her to wait. To collect as much information as she could before revealing anything.

He stared at her in the flickering lantern light. Half his face was cast in shadow, but she could see that he was straining under something. Guilt? That didn't seem right. Did he fear her reaction? She burned to know exactly what he was thinking.

After a while, he spoke. "No, Hetty. You were mourning your father; you had no reason to leave his home."

She sat with that for a moment. Much like that visceral fear, Hetty's grief had followed her through her injury. She hadn't known who it was for at first, but the loss of her father had come back to her before her own name. It had affected her deeply. She could almost recreate his visage in her mind now, a haphazard portrait of a man she knew as well as she knew herself. He was handsome, with kind eyes and a substantial moustache. Hardly ever without his pipe, she recalled the comforting scent of him, too. Tobacco and turpentine.

But she could not make out all of him. Parts were still missing. She hoped to rebuild him fully in the home they had lived in together.

Claremont was eyeing her almost warily. She supposed she couldn't blame him, after what she had put them through. "How is it you recognized me? I would have thought the mask would be limiting."

He tilted his head. "It was your laugh, in fact. I'm not sure if you noticed, but it is a tad distinct. Bell-like. I followed it through the ballroom, seeking you out long before I realized what I was doing. It seemed you had much occasion to laugh this evening." He did not say it kindly.

Hetty tried to ignore the sting of his tone. "How old am I?"

He thought briefly. "Twenty-two."

That number surprised her. "Why am I not married?"

"Your father took a rather dim view of matrimony for the sake of securing a position." He paused and sat back, looking like he wished he hadn't said anything. Perhaps he feared he was painting a negative image of her father, but she was hungry for a broader understanding of herself and her family, and that meant knowing everything she could. "My understanding is that he offered you much latitude in that regard."

"So I did not wish to find a husband?"

He quirked a brow. "I'm not sure you had many suitors," was all he offered. "My mother and I live most of the time in London. We did not spend more than a few weeks together every couple of years."

"And this ring?" she asked, pulling it from within her bodice. "Who is *JHD*?"

He looked at her like she was a simpleton. "Your father. John Henry Davenport."

Her surname did not surprise her. It was another tether. Henrietta Davenport. "So, not my fiancé, then," she concluded with relief, mostly to herself.

"No, there is no handsome, titled gentleman waiting for you at Sutton House, of that I can assure you." Why did his tone verge almost toward cruelty?

She put it aside. "What was it my father did as a profession?"

"He was an American artist. A rather accomplished one at

that, in some circles."

Her heart hammered against her chest. "An artist?" she echoed in awe, recalling how her love of art had seemed to reach through her veiled memories.

"It was why you spent your life flitting about from one place to the next, following his patronages and taking commissions all over Europe. You had only been in Sutton House for the last year. I'm sure he had plans to up and leave once more, before he died." He frowned at himself for his callousness. "I'm sorry, Hetty—"

"Did I not wish to go with him?"

"I believe it was a source of tension between you two. He liked to say he had 'itchy feet but a headstrong daughter.' He had only ever settled here because of your mother. John Davenport had no great love for England. I believe it was his sincerest wish that you would feel more at home on the deck of a ship than in the English countryside. But you had grown weary of his nomadic pursuits. This time in Surrey was something of an experiment for you both."

"I wonder why he did not see my living with the two of you as a compromise. Surely residing with family would have been a more desirable option than his continued unhappiness."

"Surely," Claremont agreed. "But the two of you did so loathe being parted. Maybe nothing would have prevented you from following him."

Hetty looked out the carriage window, suddenly overcome with a sense of rootlessness. She had felt so certain that regaining her memories would mean discovering her place in the world, but what if she had never had one to begin with? It sounded like the longing she felt to understand who she was and where she belonged was not a new sensation borne out of losing her past, but rather one that had followed her from her old life, like her grief.

Because the ache she felt when she thought of her father was grief, she knew that. But missing someone with every fiber of her being did not mean they'd never quarreled. It did not mean all was roses between them, or that theirs hadn't been a complicated relationship.

Hetty wondered why she didn't remember that, as well.

She stored away her feelings of insecurity, favoring any facts her cousin might give her. "And my mother—"

"Hetty, please," he interrupted with a sigh. "This is beginning to feel like an interrogation. Aren't you simply relieved to have been found again? We have all the time in the world to answer your queries." Hetty bit her tongue, knowing she had about three hundred more questions at the ready. She didn't wish to pester him, not after everything he had been through. "Isn't that better?" he asked, remarking upon the awkward silence that had blossomed between them. "Blessed quiet. I suspect you have much to think about before we get back to Sutton House." She nodded, afraid to speak lest a new question slip out. "If you don't mind, I shall rest my eyes until we get there. It has been a very trying time."

Before Hetty could reply, or even ask how long the journey would be, Claremont had turned away from her and closed his eyes. Only an ill-mannered person would have ignored his request for silence, but Hetty did find it odd that her cousin didn't have more patience for her, given the circumstances.

A peculiar feeling spread through her. She might have called it a chill, only this felt...emptier. It was like the feeling that had overcome her in the portrait gallery, when she had discovered how secure Jasper was, and how conversely insecure she felt.

She shivered beneath the blanket, but vowed not to give in to the tug of despair. Perhaps her aunt would be warmer. Perhaps everything would fall into place the moment she set foot in the home she had shared, however briefly, with her father. She untied the ribbons of her mask and placed it on the bench beside her. She wanted to meet her aunt again as herself. As Hetty.

It wasn't long before the carriage slowed. She hadn't thought the journey would be long, considering she likely hadn't gotten very far on horseback the night she'd fled into the storm.

It was too dark outside for her to make out much more than Sutton House's general shape. It looked to be a stately manor, much smaller than Mulgrave Hall, but still far too large for a widower and his only child. Why hadn't her father remarried? Was it his "itchy feet" that prevented him from laying down roots? Had Hetty been a burden to him? She couldn't wait to meet her aunt and ask her. She might not be a blood relative, but she had known Hetty's father for decades. If anyone had the answers she sought, it was her.

The carriage came to a stop and Claremont awoke with a start, looking right at her. "Oh, you're still here."

"Where would I have gone?" she asked with a light laugh.

"You cannot blame me for my concern," he replied. "Given your previous misadventure."

"It's not as if I ran from *you*, Cousin," she teased back.

Claremont's face went terribly blank, devoid of all emotion. "No, quite right," he responded before departing.

Perhaps it was too soon for jesting.

There was no steady hand waiting for her, so she did her best to shimmy out of the carriage, constricted as she was by Isobel's gown and the blanket both. Claremont was talking with the footman again, so Hetty took a deep breath of frigid air and studied her home.

It was a red-bricked Georgian country house, completely symmetrical and balanced in its design, with four large white columns bracketing a shiny black door with a polished brass handle. Even though she had only spent some months there, Hetty knew it would squeak when turned, and that the path to the left of the house led to a babbling brook where she liked to read in the dappled sunlight of the woods.

Her mind prickled as she remembered the small pieces of her old life, the seemingly inconsequential details that meant more to her than she could rightly articulate.

However short her stay at Sutton House had been, Hetty had had a life here. And despite Jasper's misgivings, her cousin had not led her astray.

The footman crossed her path, giving her an odd look. She almost called out to him, to find out if they had known each other before. Perhaps the strange looks were a result of her not acting the way she should have with him. Were they friendly? Did she know him very well? But before she could ask, someone cleared their throat behind her. She turned to see her cousin gesturing toward the house.

"Welcome home," he said. When she began to walk toward it, he stopped her gently. "How about I go break the happy news to Mother before we shock her into an early grave."

Hetty deflated. "You don't think she'd wish to see me straight away?"

"Do not misunderstand, Hetty. My mother's poor nerves may not survive seeing you in the flesh without adequate time to prepare." He began escorting her up the steps. "All I'm asking is that you wait until I come for you. I wouldn't want you to see her in such a state."

"Nor would I wish to upset her," she replied, finding there was a well of sympathy for her aunt within her.

They entered the home, the scent of which hit Hetty like a ton of bricks. Even with her father dead, the air still smelled of pipe smoke and the faintest hint of his cologne. She staggered, bringing her hand to the wall for some support.

"Are you all right?" asked Claremont.

"Fine, just..." she said, struggling to explain the weight of memory that was crushing her. "It's a lot to take in," she offered weakly.

"Here, come to the drawing room," he replied, guiding her to a small room off the main corridor. "Sit, sit," he implored, pushing her onto a settee. "I'll send for some tea while I break the news to Mother. Then I will come collect you when we are ready."

Hetty merely nodded as Claremont left the room in a rush. Her head ached; her body was weak. She felt like she had been thrown from her horse once more. It was almost too much to bear, being in the home she could not fully remember, without the father who had made it a home to begin with. She found herself sliding down the settee until she was horizontal, pressing her hand to her eyes in an effort to relieve some of the pressure.

How had she gotten there? It had all happened so quickly. In one moment, Hetty had been resolved to leave Jasper and the Maycotts forever, banishing herself to some unknown future as a recluse, perhaps, and the next, she was in the home she had left behind, rebuilding the broken pieces of her life with naught but her own two hands. She had hoped it would all make sense as soon as she entered Sutton House, but something was wrong. Her heartbeat had not slowed since she'd walked through the door with Claremont. Nerves, perhaps, or the lingering effects of bad memories long forgotten. But what would make her feel so uneasy in what was apparently her own home? A year might be a relatively short amount of time, but it was long enough to know when something wasn't right. She tried to remember anything else, but the effort strained her greatly.

Where was the blasted tea her cousin had promised? She sat up shakily and looked around, wondering where the nearest servant might be. She didn't expect there were many at Sutton House, but a footman, a cook, at least two maids, a housekeeper, and a butler seemed standard for a house its size. Desperate, she rang the bell that would bring a servant to her, hoping they hadn't retired for the evening and that she was not disturbing them.

But no one came. Eventually, Hetty realized she could hear laughter from deeper in the house. Laughter and jolly voices belonging to what sounded like several different people. It was odd. Was her aunt entertaining? That didn't exactly match the portrait Claremont had painted of a woman in the throes of mourning.

Curiosity got the better of her, as it always had. She had a right to know what was happening in her own home. Claremont had no doubt prepared her aunt by now. Had he forgotten his promise to her?

She walked the corridors, oddly both familiar and foreign, her feet seeming to know the way better than her mind did. Was that the tantalizing scent of a roast in the air? Was her aunt hosting a dinner party? Hetty's stomach growled at the thought. At least she might get a plate out of it.

Just before she rounded a corner she knew on instinct would lead to the dining room, Hetty heard hushed voices.

"And you're certain she recalls nothing of that night?" asked a feminine voice that must have belonged to her aunt.

"Nothing at all, Mother. It is most curious for her to have forgotten *everything*."

"Curious indeed—" The blasted floor beneath Hetty's feet creaked, silencing her aunt.

Claremont peeked around the corner. "Hetty! I thought I told you to wait for me to collect you."

"I heard voices," she said, trying not to sound weak and failing. "And I'm desperate for tea but no one came when I called."

"Darling," said her aunt, stepping around Claremont, flashing a radiant smile. "We had to do away with many comforts such as those, what with your inheritance tied up with solicitors."

It was a strange thing to say, but Hetty was too focused on her aunt's sudden appearance to make much note of it. She was tall like her son, with hair so pale it seemed stark white in the shadowed hall, but upon closer inspection Hetty could see that it was blond. Overall, she was angular and beautiful in a sharp, rather unforgiving manner.

"Lady Claremont," said Hetty, offering a small curtsy, unsure of how to greet her otherwise.

"*Psh*, we don't stand at attention here, now do we?" the woman said, arms extended, beckoning for Hetty to embrace her. "You know to simply call me Aunt Celia."

The hug was stiff. Unnatural. It wasn't the immediate warmth that Hetty had hoped for.

"But Mother, Hetty doesn't remember a thing."

"Oh, that's right," she replied. "Apologies, darling. What a wretched ailment! And to have kept you from us all this time!" She gripped Hetty's forearm and began to rather firmly guide her away from the dining room, away from Claremont, who merely offered her a sheepish look before turning on his heel and joining the dinner Hetty was being pulled away from.

She opened her mouth to protest, but her aunt was quicker.

"I'm sure you have many questions for us, but they will simply have to wait until after you've had a good night's sleep."

Her stomach growled. "I am rather hungry. Could I perhaps join your dinner?"

"That would be impossible, given your current state—"

"I am not unwell, Aunt Celia," she said, choosing rudeness as a last resort to get her point across. They stopped walking, her aunt relinquishing her grip on her arm. "Merely hungry," Hetty added, softer.

Her aunt pressed her lips together. Took a deep breath. Plastered a rather unconvincing smile on her face. "Now Hetty, I'm afraid you've caught us at a rather awkward time. My guests do not know that you were missing. How am I to explain your sudden return from Bath?"

"You told everyone I was in Bath?" She could have been dead for all they knew, and they were entertaining as though the lie they had concocted was the truth.

"My dear, we did not wish to compromise your reputation in the event that you returned to us. We have been doing our best to carry on as normally as we could, given the circumstances. I think you'll find our methods sensible when you're still able to secure a marriage proposal. Now come." She held out her hand for Hetty to take. "I will guide you to your room. A good rest is all you need. I will have a plate sent to you right away."

Hetty found she lacked the energy to argue further, and allowed her aunt to bring her through the familiar but unfamiliar house, all the way up to the third floor and into a room that seemed to embrace her the moment she entered it. There was a fire in the hearth, so someone had alerted a maid as to her sudden reappearance. Books covered nearly every surface, along with countless abandoned teacups.

"Thank you, Aunt Celia."

Her aunt looked mildly puzzled. "For what?"

"For helping me remember." Her family might leave much to be desired in terms of warmth, but they were here in this home with her, supporting her after the loss of her father. That had to mean something.

"Think nothing of it!" she replied, pressing her hands to her heart. "That's what family is for, after all. Now I must get back to my guests, but please rest, darling. I will have food sent up to you."

As her aunt turned to leave, one final question rose to the forefront of Hetty's mind.

"Do I have any other family? A grandparent perhaps? Other aunts or uncles?"

Aunt Celia turned back, frowning. "No, Hetty," she said, her voice soft. "I daresay we're all you have left in the world."

She left, and the room was colder. Hetty hadn't realized how little she wished to be alone after her accident. With the Maycotts, she'd hardly gotten a moment's peace, but she had grown accustomed to their affectionate mayhem.

Her welcome back to Sutton House was not unkind, but it was not the reception Hetty had been envisioning since Claremont had found her at the ball. Still, she could endure for a night. Her arrival had been a shock. She could not judge their reactions too harshly. They were her family, after all.

A knock at her door startled her.

"Come in," she called, desperate for company. But no one entered. Eventually, Hetty rose and opened the door herself. She was surprised to see a tray of food laid on the floor before her, its deliverer nowhere to be found. Were she not starving, she might have started snooping around the hallways, seeking a maid who may have known her from before.

But Hetty was both hungry and exhausted. Her exploring would have to wait.

She brought the tray into her room and deposited it onto her bed. Removing the cloche revealed a plate of small roast potatoes and thin carrots and a rather pitiful slice of meat. Hetty had to stop herself from devouring it with her bare hands. And while the serving size was a bit stingy, a rather generous glass of red wine accompanied the dish, which she was happy to indulge in.

When she was done, the emptiness crept back in. She put the tray on her messy desk, noticing an overturned frame amidst the chaos. Picking it up, she realized at once it was a photograph of her father. She lifted it closer for inspection, noting her memories of his moustache had been correct. The ring she wore around her neck was on his pinky finger. He looked every inch the restless artist, with paint-stained hands that blurred as though he were unable to keep still long enough for film to capture him.

The photograph was a knife, cutting clean through her. There was the bone-deep pain, the one she hadn't been able to recall, the one she felt as keenly as any wound.

Papa, she thought, remembering that someone had schooled her to call him that as a jest, playing into his long-held prejudice against the French art world, but it had evolved into something precious between them. Theirs might have been a complicated relationship, but she knew he'd loved her more than anything, and she him. They had been alone together for so long, two broken people, each missing her mother, each repairing the other.

Her tears came easily in the privacy of her room. When she cried, it wasn't just for losing him. Hetty cried for having forgotten him, too.

She stripped out of her clothes and crawled into her bed, her sobs shaking her whole body. Sleep came upon her like a sudden shift in the tide, pulling her under.

Her last thought before succumbing to the ebb of exhaustion was of Jasper.

Why hadn't she brought him with her? Why on earth had she come there alone?

Chapter Twenty-Five

JASPER

Jasper saw no reason to stay at the ball now that Jane was gone.

Hetty. Now that *Hetty* was gone.

He wasn't sure he would ever get used to referring to her as such, even if it was her name. He had no problem with it, in fact it seemed to suit her, but he had fallen in love with her as Jane. It would take some time to think of her otherwise.

Everything had happened so quickly. One minute he was on the verge of professing his love for her, the next she was gone.

Letting her go had been the right thing to do, hadn't it? In the moment, it had seemed like the quickest way to bring her back to him, but now he wasn't sure. They had parted so reluctantly, so hesitantly, that Jasper was certain where he stood with her, even if they hadn't had a chance to say it. But now he pictured her slipping easily back into the life she'd had before, discarding him. Would it be that simple? Was there any room for him in Hetty's old life, or would she come to forget him, too?

Jasper's world was rapidly crumbling down around him. He thought of Hetty's cousin, the baron. He knew nothing of the man, but that wasn't unheard of. His first instinct was to distrust him, but how could Jasper have accused him of anything? *He* knew Hetty, not Jasper. He had ostensibly grown up alongside her, known her through the loss of her mother, the loss of her father. What right did Jasper have to keep Hetty from the only family she had left?

And yet, he couldn't help but think it had been a mistake to let her go.

He turned away and Lucian called out after him, but Jasper's mind was elsewhere. His friend had stood beside him as he watched the woman he loved leave him, but Jasper hadn't heard a word he'd said.

He needed...well, he needed *her*, but a drink would suffice for now.

He was on his second scotch when Lucian and August caught up to him.

"Jasper, what on earth was that all about?" asked Lucian, who had witnessed Hetty leaving and Jasper's descent into melancholy both.

"What do you know of Lord Claremont?" he asked between sips.

Lucian's brow furrowed. "Not a thing."

"Would Edgar know him?"

"Perhaps, as he tends to know everyone," Lucian began. "Jasper, what's happened—"

Before he could speak, Isobel came upon them in a rush,

sporting a conspiratorial grin. "Beatrice claims she saw Jane leaving the ball with a man not ten minutes ago. Normally, I'd admire the woman's spirit, but that doesn't sound like our Jane, does it? No doubt Miss Bea is mistaken."

Jasper opened and closed his mouth several times, unable to find the words to explain what had happened that night.

Isobel, sensing his rising panic, turned serious. "Jasper, where is Jane?"

The question sliced through him so cleanly, so effectively that he staggered forward, scotch sloshing out of his tumbler.

August's steady arm helped to right him. "What is it?"

Helena arrived, concern creasing her features. He swallowed thickly, noting his friend and siblings looking at him as though he were mad. Perhaps he was. "Jane found her cousin tonight. Lord Claremont, a baron."

He studied them to see if the name sparked any immediate familiarity. Isobel's jaw dropped, but Helena, who hadn't heard of Hetty's departure, clapped her hands together in surprise.

"Goodness, did she really? Where are they?" she asked, looking around the ballroom. "I do so wish to know her family."

Jasper choked on the last sip of his drink. "They're gone."

Isobel's eyes narrowed upon him. "What do you mean, gone?"

"Her cousin insisted they depart immediately. Something about easing the suffering of her aunt. They've thought she was dead all this time."

"And you just let her go?" Isobel whisper-shouted.

"What right do I have to keep her?" he replied, matching her quiet but urgent tone.

His sister only glared at him. "Did you consider that Jane might be in danger with this man?"

"Her name isn't Jane, it's Hetty. She is a woman we never truly knew, with a life we don't belong in." Jasper had been so reluctant to trap her, even before they had found her cousin. Hetty had needed freedom more than anything else. The freedom to forge her own path, to live a life of her own choosing. So he had guarded his true feelings from her in order to preserve that freedom. It was a move he'd regretted as soon as she'd left the Banfields' ballroom. "No matter how much we may wish otherwise," he added, knowing that in his effort not to capture Hetty, he might have pushed her away from him instead. The thought was excruciating.

"Rubbish," said Isobel dismissively. "I know you don't believe that, Jasper, so why are you saying it?"

"Did this man have proof he was who he said he was?" asked Lucian, ever logical, ever calm.

"Well, no, none despite the fact that he knew who she was, even when she didn't. You should have seen her when she heard her name. Her entire demeanor changed. It fit her like a glove." Isobel opened her mouth to argue, but Jasper intercepted her. "He knew of her grief as well as her name, Izzie. He knew her father had died. He and her aunt have been staying with her since he did."

Helena looked between her siblings. "Why are we acting as if something terrible has happened? Didn't we hope Jane—Hetty would find her family?"

"Yes," Jasper started.

"We didn't expect said family to rush her away from us," said Isobel bitterly. "It strikes me as suspicious."

"I agree," said August, speaking up for the first time in a while.

"Do you?" asked Jasper, somewhat sarcastically.

"I do," he replied evenly. "What use is there in separating her from us, unless something sinister is afoot?"

Jasper went cold. He had thought he'd made a mistake by letting her go, but he hadn't allowed himself to fully consider the possibility that she might be in danger.

August continued. "Hetty did flee from her former life, did she not? Perhaps she was escaping *him*."

Jasper dropped his empty glass to the marble floor, where it shattered, spraying those in his immediate vicinity with Lord Banfield's best single malt. He was numb. A riot of thoughts took over his mind. He had to find her. Had to save her.

He began to walk toward the staircase before Isobel stepped in his path.

"Precisely where do you think you're going?"

"To get Hetty," he said through gritted teeth.

"Did she happen to provide you with an address and directions before you sent her off into the unknown?"

He froze. "No."

"Then let us perhaps come up with a plan before setting off into the snow without a destination in mind. Not all of us can rely on being rescued by stern aristocrats before morning."

Before they could return to the group, Edgar appeared in their path. "Izzie, you missed our waltz," he said, his tone lightly chiding. He looked at Jasper and then back at Isobel, a realization dawning. "What's happened, then? Has August absconded with someone's fiancée?"

Isobel grimaced. "Would that our problem were that simple." She looked to Jasper, who nodded and walked back to where they had started. Isobel began explaining everything to Edgar, from how they found Hetty injured in the road to how they'd lied about her identity to protect her. By the time they reached the rest of his siblings, he was almost caught up.

"And Jane—Hetty insisted on coming tonight, certain she would find the truth of her past."

"In a way, she was right," August added.

"We all knew it was terribly important to her, and I suspect her excitement was rather contagious. I am trying very hard not to blame my brother for letting her go."

Jasper gritted his teeth. "I am not her keeper, Isobel. And while the baron seemed suspicious, he might also have been overcome with relief at seeing her alive. Until we know otherwise, I'd rather not assume the worst."

Edgar had taken everything in rather calmly, despite the fact that he'd just learned the Maycotts had lied to him since his arrival. "Well, I suppose the only solution is to find her and ensure that she is well."

"Which is what I am trying to do—"

"Without a destination in mind," replied Isobel.

"Sutton House," he said, suddenly remembering what Claremont had said. "Her cousin said they've been staying at Sutton House since her father died."

Isobel looked around. "Anyone heard of it?"

They all shook their heads.

"Is the Claremont seat called Sutton House?" Jasper asked Edgar in particular.

"How would any of us know that?" asked August.

"Viola would," Isobel replied morosely before her eyes lit up. "*Burke's*!" she exclaimed, rushing away in the direction of the Banfield library. Helena and the others moved to follow her, but Jasper stopped them.

"It's going to look rather suspicious if we all tear off for the library. Stay here, there's a chance Hetty will come back." Helena nodded and August took up another flute of champagne.

When Jasper gave him a look, he shrugged. "Better I pretend all is well, no?"

Just before Jasper went after Isobel, he turned to Edgar, an idea fresh in his mind. "Find me Simon Griffith, will you?"

Edgar accepted the task without question and sank back into the crowded ballroom.

It didn't take Jasper long to track his sister to the library. They had played there with Lady Cordelia often enough as children. It was less than half the size of the Mulgrave Hall library but likely contained as many books stuffed in its shelves, giving it the appearance of barely regulated chaos. It had charmed him as a child, but now, when he needed to find one book in particular? He cursed the mess.

Isobel was already searching on her hands and knees. "What if they don't have an updated edition?" she called over her shoulder, knowing it was Jasper. The dusty library was hardly conducive to a tryst. They wouldn't be interrupted.

"If the title predates the man, I'm sure we'll be able to glean something from it." He joined her at the lower row of cobwebbed books. "What makes you think it'll be here?"

"*Burke's* isn't exactly kept near for light reading, unless you're Lady Viola Maycott." She ran her gloved finger along the shelf, disturbing a shocking amount of dust. She *tsk*ed. "Lady Adelaide would have this maid sacked immediately. Ah ha!" she cried, pulling a familiar red tome from the depths of a shelf. "1860," she said. "Likely won't contain anything useful about the current baron, but may give us information as to the family's holdings."

She flipped to the correct page and they both began reading it in silence.

CLAREMONT, BARON (Charles Warwick,) of Bassett, co. Southampton; b. 24th June, 1818; m. 4th August, 1845 to Celia Louise, daughter of Rev. John Clive, rector of Highfield, by whom he has issue Thomas Warwick, b. 11th March, 1847; s. as 4th baron at decease of his father 28th August, 1844.

"A son born in 1847, that matches the man I met," said Jasper.

"Viola would be positively thrilled to know we've finally come to understand the utility of *Burke's*," muttered Isobel, still reading. "Motto, *Ventis secundus*," She paused. "'Favorable winds'? That's not exactly descriptive, is it?"

"I'd take favorable winds over blasted endurance."

"Strikes me as rather opportunistic in a motto, but moving on." She cleared her throat. "Seat, Aldermoor House, Southampton. Not exactly close, is it?"

"Hetty didn't look like she had come all the way from Southampton when we found her." He recalled that she'd still been warm in his arms, her hair mostly dry despite the storm that had raged around them. There was no way she had gone more than a couple of miles.

"And her cousin wouldn't ride for half a day in order to attend a simple country ball."

"So she must be closer. Perhaps Lord Claremont has another home."

"I doubt it," came a gravelly voice from behind them.

Isobel and Jasper stood with a start, the former swearing as she hit her head on the shelf. Standing in the doorway were Edgar, August, and Lord Simon Griffith, the owner of the Arondelle, a notorious gentlemen's club in St. James's. He was a man whose reputation was only eclipsed by his father's debts, debts he would eventually inherit. But there was nothing Simon Griffith didn't know, no secret buried so deep he couldn't uncover and use for his own gain. He wasn't a man one wanted as an enemy, but as an ally, he could be devastatingly useful.

"Lord Simon," said Jasper with a nod, unsure of how to address the estranged son of an ailing duke. Outside of the ballroom, formalities could be done away with. He had more pressing matters to deal with than whether or not Simon and Isobel had been properly introduced.

"Simon," the man corrected with a flick of his dark hair. Jasper supposed he was handsome, but his air was mocking, cruel even. He carried an alabaster walking stick that looked more like a weapon than an aid. "It's been what, a year and a half since you graced my tables, Belhaven? Has your father's title changed you so?"

"Will your father's?" Jasper shot back, finding some of the old Jasper in his tone, despite the fact that he was relieved to find Simon so unwilling to pretend as though the Maycotts hadn't lost so much. After an evening of being treated delicately, his frankness was a welcome reprieve.

Simon studied him coldly and then grinned, his expression warming the room. "What can I help you with?"

"Lord Claremont," Jasper said, stepping around the desk. "What do you know of him?"

Simon pondered briefly before leaning against the doorframe. "Claremont owes my club a staggering sum. I'm shocked he showed his face tonight, though I'm never one to mix business and pleasure." The Arondelle was a gambling club, and Simon its exacting proprietor.

Isobel looked to Jasper. "As a guest of the Banfields, he must be known to them."

"I took the liberty of informing Banfield of Claremont's…

unsavory nature. It seems he is not, strictly speaking, an invited guest of theirs. It is only Lady Banfield's kindness that prevented her husband from having the man forcibly removed." He poured some of Lord Banfield's finest liquor into a tumbler and shot it back with ease. "I would not be so kind."

Of that, Jasper was certain. "So he is as slippery as we feared."

Simon shrugged. "He has a weakness for both cards and women that will eat him alive, if I don't manage it first."

"Do you know where he might be staying?"

Simon shook his head. "He hasn't dared return to his home in Mayfair since absconding on his debts. I've men looking for him, but he's evaded them so far. And as I said, I came here tonight for pleasure, or I would have gone after him myself." He tossed the cane from one hand to the other, threat implied.

"You don't seem overly concerned," said August.

Another wolfish grin. "As you well know, August, I always collect on my debts."

Jasper wasn't sure what to make of that, but Helena joined them, a silent but calming presence in the library that did not go unnoticed by Simon, whose eyes lingered on her a bit too long for Jasper's liking.

"Have you heard of a Henrietta Davenport?" he asked.

Slowly, Simon tore his eyes away from Helena. "Never. Is she rich?"

The man thought of nothing else. "Her wealth is of little importance. We are looking for a place called Sutton House. Are you familiar with it?"

"I know little of the Surrey countryside. And I think you'll find her wealth matters a great deal, especially if Claremont is involved."

"You believe something criminal is afoot?" Edgar asked, surprised.

"I believe you know very little of what men like him will do when backed into a corner."

Jasper's blood went cold as the pieces began to fall into place. A desperate man, with nowhere to turn, informed of the sudden orphaning of his wealthy cousin? It likely seemed too good to be true to Claremont. But how would he access her inheritance? They were long past the days of marriages between cousins, even amongst the aristocratic. Would Claremont have attempted more nefarious means?

And then he had it, the last piece of the puzzle. Hetty hadn't been fleeing some unknown assailant when she rode out desperately into the night, but rather her own family. If Claremont revealed his intent to take control of her inheritance, whether by force or otherwise, Hetty would have fought him fiercely. Jasper was sure of it. And if she'd fled, it was only because she'd had no other choice.

He sat back on the edge of the desk, the borders of his vision darkening at the thought of Hetty, *his* Hetty—a woman brave enough to set out in a storm *twice* rather than allow others to dictate her future—being at the mercy of some bastard who knew just how to snare her.

Hetty would have done anything to know her past. To know herself. And Jasper, the bloody fool, hadn't been able to disappoint her.

Now she was gone. And who could she blame but himself?

"What does that mean?" asked Isobel, no mischief in her tone now, only fear.

"It means Hetty is in danger," replied Jasper, every muscle in his body tensing. "And I'll tear the whole of Surrey apart to find her if I must."

Chapter Twenty-Six

HETTY

Hetty's sleep was not peaceful, nor restorative. Each time she managed to rouse herself, it pulled her back and held her under until she submitted once more. She had never known exhaustion could be so overpowering. But she had been through so much in so little time. Perhaps this was what her body and her mind required. Rest, even if it did not feel restful. Time to heal, even if she felt worse now than she had before.

In most of her conscious moments she thought of Jasper, and how desperately she wished to get back to him and his family. *But I'm with my family*, the vague memories of her aunt and cousin slipping in and out of her mired mind. *This feels like home, doesn't it?*

Sleep. Sleep will fix things.

And so she slept.

Once or twice, she awoke to people around her bed, though

without her spectacles she could not make them out properly, and the abyss still clutched at her viciously. She felt hands upon the borders of her injury. *Good,* she thought, *a doctor.* She must need one desperately, if she felt this poorly. Bless her aunt for seeing to it.

She opened her mouth to speak, but the words came out garbled.

"Hetty, darling, drink this." Her aunt's hand cradled her cheek, but the pressure was too strong against her skin, almost painful, almost a threat. She poured a tepid liquid down her throat. Water, she thought, but she was too addled to think clearly. "That's a good girl, sleep now."

How could she argue against it, when the desire to succumb was so strong?

She closed her eyes and sank once more into the abyss.

• • •

The next time she woke, she knew immediately that something was wrong.

Her bones ached with the need to move. Her skin was clammy. She was hot, so hot, and her mouth was as dry as a desert. She threw the covers back. Where were her spectacles? Why was the room so bloody dark?

She practically crawled her way to the water closet and saw to her needs. When she came back, a blurry figure stood in the middle of her room, gasping at the sight of her upright.

"Hetty, you mustn't exert yourself," came the voice of her aunt.

"I merely used the water closet, Aunt Celia," she said as she began feeling along her messy desk. "Where are my spectacles? I don't know if you noticed, but I am rather useless without them."

Her aunt made a strange, disapproving noise. "I hope you understand that we are doing this for your own good, dear."

Hetty paused, the hair on the back of her neck standing up. "Doing what?"

"Seeing to it that you *rest*, you have been through so much." Her aunt took her by the shoulders and began forcibly guiding her back into her bed.

Hetty resisted. "Am I ill?" she asked blankly, for she was confused.

"In a sense," her aunt said as she pushed Hetty back onto the pillows and pulled the quilt back up over her shoulders, tucking in the edges and effectively imprisoning her. She stepped back, her hands on her hips. "You may not remember this, but you were in a very delicate place before you vanished and lost your memories."

"After my father died, you mean?" She was struggling to understand her aunt's intentions. Was she simply overprotective? Or did she think Hetty a child?

"Your grief nearly consumed you, my dear. Here, I brought you some tea." She pressed the cup and saucer into Hetty's hands. "Drink."

Hetty couldn't help but huff in annoyance before taking a small sip. "Seems a normal reaction to have after losing a parent, no?"

Even without her spectacles, she could see her aunt's lips press into a thin, disapproving line. "Hetty—"

"All I want is my spectacles," she argued between sips. "You can't know how disorienting it is to be without them." Even Jasper had understood that—long before they had warmed to each other. After she'd asked, finding them had been his first, most pressing task.

"No, I'm afraid I'm going to be quite strict about this, Hetty. Doctor's orders. He said you must be kept in total isolation with nothing to stimulate you."

Hetty's nose wrinkled in confusion. "I had a doctor when I was with the Maycotts and he thought I had improved—"

"I won't risk it." Her aunt's tone brooked no argument.

Hetty, somehow more exhausted now than she had felt upon waking, found she lacked the willingness to argue further. She took another, longer sip, letting the warmth spread from her throat and into her chest, unfurling the sense of panic that had been building. "How long have I been sleeping? It's still Saturday, right?" she added, a slight jest since she felt so sluggish.

"Saturday afternoon, in fact."

So she had slept through the night and long into the next day. How odd of her. "May I at least write a letter? The Maycotts must be worried about me. And Jasper—"

"Jasper?" Her aunt's tone was sharp. Inquisitive.

Hetty felt herself blush. "The earl, that is, will want to know I am all right."

Her aunt studied her briefly. "You were...close with the earl?"

Was it that obvious? "It was difficult not to be. He found me after the accident. I suppose we grew close due to our shared grief."

"He lost someone as well?"

She nodded, unwilling to be more specific. It wasn't hers to share. "He recognized that I, too, had lost someone long before I remembered who it was. I suspect it would be difficult for him not to notice how grief wears a person down."

"Naturally," her aunt replied absently. "Drink up, dear. You may dictate a letter to me, and I will ensure it reaches its destination." She went to Hetty's desk and pulled out a new piece of paper.

It wasn't what Hetty wanted, but she could tell there would be no changing her aunt's mind. Deciding it wasn't exactly proper for an unmarried woman to write a letter to a man, she opted for the next best thing.

"Dear Helena," she started. "Apologies for my abrupt departure from the ball. I am at Sutton House, the home I shared with my father. It would seem my injury has caught up with me at last, and I am taking a much-needed rest in order to regain my strength under the watchful eye of my aunt. Please do visit at your earliest convenience, as I find I am dearly missing every Maycott, even Aunt Adelaide. Yours sincerely, Hetty."

By the time she was done dictating, weariness had come upon Hetty once more.

Her aunt continued writing for a few moments before looking back at her. "Done."

"Will you make sure it reaches Mulgrave Hall?"

"I will see to it right away."

Hetty yawned. "Perhaps you're right, Aunt Celia. I find I've never been so tired in my life."

Her aunt came to the side of her bed and leaned over her. "See, my dear, it is because your body and your mind know you are finally safe. You've been battling through it, but now you can rest at last."

Hetty sank deeper into her bed. A vulnerable thought came to her. "Would you tell me about my father?"

Her aunt stiffened. "Well, what is there to tell, really?"

"I—I don't remember anything about him," she offered weakly. "You must have known him very well, and for longer than I did…"

"He was an artist. Very famous in certain circles. I'm told he loved traveling to exotic locales more than anything, and abhorred the French..." She trailed off. "I suppose he was a complicated man. Very protective of you..." She shook her head. "That's quite enough delving into the past. Now get some rest, there will be more time for talking later."

The description was odd to Hetty's ears, but she could not pinpoint why. "The letter, Aunt Celia," she started, already slipping into sleep. "Please..."

She could not articulate its true importance to her aunt. It would not be fair to tell her of how much she had come to care for the Maycotts. To love them, really. Not yet at least.

Her aunt patted her on the head. "The footman will deliver it. You have my word, Hetty."

Only when she had the assurance that the Maycotts would know where to find her again did Hetty let go and allow sleep to take her, powerless as she was against the void.

Her last waking thought was the belated realization that her aunt's description of her father was odd. It sounded like she didn't know her brother-in-law at all.

• • •

"We'll have to get her to sign it—"

"Shh, Mother, Hetty is waking."

The room was dark. Was always dark, it seemed. Hetty's head pounded. It was more pain than her injury had caused her when she'd awoken in Mulgrave Hall, back when it was fresh and bleeding. Her hand stretched out but her spectacles were not there.

Her aunt sighed. "I told you, darling—"

"I must *rest*," she echoed bitterly. "Haven't I rested enough?

Why am I not improving?"

Claremont brought her water, which she downed eagerly, nearly choking on the liquid.

"It takes time," he offered, somewhat sheepishly.

"Not two nights ago, I was dancing every bloody waltz and polka at a ball."

Her aunt *tsk*ed. "And likely did more damage than you realize. You're paying the price now, though."

"I am not some invalid who must be coddled into wellness. I would like my spectacles, and I would like to take a bloody walk."

Claremont flinched at her tone, but her aunt stood firm.

"You are making this exceedingly difficult, my dear. But I will be blunt. You nearly lost your mind with grief before. It is why you fled from us. Madness overtook you, and we thought we had lost you for good. But by the grace of God, you returned to us, and I will not risk losing you again."

Hetty's whole body went cold. Had she truly gone mad? Was that why she was alone in the woods? Had there never been any pursuers at all?

"I don't feel mad," she said, her voice small.

"Such is the particular cruelty of madness, I would wager," replied her aunt, her tone pitying. "It was the same for your mother, Henrietta, though perhaps your father shielded you from the truth."

"My mother?" She looked toward the blurry figure of her cousin. "Claremont said she died of scarlet fever."

Aunt Celia squeezed her hand. "A fiction designed to protect you. But mad Florence Davenport was, and incurably so."

In her mind, Hetty pictured a woman she had hardly ever known, with her same dark hair and gray eyes, features she hadn't gotten from her father. But was that all she had inherited from Florence? "Why did my father never tell me?"

"He was trying to protect you, my dear, and who could blame him? He lost his darling wife to madness. I presume he could not bear the thought of losing you to that same fate."

"I suppose so..." she replied, her mind spinning under the weight of this new revelation. While she was able to recall faint memories of her father, fleeting images of the life they had shared together, she could not conjure anything of her mother, or how her madness had manifested. *Had* her father tried to shield her from it? Had she experienced what Hetty had these last few days, unmoored and untethered from her life? Had her mother been placed in a madhouse, left to succumb to it alone? The mere thought of such a loss of freedom had Hetty's heart racing. "But I am not my mother, Aunt Celia."

"But perhaps now you understand why we are unwilling to push you." Her aunt caressed her hair, tucking it behind her ear. "When you behave like this, I fear you're falling into that same madness that plagued her. I don't know what would happen to you if you allowed yourself to get so worked up again. It was disastrous before, wasn't it, Claremont?"

Her cousin stepped forward. Cleared his throat. "Terrible, really."

"This is why you must rest, Hetty. Here's a broth and some bread for you to eat. I even brought you some more tea."

As much as Hetty wanted something substantial, she was feeling so weak she wasn't sure her stomach would be able to handle much more than the meager fare before her. "Thank you."

"Eat up, dear. The doctor will be back soon to check on your progress."

She nibbled on some bread and guzzled her tea. "How long

was I asleep?"

"Some hours. It is late Saturday night now. We just came by to check on you."

"Did the footman return with a letter?"

"Hmm?" her aunt asked, still rubbing her shoulder absently.

"From the Maycotts. I assume they would have written a reply for him to come back with." Alerting her to their imminent arrival, no doubt. It had been hard to leave Jasper's grasp, to say nothing of Lady Viola's.

"Oh," her aunt replied in surprise. "He didn't give one to me. What about you, Claremont?"

Her cousin shook his head vigorously. "Not to me, either."

That was odd. She had expected Helena to write back. Truth be told, she'd expected to awaken to the stern outline of the Earl of Belhaven himself, come to collect her now that she had had time with her family. Hell, she thought the hint about the state of her health might have prompted some quick action on their part.

But what if they saw their duty as complete? Now that she was with her family, the Maycotts could move on with their lives. The food turned to ash in her mouth as she contemplated their silence. Had she lost them for good? Had she meant so little to them? To *him*?

"Don't fret, my dear. We shall write them another letter in the morning. Now you must be tired."

She thought it an odd thing to say, considering how much sleep she had gotten since arriving. But then she found it was, startlingly, true. Hetty could not escape the bone-deep fatigue that had settled upon her once more.

A thought emerged from the sinking darkness of her mind.

"What were you saying before, about me signing something?"

"Oh, nothing you need to concern yourself with, darling. Just some papers relating to the property. That falls to you now that your father is gone."

It was a reasonable explanation, she thought. Still, something lingered. Something that felt a great deal like doubt.

But she was asleep again before she could think harder on it.

Chapter Twenty-Seven

HETTY

It didn't take long for Hetty to realize there was something wrong with the tea.

What else could explain her swift descent after each cup? Her aunt was drugging her, but to what end? A misguided need to protect her? For all she knew, the doctor had prescribed laudanum, but that didn't mean she wasn't outraged at the idea that it was being done without her consent. Recommended or not, Hetty thought the effects of whatever her aunt was administering were largely negative. Her thoughts were muddled and dark, her limbs nearly numb from disuse.

So Hetty had a new plan: stop drinking the bloody tea at all costs.

A part of her wanted to get up and demand the explanation she deserved from her family. But instinct urged her to wait. To take a breath and take stock of her situation for once. Because beneath her burning curiosity and simmering annoyance at being treated like an invalid, a part of Hetty knew that something was wrong. She'd felt it in the carriage when her cousin had been so brusque. Felt it again when her aunt had revealed that they had told no one of her disappearance. Were they prepared to pretend Hetty was in Bath for the rest of her life? Surely the story wouldn't pass muster with any who might have known Hetty outside of her family.

Or was she really that alone in the world? Had her father's insistence on living abroad meant that Hetty had no meaningful friendships in all of England?

She couldn't consider it, or she risked sinking deeper into despair and accepting the cold, unwelcoming sort of affection her aunt and cousin offered her, because at least they were *family*.

Though it was hard not to compare how she felt when she saw a mere photo of her father against the vast emptiness she felt when in the presence of Celia and Claremont. Granted, an aunt and cousin would not engender the same response, but to have no response to them at all? It beggared belief. The only logical explanation that Hetty could conceive of was that they had been little more than strangers to her, even in her old life.

And if that was true, it meant they were lying to her, in addition to drugging her. Christ, Hetty wouldn't be surprised to discover her aunt had never sent the letter to Helena, out of a misplaced desire to keep her *unstimulated*. It wasn't a promising set of circumstances, and the longer Hetty puzzled over it, the more her gut urged her to do something. She needed to get out from under her aunt's suffocating control and take charge of her own life. But how?

The house was quiet, her room as dark as ever. She thought it was still nighttime, and that perhaps she had a chance at moving about unnoticed. Blind as a bat, unfortunately, since she was still without her spectacles. Her arm reached out tentatively, out of habit more than anything else, but her fingers found the familiar shape of them on her night table. Excitement and relief surged through her as she slid them onto her face.

She sat up, her vision blessedly clear for the first time in far too long. Had her aunt left them there for her to find? It didn't seem likely, given how adamant she had been about keeping Hetty confined to her bed. But then that left Claremont, and if anything, he seemed even less likely than his mother to aid her.

Did Hetty have a friend in the house? Someone unseen but perhaps aware of her impediment? And if so, would they be willing to assist her?

It didn't matter. She'd have to find a solution regardless. But she'd have to move quickly. Hetty didn't know how much time she had before her aunt would be back with another sedative tea, which she had no plans of drinking.

Hetty rose unsteadily to her feet, amazed at how quickly she had declined after days abed. The room was untidy, but there was a comfort in that. Hetty could see evidence of her old life in the messiness of it. She picked a discarded robe up from the floor and wrapped it around herself. It smelled like spring—citrus and honeysuckle. She could see the bottle in her mind, and herself reflected in the mirror on her vanity, dabbing the scent at her pulse points. It had been her mother's favorite perfume, she recalled, and Hetty had worn it in remembrance.

Odd that scent had proved the most potent link to her buried memories. Odder still to recall nothing of her mother's descent into madness. Perhaps her father truly had kept it from her.

She sat at her desk and retrieved a slightly crumpled piece of blank parchment from a stack of letters. She didn't have much in the way of a plan, but she did intend to send another letter to the Maycotts, given that there was a decent chance her first missive had not made it to Mulgrave Hall. If she had felt any better, Hetty would have ridden there herself, but she knew she'd never make it in her current condition. She quickly scribbled the barest of messages for Jasper, all but begging for him to visit her at Sutton House in rather unsubtle language, on the slim chance that her first letter had been received but deemed unimportant.

But how to send it? She knew enough not to trust her aunt and cousin, who might be under the mistaken impression that the Maycotts would not be interested in her well-being. Worse yet, they might not want the Maycotts to know anything about how they were treating her.

Then she remembered the footman, and how he had studied her quite curiously, almost like he knew something she didn't. Something she *should*. Perhaps he had retrieved her spectacles for her. Perhaps *he* was her unseen ally.

All at once, her decision was made.

The hall beyond her room was quiet and utterly dark. She tiptoed along the carpet, terrified to make a sound and alert anyone before she'd had the chance to dispatch her letter.

But the halls were empty. She hadn't seen anyone but her cousin and aunt since she'd entered Sutton House. Granted, she had spent most of her time sleeping, but she hadn't seen evidence of anyone coming to clean her room or tend to her fire. Her aunt brought the trays of food and tea herself, which struck Hetty as a strange thing for a dowager baroness to do.

Were circumstances so dire? Had her father's finances been in shambles?

Instinct guided her to the kitchens, where she found a side door to the yard. She hauled on a pair of mucky boots and made her way outside.

Hetty found the footman deep in the stables, mucking out the stalls. He dropped the broom when he saw her. She likely looked a fright—hair ratty and loose down her back, clad in a nightgown and a robe, a true Brontë heroine off to haunt the moors.

There was no time for preamble. "What is your name?"

"I'm Jack, Mistress." She guessed he was somewhere around seventeen. Still a boy.

"You know who I am, Jack?"

"Yes." He nodded eagerly. "You're Miss Davenport."

Hetty still didn't feel like it. "Did you work for my father before he died?" She needed to know where his loyalties lay.

He nodded. "Yes."

"Did my aunt recently have you deliver a letter on my behalf?"

"I've not been given a letter, Miss, not since well before you got here."

So her suspicions were correct, though she still didn't know the motive behind her aunt's actions. That could wait. She looked around the empty stables. "Are you the only servant left?"

"I am now," he replied. "There was a maid left in the kitchens, but they dismissed her as soon as you returned."

"Are they mistreating you?"

"Haven't paid me my proper wage in weeks, if that's what you're asking." He scratched the back of his neck. "They say they'll accuse me of theft if I report them."

"I'm so sorry." Hetty didn't need her memories to recall that the punishment for theft was oftentimes unduly harsh. She didn't blame him for wishing to avoid it. "Why not leave?" she asked softly. "Surely you could outrun their threats if you're willing to get as far from here as possible."

He looked at her as though the answer was obvious. "I've nowhere else to go."

She had known the feeling, only her circumstances had been so dire that she had fled into the unknown rather than staying. And she knew now that it was only luck and a certain stern bastard that had saved her from a dark fate. Sadly, not everyone had Jasper Maycott to aid them.

She had one final question for him. "Was it you who retrieved my spectacles for me?" It was an entirely unselfish action, one that would say a great deal about Jack's character and whether or not she could trust him.

He bowed his head, a blush blossoming on his cheeks. "I'm sorry for the intrusion—"

"I'm not angry, quite the contrary. I am in your debt, but I need your help once more."

He stood straighter. "Of course."

"Do you know where Mulgrave Hall is?" she asked, and Jack nodded. Surrey was only so big, after all, and Mulgrave Hall so magnificent. "I need you to ride out there with great haste and find Lord Belhaven." Jack's eyes widened. "You must give him this letter. He will be grateful to receive it, I suspect, and not at all cross with you for delivering it."

Jack nodded. "I'll see it done, Miss Davenport."

Hetty looked behind him to the horse whose stall he had been tending to. The beast looked familiar, with beautiful bay coloring and a braided black mane. When she stepped closer with her hand outstretched, the creature leaned into her touch. He was velvet soft and warm.

"Is this my horse?"

Jack nodded. "He found his way back to us a day after you left." She was so relieved to hear he had survived their ordeal.

Jack handed her a small apple. "His name is Gringolet."

"After Sir Gawain's horse," she mused, feeding him the apple, which he chomped gratefully. She looked back to Jack. "Thank you for caring for him."

"I always hoped you would return home, Miss Davenport," he said. "But why not come with me now and give Lord Belhaven the message yourself? I don't quite trust your aunt and cousin, if I'm being honest, and I don't like the thought of leaving you with them."

Hetty had considered it, but she suspected the only way she'd discover the truth was with the element of surprise on her side. If she vanished, she might never know what had happened to her, or what had caused her to flee from her home the last time. And without that knowledge, she would be haunted by the unknown.

And besides, her aunt and cousin might not have the purest of intentions with her, but they were still her family.

"I will be safe, Jack. So long as you get this letter to Lord Belhaven as quickly as possible." Once Jasper arrived, her aunt would have no choice but to cease her ministrations and actually listen to Hetty. The boy nodded and mounted the horse, urging Gringolet into a blistering gallop.

Once he was gone, she snuck back into the house and debated her next move. It was not yet dawn, and she didn't much feel like retreating to her room to wait for Jasper. She thought back to her aunt's claims that her inheritance was tied up with her father's solicitors. If she could only see the papers and documents alluding to such, she might understand her position better. Perhaps if she could prove to Aunt Celia that she was not on the verge of going mad *or* destitute, she might begin treating her like a woman grown and in charge of her own affairs.

Eventually, she found the study, which seemed to double

as Sutton House's library. It was not nearly as impressive as Mulgrave Hall's, but it would suit. For a study, the air was very Bohemian: peacock feathers and silk scarves were strewn about at random, vases of dead flowers lined the shelves, a half-dressed mannequin in a top hat leaned menacingly over the desk, and her father's sketches were littered across every surface. These she wished to collect like precious jewels, when she had a spare moment to devote to the task. But for now, she had work to do.

She lit a taper, careful to close the door behind her so no light leaked into the hall. It was cold enough for her teeth to chatter, but she could not risk a fire, not when she wished to remain inconspicuous. She pulled a dressing gown from the rack, knocking over an ornate pot beside the fireplace, the contents clanging on the floor. Wincing, she waited for the sound of footsteps above her, but none arrived. Certain contents of the pot were not surprising: a fire poker, a pair of tongs, a wire brush, and a shovel, but curiously there was more than one sword, as though her father had been as likely to engage in swordplay as he was to tend to the fire. Even more curious, the hilt of the sword felt *right* in her hand when she picked it up, so much so that she had to wonder if she knew how to use it. It was another mystery to add to the list, to be explored when she could.

Looking around at the charming chaos of her father's study, Hetty did not think the room had changed since he died. Was that her doing? Had the pain of losing him led her to crystallize his last moments, the messes he'd made and the tasks left unfinished?

She moved over to the desk and began absently adjusting the pens and inkpots, trying to recall more of the man who had left them there. She wrapped the dressing gown around her shoulders, breathing in the now-familiar scent of pipe smoke and turpentine, suddenly able to conjure images of her father humming Strauss to himself, or engaged in lively arguments with his financiers over glasses of absinthe, the only French import he would allow in his home.

With each conscious moment spent in the home she once shared with him, Hetty was remembering more of her father. Confidence surged through her. She had thought her memories were unreachable, but perhaps not.

And so, she began the tedious work of reading through reams of documents, searching for some indication as to the situation her father had left her in, hoping things were not so dire as her aunt had suggested. Maybe she and Claremont had not thought to look through the intimidating mess of papers. It didn't take long for Hetty to find a letter from his solicitor, outlining the contents of her father's will, and the legal steps that must be taken in order for Hetty to officially inherit. She didn't know much about finances, but the annual sum she was entitled to seemed more than enough to maintain Sutton House. Perhaps her aunt had been mistaken about her strained circumstances, and once Hetty was able to talk with the solicitor, matters would be sorted.

She leaned back in her father's chair, relieved to know she was not destitute, but saddened all the same by the loss of him. Sitting in his chair, wrapped in his dressing gown and surrounded by the precious remnants of his life, she could recall even more pieces of John Henry Davenport: the rich bark of his laugh, the way paint collected in the creases of his fingers, how he gladly would have eaten plum pudding for every meal if she had allowed it. But she wanted to remember everything: his joys and his triumphs, his sorrows and his grief. Perhaps once she had convinced her aunt of her good health, she would find her father's studio and study his paintings until she recalled more of him. It comforted her to have a plan.

But sudden footsteps in the hall startled her. She extinguished the taper and dove under her father's desk as the door handle jiggled, feeling half foolish for her escape and half desperate to learn what she could of her family's motives without them knowing she was listening.

"Come, you must be chilled to the bone," said her aunt, ushering someone into the study.

"The carriage ride was less than pleasant, I'll admit," said a man's voice she did not recognize. Cold air accompanied them into the study, brushing against Hetty's ankles under the desk. "I'll be glad when this business is behind us."

"Darling, the second I can sell this miserable hovel and return to London, it will be done and I'll never set foot in bloody Surrey again."

What followed was the sound of two people kissing rather passionately. Wetly, even. Hetty supposed having to hear it was her punishment for eavesdropping.

At last they came up for air. "How does she fare, then?"

"She is a loathsome bother, but Claremont does not think her memory has improved at all, to our immense relief."

"I imagine that would be an awkward circumstance indeed," the man replied. "I can hardly believe your luck in that."

"Luck or divine providence, perhaps," her aunt replied. "Well, what did your solicitor say? Is our testimony enough?"

The man hesitated. "You're certain she wouldn't recall basic facts about her own life?"

"Claremont said she did not recall that her mother was long dead from scarlet fever, nor events that occurred very recently. I think we could tell her anything and she'd have no reason to suspect we were lying to her. She is pathetically eager to trust us."

Hetty's blood went cold. So her mother *hadn't* gone mad. Before she could think further on it, the man continued. "And the story about her madness?"

"I have been planting the seed. It is not an entirely unimaginable thing, to lose one's memory after a spell of madness. In fact, I find that more plausible than the truth of the matter."

"I suppose you're right about that," he said. "Are you concerned she might suddenly come to her senses?"

Her aunt laughed unkindly. "I told her last night that her mother had been similarly afflicted. Mad as a March Hare, and dead because of it. You should have seen her face. She took to the story immediately, no doubt sensing the parallels between them. Like I said, the seeds have been planted; we need merely water them."

The man cleared his throat. "You said Doctor Poole has an existing connection with a hospital in Leicester?"

"Yes, the Leicester Borough Lunatic Asylum. We thought it best to have her committed somewhere she has no roots or connections, no friends to ask after her. Leicester seemed the natural choice."

"Well, Reynolds believes your testimony, in addition to the testimony of Claremont and Dr. Poole, would be enough for the court to side with you. Better still if she rails against her incarceration. There is little the proprietors of such institutions detest more than an assertive, ungovernable woman."

Hetty barely breathed as her body flooded with grim awareness and her heart hammered in her chest. It was far, far worse than she feared. Her aunt and cousin did not mean to see her well again. Rather, they intended to have her declared insane and confined to an asylum. Would likely have succeeded, too, had she not overheard the plot. *But why?*

Her aunt breathed a sigh of relief. "She is willful, to be certain, and she will not go quietly, if we judge her by her utter panic from our first attempt."

"Hysteria will only strengthen your claims to her insanity. Once she is deemed medically impaired, it is simply a matter of naming Claremont the trustee of her inheritance. And with no other relations, that solemn duty could only fall to him."

"And then we shall be saved," she said, relief lengthening her words. "And if my son ever bets the Claremont seat in a game of cards again, I will murder him myself."

And then she understood. Claremont and Aunt Celia were little more than strangers to her because they'd had no relationship when her father was alive. They were conniving, opportunistic predators who had emerged only when Hetty was at her most vulnerable, appearing under the guise of concerned family, seeking the fortune left to her by her dead father.

That was why Hetty had fled into the night. The bone-deep fear that followed her through her injury made sense now. There was nothing more frightening than the thought of losing her autonomy, and nothing more precarious than an unmarried, unprotected woman's position in the world, threatened by the very family who should have supported her.

That was why Claremont had been so hesitant around her until he realized that she did not remember his previous sins, and why Aunt Celia had been drugging her to keep her compliant. She felt sick at the betrayal, and at herself for falling for their deception so easily, relying too readily on her cousin's explanations. Hetty had wanted answers, and while his had been lacking, they'd provided more than she could come up with on her own, and so she had accepted them without question.

"You may be required to ensure she has access to certain resources for the rest of her life, but we are speaking of paltry sums, mere pocket change for her general upkeep, I'd expect." He spoke blandly, as though the oppression and imprisonment of a woman was a habitual occurrence for him. "What of the earl you mentioned?"

"A fantasy, I suspect. She's a commoner without any prospects. If an attachment existed between them, it will surely fade."

To be reduced to her limited prospects, and Jasper to an aristocrat's cold desperation, was the ultimate insult. Hetty would have loved him if he were a pauper, and would have parted with all of her worldly belongings if it meant they could be together. What did Aunt Celia know of love?

The armchair creaked, indicating that the man had stood. "I must return to London, but I await swift word of your next move."

"Now that we know our plan is a solid one, I see no reason to delay," said her aunt. "Send my regards to your wife," she added smugly, her voice fading as she got farther away.

The door shut quietly. Hetty didn't breathe for several heartbeats before peeking out over the table.

She was alone.

Alone in a house with two people who intended to rob her of her freedom and security both.

And she had sent away her only ally.

Hetty scrambled quickly from her hiding place and weighed her options. She might have suspected it before, but it was clear to her now that her aunt had never sent the letter to Helena. She had likely burned it at the earliest opportunity. At least now she knew for certain that the Maycotts had not abandoned her, and had she had her wits about her, Hetty would never have doubted the fidelity that had blossomed between them all so quickly.

But her aunt had taken special care to ensure she did *not* have her wits about her.

Thank God she had sent Jack to Mulgrave Hall. She didn't think the Maycotts would even know where to look for her otherwise. At the ball, Claremont had feverishly impressed upon her that they return at once to Sutton House, leaving very little time for Hetty to get her bearings or make more solid plans with Jasper as to when they would see each other next.

Perhaps he had been looking for her all along.

Maybe she needed to be patient. But after what she had just heard her aunt say, Hetty feared she didn't have much time left for patience. She could run again. Take another horse and disappear before they knew to go looking for her. But the thought of fleeing her father's home for a second time left a sour taste in her mouth, especially given her current weakened state. There was no guarantee that this escape would be any more successful than her first attempt, or that her aunt and cousin wouldn't resort to more drastic measures to silence her for good. Hetty began pacing the room. The sun was only just beginning to rise. She likely had a small sliver of time before her aunt would wish to administer another dose.

They thought her weak. Naive. Alone.

She would let them underestimate her. She would let them believe they had the upper hand. It was the only way she might emerge with her freedom intact. But she had to be careful. She had been blessedly lucky to overhear her aunt in the study. She shuddered to think of what might have happened to her if their next move had been a mystery and she had continued to trust them. But her tendency to eavesdrop had at last proven useful.

Because of it, Hetty had been given enough time to formulate a plan.

Circumstances had forced her to flee her home before, but she was in something of a better position now, even with her past still veiled from her.

This time, she would not be the one to leave.

This time she would fight.

Chapter Twenty-Eight

HETTY

Hetty fidgeted in her father's chair. She hadn't had time to change into something more appropriate, so she would be facing her aunt and cousin in naught but her father's dressing gown. She missed the armor of Isobel's dress, but this would have to do.

She could hear them already, combing the upstairs rooms, calling her name as though she were a missing pet.

They would find her soon enough, and her plan would be set into motion.

So much could still go wrong. She had sent away the young groomsman. If Claremont wished to overpower her, she would not be able to defend herself. She was relying on the fact that deep down, he was still bound by the restraints of a gentleman. That, and the threat of retribution, should they act on their plot. Aunt Celia did not believe that anything existed between Hetty and Jasper, but Claremont had seen them together and had felt the heat of Jasper's skepticism and the weight of his concern. If his mother didn't believe Jasper would come for her, her cousin did.

Eventually, they found her. Her aunt had the audacity to feign shock at the sight of her.

Hetty did not have time for games. She tried to speak clearly and give no indication of how very frightened she was to be in a room alone with them. "Claremont, Lady Celia, welcome."

"Hetty," said her aunt, clutching at her chest in a strained show of disbelief. "I did not expect to see you so..."

"Conscious?" she offered. Claremont blanched, but his mother's posture only straightened. Hetty continued. "I must say, your teas have not been the reviving sort, Aunt Celia."

She was playing for time, trying her best to keep her emotions in check lest she rush them to desperation. If Jack had gone as quickly as he had assured her he would, Jasper couldn't be that far, could he?

Aunt Celia frowned. "Isn't there a famous Latin phrase, Claremont, about the remedy often being worse than the disease?"

"*Aegrescit medendo*," he replied, before offering Hetty a smug look. "That's Vergil," he added.

"And what does Vergil say of rapacious relations?" asked Hetty, suddenly discovering a wealth of Roman poetry in her mind. "*Latet anguis in herba*, I believe." There really was much to Aunt Adelaide's theory that Hetty's deeply buried memories could be tricked into resurfacing.

Her aunt looked to Claremont, evidently not as familiar with Vergil's works. He tugged on his collar and cleared his throat. "A snake hides in the grass," he translated.

"Oh, you cannot mean that, Hetty," her aunt cried, making

her way toward the door and closing it. "We have only ever wanted what's best for you."

Hetty did not like being shut in the room with her would-be kidnappers. "I'd ask that you keep the door open, Aunt."

"My dear, we wouldn't want anyone hearing that which should be kept between family. Think of your reputation." She gave Claremont a significant look, an expression that could only be read between the two of them. Hetty was getting nervous. She looked out the window, praying a carriage full of Maycotts would appear.

Her aunt sat in the armchair by the fire. "Now, what is it you are accusing us of?"

Hetty didn't want to play her hand too quickly. She knew very well her aunt's intentions, but she didn't want to reveal the extent of her knowledge before her actual rescuers arrived. "I don't appreciate being drugged, Aunt Celia. I cannot imagine any doctor would have prescribed laudanum in such quantities."

Her aunt tilted her head. "Perhaps my hand was a bit heavy, but my aim was only to help you through your ailment and avoid another incident like before. But look at the state of you, my dear. Perhaps I was wrong for thinking your mother's fate could be avoided." She gestured to her son. "Claremont, does she have a temperature?"

Her cousin moved toward her, but Hetty backed away from him, bumping into the pot she had upturned earlier.

Her aunt made a tired, disapproving noise. "Your insistence on villainizing us troubles me so, Henrietta."

By then, Claremont had reached her, his arm extended as though to check her forehead. But Hetty knew it was all a farce, and she didn't trust either of them in the slightest. She batted his hand away, surprising them both.

Her aunt's tone was blank. "There are places for girls like you, Henrietta. Places where you can get the help you so desperately need." But Hetty ignored her, choosing instead to focus on her cousin as he advanced ever closer. Her aunt sighed. "Claremont, take hold of her. She has lost her mind entirely and there is little we can do for her except protect her from herself."

"Do not touch me," Hetty warned her cousin with a snarl.

But Claremont had no reason to listen to her, and every reason to heed his mother's command. He was on her in a flash, seizing one wrist hard enough to cause pain, and reaching for the other while she tried desperately to squirm away. But he was too strong for her, even with an arm free. Hetty might have stood a chance at her full strength, but her aunt's efforts had weakened her. She knew if he got hold of her fully, she would not have the means to escape him.

Aunt Celia rose as they struggled. "I'll send for Dr. Poole and he will attest to your madness, Henrietta. Such a shame, but we are woefully ill equipped to help you in the ways you so desperately need. But these things do tend to run in families, and we all know how it ended for your mother."

It almost seemed as though her aunt believed Hetty might be swayed toward accepting she was mad and go quietly. Perhaps there was a time when that tack might have worked. Maybe if Claremont and Lady Celia had been the ones to find her in the road without her memories instead of Jasper Maycott. They would have coddled her into further illness, but Jasper had challenged her to get better, at first out of spite, but then because the small glimpses of the life she had before gave her something to reach for. Without the Maycotts, she might not have rediscovered herself at all.

Cursing, Claremont twisted her arm behind her back, and

her vision went black with panic and rage. They meant to lock her away, to silence her in the most insidious way possible. And if they managed it before Jasper reached her, there was a good chance she'd be lost forever.

But Hetty would rather die than lose her freedom.

She reached blindly for something to defend herself with, her fingers grasping the hilt of the sword she had assumed belonged to her father. Instantly, memories flooded her mind: the clashing of steel, the jolt of pain surging up her arm, a grunt of air forced from her lungs, sweat dripping in her eyes, and the way victory tasted when she bested her opponent. In a flash, another essential truth about Henrietta Davenport locked into place: she was a most accomplished swordswoman.

Dance came easily to her because she had been trained to gracefully defeat her rival. The hard muscles of her arms came from the weight of a sword in her hand. It was like the pieces of a puzzle falling into place. Nothing could feel more right to her than the grip of the hilt. It was as familiar as breathing, as natural as putting one foot before the other.

Instinct took over. Hetty did not need to carefully plan what to do next, not when she had been there a thousand times before with opponents exceedingly more prepared than Claremont. In one fluid motion, she twisted out of his grip and planted her feet firmly on the ground in a perfect attack stance, holding the tip of the blade to her cousin's throat.

He sputtered, arms raised, his jaw slack with the shock of it. "Christ," was all he could manage.

She pushed forward, knowing she hadn't won yet. Her exhaustion was barely a factor. The threat of imprisonment had awoken every nerve in her body, and the sword in her hand did not feel heavy or burdensome. In fact, wielding it made her feel freer than she had in days.

"Hetty, please," her cousin gasped as the blade went deep enough to draw blood. He was shaking, his voice thinned to a whine. She wondered if anyone had ever given him a good beating before. Some aristocrats dabbled in pugilism, but not Claremont, she suspected, whose hands were as soft as lambskin.

"Stop!" her aunt cried from behind her. "Stop, you're hurting him!"

I might yet. She relished how the scales had shifted, now that she could defend herself. Her cousin looked upon her with real fear in his eyes. It was obvious from the way she moved that Hetty knew how to wield the weapon in her hand.

Ignoring her aunt's pleas, Hetty forced Claremont backward into a chair, where he landed with a thud and a whimper.

She gave him her most menacing look. "Move and I will not hesitate to slice you open. Do you understand me?" He nodded as vigorously as the blade would allow, and only then did she turn to her aunt, her sword arm still outstretched toward her cousin.

"Leave now and I may—"

"Hetty, this is madness! We came here to help shepherd you through your grief. How can you treat us this way when we are all you have left in the world?"

Hetty no longer cared to placate her aunt. "You claim to care for me, Aunt Celia, but it is you who would see me bound to an asylum, with my father's inheritance in the hands of your foolish son. Love could never be the impetus for a betrayal such as that."

For the first time since Hetty had awoken, Lady Celia, no longer concerned with lulling her niece into a false sense of safety, allowed her mouth to twist into a cruel grimace. "If you think this will support your claims to your sanity, you are sorely mistaken," she hissed. "One word from us and I think, given your family history, they will have no choice but to commit you."

"And what family history is that, Aunt Celia? You said it yourself, my mother was not mad, though perhaps you need be reminded that even if she were, it is not evidence against my own sanity or something either of us should be punished for."

If she was surprised that Hetty had eavesdropped, her aunt did not show it. "How long do you think you can maintain this absurdity? And who would vouch for you, when you hold a sword against your only family's throat?"

"You think me alone in the world, Aunt, and at your mercy, but that is not the case." Fear flashed across her aunt's face for a brief second, long enough to embolden Hetty. "You see, I have already written and dispatched two letters this morning, one to my father's solicitor, who I suppose now acts as my solicitor, and one to the Earl of Belhaven, alerting them to my exact whereabouts and condition, as well as informing them of your intentions as to my inheritance." It was, at least partially, a lie. Hetty hadn't had the time to pen a letter to her father's solicitor after overhearing her aunt. But by now, Jasper must have received the letter she had written him before she'd known the scope of her family's betrayal, and she felt reasonably confident he would be arriving at Sutton House at any moment, even if she hadn't known to impress upon him the very real danger she was in.

Her aunt laughed cruelly. "You have much confidence that these men will rescue you from the miserable future that awaits you?"

"What you fail to realize, Aunt, is that I am more than capable of rescuing myself." She inclined her head toward her sword as if to prove her point. Claremont let out a noise that was caught somewhere between a giggle and a cry, and Hetty straightened. "Even so, I suggest you leave before Belhaven arrives, as he will be most aggrieved to hear of your plot against me, to say nothing of my solicitor, who may yet involve the police."

Claremont whimpered. Lady Celia looked to him, disgusted, and back at Hetty. "You have no proof," she challenged, and it was true. Hetty could not prove they meant to steal her inheritance and falsely have her declared insane.

"Perhaps not," she offered, twisting the blade slightly, eliciting a gasp from her cousin. "But I do have a sword, and right now it is pointed at your beloved son, the one who would see you a pauper before exerting even a modicum of honor or an ounce of self-restraint. And I am also patient. I may not be able to prove your plot against me now, but so help me God, if you attempt to cross me again, I will not rest until a full accounting of your misdeeds, from theft to kidnapping to fraud, are read aloud in the halls of the Old Bailey."

Her aunt assessed her coolly, looking between Hetty and the blade and her son, her calculations evidently not amounting in her favor. "What is it you want, then?"

Hetty's heart began beating very quickly. She couldn't lose her nerve yet. For all she knew, her aunt was playing for time, seeking another weakness in Hetty to exploit. "For you both to leave immediately and never return. Do so, and I will not involve the police."

"Hetty, please, we are *family*," pleaded Claremont, finding his voice far too late.

She felt no sympathy for a man who would have happily seen her bound to an asylum in order to pay off his gambling debts. "I do not believe you know the meaning of the word, Cousin."

Tears welled in his eyes, but they were not born out of remorse. Rather they were the tears of a man who had been caught. She lowered the sword, the threat of capture no longer looming over her.

"Claremont, if you had simply *asked* me for help, I might have done so." She looked then to her aunt. "If you both had come to me with love in your hearts after my father had died, I would have gladly done what I could for you."

Claremont had the decency to at least look ashamed, but the same could not be said for his mother, who could not leave without delivering one final insult.

"You know, you really are sentimental and dull. No wonder your father could not bear the thought of living permanently in England with you."

The insults might have wounded the Hetty of a few days prior. This Hetty almost pitied her aunt. "Is it any wonder my father sought to place so much distance between us?"

With a huff, Lady Celia swept out of the room as though Hetty had been the one to wrong her. Claremont sheepishly followed, and Hetty allowed herself to slump into her father's chair and let go of the sword that had saved her from a grim fate.

She found she could not move as real, unembellished tiredness settled onto her like a leaden cloak, but she would not sleep until they were gone. She heard them making a racket as they packed their belongings, likely stealing what silverware and jewelry they could fit in their trunks, but Hetty lacked the energy to stop them. All she wanted was for them to leave her house.

In a little under an hour, they were done, their carriage packed. She looked out the window and did not see a footman or driver. Perhaps her cousin would take the reins. Served him right. The snow had at least been packed down or melted some since the last storm. The road away from her was not impassable.

Claremont was already at the carriage when her aunt passed the study, obviously intending to leave without saying goodbye.

"Aunt Celia," she called. Her aunt paused at the threshold of Sutton House, silent, fuming. Hetty caught up to her, suddenly overcome with the wish that things had been different. That she had found a family with them. "Did you really think it would work?"

For a brief second, her aunt's mask fell and she looked almost sincere. "My dear, how naive you are to think it wouldn't. We women have little more than what men choose to leave for us, be it money or power. Now that you are alone in the world, perhaps you'll learn."

"But I am not alone," Hetty argued. "Family is not only determined by blood; it is a choice. And just as you have made yours, I have made mine."

Her aunt gave her one last pitying look before picking up her skirts and descending, leaving Hetty in a house that did not feel like a home.

Tears fell freely as the carriage faded from view, but they were not tears of sadness. They were tears of relief. Of knowing she had saved herself from a fate all too commonly thrust upon women like her, and she had done it on her own. Jasper had cautioned her only days before that others might seek to manipulate her, and that the threat of asylum hung over every woman in need of succor whose behavior marked them as unwell or defiant. She hadn't thought to fear it from her own family.

A sob rattled through her chest as she thought of what would have awaited her in Leicester. Stripped of her freedom, of her voice, imprisoned for the crime of being unwell and guilty of possessing something a man wanted for himself. Her heart ached for the women who hadn't been so lucky, and the innumerable tragedies they faced. How easily she could have joined their ranks. How simple it was to silence a woman.

When her tears ran dry and her heart stopped racing, Hetty allowed herself some time to reflect on the circumstances that had brought her to Sutton House without a plan or an ally or an ounce of skepticism. It was the promise of belonging that had ensnared her fully. Of answering the question of Jane without-a-surname at last. But she knew now that she was wrong to think she had to belong to a place or to a bloodline.

At last, Hetty understood that a new life could begin out of the ashes of her old one. She might not ever remember all she had left behind, but that didn't mean her life would be empty. She could discover herself anew, find new passions, chase new dreams. And she knew exactly who she wanted by her side on the journey.

Hetty had awoken in Mulgrave Hall without any certainty in her life, but now she stood in her father's home and she knew the truth.

She loved Jasper. All of him. The stern bastard, the devoted brother, the lover of Jane Austen, the reluctant rescuer of kittens, and the man who had held his family together when they could have fallen apart, who cared for others long before he had ever cared for himself.

Hetty thought she'd come home to find her past, but instead she'd found her future. She wanted a new life with him, not the disparate, broken pieces of her old one.

She had left the belonging she sought behind her when she'd left the Maycotts. Hetty did not belong to a place she did not remember, or to family who did not love her. She belonged where her heart wished to be.

Jasper was her belonging, and at long last she knew Mulgrave Hall was her home.

Chapter Twenty-Nine

JASPER

For a man of six and twenty, Jasper Maycott had endured an uncommonly high number of terrible days. The day after the Banfield ball was among his worst. Knowing Hetty was in danger, but not knowing where to find her was excruciating. Explaining the circumstances to his guests had felt similarly painful. Out of all of them, only Beatrice seemed insulted by the lie she had been told about Hetty's background. Clarence, on the other hand, took to the matter rather gleefully, much to Jasper's dismay.

"A natural-born actress, I say! I simply must have her as my Ophelia!" he'd cried, as though her life were not currently in peril.

After some speculation and excitement, it had been determined that not much could be done in the middle of the night, and the group would reconvene in the morning to plan a daring rescue.

Jasper had not slept a wink, and only his last shred of sense had kept him from tearing into the night and banging on every door in Surrey until he found her. Instead, he focused his efforts on waking everyone up at the crack of dawn with a hearty breakfast spread, a great deal of coffee, and an apology in advance for how he would be treating them the rest of the day.

As suspected, he was a punishing taskmaster. First, he sent the ladies to call on nearby country houses to dig up information about where Claremont might be staying. Next, he buried Viola and Freddie in all the books he could find about Surrey's landed gentry, thinking perhaps there might be information about Claremont's other properties. He even went so far as to dispatch August, George, and Edgar to London in order to sniff about Claremont's abandoned townhome in Mayfair and convene with Simon's men, who might help lead them to the baron. Clarence he kept close because he didn't quite trust the man with a more important task, and he insisted Lucian stay in case Hetty returned to them injured.

It was a chaotic enterprise, but better, he suspected, than waiting for news of something terrible. Still, he thought he might lose his mind with worry, and those who had stayed behind at Mulgrave Hall were doing all they could to avoid him. When his sisters returned with nothing to help him, he thought he might go mad. And when another night passed without Hetty safely in Mulgrave Hall, he was sure of it.

In the end, it was Aunt Adelaide who found her. Jasper had been attempting to keep his aunt out of it entirely, worried she would be more of an obstacle than an aid, but she had sensed weakness in Freddie and dragged the information from him. She had swiftly departed Mulgrave Hall early that morning and returned to it before Jasper knew she was gone. He met her in the hallway, prepared for censure.

She peeled her gloves off. "Sutton House, home of the recently deceased painter John Henry Davenport and his only child, Miss Henrietta Davenport. Not eight miles from here. My coachman will take you."

Jasper had nearly choked. "How?"

"You don't think whispers get around when an uninvited guest weasels his way into a ball?" She raised a brow at him. "We spinsters can be quite useful; pity others choose to underestimate us." She rolled back her shoulders and gave him an evaluating look. "I'm told nearly all of the servants have been let go. I don't know what you may be walking into, Jasper, but you must be on your guard."

"But you otherwise don't object?"

"To your taking a wife?" She shook her head, her features softening. "I would never."

"No?" replied Jasper, his image of the ever-strict Aunt Adelaide not matching the woman who stood before him, urging him to behave in a rather improper manner for an earl.

She sighed and gazed out the window. "I daresay you know it was my foolish prejudice against your mother that tore a rift between your father and I, a rift I was never quite able to mend. It is the regret of my life, and the reason I avoided Mulgrave Hall like the coward I am, even after his death."

"I challenge you to find even one individual who would call you a coward."

"Not to my face, perhaps," she added with a small smile. "But it is a coward that lets the fear of what may occur stop them from living the life they were meant to."

She spoke of her own past, but the sentiment applied to Jasper as well, and only served to strengthen his convictions. "I wish you and my father had been able to mend your relationship before he died."

Her gaze over the Surrey countryside was wistful. "You know, I likely would have stayed away forever, stewing in shame. But it was a letter from Viola that convinced me to come back."

"Indeed? I didn't even know you corresponded."

"I'm not sure I'd describe it as such, but she has kept me abreast of the goings-on at Mulgrave Hall for several years now. After you lost Anthony and your parents, her letters became unintentionally revealing, which led me to believe I could be of use to you all, in some small way."

"And that you have been, and not just because you found Hetty for me."

She turned to him. "If I thought either of you less deserving of the other, I'd not approve."

"Of that I am sure," he added hastily. "But Mulgrave Hall was a terribly lonesome place before your arrival. I do hope you'll stay a while longer."

A foolish man might have commented on the tears forming in the corners of his aunt's eyes. Jasper wisely said nothing as she collected herself. "I find there is not much left for me in Bordeaux," she said before turning quickly on her heel and departing with all of the straight-spined dignity she could muster.

That was enough for Jasper.

He found Nash and August and they left almost immediately. And now he was bundled into his aunt's carriage, racing down the narrow roads of Surrey, facing the prospect of possibly fighting a man for Hetty's freedom.

"It may come to blows, you know," he warned the others, after having apprised them of everything he knew about the baron and his crippling debts.

His valet flexed his hand and formed a tight fist. "I'm not afraid to fight a toff, if that's what you're suggesting."

Jasper let his head fall back on the seat. "Christ, I haven't punched a man in years."

"In my experience, it isn't something one forgets how to do," said Nash.

"You're in luck," began August. "I scarcely make it a month without punching someone. Toffs or otherwise."

Jasper eyed him wearily. "We have much to discuss, August."

"And no time at all for a discussion," his brother replied, not entirely upset that the situation at hand would prevent one from occurring.

"Yes, well, pity I'm a bit distracted."

A small stretch of silence, before Nash asked, "You love her, then?"

"More than anything," was Jasper's emphatic reply. "I know you have your doubts as to her character—"

"Not yours, though. If you love her, that's enough evidence for me. Granted, it *is* rather early in the day to be fighting for a woman's honor, but who am I to turn down such an opportunity?"

"You know, Nash, I find the pesky matter of a woman's honor to be an inexhaustible topic of conversation," said August.

By then, the carriage began to slow and Jasper was out of it before it stopped fully, hitting the ground running. He barely saw the house, could not have told you the color of the trim nor the location of the stables. All he could think of was Hetty within, needing his help.

He took the steps three at a time and pounded on the door quite forcefully.

"Claremont, if you've harmed a hair on her head, I'll make you wish Griffith was the one behind this door!" he roared, primed and ready to do what he must in order to keep her safe.

Nash and August joined him on the landing as he knocked again, harder this time. The very last thing he expected was for Hetty to answer.

Jasper's heart burst at the sight of her. She wore a long silk robe and an overlarge dressing gown, her hair tumbling down to her waist and her eyes wide with shock. She was pale, so pale, and he could see she had been crying. Half a second elapsed before he crushed her against his chest, relief numbing the rage that had been propelling him.

"Hetty, my Hetty," he whispered against her forehead, giddy with relief. "You're unharmed?" He held her at arm's length, eyes on every inch of her, searching for injury before pulling her into his arms once more. "I never should have let you leave alone. I am so sorry, Hetty."

"Jasper." His name on her lips was an incantation he wished to hear her recite for the rest of his life. He pulled back to look at her, her silver eyes bewitching him as easily now as they had when he first beheld them in a sliver of moonlight. With her hair loose around her shoulders, she looked like a priestess of old, which made him her devoted acolyte. "You came," she said, bursting into tears.

No heavenly power could have stopped the kiss that followed, her tears staining his cheeks, the taste of salt on his tongue as she smiled against his lips. It was a kiss of relief. Of joy. Of knowing the woman he loved was safe and would continue to be so, so help him God.

August cleared his throat behind them.

Jasper looked up at his brother and back at Hetty. "I take it your cousin is gone?"

She nodded. "I sent them away this morning."

"And they left without a fuss?" he asked, hardly believing it.

Hetty blushed. "There may have been a bit of swordplay involved."

August choked, the noise caught somewhere between shock and admiration.

"And here I was, thinking I'd be the one doing the rescuing. I should have known you'd rescue yourself, Hetty." Jasper's gaze went back to Nash and August. "Return to Mulgrave Hall and call off the search, will you?"

August nodded but Nash looked concerned.

"And how will you return, my lord?"

He looked down at Hetty. "There are horses in the stables?" She nodded. "We will find our way back eventually."

Nash gave a quick nod. "Happy to see you are unharmed, Miss…"

"Davenport."

Not for bloody long, Jasper thought, feeling rather possessive.

"Miss Davenport," Nash said with a bow.

"Looking forward to better making your acquaintance, Hetty," said August with a genuine smile. "It's not every day you hear of a woman dispatching her unsavory relatives at sword point."

"And I you, August," she replied, blushing.

With that, they left, and Hetty ushered Jasper farther into the house. Her house, he supposed, even if it felt wrong to consider anything but Mulgrave Hall to be her home. They would get to that in due time. For now, he simply wanted to hold her and relish the complete lack of walls left standing between them.

They sank into the nearest settee. "How did you get here so quickly?" Hetty asked breathlessly.

"What do you mean? It took me more than a day to find you."

Her brow furrowed. "I only just sent Jack with the letter this morning, and despite everything I didn't think you'd respond quite so vigorously."

"Jack? What letter?"

"The footman. He was the only person I could trust. If he hadn't brought you the letter, I would still be at my aunt's mercy, I suspect."

"I didn't get the letter, Hetty. Perhaps we passed him on the road. But I have been looking for you since the ball. It was a devil of a time for us to find you, too. We only managed it thanks to Aunt Adelaide."

"Truly?" she whispered.

He nodded. "Why send a letter? Why not come yourself?"

Her shoulders slumped. "I was a fool to trust Claremont," she started.

"Not a fool, Hetty." He brought his hand to her chin, raising her head. "Your heart and your insistence on seeing the good in others are the best parts of you."

Her cheeks blushed pink at that. "They began drugging me as soon as I arrived, Claremont and my aunt. It took some time before I realized. And by then I had already lost so much time, and their motives were still a mystery to me. Eventually, I overheard my aunt while eavesdropping—"

"Naturally," he said, struggling to keep his voice even and light as murderous thoughts flooded his mind.

"And I discovered they meant to have me confined to an asylum in order to access my inheritance. They meant to use my lack of memories against me, and told me I had gone mad with grief. My aunt went so far as to claim my mother went mad before she died, and that I had inherited her affliction. I was starting to believe them, before I heard otherwise."

Jasper had never felt a rage so all-encompassing. "It's a good thing Claremont left before I arrived."

"I said as much when I told them to leave with the tip of my blade at his throat. But he was not the true architect of the plot. My aunt was the one who would have locked me away so easily, erasing me from the world."

"Even if they had succeeded, Hetty, know that I would have found you. There is no place on earth they could have hidden you in, no dark corner I would not have torn apart in order to find you and bring you home."

She kissed him again, deeper than any they had shared before. He wanted to be kissing those lips forever, learning what pleased her, tormenting her sweetly with his touch, cherishing her above all else.

She pulled back slightly, her eyes soft on him, her hands cupping his jaw. "Jasper, I love you."

Jasper had been so overwhelmed to see her safe and healthy that he hadn't expected her swift declaration. It rather disarmed him. "What?" he choked, barely able to keep himself together.

She smiled at how undone he seemed. "I didn't say it before, and I don't want another second to pass without you knowing my heart. I love you," she repeated, kissing him softly on his mouth. "I love you." Another kiss on his cheek. "I love you." Now his forehead. "I love you."

Jasper hadn't thought happiness such as this could ever be his again. "I've loved you since you were sick on my boots, dear Hetty."

"Don't remind me," she groaned with a smile. "I suppose I'll never live that incident down. Our grandchildren will know the manner of our meeting, whether I like it or not."

Jasper thought he might lose his cool entirely at her casual mention of their future grandchildren. "At least they will know it was true love between us."

Her smile could have warmed him in the depths of a blizzard. "Indeed, though I might hope for a more conventional path for them."

"I never had much use for convention."

Another beaming grin aimed straight to his heart. But then she yawned and frowned. "I am so tired but I desire never to sleep again, after having it weaponized against me. And I feel wretched and dirty and barely able to walk more than a few feet without risk of collapse." She looked at him sheepishly. "This is not the reunion I dreamed of."

He stood and extended his arms to her. "May I?" he asked, scooping her up before she could protest.

"This feels familiar," she said, referring again to the manner of their meeting.

"Nonsense," he said, pressing a kiss to her forehead. "You were unconscious last time."

"Where are you taking me?"

"I find there is very little turmoil in this life that cannot be solved by a steaming hot bath."

She buried her head into his neck. "That sounds heavenly."

Finding the bathroom was easy. Sutton House, while generous, was not nearly so large as Mulgrave Hall. The bathroom was a sumptuous room of white tile and brass fixtures, with various pots and vials of soaps lining the shelves. He deposited her onto an ottoman and began fiddling with the taps of the tub until the water was hot and tendrils of steam curled around them.

Satisfied, he stood and offered her a small bow, not wanting to leave her alone, but understanding all the same that a woman who had been through an ordeal such as hers might crave a moment of privacy.

"Would you stay?" she asked, her voice small. "I find I do not wish to be alone, not after…"

He joined her on the ottoman and took her hands in his. "Hetty, you need only say the word and I will never leave."

Hetty smiled and reached her hand out to tangle her fingers in his hair. She studied him then, not seeking a lie but rather relishing the truth of what existed between them, what they had uncovered after so much denial. He understood her desire to simply live in the feeling of it, of them.

"Never leave," she whispered. And then she stood, making her way to the bath and selecting a vial of oil to pour into the water, the scent of lavender filling the room. She let her robe fall to the ground, revealing a nightgown beneath. Jasper's mouth went dry at the sight of her. She gestured for him to turn away, which he did, knowing he would wait forever if Hetty wished it. He listened as she stepped into the tub and sank into the water, sighing as she went. What followed could best be described as several minutes of splashes and soft noises designed to drive him wild with speculation.

After some time, Hetty spoke. "You can turn," she said. "I'm mostly clean, save for the places I cannot reach."

She was alone in a sea of bubbles, and so achingly radiant he thought he might collapse at the sight of her.

"And which places are those?" he asked, straining to maintain what little composure he had left.

She blew an errant strand of hair from her eyes. "I'm too sore to reach my back," she said, exasperated by her own limitations.

"May I?" he asked, hardly daring to hope she might allow him to care for her so intimately.

"Would you?" she asked, apparently unaware that he would

give up everything he owned just to touch her.

He rolled up his sleeves and she handed him the cloth she had been using. He dipped it again in the warm, sudsy water and brought it to her back. He paused, awaiting confirmation. She moved the curtain of her sable hair to the side, revealing the delicate slope of her neck and an impossible number of bruises. He hadn't known she was so hurt.

"Hetty…" he started, his voice a rasp as he traced along the worst of them. He shouldn't be surprised. She had been thrown from her horse, after all.

"Shh," she whispered. "I can hardly feel them now."

He brought the cloth to her skin and scrubbed lightly, careful to also knead the sore muscles of her shoulders and neck. She was tense, but she melted at his touch, and for the first time in a long while, Jasper felt blissfully contented. To care for this woman would be the greatest honor of his life. There were so many things left to talk about, but for now he simply relished touching her, being deliberate and careful as he washed her. When his fingers wove into her hair and began rubbing her scalp, she groaned in pleasure. He went painfully hard at the sound.

"My God," she said. "I'm not sure I'll ever be content washing myself again."

Perhaps he'd dedicate his life to performing this task for her. His hand trailed down her spine, coveting the shape of her. He couldn't speak, knew his voice would crack if he did.

Hetty reached for his hand and brought it to her chest. An invitation. Her heart beat hard against his palm. He looked at her and saw her lips were parted and her eyes were hooded with desire.

"Are you sure?" His voice was ragged.

"Never been more certain." She moved his hand to cover her

breast, leaning to kiss him over the edge of the bathtub. Jasper met her hungrily. With one hand, he kneaded the delicious softness of her, while the other cupped the nape of her neck, anchoring her in place so he could taste the sweetness of her mouth. Within seconds, he was as soaked as she was, and water pooled on the tiles beneath his knees.

They parted breathlessly, Jasper doing everything he could to contain his desire lest he devour her whole.

"You should know my intentions are honorable," he said, panting.

"Mine aren't," she replied with a grin. "Take me to bed, Jasper."

He lifted her again, managing to wrap a towel around her as he did, the two of them leaving a trail of water all the way to the closest untouched guest room. He laid her down gently on the counterpane, reverently, because she was the most precious thing he had ever known. Her body was lush, her hips deliciously curved, her breasts heavy. Lit only by the pale winter light, Hetty still managed to glow from within. She was his sun, after all, and Jasper wished only to bask in her glory. He stood over her, unable to hide his own pleasure at the sight of her.

"You're a masterpiece," he said, bringing his hand to her dainty ankle, rubbing her calves, causing her to moan, the sound bringing him near to ecstasy. She lifted herself up on her elbows and bit her bottom lip, seeming to hold herself back from speaking.

"What is it you desire?" He would introduce her to a world of pleasure, if she wished, or retreat to something softer. God knew she had been through enough these past days.

But Hetty managed to surprise him.

"I wish to see you," she said, her voice low. "All of you."

He bit back a groan as he undressed carefully, allowing her to see her fill, her words somehow making him harder than before. Her gaze lowered as he stepped out of his trousers. He was straining with want, pulsing with need. The look in her eyes was hypnotizing.

"You must ask me for it, Hetty." He would not push her before she was ready.

But her desire was as evident as his. "Please," she begged. "I need you."

He crawled over her, need ruling him as well. But after denying himself this pleasure before, he intended to take his time with her. Explore every inch of her. Bring her to the edge again and again until she begged him for release.

He started with small kisses along her collarbone, down to the softness of her stomach. She curled her fingers in his hair, pushing him lower, panting with pleasure already.

"I've hardly touched you, love," he teased.

"Please, Jasper." He continued his exploration, scarcely able to believe the woman he loved writhed beneath him. It was all he'd wanted since their kiss in the library, but until she'd opened the door this morning, it had seemed impossible.

He hadn't known that happiness could be his ever again. And now that he had her, he would never let go.

He brought his palm to the center of her, his fingertips slick with her wetness. Nothing had ever felt so soft, so perfect. She arched up, pressing her delicious heat against his skin, his fingers stroking harder.

"Please," she begged again.

She cried as he slid a finger inside her, as he trailed soft kisses along the silkiness of her thighs, savoring her. She tensed beneath him as his fingers slid in and out in a relentless, steady rhythm. She was close, so close now to the edge. All thoughts of sweet torture left him. He needed her to fall apart, preferably on his tongue. He kissed her between her legs, licking and tasting her desire as she bucked against him, shaking, trembling, coming undone.

And then he lay beside her, not sure he had ever known that bringing someone else release could be so pleasurable. He tucked her against him, rubbing her back, her ribs, her belly as she practically purred in delight.

"If we had simply done that in the library, all of this could have been avoided," she mused.

"But then you wouldn't have found your home." He couldn't imagine that she regretted everything. Finding her place in the world had mattered more to her than anything else.

"I suppose that I needed to come back here to understand that this doesn't feel like home to me any longer." She rolled over and placed her palm on his chest, feeling the steady beating of his heart. "You do. And your family does. And Mulgrave Hall. I feared my life would be empty without my past, but how could it be, when you are my future?"

They kissed again, but without the urgency of before. No, this was the luxuriant kiss of two people who knew they had a lifetime before them.

"Marry me, Hetty," he whispered in her ear.

She answered by bringing her hand to the hardness of him. "Make me yours, Jasper."

Chapter Thirty

HETTY

When they had first met, Hetty had wondered how it would feel to be on the receiving end of the Earl of Belhaven's passion. She had imagined it would be a singular kind of experience for a lucky woman, and she had spent many sinful moments straining to imagine herself in that very position.

Now Hetty had the immense pleasure of knowing that being cherished by a man as attentive and diligent as Jasper went beyond what she had ever envisioned. She had almost lost her mind entirely as he bathed her, the pleasure of his touch on her naked skin too much to bear.

But what was even better was bringing him pleasure in return.

He was hot and hard in her hand. The man had brought her to unfathomed peaks with naught but his tongue and fingers. She could hardly think for imagining what he could do to her with *that*. She gripped a little tighter, watching as his head fell back against the pillow, a soft, almost disbelieving grunt escaping his lips. He was barely breathing as she moved her hand up and down the firm, silken length of him.

"Hetty," he gasped. His head still lolled against the pillow, so he did not expect it when her mouth closed around him, causing him to groan like a man on the verge of death. She relished the heat of him and how he twitched against her tongue. She hadn't known she could be so wanton, driven so wild by the man she loved. She moved her hand faster as he swelled against her lips and tongue, filling her mouth with his delicious heft.

"My God, Hetty, you must…" He gasped again, his entire body tensing beneath her careful exploration. "You must stop, love, before it is too late."

She released him, and he was on her in a flash, managing to tuck her beneath him as he kissed and licked her, nipping lightly at her breasts, seemingly desperate to consume as much of her as he could.

She gasped as the heat of him nudged at her entrance. He paused, all control, and looked her in the eye. She knew he waited for her permission, and that he would stop instantly if she wished it. There was power in knowing that. Comfort, too. But she wanted him so much she thought she might burn to nothing if she did not get some relief.

"I love you," was all she could manage to say. It was answer enough. His eyes glittered with emotion as he braced himself above her, raising one hand to lick his fingers, bringing them to where she was already wet and aching for him. He smiled at her readiness, and she gasped when he pushed inside.

She knew then that it didn't matter if she could not recall being there before with another. As Jasper sank into her, she realized their respective pasts could not touch them here, could not shatter what they shared, after all they had been through. Their fates had been sealed long ago. This joining was merely a confirmation. One of many.

Her fingers traced over his spine and shoulder blades, delighting in the firmness of his muscles, the rippling power in his body, built by the labor of his own two hands. She locked her feet below his hips, urging him deeper as pleasure tightened within her. He shook, gasping against her neck. His thrusts were bringing her to the edge once more, scorching heat welling within her.

"Yes," she urged him onward, begging for that release. "Yes, Jasper," she cried, as they fell over the edge together, Jasper shuddering, Hetty boneless with pleasure. He slumped against her, burying his head in the crook of her neck, his body twitching, fully spent. Hetty squeezed her legs tighter around him, unwilling to let go of that which they had found together.

"Keep doing that and we'll never leave this room," he said into her ear, taking the time to tease a trail of kisses along the slope of her neck.

"That isn't the threat you think it is," she replied, smiling into his soft hair.

But exhaustion tugged at them both. Jasper rolled over, putting his arm around her, and she settled with her head on his chest, listening as their hearts beat in unison and he gently traced his fingers along her spine. They lay like that for some time, silent but blissful.

Eventually, Jasper spoke. "I'd offer to bring you some water, like a gentleman, but I'm not sure where I'd find a glass."

"Allow me," she said, rising and walking naked to the bathroom. She wondered why she did not feel the need to be more modest, but she and Jasper had bared much more than their bodies to each other.

When she returned with a glass of cool water, Jasper's eyes were riveted on her. "We're going to have to go on an extended honeymoon, as I will be banning clothing until I've had my fill of you."

She laughed. "Shouldn't be more than two or three—"

"Years, give or take."

She smiled wickedly, offering him the glass and studying the room they had found themselves in. A guest room, she suspected, with very few personal touches that might bring back memories. She pulled on Jasper's shirt, wandering over to a painting of a seaside cottage, knowing before finding the signature that her father had not painted it.

Jasper joined her at the wall. "You said this didn't feel like home any longer?"

"Memories of my father won't be found here. I didn't know it but we had spent less than a year at Sutton House. Apparently, my father was something of a nomad. An *American*, in fact. Claremont said we rarely lived anywhere more than a couple of seasons." She paused, looking back at Jasper. "If he lives anywhere now, it is here," she said, gesturing to her head.

"Here, too, I think," he replied, covering her heart with his palm. She covered his hand with hers, holding him to her chest. "Do you wish to talk about what happened?"

She knew what he meant, was grateful that he asked. "No, not yet." She wasn't ready to divulge all of her dark and hopeless thoughts, the fears that had ruled her in their brief separation. Not after the joy they had just shared. It was enough that they had found their way back to each other. That they had a lifetime before them. And she was more than tired now, but the idea of sleep did not fill her with dread, not with the man she loved beside her. "Would you mind terribly if we simply slept here, for a time?"

"Mind?" he asked, incredulous. "Hetty, there isn't an activity I'd enjoy more than sleeping next to you, save for one."

They climbed back into bed, both too tired to do much more than hold each other.

Before she fell asleep, Hetty couldn't help but think Jasper Maycott had come a long way from the man beholden to an oath sworn over a deathbed. He had feared losing her, had come close to it, for all he knew, and it had not destroyed him. She imagined that back at Mulgrave Hall there were more than a few victims of the intensity of his efforts at retrieving her, but those were things that could be smoothed over. They were the people that loved Jasper for all his faults and virtues in equal measure, as she did.

Hetty's greatest fear had been discovering she was alone in the world. A woman without a past or a future, without a place she belonged in or a purpose to propel her. Now she had a foundation to build upon. They both did, together.

"Thank you for coming for me," she whispered, not sure if he was sleeping. Hetty might have rescued herself, but there was something to be said for how they had pushed each other to find a way out of their respective darknesses.

His arms tightened around her. "I will always come for you."

They fell asleep like that, entwined, unwilling to let go. When Hetty woke a few hours later, it was to the sight of Jasper studying her, lit up by the warm afternoon sun, his eyes softer than she had ever seen them, his expression utterly unburdened.

"Marry me, Hetty," he said for the second time that day.

She leaned forward and kissed the man she loved, smiling against his lips. "First you must take me home, Jasper," she said, knowing it was answer enough.

Epilogue

Four months was the longest Jasper was willing to wait to make Hetty Davenport his wife.

He very nearly swayed her toward a Christmas wedding. But Hetty, having become somewhat averse to scandal, insisted on a prolonged engagement, lest anyone think she had forced him into it.

When he woke on the morning of their wedding to the jubilant sound of songbirds, and walked the path of bluebells and primrose that blanketed the earth, the sun dappling the forest floor, he could almost admit it had been worth waiting for.

Almost.

What had distinctly *not* been worth the hardship was Hetty's moving out of Mulgrave Hall the day he brought her back to it.

I cannot live in the same house as my fiancé, Jasper. It isn't proper.

So she took residence in Edgar's country home, living quite amiably with Lady Louisa, and visiting Mulgrave Hall as often as she could. If Jasper was distressed about the arrangement, it paled in comparison to how Viola felt about it.

Couldn't you simply not get married? Then she could live here without scandal.

He didn't have the heart to tell her that nothing could be more scandalous. And besides, he wanted Hetty as his *wife*. Nothing less would do.

And so he had waited. Stretched the limits of his patience and sanity both. Took up pugilism once more. Watched Mr. Darcy grow into an orange menace. Aided with the lambing at the Hamilton farm. Hired farmhands so that Charlie Smithfield's mother could cease working in the fields. Helped to rebuild the Turners' barn, lost to fire.

The months had been busy and while he thought the work of a good earl was never done, he felt at least somewhat entitled to a break. A wedding did not strike him as a particularly relaxing event, but Jasper's whole being rested the moment he saw his wife-to-be walking toward him down the grassy aisle, a vision in white silk and delicately embroidered lace. At last, he was completely content.

Their guests were joyous, the occasion euphoric, the food sublime, but the best part of Jasper's day was sitting with his new wife and family at the end of the night, sharing in happiness—something he had deemed impossible to consider only a few months before.

"I can't quite believe we pulled it off," remarked Isobel between sips of scotch from a teacup.

"I can't quite believe that the Ton has accepted me as Hetty after meeting me as Jane," said his wife from the settee where

Viola dozed happily, her head in Hetty's lap.

"Yes, well, I'm told we have Aunt Adelaide to thank for that," replied Isobel, offering their aunt an approving salute. As a special treat, Aunt Adelaide did not chide her for the overly common gesture.

"And besides," began August, "what were they going to do, go against the Earl of Belhaven? The stern bastard wouldn't allow it. Once they became engaged, the matter was settled."

"Hetty never actually agreed to marry me, you know."

Freddie laughed. "I think it's rather late for her to back out now."

"Some things can be said without words," mused Hetty as Isobel mimed being sick.

"Get your mind out of the gutter, Izzie," Jasper warned.

She turned her nose up at him. "I reside there permanently."

"I've some news," said Helena, rather loudly so as to command the wavering attention of the Maycotts. "Now that Hetty is settled here, and Mulgrave Hall has a new lady of the house, I shall be returning to my townhouse in Mayfair. There is much in need of doing." She gave Hetty and Isobel a knowing look. "I've been avoiding both my duties and the elder Dowager Duchess of Pembroke long enough, and I'm beginning to worry about Marcus's brother. He hasn't answered any of my letters in months."

The room erupted in voices shouting over each other, some happy about the news (Isobel and Freddie), some rather incensed (Viola). Through the chaos, Jasper's eyes found Hetty's.

His Hetty. His wife. His everything.

She had pulled him from the darkness long before he had been willing to feel the light once more. But now he basked in it. In her, for she was his sun.

He looked to the portraits of his parents and Anthony, moved from the gallery to the sitting room so they would always be nearby. Before Hetty, the constant reminder of them would have broken Jasper. He'd once thought that losing them was the end. The end of happiness, the end of joy, the end of life as he knew it.

But now he knew the simple truth that had eluded him: out of an ending, a new beginning is born, if one can find the courage to chase it.

• • •

Taking Hetty to bed as his wife could not have felt more right.

"Isn't it odd that I've never been in your room?" she remarked, trailing her fingers along his bedpost.

"*Our* room," he corrected. "And, if there is anything you dislike about it or wish to change, it will be done."

"I am not thinking about furniture or linens," she said, turning to face him. "Not at this time."

"What are you thinking of, Lady Belhaven?" He would never grow tired of saying that.

She pulled a pin from her hair, letting it tumble down around her shoulders. "Mostly about how difficult it will be to remove my gown. I have no lady's maid at my disposal."

"But you do have a most eager husband," he said, approaching her. "How difficult could a row of buttons be?"

Vexingly difficult, it would seem. Undressing Hetty took him the better part of a half hour as he fumbled with minuscule buttons and mysterious hooks, his wife entirely entertained by his middling efforts. When his task was at last complete, Hetty let the gown fall to the floor, standing before him in only the most sinful-looking drawers.

"I don't think I'll be hiring you, my lord," she teased.

"Surely there are other positions I'm still under consideration for, my lady," he replied before scooping her into his arms and sinking into the bed. She giggled into his neck as he covered every inch of her with kisses, but suddenly she went still, quiet. He paused at once.

"What is it, my love?"

She pressed her hands to her face. "What if I'm a terrible countess?"

Hetty had not been raised to one day become the lady of a great house. Nor had she been primed for entrance into polite Society. It was why he loved her so. But he could not dismiss her insecurity in so blasé a manner. What good was his devotion if she did not feel comfortable in her own home?

"The simple fact that you're concerned tells me you'll be a great one." He rolled over to lie beside her, propping his head up with his arm. "Hetty, you are the bravest woman I know. You have risen to every challenge set against you. I have no doubt that you'll rise to this one, too, and make it your own."

She squeezed his hand. "I only wish the people we lost could be with us now."

"They live on in us, of that I am certain." Jasper no longer flinched away from memory or pain. When Viola brought up their mother, he happily recalled stories. When Freddie asked questions about their father, he was careful to answer truthfully. And when grief caught up with him, he allowed himself to feel it, but not be ruled by it.

"I dreamed of my father last night, actually," Hetty continued. "He spoke to me. It was the clearest I've ever seen him. I can still hear his voice in my head, it didn't fade when I awoke like it has before."

"A memory?" he asked.

"No, not quite. It was almost what I imagine he would have said to me if he hadn't died. It was a gift, to have a conversation with him on the night before my wedding, even if it wasn't real. I know that one day he will be restored to me in full." She wrapped her arms tighter around him. "I simply need to be patient."

Jasper knew from experience that Hetty's healing would not be linear. Some days were better than others, some memories more potent than the ones before. He would help her through her healing, as she had his. Whatever it took. In his mind, the actions of her aunt and cousin required retribution, but Hetty had insisted there be no legal recourse against them, and Jasper had respected her wishes, despite the fact that he was quite certain he would beat Claremont to a pulp if their paths ever crossed. He doubted they would, as the last he had heard from Simon Griffith was that the baron had decamped for the Continent, hoping to leave his debts and his troubles behind in England.

Pity for him that the future Duke of Radcliffe always collected.

"I've decided what I wish to do with Sutton House." Hetty had left it empty since they rode away from it two days after the Banfield ball. She had arranged for the footman, Jack, and the recently dismissed kitchen maid, Mary, to work at Mulgrave Hall, and had overseen the retrieval of all her father's paintings and their personal effects, but otherwise she wanted nothing to do with the house she was entitled to. Jasper had suggested selling it, but Hetty had wanted to think on it. To make a plan, as she had always done. "I'd like to make it a refuge for vulnerable women. A place they can escape to when they lose their protection in Society. They can come there and feel safe and supported, and perhaps learn new skills to make them employable. I'll have to do much planning, but I think it could work."

"So this is what you and my sisters have been plotting for months?" he asked, relieved to have his curiosity satisfied at last. "I think it's a brilliant idea."

Hetty nodded. "And I'd like to advocate for women committed against their wills to asylums, bound there only by the testimony of their wicked husbands or cruel fathers. There needs to be a place for women to retreat to when they have no other options."

"Annabelle often said as much, of the women she encountered. It would have been her life's work, helping them."

Hetty smiled and took his hand. "Isobel has told me much about her efforts. Perhaps we could even call it Annabelle House, in her honor."

She said it mildly, as though willing to abandon the thought at a moment's notice. But Jasper had come a long way from the man he used to be, the one who dared not utter Annabelle's name. He knew at once that Hetty's suggestion would be the most fitting tribute to her, a way for her name to live on as a beacon for the women she had advocated tirelessly for.

"I can think of nothing better," he replied, his voice slightly weighed down with emotion.

She squeezed his hand a bit tighter. "And I've already enlisted the help of your sisters. When Helena returns to Mayfair, she will use her extensive Society connections to elicit donations, as I imagine the running of a women's refuge will require a great deal of capital, and Isobel, Louisa, and Lady Lydia Coventry are already bursting with ideas for different services we can offer to these women. I also discovered that Lydia is a part of a committee that works with like-minded members of Parliament to put forth private members' bills that promote women's rights.

They are almost universally defeated in the House of Lords, but incremental progress is better than no progress at all."

"You know, my seat in the House of Lords has been gathering dust for long enough. Perhaps I can be of use in that regard."

She practically dove atop him, pressing an enthusiastic kiss to his lips. "Have I told you how much I adore you?"

"Yes, but I shall never tire of hearing it."

She grinned and settled into the crook of his arm before jumping up again. "Oh and Lady Adelaide!"

"Oh no," Jasper began, fearing the worst.

"You mistake me." Hetty laughed. "Lady Adelaide wishes to be *most* involved in our charitable venture."

"You'd be hard pressed to find a more suitable patroness. Though I should hope her capable of softening her edges. God knows these women will have been through enough without having to contend with her sharpness."

"*Mmm*," she replied, burrowing once more into the crook of his arm. "Too true, not all of them can rely on being rescued by a dashing earl."

"You rescued yourself, love," he said, kissing her forehead. "I was merely an accessory."

She looked up at him, pressed her hand to the steady beating of his heart. "Rescue me again, Jasper."

He was happy to oblige.

Acknowledgments

Writing a book is a journey, and I never would have made it this far in mine without the help of so many wonderful people.

Firstly, to my agents Katie Gisondi and Carrie Pestritto. You two were the first (and most enthusiastic) cheerleaders for *ALWKB* and I cannot thank you enough for all of your faith in me and my book, and your insight which helped to shape it. And another big thank you to everyone at LDLA for all of their hard work.

A massive thank you to my editor, Erin Molta, whose brilliance made this book shine. Sorry for basically always getting the forms of address wrong (despite exhaustive research). And a huge thank you to everyone at Entangled for their tireless efforts behind the scenes, including Liz Pelletier, Jessica Turner, Lizzy Mason, Heather Riccio, Lauren Cepero, and Aimee Lim. Special thank you to Elizabeth Stokes for designing and illustrating my gorgeous cover.

I was inspired to write this book in the midst of debuting

(shout out to my firstborn, Rebel Rose!) in 2020. The stress, isolation, and uncertainty of those early days of the pandemic led me to seek comfort in the arms of historical romance (seriously, I read about seventy-five in a row), and I would be remiss if I did not thank some of the romance authors I admire who so graciously helped me along the way:

Martha Waters, your books hold such a special place in my heart and I cannot believe I tricked you into being my friend. Thank you so much for your generous notes and for crafting the most perfect blurb ever for my cover, and for becoming my most cherished pen pal.

Evie Dunmore, *Bringing Down the Duke* was the first book to ignite this journey, and it has meant so much to me ever since (so much so that I borrowed a few names from it and wove them into *ALWKB*, I hope you don't mind!). Thank you for all of your kindness, and for giving me such a wonderful blurb, and for making sure my (very brief usage of) German was correct.

I'd also like to thank the outrageously talented authors who so generously gave me such beautiful blurbs: Liana De la Rosa, Alicia Thompson, Emma R. Alban, Sarah Hogle and Amy Lea.

I really leaned on my writing community while I wrote, queried, and subsequently went on sub with this book.

In no particular order, I have to thank Rosiee Thor, Alwyn Hamilton, Jordan Gray, Megan Scott, Leanne Schwartz, Brendon Zatirka, Elle Tesch, and Hailey Harlow for being my first readers as I stepped uncertainly into a new genre and age category.

Next, I have to thank the friends who have been there since day one (or who have become so important to me that it really *feels* like it): Rory Power, Hannah Whitten, June CL Tan, Kat Dunn, Claribel Ortega, Kara Thomas, Kelsey Rodkey, Tori Bovalino, Sara Raasch, Adrienne Tooley, MK Lobb, Alexandra

Monir, Livia Blackburne, and Suzanne Samin. You are all so quick with support and willing to listen to me vent and I cannot thank you enough!

To my local friends: Pascale Lacelle, thank you for all of the writing dates we seem to exclusively use as an excuse to talk shit about publishing. Amal El-Mohtar, thank you for being an endless well of sage wisdom. Ruby Barrett, thank you for being so kind (and for agreeing to co-host my launch a good eight months before any actual plans for it were made). And to Christina Matula, who is only occasionally local, but worthy of thanks all the same.

Huge thanks to one of my oldest writing friends, Victoria Aveyard. There's no one I'd rather have by my side in these publishing trenches, and since 2013 no less!

And a special thank you to the inimitable Laura Steven, without whom I would have given up on this whole writing thing long ago. I don't know how people without a Laura Steven in their lives do it, tbh!

And of course, my IRL friends deserve the biggest shout-out for putting up with me when I'm on deadline or simply annoying them with my latest hyperfixation. Special thanks to Steve and Michelle for the dance parties (Taylor Swift or otherwise).

To the readers who followed me from my first book, thank you for the DMs demanding to know what was next for me. I hope *ALWKB* was worth the wait! And to the new readers, thank you for taking a chance on me and my book. Eternal thank yous to every librarian, bookseller, or bookish influencer who has ever shouted about my books or placed one in the hands of someone who needed it.

Thanks to my coworkers for being such a supportive and well-read bunch. Special thanks to Michael in particular, for ordering a carton (thirty-two copies!) of my book for the store the second it was available to preorder.

Thank you to my family—Mom, Dad, Lauren, Wade, the Theriaults, the O'Rays, and the Williamses. You have made this dream feel possible. To my mom, Kathie O'Ray, in particular: thank you for filling my childhood with books, and for supporting me in every endeavor.

And lastly, thank you to my own little family—Byron, Gatsby, and Harriet. G & H, you are both so special and perfect I can barely stand it. Byron, thank you for never letting me quit once, and for believing in me more than I believe in myself. You are more perfect than any love interest I've ever written, because you are real and you're mine.

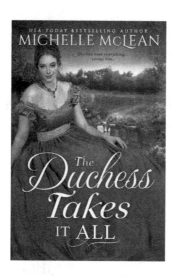

USA TODAY BESTSELLING AUTHOR
MICHELLE McLEAN

A widowed duchess in possession of a fortune must be in want of a husband...or is she? It's a battle of wills in this delightfully clever, enemies-to-lovers romance that's perfect for fans of Tessa Dare and Beverly Watts

Tamsin Palmer—the recently widowed Duchess of Clevesly—has almost anything a woman of common birth could want: wealth, title, estate, and even her adored toddler son. But it's not exactly easy. She's been ostracized by the *ton* due to her decidedly *un*blue blood. And worse still, her dearly departed duke has assigned a co-guardian of their son: the handsome (if insufferable) Count of Rauchberg, who seems most insistent on dictating the terms of Tamsin's duchy. But not if *she* has anything to say about it...

Christian August has never been so vexed in his life. He's come to help raise the duchess's son, and in return, she's doing everything she can to destroy his peace of mind. Unleashing goats, secretly shortening the cuffs of his shirts, and—damn the infernal woman— driving him to distraction with her flashing eyes and soft, kissable lips. It's enough to make a man forget his duty...

With every argument, the longing grows stronger. With every diabolical prank, the temptation becomes greater. And they'll risk everything to win...even if it means surrendering to a passion that will destroy them both.

*Don't miss the exciting new books
Entangled has to offer.*

Follow us!

@EntangledPublishing

@Entangled_Publishing

@EntangledPub